BURNING
SAND

BURNING SAND

a novel by
R. J. RUGGIERO

Beaconridge Press
Boston

FIRST BEACONRIDGE EDITION 2022

This is a work of fiction. Names, characters, places, and incidents either are the
productof the author's imagination or are used fictitiously. Any resemblance to
actual persons, living or dead, events, or locales is entirely coincidental.

Published in the United States by Beaconridge Press, Boston

Copyright © 2022 by R.J. Ruggiero

10 9 8 7 6 5 4 3 2 1

Cover design by Greg Anthony
Cover photography by Isabel Leon
and USDoE/NASA/USFWS

Publisher's Cataloging-in-Publication data
Names: Ruggiero, R., J., author.
Title: Burning sand : a novel / by R.J. Ruggiero.
Description: First Beaconridge Edition. | Boston, MA: Beaconridge Press, 2022.
Identifiers: LCCN: 2022941317 |
ISBN: 9780970413550 (paperback) | 9780970413574 (ebook)
Subjects: LCSH Volleyball players--Fiction. | Organized crime--Fiction. |
Beach volleyball--Fiction. | Sports--Fiction. | Amnesia--Fiction. | Adoption--
Fiction. | Boston (Mass.)--Fiction. | California, Southern--Fiction. | Thriller
fiction. | Mystery fiction. | BISAC FICTION / Thrillers / Crime |
FICTION / Thrillers / Psychological | FICTION / Thrillers / Suspense |
FICTION / Action & Adventure | FICTION / Mystery & Detective / General
FICTION / Romance / Sports | FICTION / Sports
Classification: LCC PS3618 .U437 B87 2022 | DDC 813.6--dc23

PRINTED IN THE UNITED STATES OF AMERICA

For my mother, whose wisdom inspires,
and my father, whose humor captivates.

To my brother, whose passion for the sport
inspired my own.

———————●◆●———————

For those who continue to persevere through
adversity, and strive to maintain their
integrity in the face of injustice.

For those for whom the game awakens the spirit.

He who knows when to fight
and when not to fight
is victorious.

- Sun Tzu, *THE ART OF WAR*

Boston's Beth Israel hospital room 342 seemed desperately in want of light. It was two in the morning and its sole source of illumination came from the green-fluorescent peaks and valleys of the ECG monitor. With each arc, the monitor let out a quick beep in a monotonous, never-changing pattern of sound. The green light barely illuminated the room's lone occupant lying prone in his hospital bed. He had been there for quite some time. His face was heavily bandaged. Only his eyes were visible and they were closed. Clear plastic tubes ran out of his nose and into an oxygen regulator by his side.

As the night wore on, the spirit within the man began to stir. His eyes began to twitch for the first time since his arrival. Ever so slightly, the pace of the ECG monitor began to quicken. Consciousness came slowly. As the man began to break through the icy surface of his comatose state, he became aware of a blockage in his nose. He instinctively reached up and pulled out the tubes. The sudden lack of pure oxygen induced rapid heart-rate within his fragile body. Consciousness came quickly. The man jolted awake and started to gag. The ECG monitor began to beep uncontrollably.

The night nurse rushed into the room. The man on the bed

began to panic, terrified. He tried to talk, to cry out, but it hurt. He brought his hands up to his throat to feel the source of the discomfort. To his surprise, they felt nothing. He brought them into his field of view. Shocked, he stared down at completely bandaged hands. The man was horrified. The nurse managed to replace the oxygen tubes and tried to calm him.

"Don't try to talk until you've seen the doctor," she said gently. "You've had throat surgery."

The man opened his mouth to scream, but no sound came out. His eyes bulged in fear and confusion. The nurse pushed the call button by his bedside. A second nurse ran into the room.

"Sting him," yelled the first nurse hurriedly.

The second nurse quickly readied a syringe.

"The doctor's coming," she said soothingly, and gave him the shot.

The bandaged man's breathing became less labored. His body became more supine, but his eyes continued to dart around the room. They finally came to rest on his trembling hands. The doctor on call hurried into the room. He stood over the patient, putting a hand on his shoulder.

"Mr. Squid, calm down. Everything is going to be all right. Do you know where you are?"

Quinton Squid shook his head 'no.'

"You are at Beth Israel Hospital in Boston, Massachusetts," said the doctor.

Quinton looked up at the doctor, his eyes full of desperate confusion.

"Your plane to Bonn was in an accident," the doctor continued.

Quinton's eyes froze. The hospital room was no longer before him. He found himself drawn into the metaphorical jumble of his own mind. In his mind's eye he saw a wall of flame raging in the distance. The flames seemed to advance toward him. But it was he who moved. Within seconds he felt himself hurtling towards it. As he flew into the fire, he heard a disembodied scream emanate from somewhere deep inside himself. His mind thrust him back to the hospital room. The doctor stood above him. He could see the man's lips move, but his voice was obscured by the latent sound of the distorted scream and the crackling of flame.

The doctor saw Quinton staring at him with a glazed expression.

"Can you hear me, Mr. Squid?"

Quinton Squid could not answer.

As Quinton stared around the room, the walls in front of him burst into flame. The ceiling caught fire, then the floor. Quinton Squid became agitated. The second nurse restrained him. The first nurse began rattling off his suddenly rising blood pressure to the doctor.

"One-ten over seventy...one-twenty over eighty...one-forty-two over ninety-seven...it won't stop rising."

"Give it a second," the doctor barked.

"It's crowning one-seventy!" she warned.

"All right, put him out. We don't need a stroke."

She gave Quinton a stronger sedative. He went limp. The night doctor turned to her.

"Call Dr. Collins and tell him his patient has woken up. And get Coach Murphey in here. It looks like his star boy is going to make it."

The sun streamed in through the hospital blinds. It cast alternating patterns of shadow and light over the bandaged man as he lay unconscious in his hospital bed. He slowly emerged from his medicated sleep.

Quinton Squid awoke to find himself strapped to the bed with velcro restraints. He tried to speak, but wasn't yet fully conscious. He saw the first nurse from the previous evening standing next to him. She injected a syringe of medication into the IV attached to his left arm. Quinton's escape from the murky depths of his subconscious became easier. Within a moment he was fully awake.

He saw an older man with narrow eyes standing over his bed. The man wore a white lab coat over green surgical garb. His ID badge read 'Dr. Collins.' Quinton's eyes searched the room. There was one other person present. A middle-aged man slouched in his chair directly across from the bed. He wore a Padres cap and bit furiously at a frayed fingernail. Quinton looked down at his own bandaged fingers. Collins moved in closer.

"Mr. Squid. Can you hear me?" he asked.

Quinton didn't react, as if he hadn't heard him. Dr. Collins tried again.

"You are suffering from serious head contusions, but you'll be all right. You've been in a coma since your plane crash five weeks ago."

A look of fear and confusion played briefly through Quinton's eyes, but he remained silent. Collins cautiously removed the restraints.

"Can you hear me, Mr. Squid?" he asked, again.

Quinton looked up at the doctor. He touched his bandaged hand to his throat. Collins smiled.

"It's okay to talk now, Mr. Squid."

Quinton opened his mouth. He tried to speak, but it felt strange. It was a strain to get the breath up past his vocal cords.

"Why are you calling me that?" he rasped.

Collins looked directly into Quinton's eyes.

"I know you might not remember this, but your name is Quinton Squid."

Quinton squinted at the doctor. His eyes strained, as if trying to focus on something very far away.

"Can you remember anything?" Collins asked.

The doctor's voice drifted away as Quinton's mental awareness retreated quickly from the hospital and back to the inner wall of flame. The flames began to billow and howl. He felt himself sucked again toward the blaze, at an ever-increasing rate. Just as he was about to be swallowed whole by the burning apparition, a frantic Quinton thrust himself back to reality. His eyes darted around the room, his breathing quickened.

"Anything at all?" the doctor probed.

"About what?" snapped Quinton.

Collins spoke softly, trying to calm his agitated patient.

"About what happened to you. About who you are. What is your last memory, for example."

Quinton forced himself to focus on his bandaged hands. He tried to let his breathing become more temperate. He heard the sound of crackling flame fade in and out of his brain.

"Fire," Quinton whispered out loud as he stared off into space.

His gaze hardened and shifted back to the doctor.

"Who are you?" he demanded.

Quinton's gaze softened again, as quickly as it had hardened. His eyes began to focus slowly inward.

"You're a doctor, right?" was all he could say before he was thrust once again into his vast subconscious. There were no flames this time. Instead, he found himself looking out the window of a moving vehicle. Street lights flashed by outside. It was nighttime. He could barely see. His eyes were nearly swollen shut and he felt searing pain all around him.

The memory of the pain echoed in Quinton's mind as he shifted once again back to the doctor and outer reality.

"I was burned. There was a fire. Wasn't there?" Quinton asked.

Like a holographic image appearing in the center of the room, he saw his view from the vehicle as it pulled into the emergency room entrance. The door of the vehicle was flung open. He watched as a large man with brown eyes and a mustache reached in and grabbed him.

Then, just as quickly as the hallucination had appeared, it dissolved. Quinton's eyes were drawn back to the bandages on his hands. He felt he was wavering between two worlds and did not know to which he belonged.

"Yes, there was a fire," said Collins. Quinton stared blankly for a moment.

"Was it bad?" he finally asked the doctor.

The man under the Padres cap listened intently.

"You were burned badly, and had severe facial lacerations," Collins explained. "You had severe contusions to the skull, the most serious of which caused a slight bruising of your frontal lobe. This is why you may be experiencing some memory loss or temporary amnesia."

Quinton laid his hands by his side and gave the doctor his full attention. The man continued.

"We had to perform several risky reconstructive and grafting techniques while you were in the coma, but your body responded well. One of our interns is a serious fan of yours. He happened to have a current full-face picture of you in a magazine. You are a very lucky man, Mr. Squid. We believe we have almost fully restored your previous facial features."

"Could I see the picture?" Quinton rasped.

The doctor handed him a picture from his file. It was a

signed magazine endorsement for Sand Dune Activewear. The top of the page read January 1991. The signature over the picture read 'Quinton Squid.' The picture itself revealed a man with dark hair and blue-gray eyes. He was a handsome man with chiseled features and a wry, condescending smile. Quinton inspected the picture. He eyed the doctor suspiciously.

"Why don't I know who this is?"

"Often, when people lose their memory, the first thing to go is the memory of their appearance," explained Dr. Collins.

"Why?" asked Quinton.

"Because none of us view ourselves in exactly the same way as we appear to the rest of the world. The subconscious mind, especially under the influence of amnesia, doesn't always initially acknowledge a photographic image of its former self."

Quinton snorted in derision, then looked at the doctor more seriously, as if he understood.

"I don't know what's going on. I can't remember anything."

He turned abruptly to the man brooding under the Padres cap.

"Do I know you?" he demanded.

"Yes," answered the man awkwardly. "I'm your coach on the Olympic Volleyball Team."

Quinton blinked. The Olympic what?

"We thought we'd try a bunch of things to help jog your memory," Collins added. "But you should rest for now. We'll have your friends come by tomorrow."

"No," said Quinton. "I want to see them now."

But Quinton's eyes went suddenly dark. Without warning, something inside pulled him into a cold blackness.

A light shone in the distance. It was that same wall of flame. He felt himself hurtle toward it once again. His ears registered Dr. Collins yelling, "Mr. Squid, are you with us?" He tried to pull himself back to the hospital, back to reality, but that was not where his mind wanted him to be.

"He's out. We'll try again tomorrow," was the last thing he heard before passing out cold.

2

Amidst the din of the surrounding festivities, Michael Delaney stood wooden, staring indignantly at the passport in his hands. The photo wore a grin which his mirror hadn't seen in quite a while.

"Do you have a death wish?" a voice whispered over his shoulder. "Put that thing away, for Christ's sake." The large, powerfully built man standing behind him quietly palmed the passport and slipped it into his own tuxedo jacket. Michael turned around.

"Nicky…," he said, holding his hand out for the passport.

"No way, they're looking right at us." Nick glanced at the small group of partygoers standing by the main buffet table. "I'll give it to you at the airport."

Michael clanked the ice around in his plastic cup.

"You're paranoid," he said softly.

"Look around this place. Everyone's here. Even Buster and Georgie, for god's sake. What are you, drunk?"

"No, I'm drinking Moxie," answered Michael.

"That's an old lady's drink."

Michael looked down at his Moxie. So what if it was an old lady's drink. He had one good slug left.

"Jesus Michael, I'm going nuts here," Nick said as he withdrew a handkerchief from his pocket. He dabbed the sweat forming above his dark eyebrows and mustache.

Nick Avanti never perspired. It was rumored he had been born without sweat glands. But Michael saw a small droplet of sweat fall from his nose onto his black wingtips. Only then did he realize how nervous Nick must have been about this evening. But nothing could be done now. It had already been set in motion.

Michael averted his gaze from the beads forming below Nick's hairline and looked around the rented birthday hall. All he could see were rented tuxedos and rented smiles. Maybe a few days ago he would've seen the group of teenage boys playing grabass by the stuffed mushrooms, or been amused by the humorless clown making balloon animals for the young girls while simultaneously regurgitating ancient Victor Borgé routines for the old timers. But now all he could see was that group hovering by the main buffet table, and that walker perched in the center of it all. A wry smile crossed his lips as he saw the aluminum edge of the walker glisten. This must be killing Victor. She had made it another year. A purple-veined hand reached out of the group and summoned Michael and Nick over.

There she stood, the birthday girl herself. Nana Rosetta was one hundred and two this December 22nd, and as stooped and brash as the day was long. She didn't have wit. She didn't have style. But she had balls that hung down to her knees. Walker, purple veins, and all. How many times had Michael seen those varicosed hands rip Frank's fists away from his face. Twenty-seven. He gratefully remembered each one.

"Michael," a familiar voice called to him from behind as he and Nick neared the group.

Michael swilled down the last of his Moxie and turned around. It was Victor. Michael could feel his heart begin to race. He took a deep, silent breath in through his nostrils.

"Hi, Uncle Victor."

"You look sharp, Michael."

"Thanks."

He did look good. But then again, he always looked good. A very tall, handsome guy. Pretty almost, in an Elvis Presley sort of way. But he had a little Vic Morrow thing happening at the same time –"whatcha-gonna-do-daddy-o?"– puppy-dog eyes with a pretty face that could turn cruelly handsome in an instant.

Nana Rosetta flashed him a birthday smile with her infamous pearly whites. A hundred and two years and she still had all of her own teeth. A fact of which she was immensely proud. She had honed and strengthened them over the years – not a day had gone by when she didn't crack at least one walnut with her bare back molars. Victor Russo, never wanting to be outdone by anyone, especially his own grandmother, had tried that trick once as a teenager. He subsequently lost three teeth and had to wear dentures since the age of fourteen. He had to settle for cracking walnuts in his bare hands. But he'd perfected his own unique style of which he himself was immensely proud.

Michael had always been struck by how strangely important cracking walnuts was to this family. He didn't remember his own father cracking any walnuts. Or his mother, for that matter. He didn't remember much about either one of his real parents.

Spilled milk, Victor had always said.

Victor Russo, toothless patriarch. Michael's head began to spin. He wanted to run screaming. Wait. Just wait, he told himself. It will all be over soon enough.

"Michael. Michelangelo," the four and a half foot Nana Rosetta called out to him, her six foot, four inch pseudo great-grandson. She liked calling him Michelangelo. She was convinced his resemblance to the sculptor's 'David' was of religious significance.

Michael stared blankly at the faded red exit sign. Nick poked the distracted Michael in the ribs. Michael looked down at Nana Rosetta's blue-tinted head with a strange combination of genuine affection and mortal dread. He had to keep reminding himself that she was still the head of this miserable family, even though she had always covered his ass. She would give you the shirt off her back, he mused, but if you tried to take it from her, she'd kill you.

He had been measuring his height against hers since the age of eight, twenty years ago. At the age of ten he made it up to her nose, and by the age of twelve she only came up to his eyes. Italian women don't die; they just shrink out of existence.

"Michelangelo, this is for you."

She handed him a chunk of asphalt the size of a softball. Michael was amused.

"Nana, what's this?"

Before she could answer, a large bodybuilder of a man barged into the conversation.

"It's the Mussolini rock from '45. Nana cracked him one right in the skull."

Michael hadn't noticed Frank was there.

Frank Russo could have easily been the poster boy for illegal steroid abuse. He was a huge, hulking man who looked like a live-action Rock-'em Sock-'em Robot.

Annoyed, Nana Rosetta continued. "After the crowd shot him and hung him upside down."

"By the balls?" Frank asked.

"No, meshugina, by his toes," Rosetta shot back. Michael could see her look at Frank with the same disdain that had always colored her perception of him. He had to smile.

Frank pulled out a comb from his pocket and began to set his blonde hair back into a perfect duck tail. Victor looked on with disgust at his son's preening. He took the rock from Michael's hands and felt its weight. Victor studied the reddish discoloration on one of its pointed edges.

"Boys, a little history lesson for you," he said as he handed the rock back to Michael. "We take care of our own when we fuck up. That's why we don't get bitched at about the war like the Krauts and Japs do."

"Salud," grunted Nana Rosetta.

"Salud," Victor offered.

Plastic wine cups clicked as best they could, and all was silent in the group as each downed the last of their liquor. Michael hadn't noticed that Uncle Louie was there. Or Sal. Or Vinny. Or Vinny's armpiece, Rosie. Aunt Rita, Victor Russo's well-preserved, highly bejeweled wife, was part of the circle as well. She was silent as usual.

Victor must have left Frick and Frack back at the warehouse. Just as well. Victor and Frank were enough for Michael to handle for now. The rest of the East Boston Knights of Columbus hall was filled with what looked like wops from central casting. Columbus wouldn't have knighted anyone in this ocean of 'Tonys,' thought Michael. He wouldn't even have gone bowling with them, he chuckled to himself.

Frank whipped out his comb for the fifth time that evening, but no matter how many times he tried, that duck tail refused to cover the large scar running across the left side of his forehead.

"Frank, put that damned thing away," Victor commanded.

Frank obeyed.

"What's this rock for, Nana?" Michael asked.

"For you and Gina. It's my wedding present to you both."

Oh Jesus, when was *she* gonna show up. Michael resisted the urge to check his watch. Where had Nick wandered off to? He spotted him hovering by the brocciole and motioned him back over. Nick sauntered back with a plate full of stuffed mushrooms.

"These are great."

He stuffed one into Michael's mouth. Victor laughed.

"You'd better get your fill now, Michael, 'cause Gina can't cook for shit."

"I know. I do all my own cooking, Uncle Victor."

Victor eyed him curiously.

"You're a strange bird, Michael Delaney. Gina called from Boca. Her flight's not coming in 'til morning."

"These Depends are for shit," Rosetta blurted out suddenly. "Excuse me, but June Allison can kiss my wrinkled ass," she declared, and headed off towards the restroom with her walker. When she was safely out of earshot, Frank whispered hurriedly to Victor, "For Christ's sake, Pop, she smells like mothballs."

"She's family. Show some respect. Besides, her party is our cover for the Callabrisi job tonight."

"You're using your grandmother's birthday party as a cover for a job?" asked his wife Rita, aghast.

"What of it?" challenged Russo.

"I was just asking," said Rita, as she lowered her eyes.

"It's not your place."

"Victor, I meant nothing..."

"So say nothing. Just get me more seltzer."

He handed his cup to her. Michael looked at his adoptive father with thinly veiled disgust. He reached for Victor's cup.

"I'll get it, Aunt Rita."

She looked Michael up and down.

"What am I, a fuckin' cripple?" she asked, then snatched the cup from Victor and headed off for the bar.

Frank continued.

"The whole damn hall smells like mothballs. Even the food here tastes from the stuff."

"Enough with the friggin' mothballs, Frank!" Victor yelled.

"But you said she wouldn't make it through to the holidays again this year."

"She's a hundred and two and can't get out of bed in the morning without two rum and Cokes. She should be on life support, for chrissake. What am I supposed to say, Frank? She's in God's waiting room."

A disgruntled Frank turned to Michael.

"T-minus nineteen hours and counting, bro. Has Gina wore it down to a nub by now, or do you still have enough left for the honeymoon?"

Victor slapped the back of Frank's head, mussing the blonde duck tail again.

"Show some respect. And if you reach for that comb one more time, I'm gonna break your frigging fingers. You look like a goddamn show dog."

Victor turned to Michael. "The three of you are scheduled to go at eleven p.m. I'll call you from the warehouse if it's any earlier. Everyone in this room will vouch you been here 'til midnight."

"I'm running this one, right Pop?" Frank asked.

"You couldn't run water, Frank. Tonight's Michael's call. Think of it as his bachelor party."

Victor stalked off after Rita. Frank glared at Michael. Michael stared back at the stupid, ape-like eyes trying to bore into his skull. He knew they couldn't do much damage. Over dessert last night at Nana Rosetta's, she had to explain to Frank that Neapolitan ice cream had nothing to do with neo-nazis. Michael unlocked his eyes.

He looked around the circle for Nick, who had apparently wandered off again. His eyes darted around the room. He wasn't playing grabass with the boys near the stuffed mushrooms. Not with the guys playing dice on the pool table. Not over flirting with the girls giggling over the boys. Ah. He spotted Nick sitting with the toddlers just as Bozo handed him a balloon animal. Nick was always wandering off, but in the end he usually came back.

3

In the drowning blue of an ethereal basketball court, a man dribbled a volleyball towards the hoop at the far end of the court. White bandages on his face, and a basketball jersey embossed with the number seven on his back, the man crossed center court. A volleyball net appeared suddenly before his eyes. The man slowed, but it was too late. He was caught in the net and began to pull it along with him. The squeak of the dragging poles echoed through the court. The squeaking sound continued as Quinton Squid woke up in a cold sweat.

He looked over at the squeaky wheel of a TV cart being wheeled into his hospital room. Two people followed behind the cart: a man and a woman he didn't recognize. The woman pushed the cart, the man hobbled behind her on crutches, a cast on his leg.

The man was large, standing six-three with the build of a first-string quarterback – sturdy and toned, but without excessive bulk. The woman was big too, about five-nine. She was beautifully tanned, and the fine toning of her musculature suggested long workouts at the gym.

Quinton's weary mental machinery tried to formulate

some kind of thought. 'Tall couple' was the best his mind could produce.

The woman noticed Quinton staring at them. She whispered to her companion.

"Stu, go get a doctor."

The man hobbled out the door.

The woman moved closer to Quinton. She smiled at him with what he could instinctively feel to be genuine regard.

"Quinton, it's Emily. Do you remember me?"

Quinton shook his head 'no.' Nothing about her felt at all familiar.

"Stu and I are your friends," she said. "He was on the plane, too. He's your beach partner."

"Beach partner," Quinton repeated.

The words made no sense to his empty memory.

"You'll see," Emily reassured him. "I brought you some tapes, some magazines, and books from the Coast to help jar your memory. The doctor said it might help."

Stu entered with Dr. Collins. The doctor examined Quinton's eyes with a penlight as he spoke.

"Good morning, Quinton. We suggested to Ms. Gardner – "

"I'm sorry doctor, but he knows me as Roeg," Emily said.

"Aren't you married to him?" Collins asked, nodding at Stu.

Quinton looked on indifferently.

"Yes, but I'm Roeg, and he's Gardner."

"We're from California," Stu explained.

Collins looked at them with a raised eyebrow. He turned back to Quinton.

"Anyway, we suggested to Ms. Roeg that your memory might be jarred by some personal interaction and information.

You can use it at your leisure. You're going to be here for four more weeks. We have two more skin grafts to perform. You'll have the final one in San Diego."

"What's in San Diego?" Quinton asked.

"Olympic Training Center, dude," Stu said.

Quinton stared blankly at the man he assumed was his best friend. He didn't recognize him or what he was talking about.

"I've gotten everyone to sign my cast. I left a big space for you," said Stu.

He handed Quinton a pen. Quinton held it and stared at Stu's cast for a moment. He looked up at Dr. Collins like a puppy-dog, his eyes filled with confusion.

"What's my name again?"

Over the next few days Quinton drowned himself in the volleyball magazines, books, and videotapes Emily and Stu had brought him.

So this was who he was. It was like cool water to the desert of his mind. He had done his best to absorb the rules of the game from the AVP Rule Book, and tried to memorize the glossary of terms. There was a lot to learn. He wondered how he could have forgotten it all.

He pushed aside the magazines and books strewn across the bed and found the TV/VCR remote. Grasping it with his bandaged hand he turned the TV on and pressed play, eager to see exactly what he did for a living. He watched the blank screen in anticipation, a sponge waiting for any memory to soak in.

The tape began. It was the Cable Sports Network broadcast of the Hermosa Kings of the Beach Championship from one year earlier. On the screen was a beautiful California day.

The sky was blue, the sand was hot, and the waves roared as loud as the crowd that had gathered to watch the championship finals. The scene held no familiarity to Quinton, but interested him nonetheless.

The court consisted of a sectioned-off area of sand twenty yards from the water, divided down the middle by a net. Each side of the court was about thirty feet by thirty feet. Tape lay across the sand to mark the court boundaries. Sixteen feet beyond each side of tape was a two-foot-high barrier to keep the crowd back and the ball in the court area. The barrier was prime advertising space and showcased anything from Coca-Cola to *Volleyball Magazine.*

On each of the four sides of the court, a simple set of bleachers loomed into the air, packed with people. They blocked the player's immediate view of the ocean.

Everyone, including the players, seemed to be dressed in the requisite bathing suit and surfer tank. It was a cavalcade of color and motion. A gigantic inflatable volleyball stood twenty feet high over the proceedings. A remote Cable Sports camera boom-arm swung back and forth over the game like a pendulum. From a stage overlooking the court, an announcer oozed play-by-play and kept the audience energized.

Quinton Squid and Stu Gardner were playing in the finals against two other top-seeded volleyball players, Bill Johnson and John Steeles. As they dove and scrambled for the ball, arcing and smashing it into their opponent's side of the court, the audience went crazy.

The bandaged man in the hospital room sat transfixed by the action on the TV. Onscreen he saw the man he was desperately trying to remember that he was. As he watched, Quinton sifted his bandaged hands through the shoe box full of sand Emily had brought him from Manhattan Beach,

California. Quinton let his mind melt back into the action on the screen.

The score was sixteen to fifteen. Squid and Gardner were leading. The games went to fifteen points, but a winning team always had to beat the other by two. Two out of three games won the match, and it was one game all. Squid-Gardner were one point away from winning the championships, and three points from losing. Quinton stood behind the service line and served the ball hard and deep into the other court. Steeles lurched for the dig, narrowly bumping it to Johnson, who meticulously set him at the net. Steeles approached and swatted the ball into the other court.

Quinton easily got to the ball, and popped it up so Stu could set him for a spike. Stu maneuvered to the ball with a dancer's grace and tapped it so it floated to Quinton. Quinton jumped his infamous forty-two inches into the air, and was in perfect position to meet the ball. He slammed it into the other court with a power that reverberated through the stands.

Quinton and Stu worked together like a perfectly synchronized machine, but Johnson and Steeles were just as well oiled. Johnson leapt backwards at Quinton's spiked ball in an almost futile attempt to get a piece of it. He caught it on his right forearm just before he hit the sand. The ball feebly floated deep into backcourt, Steeles lunged for it.

Johnson leapt to his feet. "He's up," Stu yelled to Quinton, ready at the net. Steeles got under the ball and put his forearms together, fists locked, to bump-set Johnson at the net for a killer spike. Quinton readied for the block. Steeles bump-set the ball, but it missed his forearms, hitting the ridge of his thumbs instead.

The shot went awry and began skyballing upward. It accidentally floated towards the net. Easy prey. Quinton leapt off the sand and smashed down on the skyball, sending it back into the opposite court.

"Over. Fault. Sideout. Johnson and Steeles to serve," the referee said.

The crowd began to boo furiously. Quinton, hands on his hips, walked to the referee standing on his raised platform attached to the net.

"The shot was good. It's seventeen-fifteen. The match is over," Quinton said.

"No," the referee retorted. "Your hand overstepped the net. Johnson and Steeles to serve."

"That was match point, man. Championship point," Quinton insisted.

The referee took off his sunglasses and addressed Squid directly.

"Your hand contacted the ball before it crossed over to your side of the net plane, Mr. Squid. I've already given you a yellow card. No more warnings. I don't want any more outbursts. I'm not going to warn you again."

Stu called for a time out.

"Mr. Gardner, you've used up all your time outs. Johnson and Steeles to serve," the referee barked.

Quinton became more agitated. He paced around in a circle and walked toward the referee again.

"That's fifty thousand dollars man!" Quinton yelled.

"Mr. Squid, I've given you ample warning throughout this game. Johnson and Steeles win by default."

The crowd booed outrageously. Several blonde women in bikinis held up a banner which read, 'SQUID-GARDNER RULE.' They began to chant the slogan. The eclectic-looking crowd joined in. A group in the bleachers screamed derisively at the referee.

The grumbling from the crowd grew louder. Quinton Squid was their man.

"No way!" yelled Quinton.

"Mr. Squid, get away from the net and get off the court. The championship has been called," the referee shot back.

"Bullshit. Why don't you kick your seeing eye dog, you blind fuckhead!"

"That's it, Mr. Squid!"

"If you had another eye you'd be a cyclops, you bony-assed rent-a-ref!"

"That's a two thousand dollar fine. Get him off the court!"

"Fuck you!" Quinton bellowed.

"Three thousand!" screamed the ref.

"Fucking pendejo!!"

"Five thousand!" the referee bellowed back.

"FUCK YOU!!" were Quinton's final words before he grabbed hold of the net and yanked with all his might.

The referee and his platform slammed hard into the ground. He got up and ran after Quinton. The ref reached him and kicked him in the shins. Quinton turned and punched him in the face. The crowd went into a complete frenzy. Officials ran onto the court to intervene. It took six men to pry the two apart.

Suddenly, the video image of the two men fighting froze and shrank into the upper left corner of Quinton's TV screen.

Left in its place was sports anchor Bob Esterhaus, sitting at the CSN studio sports desk. The graphic logo behind him read: 'Hermosa Highlights.' He began to speak.

"And that was the scene one year ago today at last year's Hermosa Finals, where top-seeded player Quinton Squid was fined twenty thousand dollars for breaking the jaw of net referee John Alonzo. And what does Quinton say now about last year's ruckus, considering he's in the same position to win this year? Let's go down netside. Quint, can you hear me?"

Standing at Hermosa Beach wearing a headset microphone was the man from the previous highlights and the magazine endorsement photo. He was dressed in bright blue shorts and a designer t-shirt. He was cut like a Greek god, and at first glance seemed to have about as much heart as a stone statue. He looked into the camera with a shit-eating grin on his face, but his spiteful blue-gray eyes were cold and piercing.

"Yeah, Bob. I can hear you," Quinton said.

"So how about last year?" asked the sports anchor.

"Well, Bob, you know how I feel about explicit violence, and I do apologize for any injury I caused, physically or emotionally. But let's be honest. There weren't any more bad calls the rest of the season with that motherfucker's jaw wired up."

The bandaged man watching from the hospital bed shook his head. What an asshole, he thought.

The anchorman came back on.

"Well, that's Quinton Squid, dubbed the 'Deep Sea Diver' due to his incredible beach digs. Always amusing and always controversial, but unmistakably one of the best players since Ron Von Hagen. We'll be right back to catch up with the rest of the Hermosa Finals, after we do a little business with America."

A beer ad came on. There was a sudden determination, almost desperation in Quinton's eyes as he fast-forwarded to the broadcast's next segment. Why, he wondered, did he no longer feel any trace of the mean-spiritedness he had exuded on the videotape. It didn't feel familiar. He could feel some sort of darkness brooding deep within, but somehow knew it wasn't colored by spite. Perhaps as he began to remember the exact events of his life this rancorous nature would return. He hoped not. He did his best to shrug it off.

He began to watch more volleyball action at the Hermosa Beach Championships.

4

The music from the radio and the chatter of the TV news battled for Michael's attention. He quickly but carefully packed a large duffle bag lying on his bed. His apartment was across town from the Knights of Columbus, in the Orient Heights section of East Boston. He lived on the second floor of an old duplex on Baywater Street, near Orient Heights Beach. Most of the streets in the area were lined with similar houses, built just after the first World War. They were painted in dark tones – blues, browns, and grays. At night, when the streets were empty of flashy cars and trendy clothing, it may as well have been 1929. During the day, the smell of olive loaf, fried peppers, and jet engine fuel filled the air. Boston's Logan International Airport was barely a mile away. Very convenient. Especially for tonight.

Michael continued to pack feverishly. He tossed a nine millimeter Beretta with silencer, several rolls of black duct tape, and a small leather pouch next to the dufflebag. The usually tidy room had been turned completely asunder.

Lou Reed's 'Walk on the Wild Side' and Channel 4's Jack Arnold continued to battle it out.

"The Senate begins its deliberations tomorrow on a bill

the House passed several weeks ago to institute a longer waiting period for the purchase of handguns."

Lou Reed spun his off-color weave.

"...supporters of powerful gun lobbyists, including the NRA, are planning to demonstrate on the steps of the Capitol building in protest..."

Lou's plot thickened.

"...The president has yet to indicate whether he will support the bill if passed by the Senate..."

The clashing audio signals were strangely soothing to Michael's racing mind. A phone call interrupted the media melee. Michael killed the radio and muted the television. He looked at his watch. Exactly 9 p.m. He wiped the perspiration from around his mouth and picked up the phone.

"Hello?"

Victor Russo spoke on the other end.

"Michael. We're gonna have to move things up an hour. You'll meet at ten."

"Okay," Michael answered. He checked his watch again. Still nine. Had time stopped or did he need a new battery? He grabbed a butter knife and forced open a large bureau drawer that was jammed shut. It jerked open with a loud clatter.

"Is someone else on the line, or is that you?"

"No, Uncle Victor. I'm cleaning up around."

Michael searched through the drawer. He drank in its contents. Old photographs. Mementos. Rosary beads. Basketball trophies. Michael held up a green basketball jersey, the phone cradled between his shoulder and ear. In white letters, the jersey read 'All-State - Delaney – # 7.' His eyes fell inside themselves, and Michael closed them for a moment. A nostalgic smile played over his face. His eyes opened and he looked at the shirt again. He wrapped it around one of his basketball trophies and packed it and the rosary into his bag.

Michael pocketed the small skeleton key taped to the back of the drawer, and zoned back to Russo's authoritative voice on the phone.

"Michael, you're just like your father. Always cleaning. When things got tight, he always smelled from Ajax. I always told him to drink, like a real man. You're good for Gina though. She is my niece, but she is also a pig. Slob, I should say. Hold on a second, Michael." The line clicked as he put Michael on hold.

Victor Russo sat in his glass-walled office. It was situated in the middle of an enormous warehouse loading dock in Boston's North End. Nana Rosetta always felt Victor was uppity for moving out of Eastie. Victor said he just couldn't stand the jet planes any longer. And he wanted to be closer to his warehouse.

"It's still Italiano, Nana," Victor had howled at her, "it's the North End, for crissake!"

"It's not the same North End since the pazzo yuppies moved in and made us trendy," she shot back. "For God's sake Victor, they put in a frigging Papa Gino's!"

And then the cursing in Italian would start. If Victor had his way, he would've moved his whole operation to Saugus or Lynnfield, where all the nouveau-riche Italians seemed to be migrating. But Nana Rosetta would never have stood for that. And Victor wanted to stay in that will of hers. The almighty Will. She wielded it like a samurai sword. "I'll only leave you the pins in my hip after I die, Victor!" Rosetta had threatened on numerous occasions. Michael had to hand it to the old broad. She was the only one who could grab hold of Victor's cajones and hang on for the ride.

So Victor had to settle for a nice little home on Salutation Street, a few blocks from his Battery Wharf warehouse. It was a gorgeous piece of property by anyone else's standards. But Victor was never content. It was a disease with him. Thirty years ago, the warehouse had two loading docks. His partner Phillip Delaney, Michael's father, had been content with just those two. They were large, but Victor wanted more, wanted to expand.

Now the warehouse had six docks. And the pace of movement was tense – loading and unloading, all night and day. It would've driven a normal man to drink. But for some reason it seemed to calm Victor's mind. Michael always figured it distracted him from thinking about things he didn't want to think about.

Michael didn't know the half of it.

Victor watched as a shipment of TV/VCR combo units was unloaded onto one of the docks. He looked back from the dock and stared intently at one of the six similar units set up in his office. They were stacked together, each tuned to a different sports game. Each combo unit's VCR recorded its respective game, insuring complete viewing access at some later time.

Carlo and Muncie, or Frick and Frack, as they were quietly referred to, were setting up three more units in Victor's office. Carlo was the more muscle-bound of the two. He wore a t-shirt that read 'Home of the Whopper,' with an arrow pointing down to his pants. He literally had no neck. Muncie had a neck, though it could only be seen in silhouette with a tungsten bulb. His breath could blind a buffalo.

Victor spoke to them like a kindergarten teacher. He made sure to stand back from Muncie.

"Carlo, put them three, three, and three across. Like a square."

A confused Carlo scrunched up his eyes.

"Like *The Hollywood Squares?*"

"Yeah, like *The Hollywood Squares*. Muncie, show him. Jesus."

Victor picked up the phone and took Michael off hold, just as the Boston Celtics scored a three-pointer.

"Oh, OH! You watching the Celts game, Michael? You shoulda seen that!"

Michael sat on his bedroom floor. He carefully ran his hands over more of the awards he had unearthed from the bureau. With one hand on the receiver and the other on his high school MVP trophy, Michael answered.

"I'm not thinking too much about sports these days, sir."

"A man always has time to think about sports, Michael. After you and Gina are married tomorrow, you should go away for a while. Take a vacation. We'll discuss it Saturday."

"I should go, Uncle Victor. I only have an hour."

"Remember, just the plates. A friendly competition. A little game of cat and mouse. We don't want a full scale war on our hands. The Callabrisi's can be real sonsabitches."

"Yes, sir."

Michael hung up. Their conversation had made him uneasy. He began to pack more fervently. Toothbrush, razor, and other toiletries were tossed into the dufflebag. He glanced across the room for any other stray items.

The billowing flames and five-ring Olympic logo flashing over the television caught his attention. He un-muted the TV and listened to Jack Arnold's report.

"At Logan Airport this evening, a VIP aircraft en route to the Goodwill Games in Bonn, Germany was struck just before takeoff by a smaller aircraft attempting emergency landing. Members of several of the men's US Olympic Teams scheduled to appear at the games were on board. No reports of injuries or casualties are available as yet.

"A Revere woman was the lucky winner in the Mass Megabucks lottery drawing last night. She takes home an estimated eight million dollar Baystate jackpot –"

The phone rang again. Michael turned off the television and picked up the receiver. Before he could speak, Nick bellowed into the line.

"Well?"

"Well what?" asked Michael.

"Well what, yourself. You must've talked to him, too. You've been on the phone for a decade. I'm not hanging around the airport for an extra hour like a sitting duck."

"So change the flight."

"We can't. There's nothing sooner."

"So what? What do you wanna do? You want to forget it?" asked Michael.

"Yeah," Nick answered. "We stay straight with Victor. We haven't burned any bridges yet."

"You stay. There's no way I'm marrying into this sea of Coney Island whitefish, you dago wop cugine."

"Cugine yourself."

"And if I'm out of the picture, Nick, you're next in line. Gina told me she always thought you were cute, so you better bone up on your two a.m. bungie-fucking techniques."

"Fungule. I'll see you in an hour."

"In an hour. Paesan, Nicky. We can do this."

"Paesan."

Michael hung up. Done packing, he zipped up the dufflebag.

He went to the closet door and unlocked it with the skeleton key. The closet was empty save for one large item.

Staring back at him from inside was a well worn, five foot tall, Wing Chun dummy, or Chinese wooden-man. Michael carefully placed the dufflebag on the top shelf of the closet. He ran his hands gingerly over the wooden-man's arm extensions. The dummy consisted of one large central post, from which protruded three wooden arms and one leg, looking like a large, rigid octopus.

The wooden-man was a training device – a very advanced training device on which to practice stop-hand or stop-foot blocking and striking techniques. Without years of proper training and carefully developed technique, to strike at it meant certain bone fragmentation.

Michael looked at the palms of his hands. Still calloused. Still beautifully calloused, he thought to himself. They were the marks of right action, the marks of his calm through the storm. They were the marks of his father, Phillip Delaney. Michael closed the closet door and locked it behind him.

He threw the remaining mess of clothes and trophies back into the bureau. Preparing for the evening ahead, he holstered his gun and filled his baseball jacket with the items left on the bed. Two ammo clips, duct tape, ski mask, and black leather gloves.

The door bell rang. Michael froze. It rang again.

Michael moved quietly through the bedroom and into the spacious living room/kitchen area of his apartment. It was a tightly kept, almost compulsively clean home, which didn't seem to coincide with his brash outward appearance. Sitting on the kitchen table was a wire mesh cat carrier. A beautiful black cat named Sheba slept inside. As Michael passed the table, she began to purr. Michael could hear her over the door bell. He smiled at her.

"You love me, don't you," he whispered.

Her green eyes winked at him and he crouched down to stare into them. He saw the past, present, and future in those eyes. A record of time immemorial. Those eyes could still calm him, no matter what kind of hurricane was going on around him.

Unless the hurricane was persistent. And the one outside his door now definitely was. The ringing turned to knocking and the knocking turned to pounding. A woman's voice bellowed at him from the other side of the door.

"Michael? Michael! I know you're in there, you son-of-a-sonofabitch! Open the door!"

Michael scratched the inside of his right ear with his pinkie. Shit. That voice was supposed to be in Boca tonight. Maybe she'll go away.

No such luck. Michael heard her key unlock the deadbolt. He saw the doorknob spin. For the first time in his life he wished he wasn't so tall. He wished he was small enough to fit into the cat carrier with Sheba, or under the cushions of the couch. The door began to open. He braced himself for the inevitable.

But wait. What was there to be afraid of? She didn't know anything. No one knew anything. Only he and Nick. But Gina was smart. Smarter than any of them. Smarter than Victor. It was what had attracted him to her. That and the fact she was drop-dead gorgeous.

The door opened six inches and came up against the chain lock. Five 'Whisp of Rose'-colored fingernails attached to five fingers and a wrist groped the inside of the door for the chain release. A flick of the wrist and she was in. Michael always wondered how she managed to do that.

He stared at Gina as she yanked her keys out of the door. He had decided long ago that if she was ever a guest on a talk show, the caption below her would read 'A Petite Woman

With An Exterior Beauty Unbefitting Her Cross Demeanor.'
Somehow he was sure Gina would disagree.

"Hello, Gina," he finally said.

Gina turned around, startled. Another yank and the keys
came free.

"You putz. Why didn't you let me in?"

Ah, music to his ears. Gina slammed the door shut and
threw her jacket and bag onto the couch. "All right, where is
it?"

Michael ignored her question. He was temporarily hypnotized by how garishly her Corinthian hoop earrings clashed
with her crepe goldtone pants and olive Heraldic print blouse.
Standing there in his tuxedo pants and baseball jacket with
a nine millimeter Beretta stuck in his cummerbund, he wondered who looked more ridiculous.

"Where the hell is it?" Gina demanded. The cat purred at
her as she walked by the kitchen table.

"What?"

"It. It. I know you have it."

"What 'it'?" pleaded a confused Michael.

"My diaphragm, you stupid moron!" Gina screeched as
she began crashing through the living room, searching under
cushions, through cabinets, and inside drawers.

"What the hell are you doing?" Michael asked, glancing at
his watch. "Don't you know it's bad luck to see the bride the
night before the wedding?"

Gina paused just long enough to answer his question.

"Suck my dick."

With a flip of her hair she attacked the La-Z-Boy, throwing
off the cushions and feeling along the frame with her hand.
No luck. She stopped for a minute and stared Michael right in
the sockets.

" 'Cindy Lou, the Petting Zoo.' Frank told me. You're a pig."

"What are you talking about?"

She walked up to him as he opened his mouth to continue.

"Look, I'm on my way out the – "

Before he could finish, she slapped him hard across the face. He was stunned, but didn't flinch. She slapped him again, harder. His eyes burned, but he still didn't move. Thoroughly frustrated, she groaned and belted him a hard right cross. He was taken aback this time, visibly upset. His mouth began to bleed.

"Shit, that hurt! I'm sick of this bullshit. Here. Here..."

He took out his money clip and grabbed two hundred-dollar bills.

"Here is enough money to buy yourself a goddamned, goldplated, diamond-studded diaphragm. And you can wear it around on your charm bracelet for all I care!"

He shoved the bills into her cleavage. Wrong move.

"Screw you where you live, Michael!" she fumed and abruptly kneed him in the groin. Slapping him hard across the face, she grabbed the gun from his cummerbund and kicked his stunned body to the ground in one flowing motion. He writhed on the floor in agony. She ran into the bedroom.

Gina, adrenaline pumped, gun in hand, dumped out his bedroom drawers and filed through the bureau. Nothing. She ransacked the bed, tearing down the bedcovers and pillows. Nothing. She tried the closet door. It was locked. With practiced precision she began to shoot around the doorknob. The sound of the silenced gun popping out a barrage of stifled shots rang through the apartment. She kicked the loosened doorknob to the ground.

In the living room, Michael regained his ground. He moved determinedly towards the bedroom after her.

Gina found the carry-on in the closet and pulled it to the floor. Its contents, the toothbrush, razor, toiletries, fell out onto the ground, as well as the contents of the small leather pouch: dozens of uncut diamonds. She was stunned at her discovery.

Michael entered the bedroom, the embodiment of rage. She pointed the Beretta at him and demanded, "What the hell is going on here, Michael?"

Michael stood in the doorway. "Leave it alone, Gina."

She cocked the gun and aimed it carefully at him. Her mascara was beginning to run.

"You're leaving, you crud. Aren't you? You've been scamming off Victor and now you're leaving!"

At this point he felt the best answer to her question would be a tackle, so he rushed her. She was able to squeeze off one last round before the gun hit the floor. The shot missed Michael and landed in the doorjamb. They struggled on the floor amidst strewn clothing, broken glass, and old basketball trophies.

Gina managed to get one foot on the floor, but Michael yanked it out from under her.

She scratched his face and he slapped hers. She managed to get a leg up, and swung at him with her hands cupped together like she was swinging a nine iron. He fell backwards into the bureau.

Though her appearance may not have suggested it, Gina was a worthy opponent. But Michael was still physically overpowering. Badly beaten and overtaken by fury, he rushed her again, grabbed her by the collar and backed her against the wall. Without realizing what he was doing he began to choke her. She couldn't breathe. Suddenly he focused back to the moment and let go of her. Gina fell to the ground, coughing.

As if on automatic pilot, Michael picked up the gun and changed the clip. He yanked her disoriented body up from under the shoulders and sat her down in a chair. He took the roll of duct tape from his jacket and began to bind her wrists and ankles to the chair.

"You're dead," Gina exhorted through choking gasps. "You're a dead man. I'm looking at a dead man." She went on.

"What are you planning tonight, Michael? You schmuck. When they catch you, they're going to cut off anything that can be cut off and shove it down your stinking throat. You make me want to puke in my shoes, you pile of horse – "

He put a small piece of duct tape over her mouth and shook his pinkie irritably in his right ear.

"Shut up."

Michael continued binding her to the chair, but the banshee regained her strength and struggled all the way. She desperately tried to speak through the tape. Finally she bit through and spit it out.

"– who do you think you are? Mr. Big Man, my ass. You don't have nothing in your pants, not a thing."

Michael put the gun to her face.

"I ought to blow that filthy mouth of yours right off your face, Gina. You're lucky I'm not as much of a pig as you are."

"You're just the same as me, Michael, you just never had the stones to admit it. I'll see you burn in your shorts for this, you –"

Michael managed to get another piece of tape over her mouth, this time wrapping it all the way around her head. Her eyes bulged with fury, as if they would pop right out. She struggled in earnest but uselessly, for he'd taped her completely to the chair.

"What? Nothing to say, Gina?" Michael asked facetiously.

"The sick thing is, I'm actually sorry about this, but there's no other way out of this rat's nest."

He walked to the bathroom, then came out with a box of sleeping pills. With his left hand he held out the box out in front of her. With his right he held out his naked fist.

"You choose. Sleeping pills or a hard right cross."

Gina nodded to the right.

"You think I don't have the stones to belt you. But you don't realize it takes more stones not to. That's what's wrong with you people."

He poked a small hole in the tape, fed several pills into her mouth, and put a fresh piece of tape over the hole.

"They'll find you in a couple of hours when they come looking for me. You'll be okay. Goodbye, Gina."

It was early morning and the TV was still on, the screen flooded with electrostatic snow. White noise echoed and flashed through the spartan hospital room. The day nurse entered Quinton's room and opened the venetian blinds. The snow on the screen dissolved into a white dot as she turned off the set. The sudden onset of silence woke Quinton up.

"Good morning, Mr. Squid," said the nurse as she straightened up the mess of books, videotapes, and magazines scattered on his bed. "You don't want to get this stuff caught up in your IV tubes. You could get all tangled."

She looked to him for a response she knew would not be forthcoming. The nurse was used to having one-way conversations with the mysterious Mr. Squid. He was barely conscious of himself, let alone anyone else. Most other patients she'd worked with for this long would already be calling her Jean by now. They'd know she had two kids, a wonderful husband, and was taking night classes to become a surgical nurse. But Squid was different. He was too busy figuring out who he was, let alone wonder about anyone else.

The situation intrigued her. A living, breathing Agatha

Christie novel, with a little H.G. Wells thrown in to boot. She'd come to notice how Squid's eyes inhaled everything that went on in the room, whether it was a nurse checking his IV, or how the patterns of light and shadow formed by the blinds changed throughout the course of the day. She assumed he was tucking the information away, hoping it would help clarify something for him at some later date.

"You have some visitors," she told him, and left the room to let Stu and Emily enter.

"Hi, Q," Emily said with a smile, but there was no response. Quinton simply glared at the becrutched Stu.

"Hey, uh, Quint. I'm going back to San Diego tonight and I just wanted to say goodbye, maybe talk," said Stu. He sat down on the corner of Quinton's bed. Quinton continued to stare at him.

Stu felt uncomfortable. A little edgy. Like he was in a bad episode of *The Twilight Zone*. Only this was his life, and he couldn't handle it. Stu couldn't handle much. He had barely managed to handle his own wedding. If it hadn't been for Quinton...

Stu was a follower, not a leader. And he was aggravated by the recent turn of events. He sifted distractedly through the small volleyball library of books, magazines, and videos that Emily had brought from California. It was all there. Nearly everything in print about the game of volleyball. Various rulebooks, from pro beach to six-man hardcourt; books on hand signals, drills and strategies; everything Gene Selznick had written about the Olympic Games; two years of *Volleyball Magazine* back issues; Jon's *Hot Sand*, Karch's *Championship Volleyball*; and every other volleyball reference guide Emily had been able to scrape up.

"You've been catching up here I see," said Stu, hoisting a

copy of Sinjin Smith's *Kings of the Beach*. "A lot of reading. How are you?"

Quinton took a long deep breath and slowly began to respond. He addressed Stu, his eyes serious.

"Am I an asshole?" he asked.

Stu and Emily exchanged glances. Neither could help but crack a smile.

"Well, basically...yeah," Stu said, chuckling.

Quinton wasn't laughing. Stu realized he was serious. He cleared his throat. "Okay, you're my best friend, but yes, Quint, you are an asshole. You make my sorry ass look good."

"Do I really know you?" asked Quinton.

"Yeah. Look, you signed my cast and everything."

Stu lifted his cast into Quinton's view. In large bold letters Quinton had signed his name, exactly as it appeared on the autographed Sand Dune endorsement photo.

"Is that really my signature?"

Quinton looked at Stu, almost pleading with him. Stu tried to shrug it off.

"Sure, dude. Of course. You're baked. You know, fried. Braindrained."

Quinton didn't respond. His eyes retreated back inside himself. To Stu they looked suddenly dead. What the hell was going on? Stu could not wait to get out of the room. Just hurry up and remember for god's sake! - he wanted to yell. But something inside told him to just breathe deeply.

Emily could see her husbands' jaw clench and unclench in frustration. She knew he was having a hard time accepting what had happened. Quinton had always run the show, kept things together. Right now Quinton was the student, but Stu didn't want to be the teacher. Emily went to Stu. She gently stroked his jaw.

"Stu," she said softly. "He's just confused."

Stu closed his eyes and took another deep breath. When he opened his eyes, much of the anxiety had been washed away. He looked warmly at Quinton. He felt drawn to stare into Quinton's blue-gray eyes. Quinton came out of himself. His eyes looked at the world around him, rather than at the turbulent one within. He stared back, into Stu's eyes. Quinton spoke calmly.

"Baked. Like in a fire."

Stu exhaled a huge deep breath. He felt as if a two hundred ten pound, six foot four inch weight had been lifted from his shoulders. Thank god. He's beginning to remember. The serenity Stu had found moments before vanished.

"Yeah man, we were in a fire. Right. It's all coming back. It'll catch up to you," Stu rambled at Quinton. "Just keep going. Hey, I brought you another tape, and guess what else? The new *Volleyball Magazine*. We made the cover."

Stu put the video in the VCR and tossed the magazine to Quinton.

"I'll see you in San Diego in three weeks dude," he babbled. "Okay?"

"Okay," was Quinton's only response.

They said their goodbyes and Emily and Stu were gone. Quinton was left alone in his virtual Volleyball Hall of Fame.

He stared down at the magazine Stu had tossed him. On the cover was a picture of the US Volleyball Team's plane on fire at Logan Airport. The copy below read 'Goodwill Games Up In Flames.'

The sound of crackling flame faded in and out of his mind. As he stared at the picture, his gaze turned inward once again. Strangely, the turbulent blackness within was beginning to feel familiar. He waited in it silently for anything to appear that would remind him of who he once was. He had the feeling he'd be waiting for quite some time.

6

In the heart of the North End, Michael stood in one of the dimly-lit alleyways a few blocks east of Haymarket Square. The moonlit December night was occasionally dotted with groups of restaurant-goers hurriedly rushing by. A light fog mounted, as it had just finished raining, and a cold sea breeze blew in from nearby Boston Harbor. The moonlight streamed across the wet pavement in shafts of light which made their way through the deluge of old-style architecture.

Michael looked down as several large rats began to nip at his feet. He tried to kick them away, but they were annoyingly persistent. One managed to crawl under his pant leg. It clawed at his calve. Michael shook his leg violently. He took out his gun and shot the rodent as it fell back to the ground. He looked up, fearful someone had heard the muffled shot, but the noise of the city had been loud enough to cover the quick pop.

Michael returned the gun to his shoulder holster, took out a cigarette and lit it. He dropped the match onto the dead rat's carcass. The fur ignited, then fizzled out as Michael kicked it into a puddle. He gazed at the rat's dead eyes staring up at him. It was not an unfamiliar sight. On his eleventh birthday,

Michael had received a beautifully wrapped gift from a twelve-year-old Frank. He had come to expect nothing from Frank but the occasional trip down the stairs or the usual fist in the face. He was smart to be wary. As Michael unwrapped the present, a shit-eating grin began to envelop Frank's face. Michael saw Frank move slowly out of Victor's arms' reach. The paper tossed aside, Michael carefully lifted the top off the box. He looked down, horrified at its contents. Staring back at him were the same jelly-dead eyes he had seen when his goldfish had floated to the top of the bowl. But these eyes didn't belong to a fish. They belonged to a dark, calico-striped house-cat which Frank had found in a dumpster behind the local veterinary clinic. Victor moved closer to see what had shocked Michael so deeply.

To Frank's amazement, Victor let out a chuckle when he peeked inside. Victor put the lid on the box, and he and Frank left the room to show Rita Michael's present. Michael stood there in the living room and pinched himself, hoping he would wake up. A strange chill entered his being when he realized he was, in fact, awake.

Michael looked up from the dead rat to see Nick edging his way into the alley.

"Nicky, where's Frank?"

"I don't know. Flogging the bishop," Nick chuckled.

"He should be here. What an ape. Where's your car?"

"Out the side door, in the other alley."

"Do you have everything?" Michael asked.

"Yeah. Just a carry-on."

"Okay. Just one stop at my place and then the airport. You get the flashlight?"

"Steel reinforced," Nick answered. "Mikey, just use some of that won-ton stuff on him."

"No. Remember, left side."

"Right."

"Your left. His right," Michael reiterated.

"But I'll be behind him."

"Yeah. Then your right."

"Got it. Right side. Mikey, why does he have a steel plate in his head, anyway?"

"It's a long story. Later."

Nick flicked on the flashlight. The light hit Michael's face. It was severely scratched.

"Jesus. What happened to your face?" Nick asked.

"Gina."

"Oh."

Enough said. Michael flicked his cigarette into the puddle near the dead rat.

"I am outta here, Nicky. No more Lucan."

"What's Lucan?"

"That's what I am. Lucan. The guy in the TV show."

"Never heard of it."

"It was about a boy raised by wolves in the forest. He never knew he was a human being until he met one. I want the chance to find out if I am one or not."

"Well, you're getting off to a good start here, Mikey, ripping off your adoptive father's golden hen."

"Hey, I'm still part wolf until I'm on that plane. Besides, if Victor would've let me go to college, who knows, I might be playing for the Celtics by now."

"You really think you were that good?"

Michael looked upward into the cool night air. He squinted at the full moon.

"Who knows? Spilled milk, I guess."

Nick looked up at the full moon which had caught

Michael's attention. "What are we getting tonight, anyway?" Nick asked.

Michael smiled. "You wouldn't believe me if I told you."

"Try me."

"Plates."

"Plates. What, twenties? Fifties?"

"NBA Championship rings," Michael answered.

"You're shitting me." Nick laughed.

"Would I lie to you? '86 Celtics. When they beat Houston."

"At the Callabrisi's?"

"It's a gentlemen's whatever-the-fuck wop game."

In the foggy distance, Frank entered the alley with two metal cases. Michael nodded his head at Nick.

"It's Howdy Doody time. Here comes Bam Bam."

"After he's unconscious I want to pull one of his nuts off," Nick whispered.

Michael flashed an old-fashioned straight-edge razor from inside his jacket. "Would you settle for shaving his head?"

Nick's brown eyes flashed and he grinned wickedly. "What? Remove the lion's mane? We'd better make it to Logan, or we're roadkill."

They both knew he was only half kidding.

"Go! Go! Go!" Frank yelled as he, Michael, and Nick burst into the outer lobby of the Callabrisi office building with their guns drawn.

The two lobby guards froze in their tracks when they saw the three masked men.

"Move it and lose it!" Frank barked. "Simon says, 'hands up.'"

The startled guards immediately raised their arms. Nick ran up to one of them and jammed a gun in his back.

"Don't move. This ain't my dick you're feeling," Nick

whispered loudly as he took the man's sidearm. He took the other guard's as well.

Frank looked the guards over. They were older and a bit overweight.

"Jesus, are you old," he laughed, amused at the watchmen's obvious state of decay.

A third guard ran around the corner into the group of gunmen, but an alert Michael was ready to cover him.

"Drop it now!" he ordered.

The guard abided. Nick picked up his weapon.

"That's it. That's all three," said Nick.

"That's all?" Frank chuckled. "Nothing to write home about, are they? Are you Porky? Talk about cutting corners. Old man Callabrisi's a cheap sonofabitch."

Michael and Nick couldn't help but laugh in spite of themselves at Frank's astute observation.

Turning silent, the gunmen palmed the guards' key rings and walkie-talkies and herded them into the elevator.

Frank sat at the head of the long mahogany boardroom table in the Callabrisi suite of offices. He chewed a large wad of bubble gum, with which he proceeded to blow enormous pink bubbles through the mouth opening in his ski mask. His gun was cocked. He pointed it at the other end of the table, where an unmasked Nick and Michael taped the three guards to the boardroom chairs. They had been gagged and blind-folded. One was in his underwear. Nick was quickly changing clothes with him.

"This little piggy went to market," Frank commented to no one in particular, got up and began to stick wads of used chewing gum in the guards' ears. He sat back down.

Fully dressed in the guard's uniform, Nick headed for

the lobby. "I'm going out front. Call me when you get into the safe. And Frank, you can take off your mask now. They're blindfolded."

Nick left the room.

Michael quickly put the two metal cases on the table and opened them. The first was filled with various sonic lockpicking devices and digital safebreaker counting machines. The second was filled with jeweler's drills and several small explosive charges. While Michael concentrated on the task at hand, Frank looked at the guards and began to pound on the table. He blew a huge bubble that broke all over the outside of his ski mask.

"Hey, flatfoot," he yelled across the table at a particularly decrepit-looking guard.

The guard didn't budge.

"Hey, look at me when I'm talking to you."

The guards were unable to move and didn't even try. Frank took the mask off his face and tried to remove the bubble gum. He took the comb from his pocket and carefully combed his blonde hair back into place. He looked over at Michael, who was hard at work on a safe hidden behind a reproduction of 'American Gothic.'

"Whoa, did you see that bubble? What a beauty. Hey, Michael."

Michael didn't make eye contact. He was doing his best to ignore Frank's buffoonery. He checked his watch.

"Frank, quiet. Keep it down to a dull roar, huh?"

"'Dull roar?'" Frank mimicked. "What a pussy. You always were a pussy, Michael."

Michael looked up suddenly, as if he'd just remembered missing a dentist appointment.

"Frank, who the hell is Cindy Lou?" he asked.

Frank ignored the question and smiled mischievously to himself. He blew another bubble.

Inside the bedroom of Michael's apartment, Gina had regained consciousness and struggled to break free. Her mascara had run and her face was red from the battle. She was truly a mess. She tried to jump up and down to break the chair she was taped to, but it accidentally tipped over, crashing to one side.

She groaned in frustration. Lying on her side, taped to the chair, she spotted a broken picture frame a few inches away. It was a picture of her and Michael together. The picture fueled her fury and she found new strength. She began to inch her way towards the broken glass.

Michael finished hooking up his equipment to the safe. The electronic safebreaker began systematically searching through all the possible number combinations. He checked his watch again and sat on the desk to wait it out.

Frank put his ski mask on the table, and took out a large horseshoe magnet from inside his jacket. He moved around to the other end of the boardroom table. He yanked the blindfold and gum off the nearly naked guard. The guard began to tremble.

"Don't worry," said Frank, "just don't remember my face."

He held the magnet up to the guard menacingly. Satisfied with the man's terror, Frank put the magnet down on the table to the left of the guard, and slowly moved around to the man's right. As Frank put his head on the table, the magnet shot suddenly past the petrified guard and into the left side of Frank's head, connecting with a clang. Relishing the guard's fear as he stood up with the magnet jutting from his skull, Frank dissolved into a fit of laughter.

"Hey, what time you got?" asked a distracted Michael, breaking the moment.

"Fifty-two minutes. Little less than an hour."

Michael checked his own watch for synchronization. Irritated, he began to scratch the inside of his ear with his pinkie.

"Frank, will you answer my first question?"

Frank turned his attention away from Michael and back to the guards.

"You know," he said to them, "you're lucky I'm a man who enjoys his work. Look what I brought you."

Frank took three plastic pig noses from his pocket and proceeded to put them on the guards.

"This little piggy went to market, this little piggy ate roast beef, and this little piggy puked in his shoes all the way home."

Nick entered the room, his uniform soaked through with sweat.

"What's taking so long?" he asked anxiously. "We need at least half an hour in case we have to blow the safe. The late shift comes on in fifty minutes."

Magnet still jutting from his head, Frank glared at Nick.

"Nicky boy, sit your body down and shut up."

Nick couldn't help but stare. He just had to ask.

"How did you get that steel plate in your head, anyway?"

"Ask Michael," Frank retorted, as he removed the magnet. The safebreaker's four digit number locked into place. They were in. Michael signaled Nick to get his flashlight ready and get behind Frank.

"Come clean, Frank," Michael asked. "Who is Cindy Lou?"

"She's a hooker," Frank smiled. "I told Gina she was the main attraction at your bachelor party."

"I didn't have a bachelor party. You're a real fuck, Frank. You know that?"

"Yeah, well, you should've given me what I wanted for Christmas."

"I got you the Nintendo Mortal Kombat series."

"No. What I always wanted for Christmas. Same vein, but a little more fleshy."

"And what would that be?" Michael asked.

"For you to misplace your merit badge in passive resistance, oh grasshopper. And just put up your fucking dukes for once."

"Sorry, Frank," Michael smiled back. "That will never happen. Nick, its Howdy Doody time."

Nick lifted his flashlight high and let it come crashing down on the left side of Frank's head. As flashlight and steel plate connected, the sound of metal clanging together rang through the boardroom. Frank was stunned but still conscious.

"Your right, his right, both your rights, dammit!" Michael screamed.

Nick let the flashlight come crashing down on the right side of Frank's head this time, and he went limp. They quickly bound him like a heifer and opened the safe. Nick opened the top drawer and pulled out a black velvet pouch. He reached into the pouch and pulled out a handful of diamonds. Michael and Nick smiled at each other. As Nick pulled the '86 NBA Championship ring plates from the bottom drawer, Michael took the straight edge razor from his jacket.

"You got any shaving cream?" he asked.

A fifteen minute cab ride away, Gina had cut through the tape binding one wrist and both ankles with a shard of glass. She had one wrist to go. Done, she crawled to her feet and searched for the phone. Through the mess their earlier combat had created, she pulled at a white cord until Michael's phone surfaced.

She picked up the receiver. It turned red from the blood of her glass-cut hand. She dialed the phone trembling with anticipation and screamed in pain as she ripped the tape from her mouth. Her eyes widened as someone picked up on the other end. In anguish, she cried out, "Uncle Victor!..."

Michael and Nick rounded the Orient Heights MTA station in Nick's Ford Fiesta and pulled up in front of Michael's second-story apartment. Nick kept the car running as Michael ran upstairs to get his bag and Sheba. As he keyed into the apartment, Michael smelled a strange odor coming from inside. He opened the door slowly and slipped in with his back hugging the wall. A flick of his wrist and the lights came on. For some reason the smell was more familiar in the light. Gas. Sitting across from him on the kitchen table was his bag and the cat carrier right where he had left them. Sheba was inside, limp. He opened the cage and cradled her in his arms. He ran to the kitchen stove and quickly shut off the gas.

"Oh no, oh god," Michael muttered under his breath.

He looked down at Sheba. She was dead. He clutched the cat to his chest and moved quickly towards the bedroom, screaming.

"Gina! Gina!"

He slammed open the bedroom door and ran inside. He quickly saw the chair was empty, and there was a trail of blood leading to the phone. No Gina. His ears perked up as he heard a distinctive metal-jingling sound coming from behind. Startled, he turned around to see a half-dozen grenade pins stapled to the doorframe. The corresponding grenades were taped to the bedroom door.

Their arming handles snapped open. Gas fumes flooded Michael's nostrils. He began to count down as he ran headlong for the bedroom window.

Five, four, three, two...

Just as he broke through the glass, the explosion caught him at his heels and completely engulfed him. A huge cloud of blue and orange flame, fed by the gas, billowed out from the second-story window. Michael's burning body fell onto the hood of Nick's car parked below. His face crashed through the windshield, the dead cat still in his arms.

Nick jumped out of the car, horrified. Flames covered Michael's body. Nick doused them urgently with his coat.

He saw the headlights of a car parked further down the street suddenly snap on. He knew that Lincoln. It was Carlo and Muncie. Nick pulled the unconscious, severely burned Michael into the passenger seat and sped off toward the McLellan Highway. The Lincoln tore after them.

Nick didn't know where he was heading. He just knew he needed to get the hell out of there, and fast. The routes in and out of the isthmus of East Boston and Logan Airport were locked up tighter than a drum. Of the three routes out of town, only one took you into Boston proper – the Sumner Tunnel, a mile-long, underwater canal that brought you right into the North End, near the Central Artery. And Michael needed a hospital. Fast.

Nick hit Bremen Street and took a sharp left. He looked in his rearview mirror. Carlo and Muncie were close behind. Nick ignored the 'reduce speed' signs leading up to the Sumner, and hit the gas instead. Weary toll cops looked on in disbelief as Nick smashed through the wooden toll gate doing sixty-eight miles an hour. The Lincoln raced close behind, screaming through the broken gate after them.

Driving through the Tunnel was like driving through a worm hole. It was dank and moist and smelled like the muck at the bottom of Boston Harbor. The tiles were yellow, and always seemed to seep with water. Nick hated the tunnel. He liked it even less now, as he peeled down the two-lane tube trying to maintain seventy miles an hour. He didn't see the Lincoln behind him. He blew through the other end of the tunnel, turned sharply right, then up onto Rte. 93 North.

He needed to get onto Storrow Drive then take the Mass. General/Kendall Square exit. There were back ways that were easier, but he wasn't sure of them and didn't have time for mistakes.

As he ducked off and under 93 onto Storrow, he saw the Lincoln's high beams come up behind him. He burned into the left-hand lane and buried his foot on the gas. Seventy. Seventy-five. Eighty. Eighty-one. Eighty-one. Shit, why did he buy a used Fiesta? The Lincoln caught up fast. It had to be doing ninety, easy. Think. The Mass General exit was coming up ahead.

The exit took the form of a split; the Mass General lane peeled off and up to the left, and the right side continued on as Storrow.

Nick swerved his car into the left lane. The Lincoln followed. The car in front of him put on its left signal and slowed down. Nick slowed. Sixty. Fifty. Forty. The exit loomed. Shit, we're dead. Carlo and Muncie came up from behind, hugging his tail. They were bumper-to-bumper.

The car ahead of Nick sped up suddenly, creating a long space in front of him. Nick looked up at the sign above him, 'Danger, all trucks and buses must exit left.' The eighteen-wheeler in the right lane, a car's length ahead of Nick, put on his left signal. Just ahead was the split. Wait. I'm driving a fucking Fiesta! The truck slowed and started to move left into his lane. Nick gunned the engine, causing the Lincoln to speed up behind him. He knew he had a split second and ten feet to work with. He threw the tiny car into neutral and made a quick swerve to the left.

Before they knew what was happening, Nick dropped it into third and stomped on the gas. The wheels burned into the pavement, then maneuvered around the truck to the right, into the rapidly decreasing slot between the slowing truck and the oncoming split. Nick skinned through the slot and onto Storrow.

The Lincoln was forced off the highway and into the Mass General exit by the eighteen-wheeler. Nick kept going on Storrow. He pumped the Fiesta for all the power its little engine would give him.

Storrow Drive wound like a rattler. It followed the weaving pattern of the Charles River. It took no prisoners. It's what made Boston drivers Boston Drivers. And Nick was one hell of a Boston Driver.

He screamed down Storrow, winding and weaving his way clear to the Kenmore Square exit. He exited left, then headed through Kenmore, past Fenway Park, to Hospital Row. Hospitals lined Brookline Ave; Brigham and Women's, The Joslin, Dana Farber, but Beth Israel was the one he chose. Michael had been born there, and they would have most of his medical records.

Nick's car screeched to a halt outside the emergency room entrance. He quickly got out and opened the passenger door. He grabbed Michael, removing the dead cat from his arms. He slung one of Michael's arms over his shoulder and dragged him inside.

Michael's burnt watchband gave way and his timepiece fell to the ground outside the entryway.

As he dragged Michael through the holding area's sliding glass doors, he saw the emergency ward engulfed with burn victims from the airplane collision earlier that day. The receptionist was swamped and Nick carried Michael directly into the ward's hallway. A nurse rushed past him pushing an IV unit. Nick called to her.

"Nurse! Nurse!"

She ignored him. He pleaded.

"Nurse! Help me!"

She turned around and handed him a form from her clipboard.

"Fill this out and attach it to a gurney."

The nurse helped him carry Michael to a gurney, and Nick began filling out the form. He looked back down the hallway. Carlo and Muncie were already poking around the reception area. How did they get here so fast? Nick quickly ducked beneath the gurney. He finished filling out the form and attached it to the gurney's head.

A man lying on another gurney nearby began to gasp for air. The noise caught Carlo and Muncie's attention. Shit. Think. Shut him up. Nick crawled under the man's gurney. He slipped a small pillow up over the side. The man above Nick began to gurgle. Nick started to bring the pillow down over the man's face, but before he could, the gurgling stopped. The man's burnt wrist flopped down off the gurney. Nick checked the pulse. He was dead.

Nick peered over the side of the gurney. The man had burn wounds similar to Michael's, and had the same basic build and eye color. Like Michael's, his face was horribly burned and torn, beyond any semblance of recognition. Nick looked up to see

Carlo and Muncie walking into the hallway. Any minute now they would see him. Think. Think. He wasn't used to thinking. It was Michael that did all the thinking. He pulled a sheet over the dead man's face and yanked the form from his gurney. He crawled back over to Michael and switched the forms. The new form identifying Michael simply read: Quinton Squid. White male, late twenties. Logan. NorthAir International 238.

Nick crawled back and put Michael's form on the dead Quinton's gurney. He pulled the sheet off and checked the man's body for any identifying jewelry or ID. There were none. Michael had none either. And Nick still had his passport. He hoped this would work. It had to.

When Nick realized he'd been spotted by Carlo and Muncie, he ran down the hallway in the opposite direction. Chasing after him, they ran past Michael to the dead man Nick had just been standing over. They checked for a pulse, but the real Quinton Squid was dead. They ran after Nick.

Nick ran out a side exit and quickly looked around. He spotted an apartment building across the alley and ran for it.

Nick bolted through the doors and into the lobby. He spotted an elevator. A staircase next to it spiraled upward. The elevator closed as he ran toward it. The arrow above the door clicked into the UP position.

"Mingya," he groaned.

He peeled up the staircase after the elevator. Carlo and Muncie skidded into the lobby and chased up the stairs after him.

Nick was one floor ahead of them. Rounding the staircase on the second floor, Nick saw he'd missed the elevator again. He took a deep breath and ran for the third floor. The two thugs were close behind. Nick reached the third floor and slid in the elevator just as the doors closed. The DOWN indicator came on. As Carlo and Muncie rounded the third floor corner, they pried open the door and safety gate with their handguns. The elevator continued to descend below them. They shot at it with their pistols.

"Gimme the shotgun," Muncie demanded.

Carlo handed Muncie a sawed-off from under his coat. He cocked it and fired six shots into the shaft at the descending elevator. The shots echoed through the building, across the narrow alleyway, and back into the hospital.

"Who is behind these eyes?" Quinton wondered aloud, staring into the mirror of his hospital room bathroom. The blue-gray eyes that stared back looked oddly familiar. When the bandages were removed, would the face that surrounded them be just as recognizable? Turning his head from side to side, pressing the cotton mask gently against his cheekbones, he tried to make out what he looked like through the bandages. It was no use. He would have to wait. Wait in the dark impasse of his memory until something familiar ignited a spark of recollection. His patience was wearing thin. He needed something solid for his mind to latch onto.

The nurse Quinton now knew as Jean entered behind him. He continued to gaze at his own bandaged reflection.

"You shouldn't be in here alone," she said. "You should call a nurse when you need to use the bathroom. They're on the way down to bring you for your final facial graft."

The final graft. Hope. Fear. Quinton didn't know which he was feeling. He walked out of the bathroom, his legs somewhat shaky, and sat down on his bed. He looked at Nurse Jean.

"Will my legs stay like this?"

"They'll take care of that in San Diego," she said. "But that's why you shouldn't be walking just yet."

She smiled at him, but couldn't tell if he was smiling back from underneath his mask. She had since gotten to know Quinton Squid a little better. The man she knew didn't seem anything like that jerk on the videotapes he played constantly. She hoped he wouldn't return to that state of mind when he regained his memory. It was possible he wouldn't. On more than one occasion she had been witness to a strange but wondrous occurrence: surviving mortal wounds often caused a man to question the darker sides of his nature, and change for the good of others as well as himself. She hoped this would happen with Quinton Squid.

An anesthesiologist entered the room.

"I need an arm for an IV," said the short man in a lab coat.

Quinton offered his right arm but it was black and blue. The man asked for the other arm, but it was the same. There was barely space for a final IV.

"How many ops is that?" the man asked.

"Four grafts total here," Quinton answered. "I'll get one more, then two plastics in San Diego."

San Diego. The Olympic Training Center. He knew Stu and Emily would be there. He hoped something would click in his head the next time he saw them. On his home turf. He would just have to be patient.

Quinton's hospital bed was neatly made. His bags were packed and sat atop the bed. He stood in the bathroom, in the pristine blue and white Nike cross-training suit Stu had sent him from the Coast.

He held his hands up to the mirror. Their bandages had

been removed. He wore a white glove on his left hand, the right had no covering. It was pale red from the scarring.

Quinton looked at his face. In the mirror he could see the fresh set of bandages covering it. Many a night he had woken up to get a glass of water, only to see Boris Karloff's 'The Mummy' staring back at him. But these weren't that bad. This new set of bandages were soft, unlike the hard, almost cast-like feeling of the originals. The first set needed to be rigid in order to maintain the structural integrity of his soft facial tissue. But they'd felt claustrophobic. He breathed easier with this new set.

Quinton turned on the faucet and filled a glass with water. He sipped it slowly as he stared at his own reflection.

Two orderlies came in the room to take his bags. They made themselves at home, pawing through his box of books and magazines, unaware he was standing in the bathroom. One of the orderlies found the 'Goodwill Games Up In Flames' copy of *Volleyball Magazine* and began to flip through it. The other read his bag tags.

"Quinton Squid," the orderly said aloud.

The first orderly stopped flipping. He held up an old Sand Dune endorsement photo of Quinton.

"I wonder what he looks like now," he said, and tossed the magazine back into the box.

"Shit. I wonder what he woulda looked like if Daniels hadn't had that picture of him."

"Probably like Freddy Krueger," the second orderly said with a chuckle.

"Did Freddy Krueger have any skin grafts?" the other asked.

"You're a sick son of a bitch, Nelson."

"I was just asking," Nelson said, as he picked up the box

of volleyball books, magazines, and videotapes. The other orderly grabbed the two bags, and they were out the door.

Quinton continued to quietly sip his water. Fear began to build in his eyes. 'I wonder what he looks like now.' The words bore into him like a drill bit. He looked down at the pinkish scarring on the skin of his right hand and wondered what kind of monster lurked beneath his facial bandages.

Or worse, what lurked beneath the skin. Why did he feel nothing like the man he had been before the plane crash? The question nagged and bit at his brain. Nurse Jean had shared her experiences with mortal trauma survivors and their change of life attitudes. Dr. Collins had confirmed it as a possible explanation.

"People change," Nurse Jean had explained.

What other explanation was there?

The water glass Quinton drank from suddenly broke under the pressure of his gloved fist. Quinton was startled as glass and water cascaded off his nylon windbreaker into the sink. He looked down at the broken glass, shocked at what he'd done. He brushed the glass and water from his chest, his hands trembling.

'Did Freddy Krueger have any skin grafts?' The words gnawed at him. He took a deep breath to steady himself, then searched his pockets for the full-faced Sand Dune photo the doctor had given him. He found it in his back pocket and unfolded it.

As he looked at it, he realized for the first time that this had been the blueprint for his new face. He stared at his own eyes in the mirror, then back to the eyes in the photo. They looked like the same eyes, but he couldn't be sure. Was he really the man in the photo? He had to be. Quinton folded the photo to highlight the eyes. He leaned into the sink, nose almost touching the mirror. He put the photo's eyes next to his own and compared them. They were physically similar, and roughly the same color, but somehow different in spirit.

'I wonder what he woulda looked like if Daniels hadn't had that picture of him.' Desperate, Quinton slammed the clipping down on the edge of the sink and unfolded it once again. With his gloved hand he picked up a piece of glass from the sink. He slowly brought it up to his neck. He looked at his eyes in the mirror. They were full of anger, fear, and utter confusion. The orderly's words rang in his ears. 'I wonder what he looks like now.' So did he.

Quinton stared at the shard of glass in his hand. He brought it to his throat, then carefully cut one of the bandages of his facial mask. He began to unravel it.

Carefully, he removed his bandages piece by piece until he reached the layer of cotton set against the skin. Quinton removed the cotton with jittery fingers. He looked at his face for the first time. It was badly bruised, scarred, and sutured, but its resemblance to the face in the photo was uncanny. His lips began to curl upward. He smiled at himself and closed his eyes.

"My God, it is you," he whispered to the man in the mirror. A wave of relief rushed through him. He would go to California and rebuild his old life. Or start his new one.

Victor Russo sat behind the desk in his warehouse office. In front of him stood a wall of twenty-five TV/VCR combo units. Seventeen were turned on. Each displayed a different sports channel, but Victor was riveted to the large-screen master monitor directly to his right. Onscreen, Notre Dame battled Stanford for the basketball playoffs.

Frank stood next to him. Victor viciously cracked walnuts

with his bare hands as he watched the game. It was as if Frank wasn't even in the room.

"Pop."

"Shh."

Frank sat on his father's desk.

"Move your ass," directed Victor.

Frank got up. He stared at the four small black and white security monitors surrounding the large-screen TV. Nothing exciting was going on in the warehouse.

Frank whipped out the comb from his back pocket and walked over to one of the blank screens. He could see his own reflection leering back at him. His head sported a two-month wiffle cut. Nothing he could do with the comb would cover the scar. His hair was growing back very slowly.

A commercial came on the big screen. Victor popped the pieces of walnut into his mouth. He finally addressed his only son.

"I gave you two months to look into it, and you came up with nothing."

Frank holstered the comb and turned to face his father.

"He kept all his dental records in his own apartment. Who the fuck keeps their own dental records?" Frank asked.

"We do, you dumb sonofabitch. It's rule one. Where the hell do you keep yours?"

"I won't believe he's dead until I see his guinea-wop face myself."

"Oh, for crissake. He's dead already," Victor grumbled. "You and your cousin are driving me up a friggin' wall."

"What does Gina have to do with this?" Frank asked.

Victor looked him up and down, distantly.

"He left her at the altar. You only got your head shaved."

Frank shoved his face in front of his father's.

"Only got my head shaved? Look at this fucking scar! Now you can see the scar. Michael's scar."

"It suits you. So quit whining."

"How the fuck does it suit me?!" demanded Frank.

Victor moved away from his son and glanced over at the large TV screen. The game was back on. Frank walked around the desk to block his father's view.

"I'm talking to you, here," he growled.

"Don't you raise your voice with me."

"I'll raise any goddamn thing I want to!"

"You couldn't raise your cock if Lady Godiva rode in on a white horse."

Victor laughed at his own joke.

"Stop it," Frank demanded.

Victor stopped laughing and abruptly stood up.

"No. You stop it, you pathetic piece of worm shit. Michael is gone. He's dead. I crushed his head like a friggin' walnut, and if you don't get outta here, I'm gonna crush yours too. He left you with what you deserve. To stare at that scar until your ugly hair grows back."

Frank moved in closer, fuming. He spoke in a whisper through gritted teeth.

"It's your scar, old man, not my scar. I may have to wear it, but you were the cause. It's why you can't stand the sight of me."

"I don't know what the hell you're talking about – "

"Don't, Pop. I was there. You sent me there."

"He's dead. They're all dead. You were never anywhere."

"This scar proves I was."

"It only proves you were a stupid little boy."

"And you are a fool. A stupid old fool. You wall yourself up in here, like it was a glass coffin. A glass coffin with cable.

Watching games. Watching other people play games. Sitting on the sidelines. Ever since I got this scar, you've been sitting on the sidelines. You did what you did to them and you should be proud of it."

Victor sat back in his chair.

"Get out."

Frank inhaled a long deep breath in through his nostrils, then left the room.

Victor turned his attention back to the college basketball playoffs. He popped in another piece of walnut and mumbled to himself.

"Shit, Michael. I should've let you go to college."

He raised the volume on the game and sank into the upholstered leather of his swivel chair.

8

The airport shuttle rounded a rotary near Balboa Park. It moved toward the San Diego Olympic Training Center's inconspicuously bland entrance. Quinton eagerly looked out the passenger window. Palm trees, flagpoles, and faceless statues passed by as the van neared the parking lot.

His face was bandaged again. Dr. Collins had hit the roof when he found out what Quinton had done. In his carelessness, Collins lamented, Quinton could've accidentally opened the sutures, or inadvertently caused an infection under the skin. He hadn't been thinking, Quinton explained, and promised never to do it again. He wouldn't have to. He had been satisfied.

The van parked in front of one of the many earth-colored brick buildings at the end of the large parking lot. Murphey reached for Quinton's bags.

"What are you doing?" Quinton asked.

"We're here."

Quinton looked up at the large brown box-like structure.

"I thought we were going to the Training Center."

"This is the Training Center."

Quinton looked at him oddly. This was not what he'd expected.

"Not too sexy, is it?" Murphey said with a twinkle in his eye. Quinton smiled under his bandages.

"Don't worry, its got what you need inside," Murphey said as he slid open the van door.

He hopped out of the van. Quinton tossed him another bag. Murphey caught it easily.

"It's an old converted building. It was a post office or something, I don't know. But we're lucky to have it. It's not just ours, though. Whenever the National Volleyball Team isn't here, it's used for league play, or for ref training. Gymnastics too. And ping pong."

"Ping pong?" Quinton asked.

"Yeah, some kind of older Asian men's league. Don't know much about it, but I hear they're pretty good. You coming out of there or do I have to drag you?"

"I'm coming."

Quinton grabbed his box of books and videos.

'Not too sexy...its got what you need inside.' The words resonated within him. They felt like a description of himself.

He hesitated, then edged his way out of the van.

When he stepped onto the pavement the sun shone down on him like a familiar spirit. He didn't know the last time he'd felt the warmth of the sun. In the hospital back East he'd been required to stay away from the windows in daylight and remain in his temperature-controlled room. The heat of the sun and its ultra-violet rays could cause a variety of painful complications in burn victims. Quinton had longed for the day when he could lie in the sun and let its rays dance gently on his bare skin. Soon.

The sun, the palm trees, the Training Center; dry, warm air filled his nostrils with the scent of eucalyptus and orange blossoms. It was a world he'd never seen before. The only world he'd ever known had been within the hospital walls. This would be a new adventure.

Quinton and Murphey walked into the Center. The front door led directly into a narrow passageway lined on both sides and on top by wire athletic cages filled to capacity. Gymnastics equipment tried to pour through every crevice it could find. An oak balance beam had dented in the cage door, and Quinton could see a set of parallel bars poke through from above where the cage had begun to buckle. He walked quickly through the hallway.

"The office is on the right," said Murphey. "We've set this place up for you and some of the other players who were injured in the crash. Most of them are gone now, but don't worry, we'll take care of you. Why don't you go in and check it out. Your room is twenty-seven. Stu's in there waiting for you. I'll call the doctor."

Quinton turned into the office and out of harm's way. Or so he thought.

An attractive woman of twenty-five sat behind the desk. She wore fire-engine red fingernails and lipstick to match.

"Marla, you know Quint," said Murphey. "Give him room twenty-seven."

Marla looked at Quinton. She raised one eyebrow, unimpressed. As far as she was concerned what had happened to him wasn't an accident. It was more like instant karma. No matter how much pain he had endured, there would be no sympathy in her eyes. She handed him the key to his room with an overtly insincere "hello."

Quinton looked at her. Why the attitude, he wondered. He looked at Murphey. Murphey looked at the floor. Murphey knew why. Quinton would grill him later. For now though, he just took the key to his room, smiling gently at Marla under his bandages.

"Just go straight through the fire doors, and the volleyball courts," Murphey said. "It's the last door on the left."

Quinton started his trek down the long hallway. His steps echoed softly over the tile floor. The building looked like a refurbished junior high school. The water bubblers seemed a little low for postal workers. He passed several rooms, most of them marked 'storage.'

When he passed through the fire doors, he found himself standing in a huge volleyball court. It was actually six volleyball courts, each sixty feet long by thirty feet wide. The ceiling was easily fifty feet high. The left wall of the gym was lined with ping pong tables, and the room was illuminated by a single large skylight. Quinton walked into the beam of sunlight reflecting off the polished wooden floor.

He let it kiss his eyelids. He felt a warm breeze from the opposite hallway. He opened his eyes and gazed in that direction. The breeze faded. But his eye had caught something hanging on the far hallway wall. He walked through the courts, through the second set of open fire doors, to take a look at it.

High on the left wall, framed in a glass case, was a photograph of the US Volleyball Team. The caption below it read 'World Cup Champions.'

Quinton searched the photograph for himself. His eyes scanned the team roster listed under the picture; 'Left to right: Jeff Winger, Pete McIntyre, Stu Gardner, Quinton Squid.'

He searched the photo for that fourth person, fascinated by this picture he didn't remember taking. He saw himself standing next to Stu, their arms around each other buddy-style. Their faces beamed as they grinned ear to ear. Stretched out behind them was the court he had just stood on.

Quinton's eyes shifted inward for a moment. Nothing.

Blackness. His eyes returned to linger on the picture a moment longer. He then turned and looked back down the corridor from which he had come. He saw the sunlight shining off the volleyball court.

Quinton turned back to the photo and blinked. His inner monologue was running too fast for even him to understand. He turned right and continued down the hallway in search of room twenty-seven.

Quinton keyed into his room. He saw Stu sitting on his bed, back to the door, eeking out the bass line to George Thorogood's 'Bad to the Bone' on an acoustic guitar. His attempt to sing was truly an exercise in pathos. Quinton stuck his pinkie in his ear and began to shake it vigorously. Stu changed gears in mid-croak and began to wheeze 'Peaceful Easy Feeling' by the Eagles. When Quinton dropped his keys on the counter Stu turned around, startled.

"Hey, is that you Quint?"

"No, it's Claude Rains, pendejo," offered Quinton.

" 'Pendejo.' You remember!" beamed an excited Stu.

He lunged off the bed and gave him a big bear hug. Quinton stiffened. Stu pulled away and took a step back.

"Oh. You don't remember, do you?"

"No. Not yet," Quinton responded sheepishly.

Stu tried to smile for his friend's sake.

"It's okay. Don't worry about it," he said as he extended his right hand to Quinton, palm up.

Quinton looked at his own right hand. The bandages were off, but it was still burned. Still ugly to his eyes. Stu continued to hold out his hand. Quinton looked him in the eyes and gave him a hard low five. For the first time, Stu saw Quinton smile through his bandages, his eyes warming. Quinton looked down at Stu's leg.

"I see your cast is back on."

"I re-fractured the knee. Gotta have another surgery next week."

"Me too. My first plastic."

"Have you seen what's under the bandages?" Stu asked.

"Yeah, I've seen it."

"Does it look like you?"

"I don't know. What do I look like?" Quinton said, only partly kidding.

"You know what you look like, sparky. Stop messing with my mind, you ugly mug."

Stu grabbed his crutches from atop the bed.

"Come on, Casper, let's go shoot some pool," he said, and hobbled out the door.

Quinton followed close behind.

Dr. Richard Jennings was head of reconstructive surgery at San Diego's Alvarado Hospital. He and Dr. Collins had done their residencies together at the Boston Burn Institute after graduating from Harvard Medical School. His practice was very exclusive and usually had a three to four month waiting list. Quinton was lucky he was a celebrity.

"What about my back and legs?" Quinton asked him, glancing at the medical degrees hanging on Jennings' office wall.

Jennings sat back in his chair and poised himself for a long explanation.

"The burns to your back and upper legs didn't go below the skin. They're healing nicely. But the burns to your lower legs went through to the muscles, especially your calves. They sustained the most damage. You won't be a forty-two inch jumper anymore, Quinton."

Quinton took a deep breath and looked around the office

for a moment. Medical books and more medical books. He looked over at Coach Murphey, hunched in his chair as usual, staring down at the floor.

On the shelf above his head Quinton noticed a small scale model of the starship *Enterprise*. He was suddenly struck by the fact that he could remember things like TV shows, music, and the alphabet, but not remember where he was in relation to learning about them in the first place. He had a general knowledge of the world, but nothing that specifically tied him to anything in it. He picked up a mirror on Jennings' desk and stared at his bandaged face.

"How many inches do you think, doctor?"

"I don't know. Maybe thirty. Thirty-two inches if you work hard enough," Jennings answered.

Quinton looked up from the mirror.

"Can I start now?"

"Yes. You can do anything at the Center except the pool. And stay out of the sun. You still need to be careful of your face for the next few weeks."

Quinton looked in the mirror again.

"Yeah. This face. I paid for this face."

9

Inside the state of the art weight room at the Olympic Training Center, Quinton worked himself mercilessly on the Nautilus pec machine. Bare chested, he wore new sweats and Reeboks. His face and left hand were still bandaged. Quinton breathed hard in rhythm as his beautifully sculpted torso went through the motions of a rigorous workout. He found himself counting internally, as it seemed to steady his mind. It kept him from thinking about things he didn't want to think about.

Without warning, Stu bombed into the weight room in a wheelchair. It scared the hell out of Quinton. The arm pads slipped out of Quinton's hands and the weights slammed together with a loud bang.

"Holy Crap!" he shuddered.

He looked over at the wheelchair.

Stu's leg was encased in some kind of metal contraption, and he was butt-naked except for a jock strap. Stu sweated profusely. His eyes weaved as if he was heavily sedated. He looked like a fugitive on the run.

"Aren't you supposed to be in bed?" Quinton asked.

"I couldn't stand it anymore, Q. Don't leave. Don't leave me here," slurred a medicated Stu.

Quinton took a large gulp of Evian water. He offered some to Stu, who chugged voraciously.

"Don't be bogus, Stu. You've got a pin in your knee."

Water dribbled down Stu's chest. Quinton took the bottle back.

"Have you seen her?" Stu frothed. "She's going to give me a sponge-bath. She's one heinous looking biker-mama, faded tattoos everywhere."

Quinton laughed.

"It's not funny," yelled Stu.

An elderly nurse with a blue rinse and a butterfly tattoo on her collarbone poked her head into the weight room.

"Mr. Gardner, it's time for your bath."

Stu turned his wheelchair around to face her.

"I'm not taking off the jock," he stated emphatically.

"Believe me, I'd appreciate it if you didn't," said the nurse, and wheeled him out of the room.

"Stu," Quinton yelled after him. "I'll be back on Thursday from Alvarado, after my plastic..."

Another plastic. The last plastic. Quinton figured his face looked like it had been shoved in a waffle iron by now. Those plastics hurt like hell. Like ten thousand pins sticking into his face at once.

He closed his eyes and looked inside again. Blackness. Still the blackness. It scared him. He wondered when something was going to fill that void. And yet, at times he wondered if some part of him kept it dark for a reason. Sometimes he would go so far as to say there was something almost comforting about the stark expanse of nothingness. He knew it to be a constant, frightening as it was. Someday something would fill in this chasm in his soul, but for now he just had the void to keep him company. When he really needed to, he could cling to it.

● ● ●

The days went by quickly. Quinton's time at the Olympic Training Center seemed like one long Nautilus workout. He didn't measure time in hours, days, or weeks, but by his exercise progression. Murphey was impressed. He said Quinton was operating at about eighty percent. Eighty percent. If eighty percent was bench-pressing two hundred and sixty pounds and pec-ing two-forty, he wondered what a hundred percent would feel like. Just what kind of mutant athletic machine had he been before the plane crash, he wondered.

Quinton looked just as cut, contoured, and toned now as he had on all those videotapes. He had sculpted his upper body into a stunning work of art, but he knew what Murphey was talking about. The twenty percent he lacked was in his lower legs and knees. He had worked his lower body with the machines as well; Universal, Cybex, squat press. They had helped him gain a lot of strength in the legs. But not even the plyometrics could help him regain the one thing he still lacked – his jumping ability. He knew he'd find it only one place – on the battlefield, on the court.

But he couldn't be a gladiator with that tender face. In order to push his legs, he needed to know he wouldn't cause permanent damage if he fell flat on his face. His last plastic was over. He anticipated the day the bandages came off, to see if he could regain his forty-two inch jump. That day would come quicker than he thought.

Quinton sat in the Alvarado hospital room staring intently at the mirror in front of him. Dr. Jennings began to unwrap his bandages.

Quinton's inner monologue now ranted so feverishly he thought he might implode. The pressure of having to regain the twenty percent. The uncertainty of not knowing what kind of ghoulish facade he would have to live behind for the rest of his life. The frustration of having to live up to the expectation, the legend, of Quinton Squid. And the fear of never remembering the inner architecture of just who the hell that really was.

Or worse – the fear that he would remember.

Quinton began to count to himself. One, two, three... Jennings continued to unwrap the bandages from around his face. They were curdled with dried blood, and unwrapping them had unearthed a sweaty, saline scent that made Quinton sick to his stomach.

He tried to look inside, to see if the black void was still there for him, or if something had at last begun to fill it. But instead something struck him suddenly, like an electric shock.

He didn't feel it physically. He felt it in the shadows of his mind. In a place between the world around him and the blackness within, he saw a brilliant purple flash. It lit up his vision for an instant, like the violet spark from a backyard bug-zapper in summertime. He looked at Jennings and Murphey. They said nothing. They must have seen nothing. Whatever had taken place had happened within the confines of his own mind.

He was both elated and anxious. He didn't know if his memory was coming back, or if his brain had finally short-circuited. He took a few deep breaths to try and calm himself.

Jennings finished unwrapping the exterior bandages. Underneath was a layer of cotton padding on his cheeks, nose, forehead, and chin. Jennings began to remove it slowly.

Quinton looked in the mirror as he watched the doctor remove the final dressings. He stared directly into his own eyes, then slowly allowed himself to expand his field of vision. He saw four large scars first. They were the most visible. One on his forehead, two on the left side of his face just above the cheekbones, and one that cut from his chin to his right cheekbone. They were all stitched with black sutures, appearing more menacing than they actually were.

The wounds were not as gaping, however, as they'd seemed to be when he had hastily removed the bandages in Boston. Quinton's face now bore little of the discoloration he had seen at that time.

"It looks like the surgery's holding," Jennings commented. "The swelling's gone down completely. Continue to put the cotton on your face at night when you go to sleep. Let it breathe during the day. Put the facial ice pack on for five minutes every four hours or so. I'll see you back here in four weeks unless you have a problem." He inspected the sutures one last time.

"Let's get that jumping back up to par, huh Coach?" said Quinton. Murphey smiled back. "Damn right," he said quietly, and asked Jennings, "Is that okay?"

"Sure. He can play on hard court, but no sand. Quinton, you understand? No sand until I see you back here."

"You got it," Quinton said. He got up from the chair and shook Jennings' hand.

Victor Russo was cracking walnuts like a mad man. Crack, crack, crack, crack. Four going off at once. Two in each fist slamming together every time the Boston Bruins got the puck.

He watched a small black and white TV in Gina's breakfast nook. His hands full of empty shells, he yelled at her. "Gina, where the hell's an ashtray?"

From the kitchen she barreled back, "Just leave them on the table."

A swinging door divided the two. Gina stood over her kitchen stove cooking pasta and a large batch of home-made spaghetti sauce. She stirred the sauce mindlessly as she watched *Prizzi's Honor* on her seven-inch Spacemaker TV. Onscreen, Angelica Huston gave herself a self-satisfied grin as she ran the water in her kitchen sink, but filled her father's glass with vodka instead. God, did Gina love this movie.

She tossed a piece of cooked spaghetti at the fridge to see if it was sufficiently done. It fell to the ground onto a pile of previously tossed, undercooked pasta. There was enough on the floor now for a whole plate.

The next piece of spaghetti she threw stuck to the refrigerator. The cooked pasta was ready to be drained. After draining it carefully in the sink, she drew herself a good-sized plate. She covered it with sauce and extra garlic chunks. She then picked up the undercooked pieces off the floor and rinsed them off. In celebration of her own passive-aggressive nature, Gina tossed them on a plate for Victor. Sauce and garlic were heaped on top.

"Uncle Victor, supper's ready," she said, and backed through the swinging door into the breakfast nook.

She snapped off the TV and put the undercooked plate of pasta in front of Victor. She walked back into the kitchen to retrieve her own plate. Victor clicked the TV back on and took a bite of his spaghetti. His eyes scrunched up and the creases around his forehead became more apparent. He looked for a napkin, a towel, anything to get rid of that mouthful of food. But Gina came back in with her own plate and a bottle of wine. Victor was forced to swallow.

"How's your meal," asked Gina.

"Good," Victor mumbled.

"Why are you here?"

"I haven't tasted your cooking in a long time."

"You always hated my cooking, Uncle Victor."

"Your Nana Rosetta said you weren't getting on so good."

"What the f-, did she have my apartment bugged?"

"You don't talk about your Nana like that. She's your family. She cares about you."

"Just like you cared about Michael."

Victor was silent for a moment. He pushed his plate away.

"I cared about Michael," he finally said.

"Is that why you had him killed?"

"I just wanted them to stop him," snapped Victor. "I never meant for them to kill him."

"Bullshit, Uncle Victor. You know how much they hated Michael, and in their eyes he disgraced you."

"He respected me," Victor shouted as he pounded the table with his fist.

"He feared you," Gina came back at him. "He didn't want to become like you. All he did the last few weeks he was around was watch old episodes of *Lucan* and *Little House on the* fucking *Prairie*."

"Enough already. You were crazed over the phone."

"But I didn't want him dead. I just wanted him back."

"Like a puppet on strings."

"No, Uncle Victor. My hands are clean."

"But your cooking stinks."

"And you have the eyes of a guilty man."

"Fungule," he growled, and stood up to leave.

Victor wasn't used to being met thought for thought, shout for shout. Especially by a woman. On his way out the door, he grabbed four more walnuts.

The crack of the volleyball auto-server arm smashing into its stopper bracket reverberated through the volleyball court. Every five seconds a new ball would arc over the net to Quinton. He slammed them back over, sweating and breathing hard. He grabbed a hand towel from the sidelines to wipe the sweat from his face. The ball from the server flew over the net and hit him smack in the head.

"Oh, *come on!*"

A becrutched Stu quietly hobbled through the fire doors and onto the court. He stood silently in the corner behind Quinton's field of view.

Another ball hit Quinton in the head. Stu had to put a hand over his mouth to cover his snickering. Quinton was too busy dodging balls to be aware of Stu's presence. The machine stopped when it ran out of balls. Quinton dabbed his face carefully with the towel. His face bore no discoloration and with the sutures now removed, the scars were barely visible.

Quinton walked over to the long tape measure glued to the wall at the right of the net. There was a myriad of scuff marks on the wall to either side of the tape measure. The highest scuff mark read forty-two inches. It had a large letter "Q" penciled in next to it. Quinton took a deep breath, jumped in the air, and kicked a mark into the wall at the top of his jump. Back on the ground he checked the measurement; twenty-five inches.

"Twenty-five lousy inches. Seriously?!" he yelled out loud.

Stu wobbled up behind him, a small plastic cast on his leg.

"What's up, Q?"

Quinton turned to greet his friend.

"You. Look at you. You're out of your chair. When did you get back?" he asked Stu.

"Just now. It's good to actually see your face again."

Stu smiled brightly. It really was a relief to finally see his friend's face.

"Yeah. Here I am," said Quinton, his smile just as big.

"Have you been cleared for the pool?" asked Stu.

"Yeah, just today, actually. How's the knee?"

"Same old, same old," said the obviously pained Stu. Was he trying to be a volleyball martyr, or was he just a hardy Californian? A hardy Californian, Quinton concluded. Like himself, his brain added, almost as an afterthought.

"So how's your playing coming along," Stu asked, biting his tongue.

"How long you been standing there?"

"Uh…not long…" Stu managed to say, without cracking too much of a smile.

"Long enough, I bet." Quinton grinned.

They both broke into hysterical laughter.

"Man, you really suck," howled Stu.

"Yeah, and I bet you're a real fucking prize with that knee," Quinton retorted, amused.

"Yeah, but I could still kick your ass any day of the week," said the one-legged wonder.

"Try me," Quinton challenged.

The game was afoot.

Stu stood on one side of the net, wielding each crutch like a tennis racquet. Quinton stood on the other, basking momentarily in the sun streaming through the skylight. He turned back to the net.

His face wasn't ready for extended sun exposure yet. Yet was the operative word. It gave him hope. It meant that someday he would be free. Someday soon.

Quinton stood behind the serve line, the ball in his left hand, ready to be popped up and smashed by his right over the net into Stu's side of the court. He hesitated. He took the ball in his right hand as he wiped the sweat from his left on his t-shirt. He took a long, slow breath. The breath felt deep enough to oxygenate every blood cell in his body.

He began to count again involuntarily. Four. Five. Six...It seemed to regulate his mind's anxiety. He couldn't stop it, so just let it continue.

Quinton placed the ball in his left hand and raised it like Lady Liberty holding the torch. He shifted all his weight onto his left foot, and raised the heel so that all of his two hundred ten pounds were balanced on the ball of that foot. His calve muscles tightened and began to tremor. The skin that covered them was nearly healed, but below the surface the tissue was still weak. It would take a lot of hard work to stretch and strengthen the muscles themselves.

He had no choice but to return his body weight to both feet. He tossed the ball high above his head, leapt into the air, and let his right hand come crashing down on the ball's face. The ball shot forward and began to plummet down on the other side of the net. Stu looked pathetic as he tried to hit it with a crutch. He missed it by two feet. Ace.

Quinton looked up at the sun and howled like a wolf. One to nothing.

Stu tossed Quinton the ball under the net. An overconfident Quinton served again. Stu horsed around with his crutch-bats until the ball came at him over the net. At that point Stu's eyes, ears, and his entire body became focused on the ball, and he slammed it with his right crutch back over the net. Quinton was incredulous. He could do nothing but simply watch the ball pelt his side of the court.

"Sideout!" Stu yelled gleefully.

Quinton searched the glossary of his mind. Sideout. The name of a movie about beach volleyball Stu had given him to watch in the hospital? No. Sideout: when the non-serving team wins the volley, they don't win a point, but win the serve. The score was still one-nothing, Quinton's lead, but it was Stu's turn to serve.

Quinton threw Stu the ball. He stood on his side of the court wondering if Stu could come up with the same juice twice in a row. Stu served it hard. Quinton was barely able to hit the ball back over the net.

As the ball came toward him, Stu faked one crutch for a cross-court right side spike, but instead brought up his other crutch for a left side spike, into Quinton's left-court. Quinton had read his first move and ran to the right side of his court. He was caught on the wrong side when Stu brought up the left crutch instead. One-all.

After twenty minutes of crutch-volleyball, Stu's arms felt like lead. But he kept wielding those crutches like samurai swords. Quinton was huffing and wheezing. He didn't look well enough to be conscious. His engine was running on fumes.

The ball had been in play for five hits. This was the longest rally of the game so far. Quinton barely got a piece of the ball with his left wrist.

The ball arced slowly over the net. He hadn't gotten a big enough piece to control the shot. He watched in agony as the ball seemed to hover in mid air just above Stu. It was the kind of fat air ball that volleyball players had wet dreams about.

Stu poised himself on his one good leg. He threw a crutch out of the court area. He held onto the other with both fists and waited with drooling anticipation. The ball finally came into reach. He pounded it over the net with all his might.

Too much might. Stu toppled onto the floor, just as Quinton was hit in the stomach by the ball. The wind knocked out of him, Quinton doubled over onto the ground himself. Dozens of multi-colored volleyballs swam around the two of them as they lay on the floor, their storage net broken open by Stu's flying crutch.

Quinton and Stu stayed on the hardwood floor, prisoners of gravity. They moaned and groaned, each trying to out-groan the other. The belly-aching quickly turned to laughter as they were overtaken by the colored balls rolling around them.

"Fifteen to seven. I win," were Stu's first words after decimating his beach partner.

"I just humored you, you cripple," Quinton smirked.

"I don't think so. I think it's time to call the Volley God for you, my friend."

"The Volley God?" Quinton asked.

"It's an ancient Japanese ritual."

Quinton slowly rose from the ground.

"Get up you gimpy fuck," Quinton chastised the beleaguered Stu.

"Shut up and put your balls away. Or did you forget how to do that too?" Stu needled.

"Oh, now that's low," said Quinton as he offered Stu a hand up.

"To the curb, my man," said Stu.

Quinton lifted him off the ground with a mumbled "Wuss."

"Blow me."

Stu and Quinton tended to the task of securing the rainbow of circling volleyballs.

Marla popped three pieces of Bazooka Joe into her mouth as she painted a second coat of ruby red on her Lee Press-Ons. She didn't notice the shiny new Jaguar pull into the Training Center parking lot. The car was painted the same garish red she was applying to her fingernails.

A well-dressed man with blonde hair and brown eyes got out. The suit had to be Armani. And those wingtips weren't Florsheims. Gucci to the end.

The man headed for the main entrance, carrying a box under one arm. He swung open the heavy lobby doors like they were made of tin foil. He was a large man who looked as if he could bench-press a Buick. His face was obscured behind an expensive pair of sunglasses. He strode boldly through the corridor into the reception room. He sidled up to the desk and put down the box he was carrying.

The side of the box had air holes punched in it. It read: Pacific Airlines Kitty Carrier.

"Can I help you," Marla asked indifferently as she blew on her freshly painted nails. She snapped her gum in his direction.

The man smiled and took off his sunglasses. It was Nick Avanti, clean-shaven with a really bad dye job. Bleached blonde. They hadn't even bothered to do his eyebrows.

"I understand a friend of mine, Quinton Squid, is staying here," he said.

Marla looked him up and down. She couldn't help but notice the eyebrows.

"Yeah, he is. Do you have an appointment?"

"No I don't, but I haven't seen him for a while. I have something for him," Nick said. He started to tap his NBA Championship ring nervously on the desk.

"Okay. What's your name?" Marla asked him.

"Nick Avanti."

Inside the volleyball court, Stu and Quinton continued to put volleyballs away. Through the intercom connecting the gym with the reception area, Marla asked, "Quinton, do you know a Nick Avanti?"

Quinton walked to the intercom and pressed a button.

"Hang on a minute," he said.

He turned to Stu.

"Stu, do I know a Nick Avanti?"

Stu shook his head.

Quinton searched his mind for something, anything but darkness, but there was nothing. Not even the purple glimmer. He pressed the send button.

"No, I don't know him."

In the reception area, Nick held a pure black kitten close to his cheek. He listened to the voice on the intercom. He kissed the kitten on its head. He knew that voice. It wasn't similar in tone to Michael's, but the pattern of speech was familiar. He'd known that speech pattern since he was eight years old.

He kissed the kitten again, then put it briskly back in its carrier. Nick winked at Marla, then told her he was going to leave the kitten there for Quinton. Marla protested, but Nick was gone in a flash. She looked down into the box. The pure bred mini-sphinx looked up at her and meowed. Marla hovered over the intercom. "Quint, can you come down here? Someone left something for you."

"Have someone send it to my room," he said.

"Quinton, I don't think you should," she warned.

Quinton asked, "It is ticking?"

"No," Marla answered.

"Then just send it to my room," he said arrogantly.

Quinton clicked off the send button and turned to Stu.

"What was that all about?"

Stu swaggered around on his cast, trying to pick up more balls than he could handle.

"Don't worry about it. Some fans do some strange shit. This nugget sent me her panties in the mail once."

"Nugget?" Quinton asked.

Stu looked at him like he was from Mars.

"Chick. Nugget. Betty. Babe. You gotta get with the mother tongue, bro."

The mother tongue. Quinton didn't know whether to laugh or cry. To laugh at how ridiculous words like 'nugget,' 'betty' or 'bro' sounded. Or cry because he couldn't remember the rest of his eccentric mother tongue. He chose not to think about it.

"That Marla has daggers for me, what gives?"

Stu raised an eyebrow. A droplet of sweat fell from his chin.

"You serious?" he asked.

"Yeah."

Stu shook his head. Naughty, naughty. He took off his shirt. He wiped his face and the back of his neck thoroughly.

"Come on, what is it?" insisted Quinton.

Stu ran the t-shirt over his chest. His matted chest hairs sprung back to life. Quinton couldn't help but stare. He looked down at his own chest. It was devoid of even the most adolescent peach fuzz.

"You slept with her eighteen-year-old sister when she came to visit from Tacoma last Christmas," Stu finally confessed.

"Ouch."

"No shit, Q. That was pretty slimy."

A soggy, sweat-soaked Quinton walked into his room. He noticed a cardboard box sitting on the counter across from his bed. He perked up, anticipating the possible contents. Maybe it was a box of panties. Hell, maybe it was the whole summer line from Frederick's of Hollywood.

Quinton went over to the box. He heard a faint rustling inside. Lingerie doesn't rustle. He opened the box cautiously. The tiny black kitten looked up at him and squinted in the sudden light. It winked at him a few times and let out a loud "meow." Quinton was beyond surprised. Panicked, he closed the box, picked up the phone, and dialed the front desk.

"Marla, there's a cat in my room!" Quinton yelped.

"Yeah. I know. You told me to leave it there," Marla answered, annoyed.

"But it's a cat!" he screamed.

"But it's not ticking!" she said, and hung up with a loud click.

Quinton took a deep breath, hung up the phone, and looked at the cardboard box. He opened the flaps again and looked inside. It was a small cat. A kitten. A beautiful black kitten with green eyes that...That what, he asked himself, but couldn't finish the sentence.

Those eyes and his curiosity got the best of him. He plucked the kitten out of the box, held it over his head, and determined it was female. He held the cat out in front of him with both arms outstretched. His hands held her gently under her front paws, while the rest of her dangled below. It seemed like this might be an uncomfortable position, but she was purring nonetheless.

Those green eyes smiled at him. He couldn't help but smile back. A warm smile. A smile out of character for the old Quinton Squid. He held her to his chest. It all seemed so familiar to him, yet he knew he had no pets. He shrugged it off as deja-vu. Maybe a past life experience. When he looked at the kitten again, he noticed something glinting on her neck.

"What you got there?" he asked her.

Quinton held the cat up to eye level. Her collar gleamed with translucent stones. He removed the collar and put the kitten back in her box. He hit the bathroom light and it flickered on. Quinton held the collar up to the fluorescent light. Probably cubic zirconia.

He could see himself looking at it in the bathroom mirror and became distracted by his own image. Any chance he had to look in a mirror he took, and this was no exception. It wasn't vanity. It was something he couldn't put into words. He felt the answers to all his questions were behind his eyes.

He looked away from his eyes. If only to humor himself, he took the collar and scratched it across the image of his face in the mirror. To his surprise it cut the glass. He breathed on the stones, and the fog dissipated immediately. They were genuine diamonds.

"Oh, man. They're real," he said aloud, and shook his head in disbelief. There's no way they could be real.

But the ground-glass particles below the mirror were his proof. He smiled contentedly, swinging the collar around on his finger. He walked out of the bathroom and back to the cat.

"Well, you're one rich little kitty," he said to her, lifting her up out of the box. "This is going to buy you a lot of cat food."

He carefully put the collar back on her tiny neck, then set her gently on the counter. The perks of professional beach volleyball were getting stranger all the time. He looked out the window at the setting sun. He sensed eyes upon him, and from the corner of his eye he saw the kitten winking at him affectionately. Amused, he looked back at her.

"You must be hungry. Let's find you something to eat."

The kitchen fridge was bathed in moonlight. All was still, but the silence was deceptive. A loud slapping sound echoed from the kitchen. Laughter quickly followed.

"It's not going in," Stu whispered in the darkness.

"Turn on the lights," slurred Quinton.

Stu flicked a switch and the lights came up. He and Quinton, both drunk, were stuffing a volleyball into the kitchen microwave. Quinton finished off the last of a bottle of vodka and tossed it in the trash. He looked at Stu, then at the microwave.

"I don't know about this Volleyball God stuff, Stu."

"We have to burn the ball, and there's nowhere to build a bonfire, so we'll just nuke it," Stu garbled.

"But you're going to cause a nuclear disaster!"

"It's just going to make a small pop."

Quinton moved to the back of the kitchen, as far away as he could get from the microwave. Stu set the digital timer for four minutes and closed the door on the ball. He stepped back. The timer began to count down.

Stu put his hands over his eyes but snuck looks through his fingers. Three minutes. At two minutes he started to chew on his lower lip. Quinton hovered in the back of the kitchen, holding a pizza pan in front of his face.

At one minute he snuck a look over the edge of the pan.

The ball was still intact at forty-five seconds, but at forty-four the microwave door blew open with a loud bang. Bits of burned leather sailed through the air. Quinton dropped the pizza pan with a loud clang.

"Shh!" yelled Stu.

"Shh?" Quinton mumbled drunkenly to himself. "You just dropped Fat Man and Little Boy and you're telling me to shhhh?" He began to laugh hysterically.

"Come on, we've got to get out of here," Stu pleaded.

Quinton grabbed a can of tuna fish and some Cheez Whiz from the refrigerator. The two hobbled out in a fit of laughter, groping towards room twenty-seven.

They tip-toed drunkenly into Quinton's room, wary of waking the kitten asleep on Quinton's pillow. But her ears had perked up when Quinton slipped his key into the doorknob. She stretched her paws in opposite directions and gave a large yawn.

"Hungry?" Quinton asked her as he opened the tuna fish.

"What's her name anyway?" asked Stu.

"Kitty."

"No. You have to give her a real name, like Felix."

"Felix the Cat? I don't think so. Something will come to me," Quinton said, and he set the can of tuna down on the floor. He looked over at Stu, who sat on the counter pumping Cheez Whiz into his mouth like an idiot.

"Give me that, you moron..." Quinton laughed as he took the can away from Stu.

He knelt down on the floor and squirted some Cheez Whiz on the tuna. The kitten scrunched her nose as she caught the scent. She jumped down to the can and began eating voraciously. When she looked up to lick her chops, Quinton could see she'd developed a cheese mustache. He began to wipe her mouth with a napkin. Stu was thrown into an uncontrollable fit of laughter.

"Who's the moron now?" he howled.

Quinton flopped onto his bed. His eyes saw the fluorescent lights start to spin above his head. Through the alcoholic mist that coated his brain, he suddenly remembered the terrible void inside. At this moment it held no comfort. Just emptiness.

Panic seized him. Blind fear threatened to overtake him. He started counting again. One. Two. Three. Four –.

"Ah, stop it!" he yelled out loud.

"I didn't do anything," Stu yelled back.

"No, not you. Me. Me stop it."

Stu sat up from the counter. His eyes bobbed and weaved with intoxication.

"What?"

"I keep counting."

Stu's eyes crinkled over with confusion.

"Counting?"

"Numbers. One. Two. Three. You know."

"What the hell are you talking about?"

"It's like my mind needs to lurch at something familiar, so it doesn't have to exist in just the blackness."

"What blackness?"

"In my head."

"You see blackness?"

"Yeah. Blackness. Emptiness."

Stu studied him a moment.

"How does it make you feel?"

"Scared. Usually."

"Then that must be why you're counting, just like counting sheep," said Stu.

"Huh?"

"They go on forever. One, two, three, four...They never stop," explained Stu.

"You mean if I keep counting, my mind will never be empty?"

In his mind's eye, Quinton envisioned a numeric chain stretching into infinity. There would always be one more number to keep me company, he reflected.

"You got it."

"That's deep. I think you're right. How'd you know that?"

"Everybody counts in one way or another. I guess you could say we all find something to distract us from emptiness."

"You have emptiness?" Quinton asked.

"Now we're getting a little personal."

"I thought we were best friends."

"Yeah, but not like this. Not talking. You're weirding me out."

"You mean I can't just be who I am?"

"Yeah, sure you can. But this isn't him."

"What isn't him?"

"This. You."

"I'm not who I am?" Quinton asked, suddenly disturbed.

"You're not a talker."

"What do you mean?"

"You don't talk about stuff."

"Why not?"

"How the heck should I know?"

"Well, I'm me now," Quinton asserted. "And me now is a talker. Me now doesn't remember why I don't like to talk."

"Fair enough. Try breathing."

"I am breathing."

"No, I mean instead of counting, try and concentrate on your breathing."

"Why?"

"It might calm you down."

"How do you know?"

"Because that's what I do, I breathe. Emily taught me. She's very smart, you know. You should talk to her sometime."

"Okay."

"And she's cute, too," Stu added.

"She's gorgeous."

"Hey, that's my wife."

"I know."

"Thanks to you she's my wife," said Stu.

"What do you mean?" asked Quinton.

"I don't want to go into it."

Quinton rolled his eyes. Stu was quiet for a moment.

"You really didn't recognize us at all the first time you saw us in the hospital room, did you?"

Quinton reflected briefly, then shook his head 'no.' Stu lay back on the counter and sighed.

"Just remember to breathe. Also, I'm sure you don't recall this, but I'm not gonna remember any of this conversation in the morning."

"Why not?"

"I never do. It's the booze."

"Oh."

Stu got up from the hard countertop and lay down next to Quinton.

"So when I wake up in the morning, explain to me why I'm in your bed. Thanks. Goodnight." And he was out.

Quinton was left alone with his thoughts. Counting. Breathing. Uncomfortable darkness inside. An acute awareness of the widening schism between who he was becoming on the inside and who everyone remembered him to be on the outside. His conversation with Stu had been as disturbing as it was helpful.

Quinton rolled over on his side. He looked at the kitten lying on the floor below. He watched her lick her paws, then run them over her tiny face. She looked up at him, yawned, and resumed her cleaning. Quinton studied her.

She was on auto-pilot. She wasn't thinking about what she did, or why, or 'who she was.' She just did it. On instinct. Pure instinct, Quinton thought.

Clarity of mind and instinct; something told him that was all he needed. That would be the way back to himself, the way back to the source. He was sure of it. The blackness inside slowly faded to a deep shade of purple.

11

Quinton lay on his bed fully dressed in his World Cup uniform. His eyes closed, he took long deep breaths in and out trying to calm himself.

Over the last few weeks, he found he had developed the ability to move his breath seemingly throughout his body, directing the energy it produced to any one point in need of its nourishment. His breath felt liquid, free flowing. And he found that if his mind didn't guide the breath consciously, it would wander gently where it willed, where needed, as if alive. This phenomenon seemed to increase his endurance and accuracy while he trained.

These skills had come to him seemingly out of nowhere, occurring spontaneously at increments during the course of his day to complement his athletic regimen. Because these things felt so natural to him, Quinton could only assume they were techniques he had developed or studied before the accident in order to increase his performance.

At times his 'breath' seemed to want to encircle the area just below his chest. When he allowed it there, his abdomen became warm and gently began to reverse its normal breathing pattern. It eased-in the area around his navel when he inhaled, and slowly extended it during exhalation.

In times like these, when his lower abdomen seemed to take over and gently reverse the normal pattern, Quinton would feel an inexplicable calmness envelop his body and soul. Many times he tried to will his breath consciously into this meditative pattern, but to no avail. He hadn't quite figured out the secret.

Mostly he concentrated on his normal breathing as a simple form of meditation, to calm the storms that had begun raging through his mind. The most peaceful place he had found was at the point where the inhalation and exhalation met. When he maintained an awareness of this point, his breath seemed to blend effortlessly into one circular, fluid motion. But it took a lot of concentration to get to that state. For now, he breathed just to stay calm for the evening ahead.

His kitten rested comfortably on his belly, rising and falling with his breath. Four weeks of tuna and Cheez Whiz had nearly doubled her in size. She purred so loudly Quinton couldn't help but smile. He took one more deep breath and opened his eyes. His face was nearly healed.

Stu leaned through Quinton's open door, his knee fully mended. He wore the same type of World Cup uniform as Quinton.

"They're here. Let's go," Stu said.

Quinton looked up at him anxiously.

"I don't remember any of them."

Stu leaned against the doorjamb.

"That's okay, they never really liked you anyway," he said, doing his best to lighten the situation.

"Ha ha. I'm nervous."

Stu stepped into the room.

"I know. Come on," he said. "They all want to see you."

Quinton reached up and gently stroked the skin of his

own face. Though smooth to the naked eye, he could feel the rough, still-fading edges of scar tissue that remained.

Stu came closer to him.

"Q, you can't see it anymore. You don't look any different than the last time they saw you."

"No, but I feel a lot different. At least I think I do."

Quinton gently put down the kitten and sat up. Stu held his hand out to Quinton. Quinton took it and stood up from the bed.

"Who is Dan Ten?" asked Quinton.

"Who?"

"Dan Ten. Is he on the team? His name keeps popping into my head."

"Never heard of him."

Quinton stared blankly at Stu for a moment.

"Your jacket's unzipped," he concluded.

"Yours is full of cat hair."

Stu adjusted the zipper on his jacket and Quinton shook the fur from his. They left the room and headed for the volleyball courts where Quinton would meet with the rest of the Olympic Volleyball Team for the first time since the crash.

He had read about these guys and seen their pictures in books and team photos. He had watched all the videotapes Murphy had loaned him of their overseas games. When he met them in person, he hoped he would remember a face, a voice, a handshake. Anything to remind him of the real life lived by his former self.

Stu and Quinton mingled their way through the reception. It was the official pre-summer fundraiser for the Olympic Team, a two-hundred-dollar-a-plate no-dinner dinner. Quinton didn't know what a no-dinner dinner was, but felt pretty sure he didn't know before he lost his memory either. Stu was no help. He had no clue himself. But then again, Stu wasn't always the brightest to begin with.

The gymnasium was packed. All twelve members of the Olympic Volleyball Team were decked out in their World Cup uniforms. They wore stunning red, white, and blue warmup suits that would make even the most cynical ex-pat stand up and wave the flag. The team mingled with their patrons, signing autographs, making small talk, and giving pointers to the armchair jocks. Stu shuttled Quinton over to two players standing in a corner by themselves.

As Quinton got closer and could make out their faces, his heartbeat and pace began to quicken. Something felt familiar. Quinton knew he knew them. He recognized the two, but couldn't figure out from where, from what memory.

Stu made the introductions.

"Quinton, this is Jeff."

Quinton looked into Jeff's eyes.

"Hey Quint, what's happening?" Jeff nodded.

Quinton didn't say anything. He tried to look inside himself. He didn't see the void he was expecting, but again saw the purple flash now set against an inner field of deep velvet indigo. In his mind's eye he saw the framed photograph of the World Cup Team.

He looked outward once again, but the vision he'd seen in his head lingered a moment longer. Quinton saw himself in the photo standing next to Stu. Jeff Winger and Pete McIntyre were next to them.

He hadn't remembered them. He had remembered their photograph. He was not particularly comforted by this realization.

Quinton zoned back to the gym as Pete McIntyre joshed with him. "You're even prettier than you used to be."

"Thanks a lot, Pete," Quinton said.

Pete was surprised. "Hey, you remember my name."

Quinton shrugged.

"Things come and go."

Things came and went for the next few weeks. Anxiety mostly, but no memories. No time for memories. And even less time for breathing. But a strange energy had been unearthed inside him, one which he couldn't completely control, nor fully comprehend. It took him strange places in the middle of the night. Places he couldn't remember when he woke up, but that left him feeling a cold dampness inside for countless minutes afterwards.

Daytime was work time, a never-ending cycle of practice and drills. Murphey wanted to win the Gold at the next Olympics, and wanted it bad.

Murphey stood on the court like a general, day-glo orange whistle in hand, watching his team do their jump-serve drills a short distance away.

Each player took a turn behind the serve line, where he would toss a ball up with his left hand, leap into the air, and pound it over the net with his right, still airborne. He would then run to the back of the line to start over, and the next man would toss his ball up and serve across the net. They worked in unison, a perfectly-oiled machine. Crack troops. It was easy to see why they were one of the best national teams in the world.

But two of Murphey's players still weren't up to par. They worked like dogs, but continued to fall short. They needed to spark the flames that lurked deep within them. They weren't igniting on the hard court of the Training Center gym. They needed to be in their element, the coach knew, on the shifting sands of the beach, in the hot sun that fed their creativity.

Coach Murphey called Quinton Squid and Stu Gardner out of the serve line.

"Okay. You guys have been here three months already. We're just going to be doing drills this summer, and you two won't be ready for six-man hardcourt until September anyway. Spend the summer on the beach. It's your best training ground. See what you can do at Hermosa this year."

"But I can only jump twenty-five inches," Quinton protested.

"Don't worry. It'll come. What's your hurry?" Murphey assured him. Quinton Squid wasn't his son, but Murphey had sort of adopted him as one. He liked Squid's unyielding nature, even if he could be a prick sometimes.

"I guess you're right. In its own good time," said Quinton.

He and Stu returned to the serve line to finish off their last day of drills with the team.

12

The sporty red VW convertible cruised up the Pacific Coast Highway towards Los Angeles like a runaway train. Emily was doing eighty-five easily. The Beach Boys blasting through the car stereo seemed a bit redundant on the PCH, but Stu crooned along anyway.

Wearing only a bright lemon pair of Speedos, he rubbed coconut oil over every part of his exposed skin. He wanted his beach tan back, fast, and figured cancer was years away. Every few minutes Emily glanced through her sunglasses at the perfect washboard formed by his abs. He loved the attention. Hell, Stu loved any attention. He was used to it from the beach.

Quinton had the whole back seat to himself. He stretched across the cushions, the cat asleep in his lap. The ocean breeze blowing in his face and his eyes closed luxuriously, he smiled to himself. Stu turned around to talk to his buddy. He saw that Quinton wasn't taking in the scenery.

"Open your eyes, dude. You're going to miss everything," Stu said as they sailed by a particularly spectacular ocean view. Quinton, eyes still shut, answered with a satisfied grin, "I'm not missing a thing."

For the first time since his new life had begun, he let his

face bathe in the warm sunlight without any fear of tissue damage. His face was now healed, the scars barely visible. He fell asleep in the back seat. The VW pressed on, edging closer and closer to the Land of Oz.

Late in the afternoon, the convertible pulled into the driveway of a large, one-story adobe-style house overlooking the Pacific Ocean in Santa Monica.

"Why are we stopping?" asked Quinton.

Emily and Stu looked at each other and smiled.

"This is your house, man," said Stu.

Quinton turned to face the beach house head-on. The sun hung low and lazy over its slate rooftop. The white stucco walls shimmered in the hazy brilliance. The ocean seemed to stretch on forever behind it. Quinton stood up slowly from the back seat of the convertible. He drank in the ocean air, pleasantly hypnotized by the unexpected sight before him.

"This is my house? Damn. I have good taste."

He jumped out of the car onto the sandy driveway. He noticed the large Canary Island date palms framing the house. His eyes were caught by the plush yellow rose bushes, violas, and poppies growing below the large central picture window. Never in his life could he recall having seen such vegetation. It all seemed so foreign to him. He turned to Stu.

"But I don't garden," he said, taking in more of the lush undergrowth.

Stu came right back at him.

"You're right, you don't."

They stared at each other for a moment. Lips curved upward and they began to smile.

"You remembered something," said Stu.

"No, not really." Quinton paused. "It was more like I knew."

"Well that's good, isn't it?" Stu offered.

Quinton grabbed his bags from the car and dropped them on the ground.

"So who does the pruning?" he asked Stu.

Emily laughed.

"What's so funny?" Quinton asked.

"He does," said Emily, pointing.

"Stu?" Quinton asked.

"He sure does," Emily grinned.

"He's the gardener?" Quinton laughed.

He looked over at Emily. Their eyes met and they began to howl.

"Ha ha," said Stu. "So I garden. Big deal. You two have your quirks too, little Miss Soldering Gun, Mr. Lawn Ornaments, Mr. —"

"But Stu, you used to do it for a living," said Emily amidst her laughter.

"So what?" said Stu.

"Your last name is Gardner!" Quinton bellowed, his face wet with tears of laughter.

"No, really? No one ever pointed that out to me before. Thanks so much. Haven't we already had this conversation?"

Quinton's laughter slowly tapered off.

"I don't know, have we?" he asked.

Stu met Quinton's eyes. He smiled.

"I don't know. I can't remember either, buddy. Come on, let's get you inside."

Stu grabbed the bags at Quinton's feet and walked up the stone-inlay path to the front door.

"Man this is heavy, who has the keys?" He dropped the luggage on the stoop.

Emily hurried up the stoop and keyed in the front door.

The lock opened with a loud click. She looked at Quinton and tried to read his face. Fear? Annoyance? Boredom? No, not that either. She had no clue. Quinton didn't notice her looking at him. He was miles away, inside his head, breathing. He could feel his breath gently drawn to his lower abdomen, but chose not to let it wander there.

"Dan Ten," he said aloud.

Stu and Emily's eyes met. They looked at Quinton as he stared into space.

"What?" asked Stu.

After a moment, Quinton met their glance.

"It's that same name, it just pops into my head at the tail end of my breathing."

"You've been breathing?" Emily asked, half-kidding.

"Yeah, Stu taught me."

"He keeps telling me that, but I don't remember," said Stu.

"Were you drinking?" Emily asked.

"Allegedly."

"He stuffed a volleyball in the microwave and blew it up," offered Quinton.

Emily laughed out loud.

"I don't remember that either," said Stu.

Emily glanced at them, back and forth.

"Between the two of you, I'm surprised you can remember your ass from your elbows. Okay, Q, all set for the big ride?"

He nodded and crossed the threshold, through the front door of the Quinton Squid beach house. The portal entered directly into the living room. His eyes darted about, collecting information in bits and pieces. A dried steer skull on the wall. Cactus everywhere.

Quinton was pleasantly surprised.

"This is my house. I do have good taste."

As Quinton took in the details of his home, Stu and Emily grabbed the rest of his gear from the car and came inside. Each was silently hoping that something in the house would rattle his memory.

Quinton continued to glance around the room, taking it all in. As he gazed, his eager mind began to formulate an opinion. The expensive Santa Fe style decor was pleasing to him, but on second thought he could've done without the dried steer skull. Against the south wall of the living room sat a large puffy sofa with a Native American motif. In front of the sofa sat a matching coffee table adorned with shells and coral.

Along the opposite wall, the north side of the living room, sat a desk and large-screen TV sandwiched between two large speakers.

There was no west wall to the living room. It entered directly into the kitchen area, and its west wall was simply a pair of sliding glass doors leading out onto a deck. The deck, six feet off the sand, ran around the entire western side of the house, and beyond that was the beach. The ocean, not fifty yards from the deck, stretched out to the horizon. The brazen orange sun hung low over white-capped waves in the distance. Quinton stood transfixed by its brilliance.

Comfortable Quinton was suitably ensconced in his own home, Stu and Emily didn't know quite what to do next. Leering back and forth at each other, it became obvious what they wanted to do. But first things first.

"Quint," Emily said. "I restocked the fridge, and've been watering the cactuses. Cacti. Is it Cacti?"

Quinton turned to her slowly and smiled.

"I don't know. Thanks Emily."

"No problem." She winked at Quinton. "I like to help out

all my friends when they're in the throes of an identity crisis. You're just an extreme case."

Stu rolled his eyes.

She handed Quinton his keys. He looked at her with puppy-dog eyes.

"Will you go over that breathing stuff with me sometime?"

"Anytime," she said.

The doorbell rang loudly. To Quinton's surprise, it chimed the first few bars of Ravel's 'Bolero.' Startled, Stu dropped a suitcase on his own foot, spilling Quinton's clothes and magazines onto the floor.

Quinton opened the door to reveal a pair of blonde, tanned twins dressed in neon pink bikinis. Each carried a stack of mail in their arms. One awkwardly dangled a cat carrier from her fingertips.

"Hello?" said Quinton, confused.

"Hi, Quinton," the twins said in unison. "You left this in the car," they chirped, gesturing to the cat carrier.

Quinton studied their faces more closely. They weren't quite identical twins. One had more collagen injected into her lower lip. He carefully took the carrier from the less-lippy sister.

"Thanks," he said.

"Is that your cat?" asked the first twin.

"Yes."

"I never knew you were a cat man. What's her name?"

"Sheba," he answered.

"Sheba. Why'd you name her that?" she asked.

"It's the only cat food she'll eat."

"Oh."

Long pause. Pinter pause.

"So, do I know you?" he asked awkwardly.

Stu whispered into Quinton's ear from behind.

"They're your next door neighbors, and after-dinner mints."

Emily poked Stu with her elbow.

"We asked them to pick up your mail," she added in Quinton's other ear.

"You live next door," Quinton said to the twins.

Twin number one turned to number two.

"I told you he'd remember," she said.

"It comes and goes. It's a little hazy," he answered.

The twins smirked at each other and giggled.

"What?" Quinton asked.

"You don't remember everything?" the first twin inquired.

Quinton stared at her collagen injected lip. He decided it was much too large for her face.

"No," he said to her.

"Do you even know our names?" asked the other.

Quinton looked sheepishly at the two bathing beauties.

"Uh...no."

"I'm Lori," said number two.

"And I'm Tango," said number one.

"Lori and Tango. Hi."

He took the mail from their arms.

"Anything else you want?" Tango asked with a sly grin.

He could see Emily smirk from the corner of his eye. His hands became uncomfortably moist.

"Not that I can think of right now," he muttered awkwardly.

"Come-a-knockin' when your memory's back," said Lori.

"We got the trampoline restrung," added Tango.

"Oh. You did. Oh, okay. Thanks. Bye," said Quinton, and ushered them out the door.

"Bye, Quinton," they squeaked in singsong unison.

Quinton closed the door. Somewhat embarrassed by the whole encounter, he looked down at his mail. It was all addressed to Quinton Davis.

"Who is Quinton Davis?" he asked Stu.

"That's your real name."

"Huh?"

"Davis is your given name," explained Stu. "You chose Squid for yourself."

"Why would I do that?"

"I don't have a clue, Q. The squid is the stupidest animal in the whole damn ocean."

"Thanks a lot," said Quinton.

"The truth hurts, dude. They're pathetic. They lurch for anything shiny under water. Just hang themselves on the hook. The fisherman just has to haul them up. Easy," Stu said.

"Well, maybe I should change it back," said Quinton.

Before Stu could respond, Emily grabbed him by the belt loops of his jeans. As she manhandled her husband toward the door, she became aware of Quinton's eyes on her hands. She didn't know what to make of it. She and the old Quinton, well…

"Ahem. We have to get going. Gotta feed the dogs," she said, and pulled Stu closer.

Quinton smiled.

"I've heard it called many things, but never 'feeding the dogs.' "

Emily laughed. She liked this new Quinton.

"Go on, you two," he said. "Go have a life. I'll be fine."

"You're sure?" asked Stu.

"Yeah, you heard them. They got the trampoline restrung."

"Okay. Bye, Quint. We'll see you tomorrow," said Emily.

Her eyes lingered on him curiously.

"Bye, Emily," grinned Quinton.

Stu poked an index finger into Quinton's chest.

"I'll be back here bright and early. You better be ready for me," he taunted.

"I'll be here. Go on, you two. Go feed the dogs."

Stu and Emily left and Quinton closed the door behind them. He was left standing alone, a stranger in his own home. He looked at the suitcase spilled open on the floor. Its contents were the only things in the room he recognized.

Quinton still held the mail in his arms. He walked to the desk and placed it next to a stack of 8x10 promotional glossies. The pictures were all of him in mid-dive on the beach. He certainly had been a pretty sonofabitch. Just not a very modest one.

He shifted his attention back to the mail. It was all addressed to Quinton Davis. And here he'd thought all along he was trying to figure out who Quinton Squid was.

He tried not to think about it. Let go, he told himself. Explore. Accept. Live. He opened the top envelope and pulled a check from inside. It read, 'Sand Dune Activewear, pay to the order of Quinton Davis. Ninety-eight hundred dollars.' Shocked, Quinton smiled in spite of himself.

"Shit, I'm paid."

He put the check on the desk and gathered up his luggage. He dragged it through the south hallway leading to the rest of the house. The hallway turned right to reveal a large bedroom. At the far end of the bedroom, along its western wall, were two sliding glass doors. They led onto the same deck he had seen earlier through the kitchen.

The sun was lower in the sky, and the house was getting dark. He found a button on the bedroom wall and pressed it. The button set off a series of electronic devices which caused certain lights to come up fully and others to dim. Harry Connick Jr. mood music began to emanate from a stereo in the corner. A lava lamp began to bubble. Quinton, amazed by this tacky Casanova set-up, started to laugh out loud. He went into the adjoining bathroom and looked at himself in the mirror.

"My God, Quinton, you are an asshole," he said out loud, and laughed at his own image.

He opened the medicine cabinet. Empty. The sink fixtures were plain ceramic. Nothing jumped out at him in here, although the Playboy Playmate shower curtain got the once-over twice.

Quinton dumped his luggage on the bed. It jiggled. He sat on it. It was a waterbed. Not all that surprising, under the circumstances. Just another bit of information to tell him who he was. Or who he had been, anyway. One more piece of the puzzle. He wondered if he would like how the picture looked when the puzzle came together.

He went to the glass doors and stepped out on the deck. The blazing orange ball hovering over the Pacific had melted into a sherbet sunset.

As he gazed at the shifting hues of yellow, orange, and red, he felt as if he had been reborn. A strange calmness overtook him. Today was a new day. The first day of the rest of his life. He inhaled the splendor of the horizon before him.

"I am Quinton Squid, Deep Sea Diver," he declared to the world.

13

Early morning found Quinton asleep in his bed with the curtains drawn. The doorbell rang. Quinton stirred, but didn't get up. It rang again. He groaned and pulled the pillow over his head.

The few moments of silence that followed were broken by an intense pounding on the bedroom's sliding glass doors. Quinton took the pillow off his head and rolled on his back. As he looked up he was startled to see his own image reflecting back at him from a set of mirrors mounted on the ceiling above.

Jesus, thought Quinton, what the hell had he been thinking?

As the pounding continued, Quinton began to wake up. He checked his bedside clock. 6:42 a.m. He tossed the sheet off his body and got up. He wore only designer briefs. Blue. No scarring was apparent on his calves. They were strong, and his musculature now highly defined. He had sculpted himself a finely chiseled back and hard, athletic thighs.

As he moved to the window he ran his fingers through the messy mop on his head. He opened the curtains to see Stu's face smiling back at him through the glass. Quinton clicked the latch open and Stu came in toting a small cooler. Quinton headed for the bathroom.

"Haven't you heard of jet lag?" he asked Stu.

"We drove here," said Stu. "Besides, neither rain, nor sleet, nor snow…"

"I'm not a mailman," Quinton said from the bathroom. Stu stared at him through the door.

"Damn, Quint. You lost your tan."

Stu was right. For a California boy, Quinton was beyond pale. He washed his face and brushed his teeth.

"But your legs look better. How do they feel?"

"A lot better," Quinton said, his mouth full of toothpaste.

"Good. We'll give 'em a test drive today. It's time to practice. Let's see…"

Stu opened up the cooler.

"…I've got peanut butter sandwiches, made 'em myself, bananas, mucho Powerbars, a couple Bud Lights, and of course the ever popular Evian water."

"Sounds like quite a breakfast," Quinton said. He came out of the bathroom clad in shorts and a Sand Dune muscle-shirt.

"All set," he said.

Stu shook his head.

"You better have your Wheaties first. We got all day," he said, and closed the cooler.

At seven-thirty in the morning, State Beach in Santa Monica wasn't particularly booming with beachcombers. The suit surfers were in abundance; doctors, lawyers, and studio executives trying to catch a few waves before 'nine to five.' They huddled together like a gaggle of geese, floating on their surfboards in the middle of the not-yet warm ocean. They knew they had to be out of there by eight forty-five, when the turf surfers would show up with their pierced noses and Land Rovers.

By late morning, Quinton and Stu had been busy fighting the good fight at the pro-caliber net at the top of the beach for several hours. Each had one side of the net, and the game was on. Some dusty, sunbaked palm trees were their only audience.

Stu used his hand like a jackhammer. He drilled the ball into Quinton's court with such precision and strength that it looked like a sure ace. Quinton, covered in sweat, dove for the dig with all he could muster. He tried to get a piece of the ball with his right fist. He fell at least nine inches short and got a mouthful of sand. He spit it out and he stood up, trying to brush the coat of sand from his sweaty body.

"Man, you are corndogged," chuckled Stu. "I've never seen anyone so damn sandy."

"This bites," frowned Quinton as he sat down to towel off. "I've had it."

He didn't like being referred to as food. And he didn't like eating sand.

Quinton grabbed a beer from the cooler. Stu gently took his hand and removed the beer.

"No way, man, it's too early," he insisted and put the beer back. He took out a bottle of ice water and offered it to Quinton. "Here."

"I've been drinking water since breakfast. I want beer," Quinton whined.

Stu was steadfast.

"Ice water's absorbed into the system more quickly."

"What were you? A fucking chemistry major? You've been spouting that stuff all morning. I want a beer."

Quinton could see Stu's jaw clench and unclench as he debated the issue. Finally, Stu's scowl turned to warmth.

"Okay. I guess you could use the carbs."

He handed Quinton a beer. Quinton cracked it open and lay back on the sand.

"You're a vegetarian, aren't you," said Quinton.

Stu was startled.

"Yeah, you remember?"

"No," said Quinton shaking his head.

"How'd you guess?" asked Stu.

"Wasn't difficult," Quinton answered, sucking back on the brew.

As Quinton lay on the beach drinking his beer, he began to feel the tightness and strain in the back of his legs, calves, and heel cords. His left calve was beginning to cramp. He put the beer down and began to massage it.

Stu made him eat a banana. He said the potassium would help work out the cramping. Quinton didn't feel any benefit from it. Between that, the ice water, and the proto-protein peanut butter sandwiches, Quinton took Stu for some kind of psychotic volleyball witchdoctor. He knew it was the heat talking and that Stu probably knew what he was doing, but the thought made him chuckle anyway.

Stu dragged the wilted Quinton back onto the court and tossed a ball over the net for him to dig. Quinton leapt for it, his right hand extending in a fist, but missed the ball by at least two feet. He hit the sand and was corndogged again.

"Keep your center of gravity low," explained Stu, frustrated.

"What?" huffed Quinton.

"Keep your weight low," yelled Stu. "Bend your knees. Don't stand up. Always be ready to move, or you're never going to get to the ball."

Stu was playing teacher again and didn't like it very much.

His frustration had become apparent to Quinton. In turn it had made Quinton edgy.

"Okay. Can we leave now? I'm exhausted," said Quinton.

Stu squinted at him in disbelief, hands on his hips.

"A tourney lasts two days. At least five hours each day. Get used to it, spud."

Quinton glared back at him.

"Eat ball," spouted a miffed Quinton, and positioned himself on the court again.

● ● ●

The suit surfers had long since gone. The beach was well into the noontime sun. The turf surfers sat out on the blue ocean, their matted dreadlocks standing stiff in the windy surf. Quinton couldn't help but stare at them every once in a while.

The beach was loaded with sights and sounds he'd never seen before. All kinds of folks. Yuppies. Tourists. Surfers. Inner-city beachcombers. Hangers on. He'd seen them on videotape, but this was different. This was real life. His life. It was like Disneyland.

'Just wait 'til a tourney if you want your eyes to bug out,' Stu had told him. Quinton couldn't wait for that.

As they continued to practice, a small crowd gathered around them. Stu loved it, but it made Quinton feel self-conscious. He could hear a lot of whispering going on. He knew it was talk about him. He wasn't used to being gawked at. His mind was driving him crazy. Breathe, breathe, he kept telling himself. With his mind still, he could get into the rhythm of the volley.

There. He could feel himself connect with Stu on some

deeper, more primal level as they volleyed the ball back and forth. Hands cupped together, forearms locked, they bumped the ball back and forth over the net. He chalked up their earlier ornery exchange to heat, sweat, and ego. Quinton could feel Stu's 'peaceful easy feeling' settling over the game. It wasn't hard, Stu was grinning from ear to ear. He was ecstatic they were working as a team again.

"Good, good. You got it," encouraged Stu.

The crowd grew as people began to recognize the two men. They were two-time Olympic Gold Medallists and renowned Kings of the Beach.

The 3 p.m. sun found them shaked-and-baked. As Stu packed up their stuff Quinton lay exhausted on the beach. Stu looked over at his weary friend.

"Man, you are rusty."

"I'm not rusty. I'm dead," insisted the limp load of flesh draped over the sand.

"You've lost your court sense, and you're out of beach shape. You need to do some major wind sprints and extended sun exposure endurance, not to mention work on your ball handling."

"How about you just bury me right now."

The two trudged up Stu's driveway in the late afternoon haze. Quinton was still full of sand, and a bit irritated that Stu insisted they stop at his house first. Quinton's house was just half a mile down the beach. Stu could've dropped the weighted jump rope off at Quinton's later, and they'd have been relaxing in a toasty hot tub right now instead of laboring up Stu's front steps.

"I still don't know how you expect me to jump rope on sand," said an aggravated Quinton.

"I remember I said the same thing to you myself one time. You made me jump rope for an entire day down on State Beach."

"But I can barely walk on the sand, let alone jump rope on it."

"It'll help with your coordination. You're not used to the instability and resistance of the sand yet. You have to get used to it again. You're the one who gave me this leather rope with the metal bearings. It's killer, dude. I'm just giving it back to you," Stu said with a smile.

They reached the top of the stairs. Stu flung the front door open. A stunned Quinton was greeted with several loud bursts of 'Surprise!!' A wall of people in tacky party hats faced him through the open door. A wall of people he didn't recognize. Suddenly he wished he was back on the beach. Getting corndogged, even.

Emily emerged from the crowd. She closed Quinton's gaping mouth with her fingers and gave him a big hug.

"Welcome back, Quinton."

"Uh, thanks, Em."

He started to feel dizzy. He didn't know if it was from the sun or nervous anxiety. Either way he didn't like it. His collar felt tight and he wasn't even wearing a shirt.

Emily brought out the two men standing behind her.

"Quinton, do you remember Bill Johnson and John Steeles?"

"How are you, man?" asked Johnson.

There was something familiar in his voice. A purple spark ignited in Quinton's mind as the sound of Johnson's voice faded to silence. His ears rang. He could see Johnson reach out to shake his hand. He saw Johnson's mouth move, but no sound came out. The ringing in his ears persisted. There was almost a pattern to it. A rhythm. Almost syllabic. What was his subconscious trying to tell him?

Suddenly he was thrown past the purple ember, through an indigo field, deeper into his mind's eye.

Reality was no longer before him. Instead he saw a video replay of the Hermosa game he'd seen in the hospital. The tape in his mind played a few moments before he broke the umpire's jaw. He and Stu were playing against two men. They were Bill Johnson and John Steeles.

Their images melted into a sea of purple as Quinton focused back to reality. His ears stopped ringing. Recognition dawned on Quinton's face as John Steeles' voice faded up from the silence.

"...and I'm glad you made it. Otherwise who'd protect us from those bug-assed rent-a-refs?" Steeles said, and began to laugh raucously.

Quinton forced a smile. He wanted to smile genuinely, but it just wasn't in him.

"It's uh, good to see you guys," he said. But had he ever really met these guys?

Emily could see him teetering. Maybe this wasn't such a good idea.

"Come on Quinton, let me show you around."

She took his hand and guided him through the rest of the onslaught of people converging around him. He did his best to be polite to all the friends and teammates he didn't recognize, but it wasn't easy. As Emily led him through the maze of her house, he had to wonder, was he safe with these people? Did he really know any of them? He couldn't be sure. He gripped Emily's hand tighter. She pulled him through the crowd and they found refuge in the back bedroom.

"I'm sorry about this, Quint. I thought it might help, but

I guess it wasn't such a great idea," she said as she closed the door behind them.

Quinton looked around the small room. The walls were covered with Winnie-the-Pooh wallpaper. A baby's crib sat tucked under boxes in a far-left corner. Stu hadn't mentioned a child. He ran his hand over the small blue dresser in front of him. It hadn't been dusted in quite a while.

"No, that's all right," he said to her in response.

Emily sat on a cardboard box and offered Quinton the rocking chair.

"Chivalry isn't dead," he said as he sat down, still feeling a bit shaky.

He began to rock slowly back and forth.

Emily sat up.

"You look a little peaked," she said.

"I'm okay."

"Want a paper bag to breathe into or something?" She winked at him warmly.

"No, thanks," replied Quinton. "You know Steeles? I remember him, but only from that Hermosa tape. Remember? When I popped Alonzo?"

Emily nodded. Quinton took a few deep breaths in.

"Is Dan Ten here?" he asked.

"Who?"

"You sure I don't know a guy named Dan Ten?"

She shook her head.

"His name still rings in my head," he said. "When I breathe."

"How is your meditative breathing coming, anyway? Stu said you were counting a lot before."

"Yeah. The breathing's okay. But sometimes it gets a little weird."

"What do you mean?"

"It's like the breath has a mind of its own," Quinton explained.

"It sort of does," said Emily. "It's a form of energy, just like everything else in the universe. In some philosophies, breath is what links the physical body with the spiritual body."

"The spiritual body?" asked Quinton.

"Yeah, we're not just physical creatures, we're emotional, mental, spiritual, you know."

Quinton was lost. He knew he was from California, but couldn't remember any exposure to such a perspective. Emily could sense his befuddlement.

"Forget it," she said. "It gets very complicated. There are many different aspects of many philosophies. But in all of them, even some western philosophies, the breath and stillness of the mind are integrally connected. Many traditions also equate these things with self-awareness."

"Really? All I know is, sometimes my normal breathing pattern will seem to gently reverse, like my belly extends when I exhale and goes back down when I inhale, the reverse of what I normally do. It creates a sense of calmness."

"That's a Taoist breathing pattern," explained Emily. "You're talking Taoist, as opposed to Buddhist, which is more like the way we normally breathe."

"How do you know all this stuff ?" Quinton asked.

"Got my Ph.D at Stanford."

"No kidding."

"Hey, Quint," said Emily, changing the subject. "Were you staring at my hands last night, or Stu's waist?"

Quinton laughed. He rocked the chair feverishly, as if he'd never rocked one before. Ostensibly, he hadn't.

"Your hands," he said.

She inched closer to him.

"Why?"

He continued to rock with relish.

"I noticed them while you were driving. You have beautiful hands."

She folded her arms and poised one hand below her chin. She watched his movements for a moment.

"You've always thought so," she said.

"What do you mean?"

"You and me. I wasn't going to bring it up, unless you remembered."

The rocking stopped.

"Remembered what?" he asked, incredulous.

"You and me, Quint. It was over long before the trip to Bonn. We parted as friends. Stu never found out. He still doesn't know, and I don't want him to."

Quinton's eyes widened.

He searched Emily's features for the slightest hint of a 'gotcha.' Nothing. He studied her face a moment longer. He could see her nostrils flare involuntarily. The chair began to rock again. Quinton grinned contentedly.

"We never had an affair, Emily."

"Yes we did. I'm not proud of it, but we did, Quinton."

He smiled at her.

"Your nostrils flared, Emily."

"What?"

"Your nostrils just flared. They did the same thing last night when you said you had to 'feed the dogs.' You have no poker face. I may not remember anything from the past, but what I see and hear now, I don't forget."

"Why would I make something like this up?"

"If your husband can blow up a volleyball in a microwave, I wouldn't put anything past you."

She clucked. "You are such a wet rag, little mister smarty-pants."

He laughed.

"Me? How about you – lying to an amnesiac about having an affair with his best friend's wife. That's demented. That takes the cake."

She began to laugh.

"It's not funny," said Quinton.

"Yes it is."

She started to howl.

"What's so funny?" asked Quinton.

"You had to read my face to figure it out," she gasped through sobs of laughter.

"You want something to laugh about? I'll give you something to laugh about."

He quickly snatched up her left foot, pulled off the Reebok, and tickled her foot mercilessly.

"Quit it," she laughed. "I'll kick you, I swear."

"No you won't."

"Why?"

"Because you know I'm harmless."

"Who's harmless?" Stu asked as he barged in, shutting the door behind him.

Quinton dropped Emily's foot.

"Your wife just told me we had an affair."

Stu shook his head. He turned to his wife.

"Emily, I told you to let him remember these things on his own."

"Yes, hon," she said in mock agreement.

The couple made goo-goo eyes at each other. Quinton had to look away.

"You two are disgusting."

Stu knelt in front of Emily, picked up the Reebok, and placed it back on her foot. He began to lace it up.

"You know, Q, you're lucky it was just the sneaker and not the sock. If the sock had come off, well, then this would have been a whole different story."

Quinton looked at him. Stu couldn't be serious. Over his shoulder, he could see Stu wink at Emily. These people were merciless. These Californians. Stu finished the laces. He took his wife's hand and kissed it.

"Quinton told me I had beautiful hands," she said.

Stu turned around to face Quinton. He sat down on the floor.

"He said the same thing to me," said Stu, dishing.

"You both do have beautiful hands," said Quinton.

Stu raised an eyebrow in mock scrutiny.

"Are you coming on to us?"

Quinton laughed.

"No, I just admire beautiful hands."

"Ah, hand fetish," said Emily.

"No, come on, you guys. You're bugging me out. Here."

Quinton held up his hands.

"Look at these. I don't have any fingerprints on the left one at all. Most of the skin came from my backside. See the fingers, there's hardly any detail at all."

"Sorry, Q."

"No sorry's necessary."

"We were just screwing around," said Stu.

"I know, but I just wanted to explain. On those tapes you gave me, my hands were something else. Gorgeous. Like Golden Gloves. I know it sounds vain, but inside, in my heart, I can feel how important they were to me. I'm not sure why, but I know they were. The hardness of the calluses. The veins bulging through on the back. The strength. The potential. It's hard to explain."

Emily took one of his hands in hers.

"You don't have to," she said.

Quinton smiled.

"I know I don't. But you two are my best friends. You're the closest thing I have to a memory."

Stu crawled over to him and gave him a big macho bear hug. This time, Quinton accepted. After a few moments, he pulled back.

"I think I need some fresh air, maybe see if I had an affair with any other married women out there."

Emily chuckled. Quinton got up from the rocker and left the room.

Quinton found his way out onto Stu and Emily's beach-deck. It was similar to his own. He leaned on the deck's railing and looked out at the ocean. The peach neon sun was beginning to set.

He let the dry air mingle with a touch of ocean spray in his nostrils. He swilled back on a bottle of A&W rootbeer. It wasn't quite the soda taste he craved, but it'd do. Maybe if he added a little Pepsi or some cream soda…

Something on the beach caught his eye. A threesome playing volleyball below shimmered in the sun's melting hues. The ocean ripples behind them shone like fish scales.

Quinton's eyes were drawn to one of the players in particular. She was a beautiful natural blonde with eyes that seemed to glow at him in the twilight. He watched the three as they played a friendly game of volleyball on Stu's private rig near the water.

The blonde played against another woman who was equally as beautiful, but had darker, sharper features. She played alongside a big buffed dude with a cast on his arm. It set him up for a great disadvantage. Ostensibly, the game was between the two women.

"C'mon, Pam, leave me a shot," pouted the encasted man to his partner.

She turned toward him and winked.

"Next one's yours, Ray."

The blonde smiled at Ray from across the net.

"I'm not going to pull back for you, stud," she warned.

Ray dug his feet into the ground.

"Give it all you got, O'Connor. Let 'er rip. Bleed me dry."

The blonde tossed the ball into the air and smashed it over the net. It headed for Ray's head like a heat-seeking missile. He threw his cast up over his face. His block banked the ball into the sand below.

"Damn, Holly, you're merciless! But I love it. Everyone else just babies me since the plane crash."

"Are you being sarcastic?" she asked him.

"No, just honest."

"Don't mean to break up the CODA session here," Pam interrupted, "but look what's heading in our direction."

Two very large, muscular body-builders walked down the beach towards the net. As they got closer, it became apparent they were identical twins.

"Oh god, Holly, it's the Conan Brothers," said Pam.

"Who?" asked Holly.

"Those dumb idiots from down the strip. They play Conan in the Universal Studios Tour."

"You've got to be kidding," chuckled Raymond.

"No," said Pam.

She began to giggle herself. Holly grinned.

"What do you think?" she asked Pam.

Pam looked back at her.

"I think they're going to want to play us for the net."

"You're kidding me," said Ray. "This I will sit for."

He gave Pam a kiss and sat down on the sand next to one of the net poles. The two brothers sidled up to Holly and Pam. Though they were identical twins, it was obvious even to Raymond that one of them had stuffed socks in his shorts. The steroids must've taken their toll. One of the hulking toads opened his mouth.

"We saw you playing from down the beach. We're wondering if we could play you for the net," asked the artificially endowed Conan brother.

Holly smiled gently. "There are plenty of nets up and down the strip."

"Yeah, but we want to see if we can beat the great Holly O," whined the other brother.

Both brothers snickered.

"What's so funny?" asked Holly.

"Nothing," said the first Conan.

"You're so sure you could beat us?" challenged Pam, twirling the volleyball between her hands.

"Well look," explained Conan number two, "between the two of you, you only have one ball. We got four."

The brothers laughed and slapped a high five. Raymond could see Holly bite her lip. Pam's jaw began to tighten ever so slightly.

"That one's gonna hurt you boys," Ray chided the cretaceous stand-ins.

Conan number one kicked sand in his face.

"You big fuck!" screamed a furious Ray.

He started to get up from the sand. Holly pushed him back down.

"You don't need to muck up that arm any more, Ray," she said under her breath. "Two more weeks and you're back on the beach."

She flashed him a quick grin and a wink. He sat back down begrudgingly. She was right. He hadn't suffered through six months of medical BS only to screw it up again two weeks before t-time. Not for these dickwads. Besides, Holly would kick their twin asses. She tossed the volleyball to the sand kicker.

"Rack 'em up, tiny. You can serve."

She slipped under the net to Pam's side of the court. Conan number one, the sock stuffer, served the ball deep into their court. Holly got under it easily and bumped the ball with gentle precision to Pam. Pam moved to the center of the net, eyeing the bump pass as it reached her.

Quinton watched closely. Pam readied her arms to set the ball; arms three-quarters overhead, hands facing upward with index fingers and thumbs almost touching, creating a triangle. She was a devotee of the classic set – it gave more control over the ball than any other move. It was the second move in the classic one-two-three play: bump, set, spike.

Holly's bump easily reached Pam. In turn, Pam set Holly perfectly at net. The ball hovered helplessly in mid air, just waiting to be taken. Holly approached and leapt into the air, her hand cocked back, ready for the kill. As she hit the ball with enough force to knock out a rhino, brother number two leapt into the air to block the ball as it came over the net. But his arms were too far apart. The ball crashed between them into his face. He was six-packed.

"You bitch!" he yelled at her as he checked his face for non-existent blood.

"Wake up call, you cro-magnon. Sideout. Over here. And

if you use that word again, I'll hit you my damn self," Holly challenged back.

Quinton still watched from the deck, fascinated. The Conan Brothers tossed Holly the ball. It was the women's turn to serve. Quinton saw Holly jump-serve the ball hard down the center of the opposing court.

"Down the pipe," he mumbled to himself.

He stood back from the railing for a moment and smiled. 'Down the pipe.' The slang had come to him of its own volition, with no forethought involved. A good sign. He looked back at the game eagerly. As expected, Holly's serve flew down the pipe between the two brothers. Neither could get to it in time. They didn't have a chance. Ace. Raymond yelled out the score.

"That's one-zip."

Thirteen points later Quinton was out of A&W. He looked on drymouthed but in earnest. Brother number two jumped up to block Pam's attack at the net, but couldn't get any height. She jumped seven inches over him, and slammed the ball over his head into mid-court.

"Thirteen to two," Raymond exclaimed.

Holly took in several quick deep breaths to oxygenate her blood. She walked quickly to the back-court area. She didn't jump the serve this time. She hit it standing, sending it across the net with a blunt blow from the heel of her hand.

Quinton recognized it immediately as a floater, or float serve. All those hours of books and videos were beginning to pay off.

Conan number two passed the ball to number one with a bump pass. Number one set the ball for number two, who ran from backcourt to the net. He jumped up for the spike only to meet Holly, who was at least six inches higher in the air than he was. He tried to tip it, to dink it left at the last minute to get it past her, but she blocked it back into his court with a loud slam. It hit the sand before the other brother could get to it.

"Fourteen to two. Game point," Raymond yelled out.

Pam served the ball deep. Conan two barely got a piece of it, accidentally popping it back over the net. Holly bumped it easily to Pam, who set her for the spike at the net. Holly moved into position, jockeying for the spike. She faked her attack left, but instead hit the ball right.

The Conans had mistakenly anticipated her hit. Barbarian number one barely managed to get to the ball and dove headlong into the sand. He popped it up, but too high – just over the net to where Holly waited. She leapt into the air again and slammed the ball back over the net. The sand kicker dove for it but his brawn didn't make for the needed speed. He missed the ball and ate sand. Holly stood over him at the net.

"That's why dinosaurs went extinct, you fake Conan mouth-breathers," she chastised the two misogynist neanderthals.

Quinton heard this and began to laugh out loud. All eyes turned to the porch. Quinton shut up and leaned away from the railing, looking away.

The humiliated brothers dusted themselves off and shuffled back down the beach.

"Fuck you, O'Connor," they yelled back, a safe distance away.

Pam picked up the volleyball.

"Whatever, assholes," Holly mumbled.

She looked at Pam, who was busy giving a hand up to Raymond. Ray stood and dusted the sand off.

Holly looked in Pam's eyes and smiled. Pam winked back.

"Good game, girl," she said and handed Holly the ball.

"Good game, partner," Holly agreed.

Ray put his wounded arm around Pam. He extended the other hand to Holly. They low-fived.

"Always a pleasure to see you work," he cooed slyly.

Holly spun the volleyball around on one finger.

"Trying to pick me up?"

Ray held Pam a little closer.

"Nope, got my hands full."

"You mean your hand full."

Ray cocked his head to the side and grinned.

"Too clever for your own good, O'Connor."

"Think so?" she asked, amused.

"You were too clever for me."

"I won't argue with you there."

Holly caught the ball she was spinning. She smiled into Ray's gray eyes. Pam looked back and forth at them.

"Hello? Am I standing here?" she asked.

Holly and Ray averted each other's gaze. Ray laughed it off.

"Yes, you are here, honey. Sorry," Holly said as she kissed Pam on the cheek. "He's just so darned sweet."

"So why didn't you keep him?" Pam kidded.

Quinton listened intently, straining to hear the conversation over the flagrant surf.

Holly smiled. "Because he always loved you."

Pam took in a deep breath and smiled back. "Not the answer I was expecting."

Holly looked down at the ball she held.

"No, but an honest one," she said.

"Hmm..." Pam grinned at Ray.

All were silent a moment.

"Come on you two," Holly said. "Get outta here, let me practice."

"Ok, coach," said Ray.

"Love you both," Holly said with a wink.

Pam smiled back.

"Love you too, doll."

The couple walked off into the evening air.

Holly stayed behind on the empty beach and practiced her bump sets. Quinton neared the railing again and looked on as he listened to the twang of the volleyball echo in the early evening.

14

Quinton awoke to the sound of his beeping alarm clock. 5:15 a.m. He dragged himself out of bed and over to the sliding glass doors. He pulled back the curtains. It was still dark out, but the sun was about to rise. He slid the door open to let in the ocean air, and looked through the stack of CD's near the bedroom's stereo system.

Quinton had already gone through most of his knick-knacks and personal items, none of which felt at all familiar. He thought some of the stuff was downright bizarre, like the white polyester fringed 'Viva Las Vegas' Elvis costume he'd found in the back of a closet. In his sock drawer he had found an envelope full of ballet ticket stubs, which made absolutely no sense to him.

But it was the shamelessly detailed descriptions in a little black date book that made him question whether or not he really wanted to remember who he was. That guy was a piece of work, thought Quinton as he searched through the CD's. The selection ranged from 'Giselle,' to Nirvana to Dwight Yoakam to the Chili Peppers. Very eclectic.

The Eagles Greatest Hits seemed to call out to him, and he put it on. He played 'Desperado.' To his amazement he sang along word for word. He was at once fascinated yet frustrated by the fact that he knew this song, but didn't remember where or when he'd heard it before. He let the CD continue and got down on the floor to begin the stretching routine he had learned at the Training Center.

Stretching out the backs of his legs was the number one priority. Especially the calves. They had healed very tightly after the burning, and the tissue was extremely stubborn. He had to find just the right balance between stretching and straining. It was a frustrating, painful process, but there was no other way he would get his jump back. He knew he'd have trouble playing pro ball with a twenty-five inch jump.

The quad stretches were easy. Ten reps of those, then the quad sets and straight leg raises. Then, lying on his back, he held one end of a towel in each hand, then put his foot in the center of it. He pulled his leg up with the towel, trying to stretch it to a ninety degree angle, but it wasn't going to happen. He managed only sixty. If he didn't get it up to ninety within a week, Stu said he'd tie him to a Hurley stretch rack. Quinton had seen one in a magazine. It looked like a medieval torture device. How someone could use that thing and still have a vocal range below soprano was beyond him. He pulled harder on the towel and screamed in pain, nearing seventy degrees. There was no way he was getting into that rack.

Sunrise found him jogging out of his house in a fresh pair of sweats and bare feet. He wore an orange weight belt around his waist, with the ball bearing jump rope tucked inside.

After a series of toe raises, lunges, and practice squats, he drew two points in the sand, thirty feet apart, the length of one side of a volleyball court. He spent the next few hours doing wind sprints between the two points, allowing himself to get used to the sun and the awkward inconsistency of the sand.

By early evening, an exhausted Quinton sat motionless in his large outdoor jacuzzi on the deck. He stared out at the ocean lying under the slowly setting sun. The way the auburn hues danced on the water made him smile.

His energy was low, his muscles tired, and his body tight. He closed his eyes and tried to imagine his languid body was as fluid as the water surrounding it.

His breathing became more even and his head felt lighter. He could feel a peaceful breath-energy begin to build in his lower abdomen. With the will of his mind, he gently guided the energy to the muscles in need of nourishment. His lower extremities were weak and tired. The energy fed the thighs and calves and warmed the bone to the marrow.

Quinton exhaled deeply with satisfaction. He felt his back and spine become straight. The rest of the breath-energy moved up his back, massaging the tight tissue and spinal facets. His body felt beyond peaceful, almost weightless. Quinton extended his belly in exhalation and released it during inhalation. Oxygen flowed freely through his muscles. He allowed himself to enjoy the warmth emanating from within him.

At a point when he felt almost one with the stars above, his breathing pattern returned to normal. He opened his eyes. The sky was dark, the sunset long since faded. He looked at his watch. Nine forty-two. Where had he been for three hours?

He searched the sky for Orion as he felt the water roll over his skin like a thousand gentle butterflies. He looked north and saw the dark Santa Monica Mountains looming over the gently curving Malibu coastline. For the next few hours he sat there still and rejuvenated. He forgot that he had to remember.

Quinton couldn't believe the tournament grounds. He had seen them on TV, but it didn't compare to the spectacle he was now witnessing. He thought he was at the circus, not the Jose Cuervo Venice Beach Open.

Quinton and Stu slowly made their way from the sidewalk down to the center of the grounds to get their seeding for the day. Quinton tried to take it all in. Roller bladers flew down the beach on the bike lane, weaving around the slower-paced bike riders. Every dog on the hot summer beach wore sun glasses or a heat visor. Below a sign reading 'Muscle Beach – Venice' was a fenced-in area replete with weight benches, barbells, and enough muscle-bound hunks to fill the covers of the next dozen Danielle Steel novels.

'Beat the heat' was the name of the game in the hundred-degree weather. Anyone not boating on the ocean, surfing, or boogie boarding was busy dumping bottled water over their heads to keep cool. The beach smelled like a mixture of salt water, coconut oil, and stale beer.

As they neared the tournament grounds, Quinton had to drag Stu away from the Miss Venice Open contest: bleached blondes in thong bikinis, high heels, and enough silicone to stay afloat in the most treacherous of waters. Quinton wasn't impressed. He was more intrigued by the creature of a man walking on crushed glass for money. Hell, Quinton's bare feet could barely take the pain of the burning sand on this scorching afternoon.

Passing the twenty-two foot inflatable bottle of Jose Cuervo anchored to the ground, they saw the Association of Volleyball Professionals flags flying over the court area. Just outside the player's tent, Quinton spotted the blonde woman he saw playing volleyball at Stu's two nights earlier.

"Who's that?" Quinton asked.

Stu looked at him incredulously.

"Holly O."

"Holly O?" Quinton asked.

"Yeah. Holly O'Connor," Stu said, surprised.

"Have I met her?"

Stu looked at him with an eerie grin and just laughed.

"Yeah, you met her. You met her drink in your pants."

Quinton was confused. Stu continued.

"The Venice Open last year? Man, you *have* lost your memory."

Stu stared in amazement as Quinton started to walk towards Holly. He called after him.

"Dude. I wouldn't do that if I were you. Dude!"

Before Stu could stop him, Quinton walked up to her, smiled, and said hi.

"Hi," she said, smiling back. Holly slurped down the rest of her ice water.

Looking into his eyes, she pulled out the elastic of his shorts and dumped the ice inside. She turned on her barefoot heel and was gone. Shocked, Quinton couldn't help but laugh as he shivered and quickly shook the ice from his shorts. He couldn't wait for Stu to explain this one.

Quinton and Stu sat netside waiting for their game to begin. Quinton looked at the crowd. It was large for a volleyball game so early in the tournament. There had to be ten thousand people out there. He knew a lot of them were there to see him. He couldn't have been more nervous if he was walking on the moon.

The referee took his place on the small platform attached to the net. The announcer spoke into a microphone.

"This is the first matchup for each of these two teams today, in this single elimination tournament. On one side we have the No. 5 seeded team of B.J. Aaron and Steve Aimes, playing against No. 3 seeds Stuart Gardner and Quinton Squid."

The crowd cheered furiously. A large group in the crowd wore baseball caps adorned with green rubber tentacles. They started to chant "Squid, Squid, Squid..." The announcer smiled over at them.

"I think the crowd wants to see some deep-sea tentacle dives here today, and here is the man to give it to them." He waived a hand in Quinton's direction. "Quinton Squid!!"

Quinton stood and waved to the crowd as the chanting grew louder. Stu enjoyed Quinton's embarrassment and encouraged the crowd to chant even louder. Fans of the 'Double A's,' B.J. Aaron and Steve Aimes, started to boo. The crowd quickly became entangled in a vocal fist fight over who was their favorite team.

The fans quieted down when the referee announced "Quinton Squid to serve." Stu took the volleyball from the ref. He could see Quinton was nervous. When he handed Squid the ball, he winked at him.

"C'mon man, it's just a spike from the thirty foot line. Easy," Stu said.

Quinton smiled through trembling lips.

"Let's smoke," encouraged Stu.

Stu put his hand out for a low five. Quinton met it with a loud smack. Quinton walked to the serve line at the back right corner of his court. Stu stood a few feet from the net and studied Aaron and Aimes.

B.J. Aaron, six foot four, one hundred eighty-five pounds, had always been an asshole. The six foot two Aimes had only recently become one since partnering up with Aaron. The only endorsement the pair had been able to secure was from a veterinary group specializing in the neutering of pit bulls and other impetuous canines.

Stu was of course wearing his full set of Victory Beachwear endorsement patches, and Quinton wore his traditional bright copper-green Sand Dune shorts. They both wore Sideout visors, characteristically turned up as a matter of course. Stu looked at B.J.'s wraparound sunglasses and wondered if they were the same kind of rear-vision-enhancing wraparounds that had gotten him thrown out of the tournament three years ago. It hadn't really mattered, B.J. wasn't coordinated enough to be functionally aware of what was in front of him and behind him at the same time anyway.

But Stu could see B.J.'s eyes burning into Quinton. He knew Aaron was gunning for his partner. Both hands behind his back, Stu signaled Quinton. He held out one finger in his left hand, and two in his right - he would cover the left side of their court from a possible down the line attack from Aimes, or a cross-court attack from Aaron. Quinton had his hands full covering court right, keeping an eye on Aaron, who loomed in front of him across the net.

Quinton jump-served the ball hard down the right line and moved forward. On the other side of the net, Aaron dug the ball, bringing it up with a clenched fist. Aimes set the ball back to his court left, where Aaron was waiting. Aaron leapt for the spike. He crashed the ball deep into the opposite court's right corner. Quinton ran back for an impossible save. He propelled himself through the air, reaching the ball for a perfect dig to set Stu.

"On-two! Kill!" Quinton yelled to Stu.

Stu slammed the ball into the opposite court.

"One-nothing. Gardner and Squid," announced the referee.

The crowd began to cheer furiously. Quinton lay on the sand, still amazed he had reached the ball in time for the dig. Stu put his hand out to help Quinton up.

"Welcome back," Stu said to his partner.

"Nice to be back," answered Quinton.

The sun beat down on the four athletes. Fifty minutes later found Quinton dripping with sweat. It was one game all. This third would determine who progressed in the tournament. In mid-rally, Quinton ran towards the ball as Stu set him at the net for a spike.

"He's up!" Stu yelled to Quinton as he saw Aaron start to jump up for the block.

Quinton leapt into the air with all the strength he could muster, but Aaron was right there with him. His thirty-five inch jump towered over Quinton's by ten inches. Aaron blocked the ball back into Quinton's court. Point. Quinton bent over, his hands on his knees, and gasped for air. Aaron smirked in delight.

"Hey Squid," he said, "you need any shingles for that roof?"

Quinton was too tired to search through his glossary of a memory, but got the basic meaning. His defense, his roof, had holes in it.

"Can it," Stu barked at B.J. Aaron.

"Squid," B.J. egged him on, "you look like you're trying to hit in a phone booth. Did you burn your balls in that fire too?"

Quinton was too busy trying to catch his breath. Stu leapt to his defense.

"Fuck you, B.J. What does that stand for anyway, blow job?"

"Kiss my white ass, Gardner," yelled B.J. as he abruptly turned around, dropped his shorts, and mooned Stu.

The crowd went wild with laughter and the Cable Sports cameras moved in to focus on B.J. Aaron's posterior.

"Players, please," said the referee over the P.A. system. "Mr. Aaron, that's a yellow card. Don't tempt me. The score stands at fourteen to seven, Aaron and Aimes."

"Time out," rasped Quinton.

"Time out has been called," said the referee.

Stu helped Quinton to their chairs at the sidelines. Quinton grabbed some ice cubes and ran them over his face and body. He toweled off and began to chug ice water.

"I'm cramping. He keeps blocking me. I have no oxygen. I suck," he told Stu.

"Breathe slowly. Get some oxygen in your blood, it's going to reduce your muscle fatigue," said Stu, patting his partner on the shoulder.

"Okay," he inhaled. "I'm sorry, Stu."

"You're not used to the heat yet. They're going to keep gunning for you. Don't give up, just do your best," Stu reassured him.

"Okay," said Quinton as he continued to breathe deeply.

He tried to find the peaceful, healing energy he had felt in the hot tub the night before. If he could tap into it, maybe it could help with this game.

Quinton took in a huge deep breath as he sucked in his belly and blew air out as he extended it. But he didn't feel the fire of that energy, he just felt dizzy. His eyes began to spin. Stu stared at him.

"What the hell are you doing?" he asked.

"Trying to light my fire with reverse breathing. The Taoist breathing pattern. But it's not working," Quinton explained.

"Well cut it the fuck out, because you look like you're gonna toss your cookies."

Quinton started to breathe normally again.

"Maybe I am forcing it a bit," he mumbled to himself.

The buzzer went off.

"Ready?" Stu asked his partner.

"Yeah."

Quinton and Stu walked back on court with the other players.

"Aimes to serve. Match point," announced the referee.

"We own you, Squid. Get ready," Aimes threatened. He served the ball right into Quinton, hard.

Quinton managed to get a piece of the ball with his forearm and bumped it to Stu, who set him at the net. Quinton had thirty feet to gather momentum for the spike. He saw Aaron and Aimes both move toward the net to block him. As he ran forward and reached the net, he could see them crouching in front of him, ready to jump. In mid air, Quinton decided to slam the ball away from them, diagonally, for a cross-court kill. Quinton's instincts were on target, but his jump wasn't. He didn't get enough height to hit it past either one of them. Aaron loomed a good ten inches over him and again blocked it back into Quinton's court. Point and game.

"Fifteen to seven. Aaron and Aimes. Game and match," announced the referee.

The crowd booed furiously. Quinton and Stu gathered their gear together on the sidelines.

"That was humiliating," observed Quinton, exhausted.

"Naw, it wasn't so bad," said Stu. "Besides, B.J.'s hairy butt all over the TV will cancel out anything else that happened in this game, believe me."

Quinton laughed. Stu laughed with him, happy that in spite of his frustration he could still make his partner chuckle after such a grueling loss. From the corner of his eye, Stu spotted a CSN camera crew coming towards them.

"Oh shit," he said. The interviewer walked up to them.

"Quinton, Stu. Dave Woodward, CSN. Quite a game," said the generic-looking sports correspondent as he extended his hand for a shake.

Stu met his hand tentatively.

"That it was," Stu said as he forced a smile into the camera.

Woodward turned his attention to Quinton.

"Quinton, it seems as though you haven't quite gotten your beach legs back yet," he commented, and shoved the microphone into Quinton's face.

"Hopefully, it will come in time," Quinton offered, then stepped back a bit. "Getting used to the heat again is the main thing," he explained quietly.

Stu stood there wooden, a frozen smile plastered on his face. Quinton stared into the camera. It was a foot from his face. He could see himself reflected in the lens.

"When is this going to broadcast?" he asked the cameraman.

"Now," answered Woodward.

"Huh?" asked a confused Quinton.

"Now, Quinton," reiterated the interviewer. "This is part of our live coast-to-coast broadcast."

Quinton's surprised face could be seen on a television screen three thousand miles away. In Boston's North End, to be specific. In Victor Russo's warehouse, to be exact. Victor and Gina sat in his office as Victor spoke viciously into the phone. Gina stared blankly at the twenty-five TV screens, waiting for him to finish his conversation.

Five of the screens were turned on. The attached VCR's recorded all the action. There were three different baseball games on, one TV was tuned to drag racing, and the other displayed beach volleyball on the Cable Sports Network. Gina glanced from one screen to another with little interest.

"Jesus Christ, Frank. Take your prozac!" Victor bellowed into the phone.

He slammed the receiver down, snatched up a clipboard,

and stormed out of the office. Gina stood up to go after him, but something she saw out of the corner of her eye changed her mind. Sweaty, half-naked men playing volleyball on the beach suddenly seemed more interesting than Victor and his clipboard. These guys were cut like diamonds and prettier than James Dean. She wondered why the hell she stayed around here, dating one flabby 'Tony' after another since Michael.

Michael had truly been beautiful. Inside as well as out. Only now did she fully realize what she had lost.

Onscreen, the volleyball match had ended and she raised the volume to hear what these buff beach dudes had to say. Not that she really cared, but ogling their washboards on 'mute' made her feel just a little too cheap. And there was something almost familiar about the player being interviewed. Pleasantly so. She listened in as the interviewer's voice issued from the TV.

"Quinton, it looked as though the heat was really getting to you around the eighth and ninth point."

"Actually, I think it started around point one," confessed Quinton. "Yeah, I thought I was gonna to puke in my shoes," he said, shaking his pinkie finger in his right ear as if trying to remove sand.

Three thousand miles away, a mouthful of Tab spurted from Gina's nose and she gagged for air. With soda dribbling down her mock turtleneck, she looked back at the screen with a crooked, unbelieving eye. She slowly sat down and began to stare intently at Quinton as the interview continued. She focused on his eyes, and the spirit behind them.

"Well, you didn't place today, so we won't be seeing you play tomorrow, but hopefully we'll see you soon back on the court. Once again, ladies and gentlemen, Quinton Squid is back on the beach, and back on track after his recovery at Boston's Beth Israel Hospital..."

Gina wiped the soda from her chin.

"...This is Dave Woodward, netside at the Venice Open. Bob?"

The TV cut to Bob Esterhaus at the CSN studio sports desk.

"Okay folks, that's it for beach volleyball at the Venice Beach Open today. Tomorrow, the finals. We don't know who it will be, but you can expect our live coverage to start at nine a.m. Pacific, noon Eastern, check your local listings. Right now we'll go to commercial and be right back with the Hawaiian Open bungie-jumping championships."

Gina watched as the TV cut to a commercial. She reached over to the unit's VCR and pressed stop. Gina glanced outside the glass-walled office. She didn't see Victor and his clipboard, but Carlo and Muncie loading boxes onto a pushcart. Gina gazed at them for a moment, then called out through the open door.

"Yo, Burns and Allen. Come here."

Like trained mice, Carlo and Muncie put the boxes down and padded into Victor's office. Gina closed the door behind them.

15

"Wait! Wait. Go back. No, fast forward..." laughed Stu, as beer flew out of his nose.

"Hey, hey. Don't drool all over my sofa," Quinton chuckled from his kitchen as he tossed Stu a hand towel.

"Hey, bring out the marinara sauce while you're at it," said Stu.

Quinton set the microwave's timer on the four bags of frozen fries inside. It was evening and he craved food.

"Not if you're going to spew it on my furniture," he replied.

"I swear, you're turning into Felix Unger," said Stu. "You know, my grandmother has some extra plastic furniture covers if you want them."

The three other guys sitting in the living room busted a gut laughing.

"No shit, Q, I heard you started ironing your jock strap," said the smallest member of the trio.

Quinton had seen this guy on many of the videotapes he'd watched in the hospital. After the tournament, Stu had reacquainted him personally with this fire-plug of a man, Derrick Billings. Gull Becker and Todd Reynolds were also familiar to him from the taped beach matches. Gull was a huge blonde dude who stood six foot seven and rounded out at about two hundred twenty pounds. He had graduated from San Diego State, then was drafted by the NBA's Portland Trail Blazers. After two years on the bench he'd made a bee-line back to the beach, and had made a living playing pro beach volleyball ever since.

A year ago Gull had teamed up with Derrick Billings. The fourteenth-ranked duo had become known as 'David and Goliath.' Derrick stood only five foot, ten inches tall, the shortest man on the pro beach tour. But despite his height disadvantage, he had led UCLA to four NCAA Championships, earning All-American MVP honors along the way. He had also played with Quinton and Stu on the US National Team that won a Gold Medal at the last Olympics.

Todd Reynolds was relatively new to the game. Last year he had taken the tour by storm, earning his first career victory at the Seal Beach Open with B.J. Aaron.

As Quinton observed the men conversing, the information spun around in his brain. The microwave timer went off. For four whole minutes his mind had let itself wander around these players' biographies without any direct intent to do so. Quinton really needed a beer. He opened a Bud Light and chugged away.

"Hey, women and children first," yelled Stu.

"No, it's amnesiacs, women and children first," Quinton yelled back. "Besides, you already had a few."

"Hey, Quinton, I just got a card," Todd yelled.

"What?"

"I said I got a card, finally."

"Hold on, be there in a second."

Quinton scooped up the steaming fries and tossed them onto a pizza pan. He grabbed ketchup and marinara from the refrigerator.

"Mustard!" Gull barked.

"What am I, your mother? Get it yourself," retorted Quinton.

"It's your house."

"Hello? Anybody home? My hands are full."

Quinton lay the food down on the coffee table. All six foot seven of Gull Becker stood and walked to the kitchen. He was truly a monster. There was something about Gull that Quinton found annoying. Something almost...familiar? That blonde hair, that scowl. Quinton couldn't quite place it, and sat down on the sofa.

"These fries are hot, give 'em a minute or two. What card, Todd?"

Todd picked up a deck of what looked like baseball cards sitting on the table. Quinton looked on as Todd flipped through them. They were volleyball cards. On the front of each card was a color photo of a pro player in action, with their vital statistics listed on the back.

"See," said Todd, as he handed Quinton his card.

"Nice picture of you," replied Quinton.

He turned the card over, and began to read the back.

"Six foot five. One hundred ninety pounds. Not bad. You played professional basketball in Berlin for two years?"

"Yeah."

Quinton handed back the card.

"Interesting. Do I have a card?"

Todd stared at him, unbelieving.

"Of course you do..."

"Can I see it?"

Todd handed Squid his card. Quinton scanned the back stats voraciously.

"What's the Triple Crown?" he asked.

Gull came in from the kitchen with mustard and a six-pack of Bud.

"The Triple Crown?" he asked.

"Yeah."

"You are a fucking doofus, aren't you Squid?" Gull said as he sat on the sofa. "Do someone a favor and don't fill out a brain-donor card."

"Screw you. Stu, what's a Triple Crown?

Stu answered through a mouthful of fries.

"It's when you win Olympic Gold, the World Cup, and the World Championship in three consecutive years."

"I helped do that?" asked Quinton.

"Yeah," said Stu, "you were the only player who was on all three of the teams."

"Is that a big deal?" Quinton asked.

Stu shook his head in disbelief.

"Q, it's the biggest deal there is in six-man hardcourt."

"Oh."

"Squid, you are just out for the count, aren't you?" said Gull.

Quinton turned to face him quickly.

"Have you got a problem?"

"You wouldn't get me the mustard."

"I'm not your wife, Gull."

Gull pointed an elbow towards Stu.

"You got him the marinara sauce, are you his wife?"

"Shut up," insisted Stu. "You two sound like an old married couple."

All were silent for a moment. Gull tossed the Buds around. Stu pressed play on the remote control. The Venice Beach Open from one year previous came on the TV.

"What is this?" asked Quinton.

"This is the reason you shouldn't talk to Holly O'Connor," said Stu, buzzing slightly on the beer.

Onscreen, Bob Esterhaus, the present-day studio anchor, interviewed Quinton netside.

"Quint, how do you feel about the women's exhibition match this year at the men's final?" asked Bob.

Quinton winked at the camera and smiled. "If the ladies want to have their own tourneys, that's fine. But the only place they belong at the men's events is on the sidelines cheering for their man, or strutting their stuff as Miss Venice Open."

A surprised Bob Esterhaus didn't know what to say. Stu muted the TV, but the tape continued to roll. The women's exhibition match began.

"I said that? Man, oh man," said Quinton, shocked. He began to laugh, more out of embarrassment than anything else. Everyone else joined in the laughter too, but for their own reasons.

"Dude, you were lucky she just got it wet today, and didn't cut it off at the root. Ouch," said Stu.

"Dude," Quinton acknowledged.

The laughter began to die down a bit.

"Drink up," said Gull.

They all clicked their beers together in a toast. Gull pounded down his beer and chased it with a piece of Bazooka bubble gum.

"Tomorrow is the one year anniversary of the most obnoxious statement ever made about she-man volleyball," he snickered.

"About what?" asked Quinton.

"He means women's pro volleyball," Stu explained.

"You gotta get back into the lingo, dude. Rent *Bill & Ted* or something," was Derrick's enlightened observation.

"So tomorrow's the final?" Quinton asked.

"You got it, man," affirmed Stu.

"And I made it to the finals last year? Shit," said Quinton, almost to himself.

"Shit is right," said Gull, "I've never seen you wind up on the wrong end of a game like today. You shanked so many damn passes, I wouldna' been surprised if you'd smacked a fan right in the head with the ball."

Quinton's eyes burned into Gull. He opened his mouth to speak, but thought better of it and turned away. Man, this guy pissed him off.

Quinton looked at the TV and watched the women's exhibition match still running on the VCR. He saw Holly and Pam playing against Emily and her partner Tracy.

"Wait. Stu, turn that up. Take it off mute," Quinton said, intrigued.

Gull grabbed the remote from Stu's hands.

"No way. It's the bitch's match," Gull whined through the wad of chewing gum in his mouth.

"Man, she is one cold bitch, isn't she," agreed Derrick.

Todd, Derrick, Gull, and Stu began to laugh.

"Yeah, but she is one fine bitch," said Todd, raising his eyebrows.

The four clicked beers. Quinton looked at Stu in confusion.

"I should apologize to her," said Quinton.

"Why? They're not real athletes. Just a little T and A to sell a few beers," Gull offered.

The other four began to laugh again. Quinton only cracked a smile.

"That's really harsh, Gull," he said.

"They're Ivans, man. I call them like I see them," insisted Gull.

"Ivans?" asked a perplexed Quinton.

"Ivan Dragos," reiterated Todd.

"I-will-break-you-Rock-y-Bal-bo-a," Derrick said in a fake Russian accent.

The four laughed. In spite of himself, Quinton couldn't help but crack another smile.

"I have seen a few that could toss a good shot-put," offered Quinton.

"Dude, I've seen some matches between those bitches that rival Godzilla vs. Megalon," added Gull. Gull, Derrick, and Stu cackled as they slapped a round of high five's.

"Gull, man. That's harsh," said Quinton apprehensively.

Gull turned and snapped his gum in Quinton's face.

"What the fuck, Q. I saw O'Connor ice your scrote today. Are you turning bitch-guilty or what?"

Quinton returned Gull's icy stare. He closed his eyes and took a deep breath. When he opened them again, his eyes had softened somewhat.

"Man, you just don't get it, do you," he said to Gull.

Gull snapped his gum again as he relaxed into Quinton's sofa.

"Your dick must've burned to the bone in that fire, too. You've turned into a real pussy, Quinton," he sneered as he blew a huge pink bubble with his gum.

Quinton's skin felt suddenly electric. His mind and body became one-focused in the area just below his navel. The energy concentrated there expanded into his four limbs.

Suddenly, Quinton leapt to his feet and lunged at Gull with an aerial roundhouse kick. Stu, Todd, and Derrick grabbed Quinton in mid air, his foot just inches from Gull's face. Bubble gum covered Gull's face and Quinton's foot.

All were silent and shocked. Todd, Derrick, and Stu held

Quinton over the coffee table. They couldn't figure out which surprised them more, Quinton's attack, or how they were able to react so quickly. Quinton's body was taut as a bow, his belly enlarged in an exhale. His eyes bulged from their sockets, though appeared to be looking inward. Quinton extended his diaphragm further with a long inhale, then exhaled all the air out. His eyes sunk back into his skull and he surveyed the situation before him.

As he relaxed his musculature, Stu and the others let him down. It had all happened within a few seconds.

"What the fuck was that?" screamed Gull, standing up from the sofa like a rocket.

Derrick and Todd rallied behind their friend. Stu herded a confused and speechless Quinton behind him and faced the three men alone.

"I think you guys better go, Gull. You and Derrick have a game tomorrow," he tried to reason.

Gull's face was covered with pink bubble gum. His fists clenched with rage. Todd could see the hair on the back of his neck stand at attention. He guided Gull behind him, as Stu had done with Quinton.

"Yeah, you're right. C'mon, Gull. Derrick, let's go," he said as he ushered Gull out the door.

Derrick shook his head in disbelief.

"Later, guys..." he said, then closed the door behind him.

An insanely confused Stu Gardner turned around to face his best friend.

"Man, I thought you were going to take his head off! Watch too many Van Damme movies in the hospital? Jesus!"

Quinton sat on the sofa and kneaded his palms against his temples.

"There was something really familiar there for a moment," said Quinton, half dazed. He put the palms of his hands under his eyes and brushed them across his face sideways. He then put his thumbs in front of his ears and moved them down to his chin. Stu looked on. What the hell was he doing?

Stu sat on the coffee table across from Quinton.

"Q, Gull always talks like that."

"No, that's not what I mean," said Quinton.

He bowed his head forward and placed his thumbs at the base of his skull and pushed them gently downward in a circular motion. Stu watched. This was definitely some new relaxation technique he wasn't in on.

After a moment, Stu became concerned.

"You're zoning out, man."

Quinton dropped his hands from his head and sat up straight.

"You were laughing with them," Quinton said, bewildered.

"So," said Stu.

"So, what would you do if Gull went all racial on Bill Johnson?" asked Quinton.

"Tell him to shut up," Stu answered without hesitation.

"So why'd you let him cut your wife down?"

Stu was honestly perplexed. He didn't know what to say. Quinton could sense Stu's brain overloading with conflicting input. All this from a man who used to make Stu look like a feminist. A lot to take in. Quinton changed the subject.

"C'mon, help me clean up," he said, and began picking up the beer cans and french fries strewn about the room.

"You know what your problem is?" Stu said as he stood up and began to help.

"No, what?" asked Quinton.

"With all those scars on your face, you look like Pinhead," said Stu, trying to break the tension.

"Bite me," chuckled Quinton with affection. "You can't see them without a magnifying glass. I can still stop a clock."

"More like break a mirror," chided Stu.

Quinton dumped an arm full of empties into the garbage can.

"Don't you have to go home and 'feed the dogs' or something?" he asked.

"Nope. Dogs go hungry tonight. Em's got a match tomorrow."

Stu dumped out the soggy fries he had gathered in his shirt as Quinton headed for the hall closet to get the vacuum. Stu meandered his way to the door.

"Come to the match with me," Stu hollered on his way out.

"I'd like that," Quinton yelled back.

Later that night Quinton sat alone in his living room. The room was dark, lit only by the flickering TV screen. What he believed to be his own voice issued from the television.

"If the ladies want to have their own tourneys, that's fine. But the only place they belong at the men's events is on the sidelines cheering for their man, or strutting their stuff as Miss Venice Open."

Quinton grabbed the VCR remote and rewound the tape to hear the statement again. It was so different from what he felt his own perspective to be. It just didn't seem to fit. He listened to it one more time, then let the tape continue. He put down the remote and began to watch the women's match.

Venice Beach was abuzz with the results of the men's finals. Johnson and Steeles had won the Open, beating out the No. 7 seeded team of Eddie Beck and Will Powell. Quinton and Stu sat in the player's tent. They watched Emily's trainer give her a liniment rub down. Stu watched the trainer's hands obsessively, making sure they didn't touch anything they weren't supposed to. The tension was too much for Quinton to take. He ran outside when he saw Holly walk by.

"I'll be back in a minute," he told Stu.

"Where is he going?" asked Emily.

"After Holly O'Connor. I think that woman's going to be the death of him."

Quinton ran out of the tent and into the baking sun after Holly. She was easy to spot in her ice-blue one-piece swimsuit. A large circle was cut out in the front mid section, and the open back sloped down to just above her backside. The flexibility that a two piece suit allowed was overshadowed by how easily it was to pop out of one during a tough match. For the more well-endowed players, cut-out suits were the next best thing.

"Holly. Excuse me. Holly," he called to her.

He couldn't tell if she didn't hear or was just ignoring him. He finally reached her and tapped her on the shoulder. She turned around and looked at him indifferently. At least it felt indifferent, but he couldn't really tell for sure with her eyes hidden behind those tinted sunglasses.

"Hi, Holly," he said in the friendliest tone he could muster.

She stared at him blankly. Once again she slurped the rest of her drink through the straw. Quinton put his hand out for the cup.

"May I?" he asked.

Amused, she handed him the cup. He removed the straw and stared down at the ice that remained. He clanked the ice around in the cup uneasily, looked down at his shorts, then looked up to catch her derisive gaze.

He pulled out the elastic of his shorts, stared directly into her sunglasses, and poured the ice inside. He then somehow managed to force a smile.

"I figured I'd save you the trouble," he joked.

"Thank you," she said wryly, and began to walk away.

He jumped in front of her.

"Wait. Please. Doesn't such an act of self-sacrifice merit even one minute of your time?"

"Are you serious?" she asked.

"I am serious," he pleaded.

"Quote unquote, 'you're too pretty to be taken seriously.' "

His pained smile took on an edge of sincerity.

"If you look real close, you'll see this face isn't that pretty anymore," he said.

Quinton's gaze didn't leave her.

He felt something within her shift. She didn't know what to say, but her shoulders seemed to relax a bit. She took off her sunglasses. She had beautiful green eyes. They perfectly complemented the blue swimsuit.

"I am truly sorry about what happened to you, Quinton."

For the first time in the little bit of life he could remember, he knew he was in uncharted waters. The old Quinton would never have done this. Holly would never have spoken to him, and he would not have searched out her friendship. Or would he have?

"Did we know each other well?" he asked her.

"No. Not really. Why are you here?"

"Stu showed me the Venice Open tournament last year."

He saw her shoulders turn to stone and her eyes grow cold again.

"I see. So, what do you want? Penance? You want me to kiss it and make it better?"

"No. I just wanted to apologize."

"Apology rendered. You can go back to your conscience now. I think he's gearing up to watch his wife play."

Holly eyed over to Stu and Emily leaving the player's tent, heading for center court. Holly began to walk in that direction.

"I meant what I said," Quinton yelled out as she faded from view.

"Find a priest," she yelled back.

Quinton began to go after her, but froze in mid step and let out a stifled whimper.

"Oh, my fuckin' head," he said aloud as he shook the remaining ice from his shorts. People walked by him, unfazed by the strange sight of a man shaking ice out of his shorts onto Venice Beach.

Stu and Quinton sat in the player's chairs on the sidelines adjacent to center court, watching the women's exhibition match. The second-seeded team of Emily Roeg and Tracy Rollins battled it out with top seeds Holly O'Connor and Pamela Benson. A huge crowd had gathered. Quinton watched the game through dark Ray-Bans. Stu's eyes constantly fixated on Emily.

"She won't even let me apologize," Quinton complained.

"Yeah, well. Talking down to someone on the beach is one thing, but over the air? Forget it. What the hell do you want with her anyway? You could have any piece of ass on the beach," said Stu, watching his wife move-for-move.

"Did I used to talk like you?" asked Quinton.

"Worse."

Quinton looked down at his shorts.

"No wonder there's a frost over the Florida panhandle."

Stu laughed.

Out on the court Emily crashed down an incredible spike.

"Way to go, Em!" Stu screamed out. "I hope she wins today," Stu whispered to Quinton. "Man, she's good in bed when she wins."

Quinton took his shades off and looked at Stu.

"What? What did I say?" asked Stu.

Quinton just shook his head, laughed and looked back at the game. He put his sunglasses back in their case.

After the game was over, the TV crew from CSN stood by the player's tent waiting for interviews. The field anchor, an attractive woman with square shoulders and an intimidating gaze, spoke directly to the camera.

"This is Suzanne Dryer live from the down in the player's tent on the second day of this sixteen hour, two day tournament. The scene is the same as last year's tournament, in which the women's exhibition match was a specialty event. We'll hear from the first and second-place players after they have a few minutes to cool down. But right now I see a familiar face in unfamiliar surroundings. Let's see if I can grab him and get him to talk to us."

Suzanne glanced over at Quinton who was standing just outside the tent. As she went over to him, microphone in hand, the camera crew followed. She cornered him by the Gatorade cooler.

"Ladies and gentleman, it's Quinton Squid, attending what I believe to be his first women's beach volleyball game. Am I correct in assuming that Mr. Squid?" She stuck the microphone in Quinton's face.

"Uh, yes, Suzanne, I believe you are," Quinton answered awkwardly.

"Well, this is quite a turnaround from last year's auditory upset over the air. So, why did you come down today?" she asked.

"I came down with my partner to watch his wife play."

"And what are your thoughts on the match we just saw?"

Quinton answered without pause.

"Em and Tracy are really spectacular players. It's not as much of a power game as the men's, but it's just as thrilling in a different way."

Off-camera, Suzanne snorted in derision.

"And what way is that?" she challenged. She wanted him to squirm.

He could tell she wasn't buying it, but he couldn't blame her. He composed himself as best he could.

"They don't have the men's height or muscle mass, so I noticed that they rely more on better ball control and quicker anticipation of the opponent's strategy. It's pretty amazing to watch, really," was his earnest response.

Suzanne looked at him with complete contempt. Who did this guy think he was kidding?

"Are you serious?" she balked.

Quinton smiled at her, softening his gaze a bit.

"Why not?" He looked directly into the camera. "People change," he said with a wink, and walked away.

Suzanne was caught off guard. He had been serious. A wave of disbelief played over her face. She clutched the microphone to her lips.

"Well, thank you Quinton Squid. That's quite a different story. This is indeed a very different Quinton Squid from last year. Words of wisdom from an unlikely source? You be the judge. I'll see if I can't go over and get Holly O'Connor and Pamela Benson to speak with us," she said, still flustered, and walked off in search of the No. 1 seeded women's team.

16

Gina, Carlo, and Muncie strolled nonchalantly through the emergency room entrance of the Beth Israel hospital. They proceeded down the same dimly-lit corridor through which Nick had been chased several months earlier. Night orderlies passed by, indifferent to their presence. The trio made their way closer to the inner workings of the hospital. Gina spotted a lone nurse breaking down an IV unit in one of the empty rooms and pretended to faint in front of the door. Carlo and Muncie caught her before she hit the ground. They quickly carried her into the hospital room and past the startled nurse, closing the door behind them. They lay Gina down on the empty bed.

"Excuse me," barked the nurse, "authorized personnel only."

"But my wife here just fainted," Muncie pleaded with concern.

The nurse bent over to check Gina's pulse. Carlo grabbed her from behind. Muncie put a piece of duct tape over her mouth as Gina jumped up from the bed. She quickly unzipped the nurse's uniform and pulled it off over her head. The frightened nurse was left clad in just a full slip. Carlo and Muncie tied her trembling body to a chair with the tape. Gina quickly donned the nurse's uniform and security badge.

"Sorry honey. You'll be out of here in just a sec," she said, patting the nurse on the forearm. She draped a johnnie over the woman's goose-pimpled arms. Gina turned to Carlo and Muncie.

"You touch her," she warned, "and I'll fry up your balls for Sunday dinner. Be back in a bit."

Gina slipped out the door, leaving the two thick-necked bookends to stand watch over the helpless R.N. Beauty and the Beasts.

Gina made her way to the basement.

After some delicate lock-picking, she stood alone in the dark, deserted hospital records room. She flashed her penlight slowly around the room until it came to rest on an enormous filing cabinet. Gina tossed her hair back defiantly and walked over to it. She opened the file drawer marked "Dale – DiPetrio."

She put the penlight between her teeth and sifted through the files with her gloved hands. The headings read: Dale, Dalton, Debenedetto, Decole, Delaney...Gina pulled the Delaney file. She removed the penlight from her mouth, twisting its rim to enlarge the circle of light. She read.

There wasn't much to learn from this file. It contained the personal information form Nick had filled out and attached to the gurney, a certificate of death signed by the coroner indicating the patient had been dead on arrival, December 22, 11:43 p.m., and his conclusion that death was 'the result of severe third degree burns covering eighty percent of the body, burns to the respiratory tract, septic shock, increased vascular permeability, and lung failure due to acute respiratory distress syndrome.'

The only other items in the file were photographs taken by the coroner and the morgue.

The morgue photos looked familiar to her. She and Victor had been given the task of identifying the body. There hadn't been much left to identify. Gina had thrown up right there and then from the sight of the body and the smell of formaldehyde. As she looked at the coroner's photos, she realized how much the body at the morgue must have been cleaned up. And even then the face and body had been too mutilated to make a positive ID. The raw photos were absolutely ghastly. She closed the file quickly as the sense-memory of formaldehyde started to seep into her brain.

She put the Delaney file back in the drawer and the penlight between her teeth. She opened a different drawer and sifted through another set of files. Scarsdale, Scrapton, Squibb, Squid...She pulled out Squid. It was much thicker than the Delaney file.

The personal information form simply read: Quinton Squid. White male, late twenties. Logan. NorthAir International 238. There were photographs of specific burns. The left calve. The right calve. The back of both legs. The lower back, and part of the torso. There were pictures of superficial burns on the arms, and severe ones on the hands. But the explicit photographs of the face were the most grotesque. Gina could feel her stomach begin to churn again in disgust.

She closed her eyes for a moment. She sucked in a long deep breath. As she opened her eyes, Gina forced a sense of numbness to overtake her. She just had to get through the rest of this file, and that's all there was to it. If Michael was alive, she had to find him.

The file stated that the type of facial injuries the patient had sustained were consistent with severe impact as well as extreme burning. Both eyes had swollen shut. Nose broken. Left cheekbone shattered. Right jaw bone fractured. Broken glass pocked his face like buckshot. Possibly from the airplane window, the file suggested.

Gina skimmed over the rest of the dozen or so pages of doctor's scroll. She took note of certain section headings in particular:

(1.) Quinton Squid – patient admitted December 22, (2.) Severe burns – grafting recommended, (3.) Reconstructive surgery mandatory, (4.) Patient released to Alvarado Hospital, San Diego, April 5.

She leaned against the cabinet and stared down at the last page in the file, a picture of Quinton Squid's face taken upon leaving the Boston hospital. Though noticeably scarred and bruised, the face was that of a man, not the grotesque monster she had seen a dozen pages back. And the eyes looked suspiciously familiar.

"California," Gina said to herself quietly. She put the file away and slowly closed the cabinet behind her.

Frank sat back in Victor Russo's office chair, chewing impatiently on a wad of Bazooka Joe. He looked out at the otherwise deserted warehouse as Carlo and Muncie fiddled around in front of him with half-a-dozen remote controls. They pointed one after another at the TV's on the office wall, but none would activate the main large-screen television.

Carlo finally gave up and turned it on by hand. Muncie took his cue and pressed the play button on the VCR. The Cable Sports Network Champion Bungie-Jumping logo flashed across the screen.

"Why are you showing me this?" asked an irritated Frank.

"It's before this. She taped it the day before yesterday,"

Muncie said in his usual half-witted monotone. He sounded a little like Scooby Doo.

He scan-rewound the tape past the bungie segment, through the Venice women's pro beach volleyball exhibition match. Frank arched an eyebrow.

"Well, at least this is better than bungie jumping," he said.

He didn't see the four world-class athletes playing a game of skill, concentration, and power, he saw four women jiggling around the sand in bikinis.

"So Carlo, are you afraid of her too, or was this Muncie's idea?" Frank asked.

Carlo looked sheepishly down at the floor.

"What do you think she's gonna do – hit you with her purse? She's only five foot two; it's not like she's one of these Amazons," he said, nodding at the screen.

"We've seen Michael's face after a fight. We want you to protect us," Muncie insisted.

"And what makes you think I'll do that?"

Muncie rewound the video to the end of the men's volley-ball game and let it play. The interviewer's voice issued from the TV.

"...it looks as though the heat was really getting to you around the eighth and ninth point."

"Actually, I think it started around point one. Yeah, I thought I was gonna puke in my shoes," Quinton said as he took his pinkie finger and rubbed it around in his right ear.

Muncie paused the tape. He gave Frank his answer.

"Because she thinks she found Michael."

Frank stared at Muncie, then at Carlo, then back at Muncie. He sat up in his chair.

"Play that again."

Muncie obeyed. The VCR scanned backwards. The three watched Quinton's pinkie-to-ear mannerism a second time.

Frank slowly nodded as he watched the tape.

"What's she got planned?"

"We don't know," said Muncie.

"Keep me informed," Frank ordered.

"You'll protect us?" asked Carlo.

Frank looked at them like pathetic mice.

"Yeah, I'll protect you. Just keep me up to date."

They nodded quickly.

Frank sat alone in the darkened office. He had played Quinton's interview over and over again. He played the brief clip three more times consecutively, then shut off the TV. He got up and ejected the tape. He ran his hands over his wiffle-cut and started to sing 'Here Comes the Sun' softly to himself.

Smiling, he turned off the VCR and left the office.

Though neither placed first in the weekend's events, Stu and Emily threw their annual End of Venice party nonetheless. Even birds sing after a storm.

They had dressed up their house like a huge gondola. Stu was a whiz with paper mache. Give him a few days and a few beers and he could reconstruct Windsor Castle on your front lawn. The Venetian gondola had been his idea. Emily would have been just as happy with Venetian blinds. But hell, a theme party was a theme party. Besides, she'd rather have him construct a gondola for the Venice Beach Open than the entire New York skyline for the Manhattan Beach Open.

Hundreds of people converged on the small 'houseboat.' From a distance, it looked as though a giant Viking ship had run aground on the Santa Monica shoreline. Partygoers were gathered inside, dancing, drinking, and mingling. They were packed tight.

Most were athletes; surfers, beach players, or hardcourt players. Some were hangers on, wanna-be's, actors, and whatnot. The balcony was engorged with people. A few stood on the beach just under the deck, but none ventured further than that. All wanted to stay within a few feet of the nearest keg.

Twenty yards from the balcony, a frustrated Quinton practiced overhead spikes at Stu's private rig. He wasn't in the mood to party.

He'd set himself at the net, then slam down on the ball with a hard-driven spike. His spiking hand kept getting caught in the net after it hit the ball. He couldn't seem to jump high enough to pound the ball over the net, and still be able to retract his hand after the hit.

"I can't get the fucking altitude," he chided himself under his breath.

On the crowded deck above, someone was watching him struggle. It was Holly. This time it was she who observed his work discretely from the balcony. Quinton put the volleyball down and began to practice straight vertical jumps next to the net. Holly watched him a bit longer, then walked down the stairs to the beach.

The sounds of the party wafted down from the house above, but Quinton didn't hear them. Though he concentrated fully on the task at hand, his twelfth jump was inches shorter than his first. It seemed all his practice had been of no use. He continued the vertical jumps anyway. Holly came up slowly behind him as he worked.

"Didn't you hear what you said today?" she asked.

Quinton turned around, startled.

"What?" He was surprised to see her.

Holly moved a little closer to him. She could see the sweat trickling down the side of his face.

"Don't you remember? You know, in front of the camera."

"Yeah, of course I remember."

"No, you don't," she said.

"What frequency are you on?" asked Quinton, putting his hands on his hips.

She could see the lines above his eyebrows crease in confusion.

"Think about it. How high are you jumping?" she asked.

"Thirty."

"Thirty?"

"No, well, maybe twenty-eight tops," he confessed.

He wiped his face with his lime green t-shirt.

"Didn't you used to jump forty-two?" she asked.

"Yeah."

He ran the shirt collar over the back of his neck.

"My calves got burned in the crash."

She looked at him with softer eyes.

"Okay then, if this is something you are going to have to live with, you need to listen to your own advice."

"What do you mean?"

"In the interview today, you were talking about the women's game and our height disadvantage. You know, how we have to utilize other skills to get the ball over the net, blah, blah, blah."

"Yeah," agreed Quinton, perplexed.

"If this is the way you're going to make your living, you're gonna have to adopt a different style. Your old style isn't working for you. You can't do the jumping right now, maybe not for awhile," she explained. "You can't push what you haven't got to push."

"All I know is what I knew before."

"Well, you're going to have to learn some new tricks if you want to place in the top ten again. How's your cut shot?" she asked.

Quinton threw up his hands and shook his head.

"No way, I'm no dink master. No trash-man."

"Well, you're no placer these days either," she was quick to point out.

Quinton laughed.

"You got me there," he admitted and put his hands down.

Holly moved a little closer to him and spoke in a loud whisper.

"You don't have to be a total chipper, just slice the ball more. Change your wrist angle. Cut extreme over the net. Just watch your fingers, keep it clean. You won't be 'hitting like a girl,' if that's what you're afraid of."

Quinton smiled and looked down at the ball lying in the sand.

"Good read," he confessed.

"You have to do something to compensate for the ten inches you've lost," she reiterated.

"I know. I know. But I don't know what."

"C'mon. Try the cut. I'll block you."

He looked into her eyes. She didn't look away. They were the same color as his t-shirt. Kismet, he figured. Why not.

Quinton nodded his head and Holly went to the other side of the net. He stood near the front of his side of the court holding the volleyball in his hands.

"Set yourself," she said across the net.

He popped the ball into the air, then jumped up to hit it. At the top of the net, he was met by Holly's block. Her arms were outstretched vertically and she had at least seven inches on his jump. There was no way for him to hit the ball past her head-on, so he tapped the ball diagonally left. It sliced by her block and hit the sand. Point.

"There you go. You did it," she said.

She grabbed the ball and tossed it to him.

"Okay, I'll practice that. Thanks," he said, smiling.

"No. Thank you, for today," Holly said sincerely. He felt a kindness in her eyes.

She extended her hand to him. They shook.

"Can I ask you something?" he said sheepishly.

"Sure."

"Okay, I'm not the greatest when it comes to slicing and dicing, probably because I was so used to the height that I didn't need it that much. But, do you think if you have some time, you could show me a little more of what I need to learn?"

"And what will you give me in return?" she asked, smiling.

"The unyielding satisfaction of knowing you've helped another volleyball brother, not to mention, the kudos of the Volley God," he said.

"The Volley God?" she asked, arching her eyebrows.

"Yeah. You know, when we all stand around a big bonfire, and burn a volleyball in effigy to the Volley God to thank him for everything," he tried to explain.

"What are you talking about?" she laughed. "I've never heard of any Volley God. Where did you hear about this?"

"From Stu down in San Diego. It's an ancient Japanese thing."

Holly couldn't contain her amusement and chuckled outright.

"Sorry Quinton, no such thing. I think he got ya."

Quinton blushed in embarrassment and began to scratch

his ear with his pinkie. He couldn't help but join in her laughter.

"What a prick. What a little prick," he mumbled, making a mental note to get Stu.

As their laughter died down, Quinton stared up at the full moon. He looked over at Holly. God, did she look good.

"The Volley God, huh?" he said to himself.

He tossed the volleyball up with one hand and punched it high into the air with the other. Holly and Quinton watched it fly through the night sky. It flew over the moon, then fell back to earth. It landed in the ocean with a loud smack. Quinton turned to Holly.

"Do you have any time tomorrow?"

"Yeah," said Holly, almost hypnotized as she stared at the ball floating in the ocean.

She brought her focus back to Quinton and corrected herself.

"No, wait. I'm playing in that celebrity exhibition match for ESPN."

"How about Tuesday?" he asked.

"What time?"

"I have an endorsement shoot in the morning. Ten to twelve. Maybe I can pick you up for lunch or something and we can go after that," said Quinton.

"Okay. How about I meet you at the endorsement. I've got some stuff to do in the morning, too. Where is it?" Holly asked.

"Downtown at the DeCosta studio. First floor, I think. Suite 132. Just come in. I'm sure everyone there knows you anyway."

"Okay. I'll see you there around noon. I've got to go, played a tough game today."

"Yeah, you did," he said.

"Why don't you come down and watch the game tomorrow?"

"Thanks, but I think I'm just going to pack myself in ice and watch it on the tube."

"You're getting soft Quinton."

"No. Watching it in the hot tub would be soft. But packed in ice, I can rationalize that."

Holly laughed.

"Okay. I guess I'll see you Tuesday."

"Yeah. Good luck tomorrow. I'll be watching," Quinton said with a wink.

"Just watch where you put that ice," Holly said slyly, and walked back towards the gondola.

Quinton stared after her for a moment, until her form blended in with the other Venetian partygoers. There was something about her that made his heart seem to race. He couldn't remember feeling like that before. But then again, he reminded himself, he couldn't remember feeling much at all.

He knew it felt good, though. He pulled his t-shirt off, dove into the ocean, and swam after the volleyball. Thirty yards out he reached it and grabbed onto it. He held the ball against his solar plexus as he lay back and floated in the cool ocean water.

17

When Quinton woke up Monday morning, he felt as though he'd slept under an elephant's foot. Two days after his Venice match, and he still felt too sore to breathe. By early afternoon he managed to crawl to the living room couch, where he packed himself in ice and watched the exhibition match on TV. Holly and Pam were playing against two male celebrities.

By the tail end of the match he couldn't feel his limbs. He knew he wasn't supposed to leave ice on for more than twenty minutes at a time, but was too sore to take it off, and too engrossed in the game to care.

O'Connor-Benson were two points away from victory when Holly made a spectacular dig to set Pam. Pam thrust herself into the air, and crashed the ball cross-court over the net. She hit it so hard it bounced off the sand and into the audience.

"Sweet! Sweet!" Quinton yelled from the sofa. Today he was an armchair warrior.

The announcer spoke on the TV.

"This is match point for O'Connor and Benson. Coming out of deuce number four, Benson to serve."

Pam walked to the serve line, ball in hand. The two hunky heartthrobs in the opposite court readied themselves for her infamous sixty mph jump-serve. The shorter of the two, soap star Roger Miles, was six-one, a good three inches taller than the five foot ten Pamela Benson. He had four inches over the five foot nine Holly O'Connor. His partner, daytime fave Lance Derrickson, was six foot three and cut like a statue. Both were incredibly handsome. They were, after all, celebrities. Pam blew the two pretty boys a kiss, then blasted the ball into their court with her infamous serve.

Miles managed to get a piece of the ball with his forearm and bumped it to his partner at the net. As the ball flew to Derrickson, Miles could see Benson and O'Connor squinting to keep track of its position. He looked over his shoulder and saw the sun at his back. The two women faced directly into it, and their visors and shades seemed of little use.

"Sun!" Miles screamed to Derrickson, calling on him to take advantage of the situation.

Derrickson opted not to try a downward power hit, of which the women could get a piece, but instead listened to his partner and hit the ball high into the air, skyballing it upward and over the net. The ball reached its peak seventy feet above the net, then began to plummet into Pam and Holly's court. They tried to look up at the ball, but it came directly out of the sun. Pamela tried to squint and adjust her visor, but it was to no avail.

Holly stood ready at the net. She stared straight ahead, not at the sun and ball above, but used her peripheral vision to catch a glimpse of the moving ball's silhouetted form. It was enough for her brain to plot its trajectory. She readied herself in position for a spike. Holly threw herself into the air.

The height she got was incredible. As she reached the peak of her jump, she could peripherally make out the ball falling towards her. She glanced quickly at her opponent's court. Miles covered court left. Derrickson covered the right. Center court was open territory. She looked up again. The ball was within reach. With Herculean power and precision she smashed it into the opponent's uncovered center court. The two men exchanged glances. Neither dove for the ball. The ball plopped down mercilessly between them. The crowd went wild, screaming with delight.

In his living room, Quinton cheered out loud.

"Holy Shit!"

"The crowd is in a frenzy!" belted the announcer. "This is the most spectacular game of the day. Roger Miles and Lance Derrickson of 'Endless Summer Days,' two of daytime's hottest hunks, caught in the classic 'husband-and-wife formation' – No Communication! The game and match go to O'Connor and Benson!"

The crowd continued to whistle and cheer as the four players met at the net with high five's all around. Quinton watched Holly on the TV screen. Admiration played over his face.

"That was a beautiful thing, Holly. 'Husband-and-wife formation' – too damned funny," he said to himself, and clicked off the TV.

He crept out from under his ice bags and headed for the hot tub.

Later that evening, Quinton's cat sat in the living room eating tuna and Cheez Whiz from a paper plate. The room's Casanova lights had been dimmed. The cat was not disturbed by the sound of the shower running in the background, or by Quinton's singing as he bathed. He rendered a fairly good impression of Lou Reed's 'Wild Side.'

Hearing a noise from the front of the house, the cat looked up from her meal. Her ears perked up and her eyes widened in alarm as she heard a scratching sound outside the front door lock. After a moment, the lock clicked. The knob slowly turned and the door began to open.

Quinton continued to sing in the shower.

The intruder's right foot entered, and the rest soon followed. He wore dark shoes and pants, and a black ski mask. His movements were obscured by the scant light.

From the shower Quinton started another verse, oblivious to the man's presence.

As the intruder came into the room, the cat began to purr. He ignored her and moved to the coffee table in front of the television.

He took something from his jacket and set it down on the coffee table. It was a passport. The passport had been paper-clipped open to the page containing the name and picture. The name read 'Michael Delaney,' and the passport bore a picture of the man that once went by that name. From behind his ski mask, the intruder's eyes lingered on the image for a moment.

Quinton turned off the water and stepped out of the shower. He shook his head dry and wrapped a towel around his waist.

With the noise of the shower no longer covering his movements, the intruder deftly scooted out the front door, clicking the lock loudly behind him. The towel-clad Quinton came into the living room, drying the inside of his ears with a face cloth.

"Hello? Is someone there? Sheba, you see anyone?" he asked the cat.

Quinton turned up the living room lights, certain he'd heard something. Sheba looked at him. She squinted affectionately. She continued to purr. Quinton's eye was drawn to the object lying on the coffee table. He walked over and picked it up.

"What the f– " he said to himself.

He stared at the passport. He found himself immediately drawn to something in the photograph. The eyes. Michael Delaney's eyes.

Quinton's gaze narrowed until all he could see were just those eyes. He looked up suddenly and stared off into space.

He heard a distant sound echo through from his subconscious past. The jingle of pins being pulled from grenades played through his brain. Perplexed, he looked around the living room for the source of the sound, but saw nothing. Suddenly he heard the voice of a stranger in his mind, counting. 'Five, four, three, two –' then the unearthly sound of a gas explosion. Loud and unrelenting.

His attention snapped back to the present. He dropped the passport on the coffee table.

"Shit!" he gasped.

He ran to the front door in a panic. He opened it and inspected the outer lock. No traceable signs of a break-in. He could've sworn he'd secured the deadbolt earlier. But it had been unlocked.

He anxiously stuck his head out the doorway and looked up and down the narrow street. Not a soul. He went back inside and closed the door behind him. He snapped the deadbolt shut. Sheba looked up from her tuna. Quinton glanced over at her. Her green eyes had seen what happened, but she wasn't telling.

Later, in the middle of the night, Quinton tossed and turned in his sleep.

"He was hit with the bumper. He was hit with...bumper," he mumbled.

His face was soaked in sweat, his sheets stained with it. Tangled images and blurred half-truths menaced his mind and quickened his heartbeat.

"No! No!" he screamed, and was thrust awake by the sound of his own terror.

Quinton sat up in bed, trembling. He reached for the glass of water by his bedside and sucked it down. His breathing was labored and uneven. He ran his hands over his sweat-drenched face and pulled the soaked sheets around him. He drew several deep breaths to calm himself. He shut his eyes and continued a deliberate inhalation and exhalation. A relative peace began to overtake him.

"Sun stroke," he said out loud. "I definitely haven't found my beach legs yet."

He stood and wiped the rest of his sweaty body with the bedsheet. He held his hand in front of his face. It continued to tremble.

Quinton opened the drawer of the bedside table and took out a box of Sominex. He went to the bathroom, poured himself a glass of water, and gulped down two sleeping pills.

Quinton Squid stared at himself in the mirror. There were creases in his forehead and bags under his eyes. His face was red. His head felt like it was on fire.

Leaning over the sink, he poured the remaining water in the glass over his head. He shook his head fiercely and wiped his face with a towel. Making eye contact with his reflection, he began to probe the soul behind his eyes. He caught himself and abruptly stopped.

"Go to sleep, Quinton," he told the man in the mirror. "You've got a photo shoot in the morning. Get some sleep. Good night."

He shut the light off and left the bathroom.

At 8:00 a.m. the phone rang. Quinton stirred but didn't wake. A few minutes later, he heard a dull pounding on the bedroom's sliding glass doors. The phone rang again. He labored upward towards consciousness, then picked up the phone.

"Hello?" he rasped into the receiver.

"Q, it's Stu."

"You woke me up," he slurred. His eyelids crinkled with exhaustion.

"We have a date. Open your bedroom door."

"Why?"

"Because I'm standing on the other side of it."

Quinton got up and opened the shades. Stu's smiling face pressed up against the glass. He held a Motorola flip phone to his ear. Quinton slid the door open.

"Why are you here?"

Stu ignored the question. "You look like hell," he said.

"I need more sleep."

Stu walked into the house. He pocketed his phone.

"No. First you need to hang up the phone, then you need your Mikasa lesson."

"Oh, that's right!" Quinton yelled, and hung up the receiver.

He rubbed his forehead fiercely with the heel of his palm.

"Chill, dude, chill," said Stu. "The cavalry's here. You got two hours before your endorsement shoot. We'll ball-learn you in no time."

"Stu, I can barely tell the difference between a soccer-ball and a volleyball, let alone a Top Flight from a Top Flight Gold."

"The Top Flight used to get a little egg-shaped with wear. So they came out with the Gold. It's a little smaller so lends itself to faster play."

Quinton stood there with a blank expression on his face.

"Don't worry, I'll learn you, partner. Just jump in the shower and meet me on the beach."

Quinton stumbled into the bathroom and shut the door behind him.

Stu dumped his bag of balls onto the beach. There were various makes of Wilsons, Mikasas, Brines, and Tachikaras. A dozen and a half balls in all. He could tell the difference between each one with his eyes closed, and was going to prove to Quinton that in time, he could too.

Quinton dragged his weary body down the deck stairs and onto the beach. He wore a cobalt blue pair of Sand Dune shorts. He sat down next to Stu. Quinton was chowing down on a nectarine and offered one to him.

"No thanks, bud. Just ate."

"Stu, how long have I been the spokesman for Mikasa?" he asked him.

"About five years."

"They make a good ball?"

"Yeah, here."

Stu tossed him a volleyball.

"That's an original Mikasa Beach Champ. The FIVB used it in Rio a few years back. It's piece of history. How does it feel?"

"Okay, I guess."

"Here."

Stu tossed him another ball.

"Compare them. Tell me the differences between the two. The second one is an old Brine Hard Core Pro."

Quinton felt the Mikasa in his hands, then the Brine. He picked up the Mikasa again.

"This one's lighter."

"Good."

"And the surface is a little slicker. The other one, the Brine has a more…the surface has a different touch to it, I feel the leather more. But they both feel like good balls."

"Yep. Two of the all-time best. Good job."

"Thanks. Why do I have to do this, again?"

"Truth in advertising."

"I didn't realize you were such an idealist," Quinton said.

"If you get put on the spot in some interview, you better know your ass from your elbow. In this case, your 'Mikasa' from your 'su casa.'"

"But this is boring."

"One man's boredom is another man's bread and butter. You're getting paid a shitload. Catch."

Stu tossed him the current AVP ball.

"This is the ball we use in tourneys."

Quinton twirled the ball in his hands a moment.

"Guess what," he said tentatively.

"What?" asked Stu.

Quinton smiled and looked up from the volleyball.

"I have a date for lunch," he said.

"You dog, who with?"

"Holly O'Connor."

"You lie."

"It's true."

"You're serious?"

"Yeah. She's going to help me with my…"

"Your what?"

"Nothing."

Quinton didn't want to say the words 'cut shot.' Stu stared at him insistently. Quinton dodged the question.

"That thing I said over the air…"

"Yeah."

"If so many of the women players hated me, why didn't Emily?"

"Because of a lot of things. Mostly the wedding."

"What wedding?"

Stu smiled.

"Our wedding. You made me do it."

"Why?"

"Are we going to waltz down memory lane here, or get you ready for your shoot?"

"You're so evasive sometimes."

"And you're a pain in the ass. Here, check this one out. It's a little heavy, so it's good in the wind."

Stu tossed him an early SV series Tachikara.

18

Quinton looked at himself in the make-up mirror as Stacy, the DeCosta Studio makeup artist, prepared him for the endorsement shoot. There was an older endorsement photo of Quinton taped to the mirror. As Stacy worked on him she eyed the picture occasionally for comparison. Quinton glanced at the picture several times through tired eyes. Stacy blotted his face with foundation.

"You look like you didn't get much sleep," she said. "You've got huge bags under your eyes. Who's the lucky woman?"

"No, it's nothing like that. I'm just tired from the tournament," he said casually.

"Yeah, sure. That's what they all say," she kidded.

Quinton picked up a small magnifying mirror from the counter and held it up to his face.

"Are these scars going to show up on the photographs?"

"No. Believe me, they wouldn't want you for the shoot if they thought they would. You can barely notice them in natural light, and with a little makeup everything will be taken care of. And just in case, there's always airbrushing."

"Airbrushing," Quinton said absent-mindedly.

Stacy finished giving him a warm-toned foundation. Time

for the intricate work. She glanced at the old photo on the mirror.

"The structure of your face is pretty much the same, Quint, but there's something about it that's a little different. I can't quite place it."

"It's the eyes," said Quinton.

Stacy stared at his eyes in the mirror and then at the set in the picture.

"Yeah, you're right. It is the eyes. They're much kinder."

She began to highlight his jaw line with a copper shade of blusher. Quinton looked around the large studio.

There were half a dozen settings arranged in and around the enclaves of the studio. There was a French cafe scene, an elegant bedroom set, something that looked like the interior of a ski lodge, a mountain climbing set, and a cruise ship deck scene.

But the largest by far was the beach set. Fake boulders sat on a sandy surface in front of a huge rear-projection screen. It wasn't difficult for Quinton to figure out which set he'd be shooting on. He felt surreal in these surroundings. It was not an unusual feeling for him lately. Stacy finished highlighting Quinton's eyebrows, just as the producer yelled over from the other end of the studio.

"Stace, is he done yet?"

"Yeah. All set," she yelled back.

She turned to Quinton.

"All set. Maybe next time if you get a tan first, we won't have to put so much foundation on," she chided.

"But Stacy, when you tan, you age," he kidded back.

"What are you, eighty? Get your butt out there on that beach, Q," she laughed.

Quinton chuckled. He stood up and removed the makeup

bib from his neck. He wore a white muscle tank and chili pepper red shorts, both embossed with the logo for Sand Dune Activewear. He looked at himself in the mirror. He looked mighty fine. Stacy seemed to agree. She couldn't take her eyes off that jaw line.

"Thanks, Stacy," he said, then walked over to the beach set to meet the producer.

The producer was a small man with a wrenchingly overcompensating handshake, and glasses with Buddy Holly frames. His nose seemed to whistle when he talked.

"Hi, Quinton." The producer gestured to the man standing next to him. "This is Drew, your photographer for the day," he said in his excessively cheerful tone.

Quinton and Drew shook hands. Drew needed a shave, fast, and the wardrobe police had to be called at once. He wore gaiter boots with khakis and a corduroy fishing vest. At some point he must have been a European cinematographer.

"Okay. Just go over to the set and give it what you got. Drew will hold your hand if you need it. I've got to be somewhere," said the producer, and he was off.

Drew moved behind the camera, which sat on a large tripod. Quinton walked onto the set. The screen behind it now shone a sunny ocean view. He stood on the sandy floor that resembled a beach. He thought the set looked ridiculously fake, like a low-budget episode of *Gilligan's Island*. He looked extremely uncomfortable and stood there stiff as a board. Drew poked his head out from behind the camera.

"Is this what you usually do in a shoot, Quinton?"

"I don't know what I usually do in a shoot," he said, a slight titter in his voice.

Drew massaged the bridge of his nose with his thumb and index finger.

"Okay. This may take a while."

Two hours later, Holly parked her white convertible Jeep in the DeCosta Studios parking lot. The studio was located in downtown L.A., in a fancy office district bordering some of the rougher parts of town. She went in through the back door adjacent to the lot. She knew these studios well. She'd done shoots here for Brine, Reebok, and Revlon. She walked through the maze of changing rooms into the main studio. She sat down in a director's chair off to the side and watched Quinton's shoot. Right Said Fred's 'Too Sexy' blasted from a speaker above the beach set.

Holly wondered if this could get any more cliché.

"Okay! Kiss him! Both of you!" Drew gushed over the music from behind his camera.

He was speaking to the two models standing next to Quinton. The models happened to be Quinton's neighbors, Lori and Tango. The twins wore neon tangerine string bikinis. Quinton now wore hot pink volley shorts. Drew had the crew hang orange gels over the lights to give the set a warm glow, and to make it appear as if Quinton was tanned all over. Most remnants of the accident seemed to have faded. He looked more like himself than ever before.

The twins obeyed Drew's order and smooched at Quinton mercilessly.

"Stop smiling! Think sultry and smoldering!" Drew barked at Quinton's grinning face.

But Quinton was fluid. He had gotten the hang of modeling and was obviously enjoying himself.

"Okay. I want you two down on the floor, one on each leg," ordered Drew.

As if on cue, Lori and Tango each slid down half the length of Quinton's body, knelt on the ground, and held onto a leg.

Drew removed his camera from the tripod and took some shots hand-held.

"Okay...good. Good, Quint. Tango, play a little bit."

Tango ran her hand up Quinton's calve. It wandered over his knee, onto his thigh, and under his shorts. Quinton pushed it back down.

"Drew!" Quinton yelled over the music.

"Take a pill!" Drew clucked, and clicked away.

Quinton put a hand out to the two women at his feet. Each took one and he pulled them back up to a standing position. Drew put down the camera.

"Hey, who's the director here, huh?" he whined.

"This is a little embarrassing," said Quinton.

Drew looked at him blankly. Was this guy serious? The music blared on.

Drew's watch beeped. He looked at it. Twelve noon. He went back to his tripod.

"Okay. That's it people. We've got everything we need. Wrap it up for today," he said.

Quinton left the set and went over to Drew.

"We can go now?" he asked.

"Yep. Good job, Quinton. Good job," he said and began to put away his equipment.

Drew leaned into Quinton's ear and whispered.

"What are you, the man of steel? I mean those shorts you're wearing are pretty thin and I didn't see anything. I mean nothing. I have a chubby and they weren't even touching me."

'Euro trash' was the first thought that came to Quinton's mind. "I guess they just don't do it for me," is what came out of his mouth.

Quinton turned in Holly's direction.

"Be back in a minute," he called over to her. "Just have to change."

He walked towards the changing rooms. As he moved past the bedroom set, the Bikini Twins each grabbed an arm and tried to ply him onto the mattress. He barely managed to wiggle his way out of their well-proportioned clutches. He looked back at Holly.

"Be back in a second," he assured her.

Or was he assuring himself. Holly threw him a wry grin.

"Don't forget your bookends," she yelled back.

Quinton tried to hide his chuckle from Lori and Tango. They skipped after him down the hallway. They managed to capture his arms once again. What were they, tag team jello wrestlers?

"Where are you off to, Quint?" Lori asked, as they entered the changing rooms.

"Lunch. Sorry, but I made other plans after the shoot. I didn't realize you two would be working here today," he said, trying his best to sound sincere.

He still couldn't figure out what it was about them that gave him the willies. It was probably that the three of them had shared some tawdry secret that he was no longer in on. Either that or the fact that they looked too much like *The Price is Right* models. Tango turned his head gently to face hers.

"I can't believe you don't remember us, or remember the –"

Tango leaned over to Quinton and whispered in his ear. His eyes widened in disbelief. A frightened Quinton tried to force a smile.

"No. Uh, no, I don't remember that."

He stopped short at his dressing room.

"Well, we could always help jog your memory," Lori offered.

"Or make some new ones," Tango invited through her pouted, collagen-injected lips.

Quinton quickly untangled himself from their arms and backed into his dressing room. Their lips didn't look sexy to him, just swollen.

"I need to get changed now. Maybe I'll stop by sometime," he said nervously.

The twins looked at each other and smiled mischievously. They snickered and entered their dressing room. Quinton changed quickly and left the dressing room carrying a large picnic basket. He moved briskly through the studio and over to Holly. Sweat was beginning to bead on his forehead.

"I've got to hurry up and get out of here. Those two are looking for me," he said, peering over his shoulder.

Holly was amused.

"I don't believe it. Quinton Squid, running away from women."

"You don't know what they told me."

"I'll bet I have an inkling," Holly chided.

"Did you know they used to be dominatrixes?" Quinton asked her.

"Yes," Holly nodded. "And professional bullfighters."

Quinton nodded emphatically and ushered her out the back door to the parking lot.

"Stu dropped me off. I didn't bring my car," he said.

"Okay, then I guess I'm driving," she said, leading the way to her Jeep.

"But I did make sandwiches for lunch," he said.

"Well, I'll be darned. He cooks."

"Well no, actually I only deli," Quinton said with a wink.

Holly beeped off her car alarm. They slid into the leather bucket seats.

Holly looked at his face in the natural sunlight.

"What?" asked Quinton.

"You're wearing blusher."

"I know. It highlights my jaw line."

Holly laughed.

"Well, aren't we secure in our masculinity."

Quinton joined in her laughter.

"You got a tissue or something?" he asked.

"I think so."

She opened her purse and handed him a kleenex and some cold cream. He began to wipe off the blusher and facial tone.

"So, did you do Sand Dune all morning with the Bikini Twins?"

"Yeah. I can tell you're a big fan," Quinton chuckled.

Holly smiled. She handed him another tissue.

"Yeah. Huge fan."

Quinton attacked the eyebrow pencil.

"No, I did some Sand Dune by myself, and a revamp of the old Mikasa spot. You know 'Dig softly and carry a big spike?' Turns out it's a phrase coined by Teddy Roosevelt during his pro beach years."

Holly laughed.

"I guess Teddy got around. You're very well learned."

"Thank you," said Quinton. "All off?"

Holly studied his face.

"Yeah, all butch again."

"You're too kind."

"So, where should we go?" she asked.

"That's up to you. Your choice."

She started the Jeep.

"How 'bout some mini golf? I'm in the mood for knocking down windmills."

"Mini golf. Haven't done that in a long time. I think. Sounds good."

"Good," said Holly. She shifted into gear and drove out of the parking lot.

A gray Mercedes sports coupe parked across the street pulled out and began to follow them. The top of the line Mercedes had no trouble blending in with the affluent-looking midday traffic moving west on Wilshire Boulevard. It was careful to stay far enough behind the Jeep not to be noticed.

19

Holly's golf ball rolled through the miniature windmill and fell into the eighth hole cup behind it.

"That's a hole in one," she said, kneeling down to pluck the ball out of the cup.

Quinton looked around the mini golf grounds. It had a nice family feel to it. Clean and relaxed. Off to the side there were some picnic tables, children's swingset, and a giant fifteen foot checkerboard. The board was made of wood and topped with astroturf, in alternating red and white squares. Two second graders stood on it playing a game with huge red and black foam checkers.

Holly looked over at the mesmerized Quinton and smiled.

"Quinton, it's your shot."

Quinton turned around, befuddled.

"I've never seen anything like that before in my life. It's amazing."

"Yeah, I guess it is. Never really paid much attention to it before," she said.

"When the kids get off, you want to play a game?" he asked her.

"Sure," she said, a slight chuckle in her voice.

"Did you ever see *Sleeper?*" Quinton asked as he put his ball down on the ninth hole tee.

"Yeah," answered Holly.

Quinton readied his shot.

"I rented it the other night," he said as he glanced over at the checkerboard. "It had all these huge vegetables in it. Huge banana, huge carrot. I laughed my ass off. And then this. This huge checkerboard. Weird."

Holly looked at him and smiled. Who was this man? Quinton continued to practice-putt his shot. He lifted his gaze from the putter and up to Holly. He caught a quick glimpse of her smiling at him before he had to squint from the sun behind her.

"You are strange," he heard her say.

"Why is that?" he asked.

"A big ladies' man like you staying in at night to watch old movies."

"That's just part of my plan."

"And what plan is that?" she coaxed.

He moved his eyes away from her and let them rest on his hands as they guided the putter.

"Okay. Can you tell me what *Sleeper, The Time Machine, Planet of the Apes,* and *After Hours* have in common?"

"You got me," said Holly.

Quinton looked at the golf ball.

"They're all about guys who one day find themselves in a time or place they know nothing about, and have to find a way back to where they came from, or figure out how to live in the place where they've ended up."

"So, what part of the plan is this?" she asked.

Quinton looked in her direction. He put his hand over his eyes to shield them from the sun.

"This here? This isn't part of the plan. I guess it's a result."

"What do you mean?"

"In the hospital, I used to lie in bed at night and wish I was E.T. or Rod Taylor, because in the end they got to go home. And I wanted to go home, too. Now I am home, but I still feel that way. I know this to be my home, but don't feel it. I can't remember anything. I don't know…there's a lot I don't know. But I want to learn and I was down on the beach trying to teach myself, and you came along to help me out and here we are."

Holly didn't know what to say.

Quinton hit the golf ball he'd been toying with for five minutes. The shot banked off the left bumper, hit the right, and went through the waterfall. His second shot landed in the ninth hole.

"That's a birdie," mumbled Holly.

"A what?" Quinton asked.

"A birdie," she said, louder.

"What's that?" he asked.

Holly was surprised.

"It's one under par. You don't remember what a birdie is?" she asked.

"I don't think I ever knew," Quinton said, shifting the weight of the putter in his hands.

"How can you tell?"

"I don't know. The putter seems awkward, like something I've never used before."

"So how come you're playing so well?" asked Holly.

"I don't know that either," he answered. "I guess I'm just a natural athlete."

He threw her a cheesy grin and she couldn't help but laugh at his bravado.

"Cute there, Davis," she said.

Quinton dropped the putter. A purple flash appeared within him, making him feel like he'd been struck by lightening. His eyes closed sharply. In his mind he could see an endorsement check made out to the order of Quinton Davis.

He shook his head fiercely, then opened his eyes to see the golf grounds gyrate in front of him. His vision cleared.

"Are you okay?" Holly asked, as she picked up the putter.

"Yeah, I'm fine. It's just the sun. I'm not used to it yet."

She handed him the putter. He took it with an awkward smile.

"How do you know my real name?" he asked.

"I organized the women's tour. We had a listing of all the men's players too," she said, putting her ball on the ninth hole tee.

She readied her shot, then asked, "Did you bank off the left at forty-five degrees?"

"Almost. About forty-three," he answered.

"Okay. Get ready, Squid. I'm going to beat your ass," she said.

"That I'd like to see," said Quinton, a bit too hastily.

She popped the ball. He watched it bank off the left bumper at forty-three degrees, hit the right exactly where his shot had, go through the waterfall and into the ninth hole cup. Another hole in one. Quinton looked at her in disbelief. She winked at him.

A tickled Quinton walked to the ninth hole. He removed the two balls and juggled them with one hand.

"You're just full of tricks, aren't you?" said Holly, amused.

"Sure am."

He caught the balls and looked around for the next tee hole.

Holly walked over and tapped him on the shoulder.

"Quinton, there are only nine holes."

"Good. Time to eat," he said gleefully.

"So who won?" he asked, gloating, as they walked back to the golf shack.

She looked at him with one eyebrow raised.

"Please," she said with mock condescension.

They sat at a picnic table near the giant checkerboard. Quinton spread the contents of the picnic basket over the table; napkins, sandwiches, designer water.

"These are so good," said Holly, with a mouthful of pastrami on rye with extra mayo. "Where did you find these?"

"I bought the building materials at a specialty shop, and constructed them myself at home."

"How very architectural of you."

"Thank you."

Quinton glanced over Holly's shoulder at the checkerboard. The second graders were still at it.

"They still there?" she asked him.

He nodded yes, chewing on a mouthful of pepper steak. The table they ate at was worn and weathered. There were more initials etched in the wood with hearts around them than he could count. He looked for the initials Q.S. in and amongst the hearts, wondering if he had been here before with a girlfriend. No such luck.

But the checkerboard was so cool, he knew he must've played there before. He scanned the table again. There were no Q.S.'s, no Q.D.'s, and no H.O.'s. Yeah, he checked the H.O.'s too. Quinton looked up at Holly, who was busy chewing on her sandwich. He noticed she had a glob of mayonnaise in the left corner of her mouth.

"Mayo," he said, and pointed.

She took a napkin and wiped her mouth.

"Thanks. So. Everybody thinks you're fully recovered?"

"Yeah, most people," he said, finishing his sandwich.

"But you're not. You still don't remember much," she asked.

He looked up at her, not saying a word.

"Don't worry. I'm not going to tell anybody," she assured him.

He took a long pull on his bottled water, then set it down on the table.

"Actually, I don't remember anything from before the plane crash. And what I do remember is mostly from the stuff Stu and Emily gave me. Books, newspaper articles, magazines, videotapes, that kind of stuff."

"And none of it triggered anything?"

"No. But sometimes I get this weird jolt of something. Like a passageway opening up in my brain, if only for an instant. I don't know exactly what it is. I got it again when you called me by my other name and I dropped the putter."

"You mean Davis?" she asked.

"Yeah. I guess that's my real name."

"Your father was a volleyball player. Do you remember that?" Holly asked.

"He was a player?" said Quinton, surprised.

"Yeah. The '64 Olympics. A Gold Medallist."

"I didn't know that."

Holly could see Quinton's eyes slowly focus inside himself.

"Haven't you gone through all your personal stuff at home, to see if anything might click on a lightbulb, help you remember?" she asked.

"Yeah, but I haven't been able to find anything really concrete. Just knick-knack's and an Elvis costume."

"An Elvis costume?"

"Yeah, from his Vegas years, white polyester with fringe. And about forty ticket stubs from the ballet."

Holly looked at him strangely. Who was this man? Whoever he was, he was damn interesting.

"Don't look at me, I didn't buy them," said Quinton.

"Then who did?" she asked mischievously.

He smirked back. "I did, but not me me, me then. I'm me me now."

She couldn't help but chuckle. Quinton joined in.

"Man, you are total toast," she said, catching her breath.

"Thanks a lot."

"I'm sorry. Look, maybe we can go back to your place sometime and see if we can find some more stuff."

Quinton answered her with interest and vague suspicion.

"Okay. Thanks. Why are you helping me?" he asked quietly.

Holly thought for a moment. Quinton could feel the synapses in her brain going off like firecrackers. Silence. Quinton looked at her. He ignored the giant checkerboard which had held his attention previously.

"I don't know," she said finally. "I really don't know."

"Because there's something about you that's really familiar to me," said Quinton.

"What is it?" asked a curious Holly.

Quinton thought for a moment. Holly stared at his face. It was a beautiful face, but it was the eyes she was drawn to. She wondered why she had never noticed his eyes before. It was like he was a different man. Quinton let his eyes rest on hers.

"I'm not sure," he said. "It's vague. It's just a really familiar feeling. And you have the same color eyes as my cat."

A golf ball landed in the potato salad, breaking the moment.

The eight-year-old who shot the putt awry came running up to the picnic table to reclaim his ball.

"Sorry, mister," he said, and reached a hand into the salad to retrieve his Titleist. He looked at Holly apologetically, then at Quinton. The kid took a step towards the golf course and froze in his tracks. He turned back to Quinton.

"Aren't you Quinton Squid?"

"I guess so," Quinton answered.

The boy looked at him again, confused.

"You mean you don't know?"

"No. I was just kiddin' around. Yeah, I'm Quinton Squid."

"You're really good." The boy smiled. "I seen you jump on TV. You jump so high I bet you could jump over my head."

"I don't know if I could do that, you're pretty tall," Quinton said kindly.

The boy's smile beamed brighter.

"No, you're the best. You can jump over anything, and when you dive you just dig, dig, dig and never let the ball touch the sand!"

Quinton enjoyed the boy's enthusiasm. He smiled.

"Nah, we all miss a ball now and again. Believe me, a lot of my volleyballs have ended up in the potato salad, too."

The boy laughed.

"Good luck with the rest of your game," said Quinton.

"Thanks," said the boy, and skipped off to the golf grounds.

In the background, Quinton and Holly could hear the boy yell, "Dad, Dad, I just talked to Quinton Squid! Dad, he's right over there!"

Holly laughed. She looked down at her watch. Five o'clock.

"We better get to the beach. At this rate, we won't be there 'til the sun goes down."

"All right," Quinton agreed as he gathered up the picnic

basket. He stood up. "Just show me the way." Quinton paused. "You know, you cheat."

"I have never cheated in my life," Holly defended as she stood, picking up the trash.

"No, you definitely did some double-putting when I was staring at the checkerboard."

"Oh no you don't, Squid. I won that game fair and square."

She handed the trash to Quinton and pulled out her car keys.

"All right," said Quinton. "If you did then you won't be afraid to play me again sometime, best two out of three."

Quinton dropped the trash into a can by the parking lot.

"You've got a date," Holly said as she opened her car door.

Quinton got in the car. Holly turned the key and they were off. The gray Mercedes pulled out from behind the run-down taco stand across the street and continued to follow them.

Holly and Quinton reached Santa Monica's State Beach at sunset. As usual Quinton's attention was drawn to the canvas of pastels painting the sky above. It made him feel integrated and at ease. Holly was busy on the ground. She drew circles in the sand with her foot on one side of the net. Several palm trees stood watch behind them. Quinton looked down from the all-encompassing Matisse. Holly's footwork struck him as curious.

"What are you doing?" he asked.

She looked up from the ground a moment and winked at him.

"In a second."

She brought her attention back to the task at hand.

Quinton studied the ground. He could see she had made nine circles in the sand. Three rows of three each.

"I saw that game you lost to the 'Double A's,' " she said finally.

"You mean Aaron and Aimes?"

"Uh huh. You kept picking up all their trash, but they still built you a major roof."

"I know. They blocked me like an eclipse," Quinton confessed.

"Nice analogy."

"Thank you."

Holly finished up her work. Inside each of the nine circles she'd drawn a corresponding number, one through nine. She looked up at Quinton.

"Okay. I'm done."

Quinton looked at the ground amused.

"What did you do?"

"Quint..." Holly said with hesitation.

"What?" he asked.

"Don't take this the wrong way..."

Quinton smiled.

"I won't. I'm the one who asked you to help me, remember?"

"Okay. Plain and simple. They blocked the shit out of you. You can't get the height right now. You have to rely on your other strengths, or create some new ones. Slice and dice it. Poke it. Lob it. Or grunt and dink it. Do what you can to make them change their game," she said.

Quinton tried to maintain his smile.

"In other words, be a trash-man," he said.

"Slice and dice is not junk, Quinton. Look, you have the softest dig on the beach, you can get a touch on anything, but you can't get enough height on your approach to topple their block. You'll do squat until you change your strategy."

He ran his hands through his hair.

"You think I don't know that."

"No. I know you know it. So why are you tooling around?"

"I don't know."

Quinton paced around his side of the court, hands on his hips. Holly watched him pace once, twice, six times around the court.

"So what are you going to do about it?" she asked finally.

He stopped pacing. He stared her in the eye. Behind her head was the sunset's explosion of cottony reds and watered-down pinks. He wondered what the hell he was afraid of. Public perception? No. He had already screwed that up over CSN. What then?

It came to him, finally, in a flash. He wanted to be Quinton Squid. He wanted to be the man he used to be. But how could he remember who he was if he wasn't like that guy anymore? That man was an asshole. He wasn't that man anymore. He didn't know who he was now. But whoever he was, he knew he wanted to keep playing. And if he wanted to keep playing, he had to change his strategy. Holly's words had burned into his memory; 'You can't push what you haven't got to push.'

"Okay," he said aloud. "Learn me."

Holly looked into Quinton's eyes for a moment. He felt as if she could see right through him. Not through his body, but through all his bullshit and straight into his heart. He had let his guard down and she had seen the opening. He wanted to throw his wall back up quickly. But something deep inside told him to trust it. Trust it blindly. Isn't that what I've been doing since I woke up in the hospital, he asked himself. No, he knew this was the first time he had really let his guard down.

Holly smiled at him. They stood less than two feet apart. The only thing between them was the volleyball net. Why doesn't she take something from me, Quinton wondered. His guard was down and she hadn't tried to manipulate him, steal anything from him, or wound him. He wondered why he assumed someone would.

"All right," Holly said. "School's open. I'm going to set you, and you'll hit against an imaginary blocker in front of you. I'll call a number and you hit that circle. You see the numbers?"

"Yeah," said Quinton.

"And when you get the hang of it, I'll block and you'll set yourself, okay?"

"Okay."

Holly walked under the net to Quinton's side of the court. She readied herself to set the ball for him.

"Remember, we're not going for the hundred mile an hour smash, but the well placed, well-controlled touch shot," she reiterated.

"A soft shot?" Quinton asked.

"Not really soft, because it still has to have enough speed to get past the blocker. More like precise."

"Focused."

"Exactly. You have to know where in the sand you want that shot to go."

"Okay. I think I got it," said Quinton. "Before I forget. Wind sprints, six a.m. tomorrow. Sound good?"

Holly spun the volleyball around on her finger like a basketball.

"Is that an invite?" she asked.

"Yes," Quinton said as he watched her hands twirl the volleyball around her perfect waist.

"Okay," said Holly.

He stared at her a moment. She was spinning the volley-ball on her finger again.

"Nice ball-handling," he said.

"I always wanted to be a Harlem Globe Trotter."

"Oh yeah? I always wanted to be a ballerina," Quinton kidded.

"Probably explains all those ticket stubs."

"Too quick for me, O'Connor."

"Okay, let's get down to business. Imagine that big ape Aaron is in front of you, blocking."

Holly set the ball to Quinton. He leapt into the air. Just before the peak of his jump Holly yelled out, "Three." Quinton hit the ball, cutting it diagonally across the net to the far right circle marked number three.

"Good shot!" yelled Holly. "How did that feel?"

"Damn sneaky," Quinton said with a sly grin. "They won't be expecting that kind of shot from me."

"I know," said Holly. "That's the point."

"Stu's gonna fry my ass," said a suddenly gleeful Quinton.

Holly couldn't help but laugh herself.

"No, he'll be patting your ass because you're gonna be racking up the points slicing and dicing."

Quinton walked under the net to the volleyball on the other side. He picked it up and tossed it in the air.

"Quinton Squid. A trash-man," he said, almost to himself.

He caught the ball and headed back under the net.

"Quint, how many times do I have to tell you. Slice and dice is not considered trash anymore."

"Then a lot of the books I've read must be outdated."

"I can't believe all you know about volleyball is just from books. You must remember something."

Quinton smiled at her.

"No. I don't even know if I can do this," he said, and tried to spin the volleyball on his finger. To his amazement, it worked. It felt like the most natural thing in the world.

They continued to drill into the early evening hours.

20

It was late in the evening and Quinton's living room lights were dimmed as usual. Sheba sat on the couch. Quinton was nowhere to be seen. The crashing surf outside was barely audible under the din of the running shower. The bathroom lights were on and the bathroom full of steam. From the shower Quinton's voice again sang 'Wild Side.'

But he was not in the shower. His voice emanated from a waterproof boombox hanging from the showerhead. Quinton, perched in a chair next to the front door of his darkened living room, held a Louisville Slugger baseball bat close to his chest. His head leaned back against the wall, dozing.

Sheba's ears perked up suddenly. She heard a scraping sound against the door. Quinton's eyes jerked open. He didn't move. His grip tightened around the bat. He could feel his heart start to pound fiercely against the wall of his chest. His breathing became labored. His brain cried out for oxygen, but he had to control his air intake, control the sounds he made. Quinton listened to his own voice singing in the shower.

There was more scraping against the door. Quinton heard something get shoved into the lock mechanism. It turned back and forth. He stood up silently and let his back hug the wall at the point closest to the door. His knuckles grew white around the neck of the bat. The pounding of his heart rang in his ears. He heard the lock click and the knob turn.

Quinton opened his eyes wide and wiped the sweat from his brow. He was sure the pounding of his heart could be heard thumping throughout the house. He could barely hear the creaking of the door as it swung slowly open. Maybe this wasn't such a good idea. Too late.

The intruder entered the house. Quinton's hands locked like clamps around the bat. As the intruder turned around to close the door, Quinton greeted the unwanted guest with a blow to the skull. The intruder collapsed on the floor, unconscious.

Quinton bound his hands and feet with a quickness and skill he could not explain. He dragged the man out on the deck, the bat tucked under one arm. Quinton placed the limp body face down next to the hot tub. He searched the intruder's pockets.

He found a large wallet and leafed through it. It contained only an airline ticket stub reading J. Wilson, round trip, Tahiti, Pacific Airlines Flight number 386, and a money clip containing a wad of crisp, new hundred-dollar bills.

Quinton held one of the hundreds up to the light. He could see the alternating pattern of the *USA 100* thread embedded in the paper. It was genuine currency. For a moment, he wondered how he'd known to do this. He looked back down at the intruder. Confusion played over his face. He put the money and ticket stub back into the wallet, then tossed it onto the deck table.

Quinton knelt beside the bound man. He lowered his hand to the man's head, and yanked off the ski mask. Grabbing the back of his blonde hair, he quickly dunked the man's face in the hot tub. When he yanked the intruder's head out of the water, he began to come to. Quinton angled the intruder's face toward his. He didn't recognize the man Michael would've known as Nick Avanti. But there was something distantly familiar about this large man with brown eyes.

"Remember the Celts," a voice whispered to him from behind.

Quinton quickly turned around, but there was no one to be seen.

Without warning, reality left him and before his eyes he saw a white Cadillac explode into his field of vision. Burning debris scattered and the car's bumper flew towards him. Quinton shut his eyes. When he reopened them, the intruder was staring at him. Quinton's gaze softened. He looked directly into Nick's eyes, entranced.

"He was hit with the bumper," Quinton mumbled.

Nick looked at him strangely, an eyebrow raised.

"What are you talking about? Who got hit with a bumper?" Nick asked.

Quinton's demeanor hardened as he zoned back to reality. He stared at Nick.

"Who the hell are you?" he demanded.

The grip on the back of Nick's head tightened mercilessly. He grimaced in pain.

"Michael. Mikey, it's me. It's Nick," he said. Water trickled from his soaking-wet hair.

Quinton was agitated. Veins bulged from his forehead.

"I said, who the fuck are you?" he screamed.

Nick looked at him gently.

"It's Nicky. Nick Avanti. We grew up together."

Quinton's eyes shifted momentarily. His mind flooded with purple light. He found himself standing by the intercom in the

Training Center gym. Stu was putting volleyballs away. In his mind, Quinton heard the intercom come on. Marla spoke.

"Quinton, do you know a Nick Avanti?"

As Quinton saw himself turn to look at Stu, the purple light disappeared. He found himself again on the deck of his Santa Monica beach house. His eyes bulged with intensity as he looked down at the man tied up in front of him.

"You followed me from San Diego," said Quinton.

Nick smiled. Maybe Michael was remembering.

"Yeah, but I had to take a quick detour through Tahiti. I couldn't sell the stuff around here. Did you get the cat?" Nick asked eagerly.

Quinton brought his face closer to Nick's. Nick could see the confusion in Quinton's eyes. He didn't remember. How could he make him remember? Nick hadn't a clue, Michael usually did all the thinking.

Beads of sweat fell from Quinton's nose onto Nick's head.

"Yeah, I got the cat. What the fuck are you, some kind of freakazoid fan or something?" Quinton demanded. His insistence made Nick suddenly furious.

"Michael Marino Delaney, you dago mick cugine! For Christ's sake, take a deep breath and shut the fuck up a second!" he bellowed.

Quinton felt the fearful uncertainty of his delicate world being shaken. He matched Nick tone-for-tone.

"Why do you keep calling me Michael?! The name is Quinton Squid, you dumb sonofabitch! I ought to have you arrested for B and E!" he roared.

Desperate, he took Nick's head and dunked it underwater again. Quinton screamed out to the lonely California night. He held Nick there for a few seconds, then pulled him up. Nick coughed out water and gasped for breath.

"Michael…I've been…keeping an eye on you. I hear that Gina and Frank are getting itchy. You do too many interviews on CSN. You've got to learn to control that tic, Michael. You know, the pinkie in the – "

"Shut up!" Quinton screeched.

He grabbed Nick by the collar and yanked his face to within inches of his own. Nick saw the anger and fear in Quinton's eyes melt into a cold blankness. The man before him was not the man he knew at all. He was a shadow, a two dimensional version of that man. The third dimension, the one of heart and soul, had disappeared.

But not for good. Nick had seen it bubble to the surface as he watched from a distance at the mini-golf grounds, seen it come out to greet Holly O'Connor on the beach. But it was back inside now, deep below the surface. That third dimension was hiding somewhere inside of Michael, of Quinton, licking its wounds.

It would be back for good someday, Nick knew. He would make sure of it. But for now this man who held his shirt collar with white-knuckled fists lacked that dimension. Quinton's eyes were frozen on Nick in an icy stare. He couldn't tell if Quinton was going to bite off his nose or kiss him full on the lips. All Nick knew was he needed to get the hell out of there.

Quinton finally let go of Nick's shirt and let him drop to the deck floor. Quinton moved to the cordless phone resting by the wallet.

"Your cat!" Nick rasped. "What did you name your cat?"

"Shut up!" barked Quinton.

Nick strained to reach his left shoe with hands bound behind him. After a moment he retrieved the small Swiss Army knife tucked inside. Oblivious, Quinton grabbed the cordless and began to dial.

"You know what your cat's name is?" Nick asked again.

He worked covertly behind his back, sawing at the ropes binding his hands.

"Will you shut up!!" yelled Quinton. He spoke into the phone, "Yeah. I want to report a break in...1015 Ocean Drive, Santa Monica...Quinton Squid...about thirty, blonde, six foot two, big build...ten minutes ago."

"Your cat. Your cat! What did you name your cat?!" Nick insisted.

"Shut up!" Quinton screamed at him.

He turned back to the phone.

"No, not you. I was talking to him. I have him tied up... okay."

Quinton hung up the phone. Nick continued to saw quietly at his wrist bindings.

"It's Sheba, isn't it? I bet it's Sheba," Nick said.

Quinton turned to Nick, extremely hostile. This man was fucking with his mind.

"Everyone knows the cat's name is Sheba!"

"That was the name of your other cat, too! The one that died in the fire!" Nick said.

"I didn't have a cat on the plane!" frothed Quinton.

"The fire wasn't on a plane!" Nick screamed back.

Quinton became frenzied. He picked up the baseball bat and headed towards Nick. The veins in his neck bulged as his heartbeat quickened. His eyes burned with rage.

"Sonofa figlio di puttana, figlio del diavolo cornuto!" he babbled, gesticulating with the baseball bat excitedly.

"What the fuck was that?" he asked himself aloud.

"Italiano, you dumb fuck!" yelled Nick. "Yeah, everyone knows its name is Sheba, but I bet no one else knows it has a small fortune in diamonds strapped to its neck."

Quinton dropped the bat. His face contorted in confusion. "How do you know that?"

"Because I'm the one who gave you the cat. I'm the one who gave you the diamonds."

The wrist bindings were cut. Quinton moved closer.

"You came back to get the diamonds, didn't you. What is this – some sort of weird smuggling thing?"

"No – I came back to warn you. To tell you Frank and Gina are coming to –"

The doorbell rang. Still Ravel's 'Bolero.' The tune rang through the house. Thoughts of Bo Derek filled Quinton's brain.

"Mr. Squid! Mr. Squid, it's the police," a loud voice called from the front of the dwelling.

Quinton's head began to spin. He walked to the edge of the deck.

"I'm back here," he yelled around the side of the house. "In the back of the house."

In back of Mi Casa, he thought. Mikasa micasa. Mikasa es su casa. Mi casa es…His brain babbled at itself. Sweat poured down his face. His breathing became labored. He began to hyperventilate. Keep it together. Keep it together. One. Two. Three. Four…he silently counted the wooden floorboards of the deck…"fifteen," he said aloud.

"Shut up!" he finally screamed at the top of his lungs, frantically scratching his ear with his finger.

"Michael, you're counting again!" yelled Nick.

"Mr. Squid? Mr. Squid are you all right?" the cops yelled as they ran to the back of the house.

"What do you know about my counting?" Quinton demanded.

Nick could hear their footsteps edging closer to the deck.

"Call off the cops and I'll tell you."

"No way."

"Then I'll see you later."

Nick stood abruptly and pushed Quinton into the hot tub. Without breaking stride, he slashed off the ropes binding his feet. Nick jumped over the railing and ran for the labyrinth of houses stretching down the beach.

"Just breathe, Michael," he yelled back as he ran. "Keep breathing, for Christ's sake! And do your dan tien!"

"You know Dan Ten?!! Who is he?!!" Quinton screamed.

"You'll remember, Michael! You'll remember!" Nick yelled to the tortured man on the porch as he disappeared into the darkness.

"Motherfucker..." Quinton whimpered from inside the hot tub.

Two policemen ran up the back stairs onto the deck. A fully clothed, water-logged Quinton Squid tried to get out of the hot tub.

"You okay?" asked one of the cops.

"Yeah. He just went that way," Quinton pointed down the beach. "He had a knife. I should've checked him."

The police scurried down the stairs and took off in Nick's direction. Quinton managed to climb out of the tub. He felt like an idiot, dripping with water, waiting for the police to return.

He saw the Louisville Slugger lying on the deck and picked it up. It was stained with blood. He bent down over the tub and washed it off.

Minutes later the policemen returned. Nick was not with them.

"He's gone. I'm sorry, Mr. Squid," said the elder of the two officers.

Quinton stood, toting the wet baseball bat.

"No, it's my fault."

He held out a water-wrinkled hand to the officer.

"Hi. Quinton Squid."

The officer met his hand with a smile. He was obviously a fan.

"Patrick Riley, pleased to meet you. Call me Pat."

The two shook hands. The junior officer wasn't about to be left out. He too extended his hand.

"Freddie Marx. Nice to meet you."

Riley returned his flashlight to its leather holster.

"What did he make off with?" he asked.

"Nothing. I caught him in time. Hit him over the head with a bat."

Marx smiled.

"At least he'll have a nasty headache in the morning. Might make him think twice about doing something like this again. Sorry we couldn't catch him for you."

"That's okay," said Quinton, still dripping. "Thanks for coming so soon."

"Our pleasure," said the star-struck Riley, a big sappy grin on his face. "By the way, while I'm here…my daughter's a really big fan. Think you could sign me an autograph or something? If it's not too much trouble."

"No, not at all. Come on in."

Quinton led them through the glass doors into the living room to his desk. He took one of his 8x10 promo glossies from a stack.

"What's her name?" he asked.

"Pat," said Officer Riley, a bit awkwardly.

Quinton smiled. He slowly turned his face to Riley's.

"Is that Pat as in Patricia, or Pat as in Patrick?"

Quinton winked at Marx. Riley squinted his eyes in embarrassment and cleared his throat.

"That would be Pat as in Patrick."

Quinton couldn't help but laugh. Riley and Marx joined in.

"Fair enough. Patrick it is," said Quinton as he wrote on the glossy. He hesitated a moment before signing his autograph. Closing his eyes, he saw himself writing his signature on Stu's cast, the signature he'd gleaned from the endorsement photo. When he opened his eyes, he found he'd signed the photo in the exact same manner. Mild relief played over his face. He handed the autographed picture to the officer.

"Here you go."

Riley read what he'd written aloud. "To Patrick Riley. Thanks for making a bee-line to save my backside. Mikasa es su casa. Quinton Squid."

Riley extended his hand.

"Thanks a lot, Mr. Squid."

Quinton met his hand again and shook it.

"Call me Quinton, okay?"

"Okay."

"Call us again if he comes back, or if there's anything we can do for you," said Marx.

As they walked to the door, Quinton noticed the passport still lying on his coffee table. He looked away from it.

"There is one thing you could do for me," he said.

"What's that?" asked Riley.

"The burglar kept mentioning a name to me, Michael Delaney. Could you find out who that is for me?"

Riley and Marx looked at each other. Marx shrugged. Riley turned back to Quinton.

"I suppose we could put out a feeler for you."

Quinton scrawled the mysterious name on a piece of paper and gave it to Riley.

"Thanks, Pat. I'd really appreciate it."

"No problem."

Quinton shook hands and closed the door after them. Letting down the sports hero facade, he stood in the dark room alone and dripping. Shaken and confused, his teeth chattered and his hands trembled. Quinton took off his sopping clothes and carried them to the kitchen. He dropped the clothes in the sink and went out on the deck. He climbed into the hot tub to try to warm his trembling body, dragging the Louisville Slugger in behind him.

Frank sat at Victor Russo's desk looking particularly chipper. By day he had to follow orders from his barking father, but at night Frank got to sit in the old man's chair. It made him happy in a passive-aggressive sort of way. Carlo and Muncie entered the office.

"You got a time?" Frank asked.

"She's going tomorrow night," Muncie told him.

"Where?" asked Frank.

"She won't tell us, but we have to fly," said Carlo.

"What time, and what airline?" asked Frank.

"She won't tell us that either," answered Muncie with his usual dim-witted expression.

Frank looked them over, up and down, left to right.

"You two are a couple of fucking prizes, you know that?"

He snatched up a cardboard box off the floor and opened it. He took out two cell phones and two beepers. He handed one each to Carlo and Muncie.

"I'm supervising a shipment tomorrow. Victor's out of town. I'll be here all day. You call me when you get to the airport, I just need fifteen minutes to get there from here. You got it?" he asked.

"Yeah," said Muncie.

"Frankie?" Carlo asked.

"What?"

"Why don't you just ask her?" he wanted to know.

Frank looked at the two dolts standing in front of him. He rested his folded hands on the desk.

"She still loves him. She doesn't want me to ruin his beautiful Sistine Chapel face. Michelangelo's 'David,' my ass."

Carlo and Muncie didn't quite get it. They looked at him in confusion.

"Huh?" asked Carlo.

"But the joke's on her," continued Frank, almost to himself.

"How do you figure?" asked Muncie.

"Because he don't have that face no more," explained Frank as he broke into a cackle.

Quinton sat at the edge of his bed in a pair of paisley silk boxers. The Louisville Slugger stood by the dresser, drying in the breeze. His hands trembled furiously. His mind swam with 'Bolero,' unintelligible Italian curse words, and questions, so many questions. He chose not to think about the burglar, and how he had called him by another name. After all, he was a burglar. Just plain crazy. From the blow to the head, he tried to reason.

Quinton seethed at the box of sleeping pills lying on his bedside table. He didn't want to make a pact with this devil again, but wanted to sleep. Anything to get away from the mangled, confused insanity consciousness offered at this particular moment.

He picked up the box and opened it. Empty. He dropped it back on the table.

That couldn't be the one he bought a few days ago. He

opened the top drawer of the table. The new box had to be in there. There was no way he could've used it up. But he was wrong. The empty box was the new one.

There had to be more in there somewhere. But inside the drawer he found only sheets and pillowcases. He opened the next drawer down. More sheets. Sheets he hadn't folded recently, sheets he must have folded in another life.

He pulled out one sheet after another, looking for something to help him sleep. He became aware of a familiar scent. Mothballs, said his subconscious. Why the hell would he have put mothballs in with cotton bedsheets, he wondered. Mikasa es su casa. Mi casa es su casa, his brain insisted as he pulled out sheet after sheet. He finally found the source of the odor.

At the bottom of the drawer, wrapped in some rank-smelling plastic, was an old picture album. He took the album out and unwrapped it. It was musty and jam-packed with material, appearing to have been made into a scrapbook. He tossed the plastic onto the night table.

He opened the picture album and spread its contents out over the bed. It was full of newspaper articles, flyers, photographs, ribbons, and cards. Quinton picked up a small black and white snapshot. The photo was of a man and woman with a baby. The woman had dark hair and wore a miniskirt. She appeared to be in her early twenties, the man perhaps a bit older. She held a two-year-old baby in her arms. The man wore a dress uniform from the Merchant Marine. Both had strikingly good looks.

Quinton flipped the photograph over. On the back, scrawled in pen, was a note which read 'Elizabeth, Quint and Quinton, Jr.' Quinton put the picture down.

Thoughts he could not comprehend raced through his mind. His breathing grew more rapid. Wrinkles covered his mind's eye as he scanned over the other material in confusion. He began to look over the newspaper clippings, and picked up a playbill which read, 'The New York City Ballet: Giselle.' Quinton's eyes continued to roam.

He focused on another black and white photo. This was of the senior Quinton Davis as a young man. He stood on an outdoor track wearing an Olympic uniform. Tied around his neck on a ribbon was an Olympic Gold Medal. The man's eyes burned with an intensity bordering on the spiteful. A caption below the picture read '1964 Olympic Games.'

Mounted next to the photo, in one of the book's clear plastic pouches, was the actual Gold Medal. Quinton stared at it. He ran his fingers over it through the plastic. This was his father's Gold Medal, he said to himself, and let it sink in. The notion gave him comfort. This was his father.

Next to the Medal was another pouch containing a reel of eight-millimeter movie film. An elastic-band held a piece of paper against the reel. The logo on the receipt read 'Pier One Video Transfers.' Video. It must be in the house, he thought, and got up from the bed.

He walked into the living room and flipped through his collection of videotapes. In the bookshelves next to his desk he had videos from nearly every major beach volleyball event since the year he went pro. Hermosa, Manhattan Beach, Rio, the Australian Open; they were all there to be studied and scrutinized, over and over. There were forty of them.

The only other video contained in the collection was the copy of *Chariots of Fire* he had bought when he'd rented *The Time Machine*. But the Pier One video had to be there somewhere. It just had to. He sifted through the volleyball tapes more carefully. Hermosa from three years ago. Hermosa two years ago. Last year year's Hermosa. Last year's Manhattan.

Last year's Hermosa. Wait. Two copies of last year's Hermosa? He pulled the two boxes from the stack and looked at the tapes inside. One read Hermosa. The other read 'Pier One Video Transfers.' He popped it hungrily into his VCR. Quinton sat on the sofa and clicked on the television.

The eight-millimeter color image on the TV screen was grainy and slightly overexposed. There was no sound. On the screen, Quinton saw his mother, Elizabeth, clowning around near a stand of multi-hued, orange and yellow maple trees. It looked like autumn somewhere back east. The fall colors struck him as familiar, almost comforting. His mother continually shifted all of her weight onto her toes and did a series of ballet pirouettes. She stopped and plopped down on the ground in mock exhaustion. Laughing, she signaled to someone off-camera. A small boy of four entered the frame. He looked at the camera shyly.

Quinton was riveted. It was him as a child. He searched the boy's eyes for some sign of himself. He couldn't remember making this movie. He couldn't remember his mother. Onscreen, Elizabeth motioned him over to her. She stood up, pointed at the camera and nodded to him. The boy shifted his weight onto one foot and did a pirouette almost identical to his mother's. Incredibly, the boy continued to do an elaborate series of pirouettes, then the screen went blank. The videotape stopped and began its automatic rewind. The entire tape had lasted a mere two minutes. Quinton was left sitting in silence on the sofa, staring at the blank screen.

The middle of the night found Quinton swimming in medicated sleep. He slept on his bed, his body covering the pictures and clippings from the scrapbook that lay next to him. His eyes began to twitch, slowly at first, then furiously.

He was awake in the world behind his eyes. In the darkness of this other world Quinton could hear Nick's voice echo clearly all around him.

"Mikey, it's me. It's Nick. We grew up together."

The world inside his mind became a luminescent white. Nick's voice slowly faded into that of Michael Delaney's mother.

"Mikey. Mikey," she called in her pleasant sing-song voice.

The white light dissolved into a new reality.

Mr. and Mrs. Delaney sat at the top of their driveway in a brand-new, white Cadillac convertible. They were a pleasant couple in their late thirties.

The engine was off. An eight-year-old Michael walked down the driveway, away from the car, towards the street. The surrounding oak and maple trees were ablaze with the reds and yellows of New England autumnal coloring. The scent of pine trees and fallen leaves lingered in his nostrils. His mother called to him again.

"Mikey. Come on, we're ready."

She turned around to see him heading towards a large blonde-haired boy crouched at the end of the driveway. Struck by a sudden thought, she turned to her husband sitting in the driver's seat.

"Oh. A scarf. I forgot to get something to keep my hair down. Just give me a second, okay hon?" she asked.

Mr. Delaney smiled.

"Sure. Hurry up, though. I just can't wait to test her out."

She got out of the car and ran into their one-story ranch. Michael's father adjusted the rearview mirror. His eye caught sight of Michael as he was walking away. He called out to him.

"Michael, you coming? I told you it was snazzy, huh? Your Uncle Victor doesn't fool around. Come on, son. You've got the whole back seat, all to yourself."

"Yeah. Just a sec, Dad. Tell me when Ma gets back," he yelled to his father.

Mr. Delaney caressed the car's red leather interior gently with his palm.

"What a beauty," he cooed.

This week's Sunday drive would be different. They would set out at one o'clock like they always did, but not in that rickety old Dodge. Phillip Delaney caught a glance of himself as he adjusted the sideview mirror. Any vanity aside, he thought he looked quite dashing in his beard and mustache. No one had ever guessed he'd grown it to hide pockmarks from a serious case of childhood chickenpox. Mrs. Delaney had loved his rugged good-looks with or without the hairy disguise. She was equally striking, with smooth olive Italian skin and wide, blue-gray eyes. Michael had inherited those same eyes. 'Eyes that will make the girls swoon someday,' his father had always said. There was an innocence about Michael's baby blues. Come to think of it, this new car made Phillip and the wife feel like kids again themselves.

Michael had looked forward to this Sunday drive all week. He had never driven in a new car before, let alone a Cadillac convertible. But first things first. He felt a compulsory urge to see what that boy at the other end of the driveway was doing. The crouched boy's back was to him, but as Michael drew closer he could see smoke rising from somewhere in front of him. Michael went around the boy and crouched down to get a better look.

The blonde boy held a magnifying glass in his hands, focusing the sun's rays on the ground below. He was setting fire to a spider. The boy chewed bubble gum diligently while he worked. A dozen or so scorched insects lay next to him in a pile on the ground. They were the remains of the ants, beetles, and caterpillars he had burned alive.

As he burned the daddy long legs, it was clear to Michael that the boy was getting a perverse thrill from watching the poor thing perish before his eyes. Michael felt his breakfast of eggs and bacon churn in his stomach. He swallowed hard, trying to resist his body's urge to vomit. Michael was horrified, but intense curiosity got the best of him.

"Whaddya doin' Frankie?" Michael asked.

The nine-year-old Frank looked up from his gore fest. He snapped his gum several times before answering.

"Nothing, you little mick. What's it to ya?"

"My name is Mike," said Michael.

"Mike the mick," mocked Frank, still snapping his gum.

"No. Just Mike. Whatcha doing?"

Frank regarded him a moment then blew a large pink bubble. He sucked the gum back in his mouth. A mischievous grin curled over his face.

"Come here," Frank beckoned.

"Why?"

"Just come here."

Michael hesitated, then sat down next to him.

"Okay. Put your hand on the ground," goaded Frank.

"Why should I?" Michael asked.

"You want to see what I'm doing?"

"Yeah."

"Then just stick your hand out, you stupid harp."

Michael was confused, but thought it best not to ask for an explanation. He put his hand on the ground as Frank had instructed. Frank held the magnifying glass over it. As it caught the sun's rays, Frank reached out and pushed his other hand over Michael's wrist, holding it in place. The magnifying glass started to burn Michael's hand. Michael screamed out in pain.

He tried to move but Frank's grip was too strong. As they struggled, Michael managed to push Frank away. A furious Michael stood up. Frank stood as well. Though only a year older, he had a good four inches on Michael.

"What'd you do that for, you big jerk?!" Michael yelled at him.

"I don't have to tell you anything, mick, harp, half-breed dago mutt."

"Why'd you burn my hand?"

"I don't have to tell you."

"Why are you burning bugs in the first place?" Michael demanded.

"Ask your old man. He knows a lot about bugs," said Frank.

"What's that supposed to mean?"

"It's my job. I find bugs, then I burn them. Besides, your cat runs too fast."

"You leave my cat alone, Frankie."

"Maybe I will. Maybe I won't," Frank teased as he blew another large bubble.

At the top of the driveway Michael heard the car door slam. He looked back at the new Cadillac. His mom and dad were in the front seat.

"Mikey," his mother yelled, "we're ready. We're coming down. We'll pick you up at the end of the driveway."

"Okay, Ma," Michael yelled back.

Michael turned back to face Frank. They stared into each other's eyes, angry. Over Frank's shoulder Michael could see his father lean over and kiss his mother in the front seat. Michael smiled. He knew he didn't have to worry about Frank or his magnifying glass, or anything else. He had his family and they would protect him from anything bad that came his way.

"Okay, here she goes," said Mr. Delaney, and put the shield-shaped key in the ignition.

The engine didn't turn over. He tried it again. No luck. Third time was the charm. The car turned over...and exploded.

Out of nowhere, it erupted into a huge orange blaze. Glass and metal flew fifty feet into the air, landing on the surrounding lawn in flames. Michael saw a huge chunk of metal fly towards him. He ducked and fell to the ground. Frank turned around to see what the horrific noise was. Within a split second the chunk of metal, the car's rear bumper, smashed full tilt into the left side of his head.

Michael stood up in shock and began to panic. Frank lay prone on the ground beside him, bleeding profusely. The car was a nightmare of orange flame. It complemented the surrounding autumn hues with a sickening poignancy. Michael ran towards the car, screaming.

"Mom! Dad! MOM! DAD!"

The car was surrounded by an impenetrable wall of fire and radiant heat. He couldn't get near it. Nothing could be seen but the blaze. Indifferent to the blinding heat, Michael fell on the ground and began to cry. The crying turned to wailing and he began to sob at the top of his lungs.

"Mom! Dad..."

"Mom! Dad!" Quinton screamed as he woke from his nightmare.

His breathing was labored and his body soaked in sweat. A horrible dream. As his subconscious rushed to obscure the particulars of it, his conscious mind tried to hang on, to retain something, anything.

Wait. Who was the couple in the car? What was the name they had called him? It was on the tip of his brain, but he could not place it. All he could remember was that it had not felt wholly unfamiliar.

Realizing he lay face down on newspaper, he rolled over onto his back. He peeled off the newspaper article stuck to his face. Black newsprint covered his left profile. It left a woman's face portrayed faintly in relief under his left cheek.

He held the article up to the light. At first the image appeared blurry. After a few deep breaths it pulled into focus.

The top of the yellowed newsprint read 'New York Times Art Section.' Below it, a large headline read: 'New York City Ballet Phenom Dead of Heroine Overdose at 25.' Next to the headline was a picture of Quinton's mother, a very beautiful, athletic-looking woman taken during her prime. It was the same woman in the video. The article went on to describe how her only living relatives were her son and her estranged husband, a merchant seaman who had not been heard from for several years.

Quinton stared at the newspaper photo. He desperately wanted to recognize this woman. This was the woman in the eight-millimeter home movies, but had it been the woman in the dream? Or had that been someone else? He wasn't sure. It was all so hazy.

What was going on? He thought of the burglar and his bizarre rantings. What was it he had called him?

Michael. The name on the passport. He had the sneaking suspicion that was the name he had been called in the dream. His eyes searched frantically over the sea of articles and photographs strewn across his bed for signs of the couple in the nightmare. He couldn't remember their faces, just a vague impression of how safe they had made him feel.

His eyes came to rest on an old *Sports Illustrated* clipping. Quinton snatched it up feverishly. The title to the back-section writeup read 'Whatever Happened To: The Weekly

Remember When.' Quinton's eyes skimmed over the first few lines of copy.

"This week's focus is the infamous Gold Medallist Quinton Davis of the 1964 Summer Olympic Games. Shortly thereafter, the brilliant but quick-tempered player hung up his volleyball to return to full time duty with the Merchant Marine. Little is known…"

Quinton stared at the article blankly for a moment then put it down. His father was alive. But didn't he die in the Cadillac? It had felt more like an actual memory than just a dream. Was this guy the father in the dream? He could've been, but what if he wasn't? Quinton started to panic. He started to count. One. Two. Three.

Wait. Focus on reality, he told himself. Focus on what you know to be true. Twisted memories and bizarre dreams may persist, but for the sake of your sanity, look to the tangible. As far as he knew, Quinton Davis was his father, and this was real.

He began to clear his bed of the clippings and put them back in the scrap book. Left on the bed was the Gold Medal and a lone key. He picked up the key. The attached tag read 'Santa Monica Storage.' What did he have in storage? More skeletons in the closet? He gingerly placed the key and Gold Medal on top of the scrapbook, and put all three back into the drawer.

He lay back in bed and gazed at his own reflection staring back at him from the ceiling mirror. He looked at his clock. 4:15 a.m. Two more hours and he had to meet Holly on the beach. He closed his eyes and did his best to sleep.

Wind sprints were not Quinton's strong suit. Especially at six in the morning when he hadn't slept all night. Holly, on the other hand, ran like a cheetah as she sprinted back and forth from the ocean to the boardwalk at State Beach. Quinton had given up any attempt to keep up with her and was now preoccupied simply with keeping vertical. After a while even this proved futile. Exhausted, he let his legs fall out from under him and lay down on the sand. Holly sprinted over to him.

"I've got to rest," Quinton gasped. "How do you do that?"

Holly stood over Quinton and took in a few deep breaths. She studied him casually.

"I never smoked," she said, and sat down next to him.

Quinton looked at her. What else didn't he know about his old self ? Or was she just playing with him? It seemed to be a pastime with these Californians.

"Why? Did I smoke?" he asked.

"No. At least not that I know of," she said. Deadpan.

Quinton continued to look at her with the same confused expression. After a moment a knowing smile broke across his face.

"Very cute, O'Connor."

He playfully grabbed her left foot. She tried to pull it back, but he had her foot in a tight but gentle grip. He tickled the bottom of her foot mercilessly.

"Stop that! I can't stand it," she giggled, then got a better idea.

She grabbed his right foot and furiously tickled the bottom of it.

"Ah, cut it out," he laughed and tried to wrestle it from her grip but she was too strong. Pleasantly so.

"Please stop it," she pleaded, laughing.

"Promise you won't mess with my mind?" Quinton chuckled playfully.

"I promise. I won't play any more games with your fragile psyche..."

Quinton stopped tickling. Holly ceased her barrage as well and they released each other's feet.

"Okay," Quinton said as he lay back in the sand.

"...much," Holly kidded.

"You better not," Quinton warned, a gleam in his eye.

Holly removed the elastic from her ponytail and let her hair fall down around her shoulders. Quinton caught this motion out of the corner of his eye. She looked good. She lay back on the sand next to him and closed her eyes. He became aware of the closeness of her body. Her lycra bike shorts and cotton crop-top revealed much about her well-proportioned figure. The sea breeze wafted the sweet smell of her hair gently in his direction.

Holly opened her eyes and looked up at the sky. She felt his eyes on her, but couldn't be sure of what it meant. He was a hard guy to read. Quinton closed his eyes. Holly did know one thing, however. She knew how attractive this new Quinton was to her. As his finely chiseled body, clad only in shorts, lay next to her, she marveled at how much kinder, more thoughtful, and likeable this man had become since his plane crash.

Suddenly the morning sun broke out over the boardwalk. Its golden rays cascaded over the beach. Quinton opened his eyes and let himself bask in the sun's warmth. He was ecstatic.

"That. That is the Volley God," he said from a place deep in his soul.

"It is, huh?"

"Yeah."

Quinton stood up and stretched his arms out to the sides. His chest jutted out towards the sun. He began to repeat something yearningly in a whisper.

"Meus Deus, Mea Mater, Meus Pater..."

"What does that mean?" Holly asked.

"You are my God, you are my Mother, you are my Father."

"I didn't know you spoke Latin."

"Neither did I."

For an instant Quinton looked at the rising sun. It seemed to feed him somehow. He closed his eyes and took a deep breath through his nostrils. He exhaled slowly through his mouth. He felt a pervasive sense of stillness move through his body. He began to feel as if he was breathing air into his feet, his arms, his fingertips.

His body began to feel soft, almost weightless. His mind became calm and breathing effortless. He smiled as he felt his breath begin to encircle the space just below his navel. When he inhaled, his belly drew inwards; when he exhaled, it gently extended. His breathing became circular and fluid.

He opened his eyes and inhaled deeply. The dawn sky shone with a brilliant intensity he had never noticed before. His breath felt as if it ebbed and flowed in unison with the ocean waves below. He felt at one with and as light as the air that surrounded him.

"Ave maria, gratia plena," he heard himself say as he felt his arms raise naturally in front of him. The palms of his hands turned inward towards each other without effort. "Ave maria, gratia plena," he repeated.

His palms turned outward and began to push out to the sides as if doing the breast stroke: Tai Chi short form movement number one – Large Bear Swimming in Water. With fluidity and ease of motion he reversed the movement, bringing his palms back together with a large in-breath. He exhaled as he brought his hands to his waist and spread his arms out to the sides: movement number two – Eagle Attacks Its Prey.

"Ave maria, gratia plena, dominus tecum," he whispered aloud. Holly knew the words. She'd gone to Catholic school once upon a time, long ago. Without thinking, she moved her lips in unison with him as he repeated the Hail Mary in Latin. She looked on in awe. His accompanying movements were so foreign to her eyes.

"Benedictata tu in mulierbus et benedictus fructus..." Quinton continued as he allowed himself to gently rock back and forth, heel to toe. He brought his arms down to his sides and back to neutral. He stood still and allowed himself a long, deep breath. He then moved his right leg back, keeping it off the ground, raised his left foot on its toes, and spread his arms wide: movement number three – Step Back and Ride the Tiger.

He set his right leg down, crossed his arms in front of him and turned his body around one hundred eighty degrees: movement number four – Embrace the Tiger and Return to the Mountain.

"...ventris tui Jesu. Sancta maria, mater dei..."

He swung his right arm across his body, down to his waist,

and inhaled. He swung his left arm across his body to his waist and exhaled.

"...ora pro nobis peccatoribus..."

Quinton pulled his left leg in towards his body and raised his knee to a ninety degree angle. He crossed his hands in front of his body and inhaled. He spun a hundred eighty degrees again counter-clockwise on his right heel. He opened both arms and brought them to his sides, kicked upward with his left heel, and let out a gentle exhalation: movement number five – Strike the Tiger.

"...nunc et in hora mortis nostrae. Amen."

His body returned to its original neutral stance. He stood facing the sun with eyes closed and his arms hanging loosely by his sides. To Holly, his form seemed to melt into the ocean behind him. Her lips continued to move unconsciously in silent repetition of the Hail Mary.

With a deep breath, Quinton clasped his hands together and bowed down to the ground. He leaned back into a sitting position as if beginning a meditation.

Holly stared at him. This was a Squid she had never seen before. One that few, she was sure, had ever seen at all. After a few moments his eyes closed and he began to sing.

"So buy me some peanuts and Cracker Jack, I don't care if I never get back..."

Quinton opened one of his eyes. He let it look over at Holly. He opened the other eye and slowly reintegrated back to the moment.

"What was that?" asked Holly.

"What was what?"

"That stuff you were just doing on the beach. It was beautiful."

"I have no idea what that was, but the other part was 'Take Me Out to the Ball Game.' "

Holly looked at him quizzically.

"Quinton Squid, you are a strange being."

"Aren't I, though?"

Quinton felt his breathing pattern gently return to normal.

"I didn't know you had studied any of the martial arts," Holly said.

"Neither did I. The movements just came to me. Suddenly."

"Just like that?"

"Yeah, I guess so. The motions just felt so peaceful. So perfect."

"You would've had to study for years to move with such intricacy...such grace. That was just too amazing."

"I really don't know where it came from," said Quinton, still feeding on the ecstatic energy bubbling up from within.

Holly couldn't help but stare. This part of his spirit he had unearthed was sublimely magnetic. As she gazed at him closely, she could've sworn she saw a thin film of hot steam rise up from around his body.

"There's no martial arts stuff at your house?" she asked.

"No. None at all."

Quinton wiped his brow with a bare forearm. The steam around him began to dissipate.

"Would Stu know if you had studied martial arts?"

"Yeah, Stu should know."

Holly was silent for a moment. Her tone became less incredulous and more serious.

"Quinton, the sun can be your God, and I suppose the sun can be your mother in a manner of speaking, but your father is still alive."

"Yeah, I know. I found a lot of the stuff I was looking for. Pictures and news articles in an old scrapbook."

"You did?" asked Holly.

"Yeah."

Quinton and Holly sat on the beach cross-legged, facing each other. He felt comfortable around her. He scooped up a handful of sand.

"Maybe you should look him up," she suggested. "Try and find him. It might help to talk to him."

Quinton was fascinated by the granules of sand slipping through his fingers onto the beach below.

"It might," he said absent-mindedly. It would be daunting to meet his real father. He might get some real answers. Answers that could be hard to accept.

"Quint, I have a friend at the DMV. He might be able to track him down."

Holly looked at him playing with the sand. She noticed he wasn't paying attention.

"That is, if you're interested."

Quinton dropped the sand, shook his hands off and looked towards the sun.

"Yeah, I'm interested."

He looked back into Holly's eyes and smiled. She smiled back. Warmly. He was again touched by her desire to help him.

"Okay then," she said.

"Okay," said Quinton. He looked into her eyes again, then looked away.

Quinton pulled out the storage locker key from his back pocket and handed it to Holly.

"I found this in the scrap book."

She looked at the key and its inscription.

"Santa Monica Storage. What's in it?"

"I don't know. Figured I'd bring it by Stu's later. Maybe he knows. I tried to call the place, but it's not listed."

She gave it back to him.

"If it's the one I'm thinking of, it's on Marine Ave."

"Great," he said.

"Not really, because it burned down a couple years ago."

"That explains why they don't have a phone number."

"Sorry. Fire certainly has taken a lot away from you, hasn't it," she said gently.

He looked up at her. The warmth of her empathy was undeniable.

"It certainly has."

Stu opened his front door to find Quinton brandishing a lone key.

"You know what this is?" he asked Stu.

Stu took the key from him. He inspected it.

"A locker key from Santa Monica Storage?"

"No shit, Sherlock, I can read English. I mean do you know what it's for?"

"Storage?"

Quinton grabbed the key and barged past Stu into the house. He walked to the kitchen, where Emily poured herself a glass of iced coffee. Quinton sat at the table.

"He's a bright one, Em. Count yourself lucky you snagged him."

Emily laughed. She poured a second glass of coffee. Quinton's eyes scanned the fruitbowl in front of him. Kiwis, nectarines, grapes. A lot to choose from.

"Oh, I didn't snag him, he came crawling back with his tail between his legs, begging me to take him back," Emily said.

"Oh yeah? When was this?" Quinton asked, popping a grape in his mouth. Emily smiled.

"You should know, Q. You're the one who sent him back in my direction."

"Hmm. Smartest thing I ever did, I bet."

"You got that right," she said. "Iced coffee?"

That kiwi looked good. Nah, too sour.

"Quint?" Emily asked.

"Yeah?"

"You want some iced coffee?"

"Oh. Decaf?"

"No, but a great dark roast. Not too bitter."

Quinton shook his head.

"Thanks, but I'm not sleeping so great these days as it is. I found this key rummaging around at three a.m. this morning. Don't have a clue what I'd keep in storage. Don't have a clue about much these days."

Stu walked into the kitchen and sat across from Quinton.

"But you're getting a great tan," he said.

"This is true," said Quinton.

"Want some fruit juice or something, Q?" asked Emily.

"No, thanks, I'm fine." He ate another grape.

Emily sat at the table with her coffee and handed a cup to Stu. Stu winked at her and she smiled back.

"So, I'm the one who got you back together, huh?" said Quinton.

"Yep," Stu said as he clicked the ice around in his coffee.

"Marriage and fidelity doesn't seem like something I would have gone out of my way to encourage."

"I was surprised as hell," said Emily.

Stu was suspiciously quiet.

Quinton eyed him curiously. An awkward silence settled over the room. Quinton stood up.

"I think I will take that juice, Em. In the fridge, is it?"

"Yeah, help yourself."

He opened the fridge and took out a bottle of apple juice. He looked around the kitchen.

"Glasses?" he asked matter-of-factly.

"Above the sink," Stu said quietly.

Quinton opened the cabinet. Coffee mugs and glasses lined the lower shelves. The top shelf was a myriad of colored plastic cups. A Flintstones cup with attached crazy straw caught his eye.

"Cool," he said, and reached for it on tiptoes.

Quinton brought the cup down to the counter and filled it with juice. His back to the kitchen table, Emily stared at him in shock.

"So seriously, Stu, what do you think I could possibly have in storage?" Quinton asked as he turned and leaned against the counter, cup in hand.

Stu looked at Emily. She stared blankly into her coffee cup. He looked back at Quinton.

"Maybe your closets at home are so filled with skeletons, you needed room for more."

Emily laughed in spite of herself, breaking the tension. Stu smiled at her. He lifted her hand to his lips and kissed it. He brought it back down to the table, staring into her eyes. Her dark eyes began to come alive again. She stirred some milk into her coffee. Stu turned to face Quinton, who just looked at the couple with an eyebrow raised. Had he done something wrong? He awkwardly sipped his juice.

"How about we go check it out, Q?" Stu offered.

"Sure," Quinton said, with the most neutral expression he could muster. He wished he could remember why they were acting so strangely. But for now, he just tipped his head forward and bit down on the crazy straw.

23

The yellow cab screeched to a halt in front of the domestic terminal at Boston's Logan Airport. The cabbie swung around in his seat.

"Twelve-fifty," he said through the stubby cigar jammed in his mouth. Carlo and Muncie got out of the cab.

"Get the bags," Gina ordered.

The cabbie popped the trunk.

"Thanks," she said.

"No problem," he said, sucking on the soggy end of his lit cigar. He wiped his sweaty palms on his t-shirt.

Gina handed the cabby a crisp new hundred-dollar bill. Her forearm was a bevy of faux tortoise-shell bangles. He stared at the bill in her hand and smiled.

"Forget you saw us," she instructed.

Still staring at the bill, he nodded. As he reached for the bill in her hand, he let his eyes wander slowly past it, past the bangles, up her arm, and down the nape of her neck to her chest. His eyes rested there. He felt his fingers reach the bill, but Gina's fist would not let go. The cabby looked up into her eyes. The sheer coldness staring back at him made him uneasy. He tugged harder at the bill. It wouldn't budge. Stalemate.

"Hey, lady..."

"I thought I told you to forget you saw us," she said, eyeing the lit end of his cigar.

He threw her a greasy grin.

"Just trying to remember what I'm supposed to forget."

Their hands still locked in a tug-of-war, he stared down at her chest again.

"Pretty memorable."

Gina grabbed the cigar out of his mouth. He tried to snatch it back, but she held it menacingly close to his right eye. He backed off. Gina moved the cigar back and forth, from eye to eye. The cabby's eyes began to tear up from the smoke.

"Be careful what you wish for," she warned. "Some things you put in your mouth can burn you. Bad."

She lowered the cigar to their locked fists.

"Don't do it, lady."

"Let go of the bill."

"Hey, I earned it."

"You certainly did."

She jammed the cigar down on the back of his hand. He screamed and pulled away. Both bill and cigar fell into the front seat.

"Like I said, forget you saw us," Gina said.

The cabby nodded. Carlo and Muncie stood motionless behind the trunk, staring silently into the cabin. They looked at each other and took a long, silent breath. Gina got out of the cab. They closed the trunk and picked up the carry-ons sitting on the sidewalk.

"What am I, a fucking cripple?!" Gina screamed as she snatched her bag from Muncie.

"Follow me," she ordered, and they fell immediately into place behind her.

The three followed the signs to area A: American Airlines, America West, Continental, and Express Air. Muncie and Carlo took note. They passed the American Airlines terminal, then America West. Another twenty-five feet and they passed Continental. That narrowed it a bit. As they passed a sign for the restroom, Muncie tapped Gina on the shoulder.

"I gotta take a piss," he announced.

Gina stopped and turned to face him.

"You should've gone in the cab like everyone else."

Muncie began to cross his legs back and forth like a pre-schooler.

"I'm serious."

Gina was aghast at his infantile display.

"What are you, five?" she screeched.

"I really gotta go," pleaded Muncie.

Gina looked at her watch. Five forty-seven. Thirteen minutes to spare. Gina eyed him with little tolerance.

"Fine. Go. Meet us at Express, gate five. Boston to L.A. The flight starts boarding in thirteen minutes."

"I don't have a watch."

Gina wanted to belt him. She spoke to him through grated teeth.

"Okay. So start counting. Twelve-Sixty, twelve-fifty-nine, twelve-fifty-eight. Get it?"

"Got it," said Muncie, beginning to count down out loud as he walked away.

"Twelve-Sixty, twelve-fifty-nine…"

"To yourself, stugatz! And wash your hands after," Gina yelled after him.

She spun on her heel and continued toward the terminal. Carlo snuck a quick look over his shoulder and nodded at Muncie. Muncie nodded back. Carlo continued after Gina.

Muncie entered the men's room. He pulled out his cell phone and dialed a number. Thirteen minutes. Thirteen lousy minutes. There was no way Frank could make it there in that amount of time. He was going to snatch them bald-headed. Someone answered the phone.

"Hi," said Muncie.

"Cut the bullshit," said Frank. "Where and when?"

"Express. Gate five. Boston to L.A. It leaves in thirteen minutes."

Muncie closed his eyes and scrunched up his face, as if something was going to smash down on him from above. He waited for the verbal tirade on the other end of the line, but it didn't come. Frank finally spoke, but in a calm voice.

"You know, you're one lucky sonofabitch, Muncie. The two of you are lucky sonsabitches. There's an hour delay on all flights out of Logan tonight. I'll beep you when I get there."

Muncie heard the phone click on the other end. He put the cell phone back in his pocket and left the rest room. He walked to the Express Air terminal and saw Carlo and Gina sitting at the bar adjacent to gate five. He sat down next to them. Gina turned to him. She handed him a drink from the bar.

"We got an hour delay. I ordered three Sex on the T's. Drink."

Four Sex on the T's later, Muncie's beeper went off. He fiddled for it in his jacket. He finally found it and shut it off. Gina looked at him strangely.

"Since when do you wear a beeper?" she asked.

Muncie didn't hesitate, but his answer was badly rehearsed.

"It's-probably-Victor-wondering-where-I-am," he said, as if it were all one word.

He began to slide himself off the barstool when Carlo's beeper went off as well.

"Me too," Carlo said awkwardly.

Gina eyed them suspiciously. Plastered-on grins covered their faces as they slithered away from the bar to the nearest pay-phone/rest room area. Gina noticed Muncie look back over his shoulder as they walked away. She checked her left breast pocket for the plane tickets. She opened her purse to make sure her tazer gun and thumb cuffs were still secure. All were safe. A drunken businessman with an atrocious paisley tie bumped into her as he got off his barstool.

"I'm sorry, miss," he slurred.

"Keep your eyes open, pencil dick," she barked, and readjusted her suit jacket.

Frank waited patiently, standing at a urinal in the Express terminal's men's room. He listened intently to a conversation being held in one of the stalls. At first he thought there were two men in the stall, but then realized one of the voices came from a walkie-talkie. The man in the stall started talking again.

"Charlie, we might have to scrap it for today."

"Yeah. Without Michelle everything sounds like entrapment from this end," Charlie answered through the talkie.

"I know. I just hate to go home empty handed," said the man in the stall.

"Pike, give her ten more minutes to show," Charlie suggested.

"Okay," Pike said from the bathroom stall.

Frank heard the distinctive sound of an antenna telescoping shut. Sergeant Pike emerged from the stall. He was impeccably dressed in a tailored Italian suit. A 'Hi, I'm Stan' sticker covered the upper left hand pocket of his double breasted suitcoat. It might as well have read 'East Boston Vice Division,' thought Frank. The guy had cop written all over him. Pike quickly washed his hands at the sink, careful not to get water on his right-hand cufflink. Frank tried to get a good look at it. He saw a small wire snake from the cufflink up and under the suitcoat. That had to be the mic. Just as Pike left, Muncie and Carlo entered the men's room. Frank patted them both on the back.

"Good work."

"They'll be calling the flight any minute now," Muncie said.

The bad paisley tie entered the men's room. He nodded to Frank. Frank smiled.

"Vincent," he said, addressing him directly.

Vincent smiled back.

"Franklin," he said in his sober tone.

"What you got for me?" Frank rubbed his hands.

"Just what you wanted."

He handed Frank three airline tickets. Frank began to chuckle to himself. This would absolutely kill Gina. Frank handed Vincent and his paisley tie three one hundred dollar bills from his money clip.

"Thank you."

"My pleasure," said Vincent, and left the restroom.

Frank opened one of the airline tickets. The name on the boarding pass read 'Gina Lollabrigida.'

"I guess this one's for me," he smirked.

Frank pulled a pen from his pocket, laid the ticket on the counter, and changed the letter 'a' in Gina to an 'o.' The alteration took only a moment.

"There," he said and dropped the ticket into his front pocket.

Frank opened the other two tickets. He couldn't help but

laugh out loud. The names read, 'Sal Minella' and 'Jack Mehoff.' Amused, Frank handed Carlo and Muncie their passes.

"You decide who's who."

They looked at the tickets and switched them back and forth. Muncie took permanent hold of 'Sal Minella.'

"I look more like a Sal."

A ticked-off Carlo was stuck with 'Jack Mehoff.'

"I don't look like a Jack."

Frank stared at them, incredulous.

"Doesn't anything about those two names strike you as odd?" he asked the no-necked monsters.

"No," they said in unison.

Frank shook his head in disbelief.

"Then you are aptly named. Sal, Jack, stay in here until I call you."

With that, Frank left the men's room. He strode quickly into the bar across from gate five. He sat down on the stool next to Gina. Gina was too busy looking into the bottom of her drink to notice.

"Hey honey, how much for a bungie fuck?" he whispered.

Gina turned and dumped the rest of her drink in his lap.

"Shit!" screamed Frank.

The bar turned suddenly silent and everyone stared at them for a moment. Pike noticed them as well. He began to whisper something into his cufflink. Conversation in the room resumed. Frank began to blot at his crotch with every napkin he could find. Gina gave him her handkerchief.

"I'm sorry. I didn't know it was you, Frank. Sorry I got you all wet."

Frank took a moment from his blotting and looked up at her.

"Cousin, you ain't never gotten me wet."

Gina glared back at him.

"Screw you, Frank."

"Touchy, touchy."

He continued to blot away, a bit too merrily. Gina began to eye him with suspicion.

"What are you doing here anyway? Where are those two – oh, you little bug fucker."

His silk pants fairly dry, Frank tossed the wet napkins from his lap onto the bar. He stared at Gina's with an 'I'm rubber, you're glue' sort of attitude.

"If you play with fire, Gina..."

Gina started to reach into her purse.

"And don't go for the tazer, hon. You see that guy over there?"

Frank gestured to Pike sitting in the corner. Gina looked over at him.

"He has a gun tucked in the front of his pants. A very big gun, cousin. And he has orders to shoot you a new eyeball if you even move," said Frank.

"Screw that," was her response.

Frank took a serious tone.

"He's outside the family, Gina. He'll do it. Don't fuck with him. He won't scare as easy as Sal and Jack. By the way, that was very funny, cuz. I always admired your sense of humor."

Gina glared at him. Her jaw began to clench just as Michael's had a thousand times before.

"I got a plane to catch," said Frank.

He took his ticket out of his pocket. Gina reached for hers, but they were gone.

"You suck, Frank."

"Gina Lollabrigida, huh? You think you look like her? I

guess there is some resemblance. At least when you're not retaining water. Remember, not a move, cuz."

"Just you wait, Frank. Just you wait," she warned.

If she could have spit venom right then and there she would've. Out of the corner of his eye Frank could see Sergeant Pike watching them. Frank got up from the barstool and began to walk toward him. Gina sat at the bar, seething. Her anger began to build exponentially. She wanted to explode. Frank sat down next to a startled Pike.

"Excuse me, sir. The bartender said you might be able to help me," Frank explained.

"What is it?" asked Pike.

"See that woman there at the bar?"

"The one who tossed her drink at you?"

"Yes."

"What's the problem?"

"I asked if I could buy her a drink. She said 'sure,' then dumped her old one on my trousers. Then she told me to tell her how much I had liked it. When I tried to walk away she grabbed my wrist and told me I owed her a hundred dollars for the session. I didn't know what to do. I spoke to the bartender and he told me to talk to you."

Pike's curiosity was piqued. He shifted in his chair. He placed his right cuff link closer to Frank.

"Did you say anything that may have led her to believe you were willing to pay her for sex or some kind of B&D?"

"B&D?" asked Frank with faux innocence.

"Bondage and discipline. Humiliating behavior? Sex with a dominatrix?"

Frank looked shocked.

"My lord, no. As soon as I sat down she just started talking."

"Okay, thanks," said Pike. "We'll take it from here."

"Thank you," said Frank, and he walked off towards the boarding gate.

Pike stared over at Gina who was downing another Sex on the T. He spoke into his cufflink.

"Charlie, we may have a live one. I'm going up to bat."

Sergeant Pike walked from his table to the bar and sat next to a furious Gina. She turned to him immediately.

"If you whip that thing out, I'm going to fuck you so bad your dick will fall off. I've got thumb cuffs in my purse that will fit so tight around your balls you'll beg for mercy. We both know you can't stick it to me right here in front of everyone with the equipment you have. That bulge don't look big enough to have a silencer on the end of it. But I got a tazer in my purse. I could cook up that sausage of yours right here and now. And no one would be the wiser. It's your decision. Do you want to get out of here, or is it kielbasa time?"

A shocked Pike yelled into his cufflink.

"Did you get that, Charlie?"

"Holy shit, yes!" yelled Charlie from the walkie talkie in Pike's pocket.

He grabbed Gina's left wrist.

"I'm Sergeant Stanley Pike, Boston Police East Vice Division, and you are under arrest. That was that most lurid, disgusting come-on I have heard in my fifteen years in Vice."

"Come-on? What the hell are you talking about, come-on?" demanded Gina, confused.

"You have the right to remain silent..."

Gina was a ball of burning fury. Her eyes searched the bar for Frank. No such luck.

"Frank! Frank!" she screamed as she saw Kukla, Fran, and Ollie standing in line at the threshold of boarding gate number five.

The flight was called over the loudspeaker.

"Final boarding for flight 547, Boston to Los Angeles. Express, gate five, final call."

Frank waved to Gina as he, Carlo and Muncie disappeared into the boarding corridor. Pike finished reading Gina her rights, but she could've cared less. All she wanted to do right now was play ping-pong with Frank's eyeballs. How the hell was she going to get out of here? Think, she kept telling herself, but she was beyond thought.

"…do you understand the rights I have read to you?" asked Pike.

"Fuck you, yes!" Gina bellowed, then went ballistic.

She kneed Pike in the groin and elbowed him in the chest. He went down like a sack of potatoes. Gina ran past the crowd gathered at gate number five and into the main terminal hallway. Spying a security checkpoint further down the hall, she ducked into the next nearest boarding corridor, gate seven. As she ran down the end of the long tube, the attached plane sealed its hatch shut. Cut off, she began pounding on the door furiously. The plane pulled away, leaving her with two options: capture, or a twenty foot drop onto hard pavement. Pike ran up behind her. Ten airport security guards followed.

"That's one count of solicitation, and one count of assaulting a police officer. You want to try for another?" taunted Pike, enraged.

Gina backed herself to the end of the tube. Behind her was the twenty foot drop. Boston Harbor shimmered in the distance.

"Don't push me buddy. I'll fuck you blue."

In spite of himself, Pike licked his lips.

"I'll bet you would," he said, then lunged at her.

Gina side-stepped his attack. He flew off the edge, but managed to grab onto a handle on his way out.

He screamed at her. "For crissake, help me up!"

Gina leaned over the edge.

"Fuck off."

Airport security moved up and cuffed her from behind.

"Shit!" she screeched. She tried to bite one of the guards, but was restrained.

Security helped Pike up from the ledge.

"Make that two counts of assaulting a police officer!" he yelled in her face.

"Malvagie diavolo cornute, figlio di puttana!" she babbled back at him, eyes bulging.

The furious Gina was hustled off by security.

24

Santa Monica Storage had indeed burned down. It looked like three acres of scorched tin shacks. The front few units of the self-storage facility stood intact, but the rest had been badly damaged by the fire. Most of the pre-fab tin sheds were left barely standing, their metallic structures buckled and warped by the heat. All were heavily charred.

"Hey, this would be a great place to hide a body," Stu said as they pulled into the blackened facility.

"You're a sick one," said Quinton.

They jumped out of Stu's lime-yellow '68 GTO convertible and walked past the unburned storage units, into the charred jungle of burned shacks and scorched palm trees. The dusty mid-afternoon sun beat down as they surveyed the ruins before them.

"What a mess," said Stu. "Which locker is it?"

Quinton looked at the key.

"Forty-two," he replied. Stu peered at the barely-legible numbers stenciled on the row of units in front of him. Quinton searched the row behind them.

"It's probably in the fourth row, down here," Stu said as he moved away.

Quinton followed. They weaved through the maze of blackened pre-fab and vegetation.

Several of the units in the fourth row appeared to have been sheltered from the more extensive damage and were left somewhat intact. Quinton and Stu passed unit forty-four, then another, then stopped.

"This must be it," Quinton said as he bent down to wipe the soot off the number plate. "Number forty-two."

Quinton stood up and looked at Stu. The sun blinded him momentarily. He squinted, then held his hand up to shield his eyes.

"Okay, pop the lock, buddy," he heard Stu say.

Quinton looked down and readied the key. The suspense was killing him.

"Any last minute guesses?" he asked.

"Uh, the back seat of your old '75 Buick? The Passion Wagon?" ventured Stu.

"Think so?" Quinton asked.

"No," Stu replied. "Not gauche enough."

"Ha ha. Here goes."

Quinton inserted the key and turned. The lock clicked open.

"We have ignition," he said. He grabbed the soot-stained handle and yanked up on the door.

The door slid up to reveal a large storage unit, jam-packed to the ceiling with every kind of lawn ornament imaginable. The two men stared at the bizarre finding. Scores of pink flamingos, garden gnomes, gazing balls, and birdhouses sat in silence, covered by a thin layer of ash. Some of the ornaments had perished or been badly damaged by the flames, but most were left untouched.

Quinton looked confused. Stu, hit by a sudden realization, stood bolt upright.

"Sweet Sally Christmas, Quinton."

"What?"

"What the hell did you do?"

Quinton became agitated. How many fixations did he have?

"What, do I collect this stuff or something?" Quinton asked anxiously.

Stu walked over to a garden gnome. He dusted the ash from its elfin face.

"This is the one from rush week, isn't it? That was ten years ago. And these..."

He moved over to a family of half-melted pink flamingos.

"...these are the ones..."

"These are the ones that what?" asked Quinton.

Stu stared at him like he was a complete stranger.

"You don't remember, do you?"

"No, I don't remember! If I don't remember anything else, what makes you think I'd remember this? What is all this?" Quinton pleaded.

Stu walked past him, out of the unit. He took a deep breath and sat on the blackened ground outside.

"We lifted the gnome on a frat dare, from one of the professors' houses. Me, you, and...well, it was ten years ago, and you wouldn't remember him anyway."

Quinton stood next to him.

"What about the flamingos?" he asked.

"We were out drinking sophomore year, missed the bus, and had to crawl home. Went as the crow flies, over fences and through people's yards. We came up on them and you just had to have 'em."

"Why?" asked Quinton.

"You said the weirdest thing. Something about how you

needed them, how it was like stealing a piece of family. You never had a lawn of your own. Always went from foster family to foster family... And senior year you asked me if I'd help you snatch the lawn bunny at Dean Witherspoon's house. I thought you were just joking, but I guess you weren't, because there it is."

Stu pointed to a large, scorched ceramic English hare poised inside the storage unit. Quinton could hardly believe his ears.

"It used to be green and purple," Stu continued. "Like the Wimbledon colors. Witherspoon was so Brit-whipped. Jesus, Q, where did you get all this stuff...when?!...I'm speechless. You're pathological. There must be sixty lawn ornaments in there. And all those birdhouses. Why birdhouses?"

"I don't know."

"Man," Stu replied.

Quinton sat down next to him.

"I lived with foster families?"

"Yeah."

"How many?" Quinton asked. He was desperate for information about this person he was beginning to feel he had simply stepped into, like a suit of clothes.

"A lot. I don't know. You only mentioned it that one time. When you were drunk. Oh, and one other time."

"What other time?"

"When Emily was pregnant."

"That explains the Winnie-the-Pooh wallpaper," said Quinton.

"Yeah. And the Flintstones cup. I can't believe you used it."

"I'm sorry. I had no idea."

"I know," Stu sighed. He took a deep breath. "It was senior year in college and I didn't want to be tied down.

You and me had always talked about bumming around the Aussie outback, and I was just going to take off. You said no way. The kid shouldn't have to grow up without a father. You told me to grow up too. I couldn't believe it. It was so unlike you. Anyway, we got married, but Em lost the baby."

"I'm sorry to hear it," offered Quinton.

"Nah. We'll have another one someday when we're ready. Besides, marrying her was the best thing I ever did."

"So that's why Em never hated me."

"Yeah."

"Weird."

"I know. But not as weird as this storage locker. What are you going to do with all this stuff?"

Quinton stared blankly into the burnt void.

"How about we just finish the torch job," Quinton suggested. Stu smiled.

"I have some lighter fluid in the trunk, we could build a bonfire," Stu elaborated.

"Let's get to it, dude."

Gina sat alone in her cell inside the East Boston Police Station. She picked nervously at her manicured nails. Her anxiety was relentless. She jiggled her forearm and listened for that familiar sound, but it wasn't there. She got up and went to the bars of her cell.

"Hey," she yelled at the guard. "Where are my goddam bangles?"

The drunken man in the cell across from her woke up. She continued.

"I want my tortoise-shell bangles! And guard! I want to try that number again!" she screamed.

"What do you do with the bangles?" asked the drunk.

She looked him up and down. Buster Brown's, gray polyester pants, a matching corduroy suit jacket, and disheveled red power tie. Obviously a toasted conventioneer, she thought to herself.

"Eat your weasel," Gina barked back.

The drunk was persistent.

"Hey, honey, I'm over at the Marriott. How 'bout a poke after we get out of here?"

"How about I put your dick in a breast pump, you fucking soak."

"What kind of attitude is that from a pro? I got money. I hear you're one of those dominatrix, aren't you? Huh?" He leered at her. "Huh, hon? Can you pierce me a nipple ring?"

"Come closer. Let me get a good look at you."

He moved to his cell bars and put his face between two of them. Slowly, Gina removed one of her red suede pumps, and twirled it lasciviously around on her finger. She licked her lips. The conventioneer's mouth opened. She hurled the shoe at him. It hit him in the forehead dead on, and he fell to the floor, unconscious. Gina smiled ruefully, then continued to pace around her cell. Her smile soon turned back to an angry scowl.

"Frank, you fucking fuck. You frigging coglione."

She threw her other shoe at the wall in frustration. Exhausted, she sat down on the bed again. A tear fell from her eye. More tears came. As she rocked back and forth she whispered to herself.

"Michael. Oh my God, Michael..." she began to weep softly.

A guard came down the hallway and stopped at her cell. She composed herself immediately.

"The chief says you can try that number again."

He unlocked her cell and hustled the barefoot Gina to a pay phone. She dialed a number. Her eyes widened as someone picked up on the other end.

"Uncle Victor!" she yelled into the receiver.

25

Quinton stared blankly at the seeding chart for the Miller Lite Long Beach Co-Ed Challenge. He couldn't figure out what was going on for the life of him. A large number twenty-six was pinned to his teal-colored t-shirt. Stu walked up to him, amused. He wore a number eight tucked into the rim of his Victory visor.

"Dude, I can't believe you placed for today," said Stu.

Quinton turned to him.

"Thanks. Thanks a lot."

"No. I'm serious. Quarterfinals. I'm impressed."

Quinton caught a glimpse of Holly walking towards them in her sunglasses. She also wore a number twenty-six pinned to her coral blue t-shirt.

"It just goes to show what a couple weeks with a good coach can get you."

Quinton's eyes didn't leave Holly. Stu looked him up and down.

"Man, you? Not you…"

"What?"

"Quinton Squid, in love," Stu said, incredulous.

"I am not. With who?"

"Who do you think? You'd better find a bib before that twenty-six you're wearing gets all soggy."

"Oh, blow me."

"Eat ball."

"Eat ball back."

"Quinton's in love," Stu insisted, a wry smile covering his face.

"I am not," insisted Quinton.

"Or at least seriously infatuated," Stu egged him on.

Quinton smiled.

"Okay, I'll cop to that."

Holly and Emily sidled up to them. Emily's tank top sported a number eight as well. Stu gave Emily a kiss, then looked over at Quinton. Quinton gave him a dirty look.

"I think I found our competition," Holly told Quinton.

Quinton pointed at Stu and Emily, aghast.

"These two?"

"Yep," confirmed Emily.

Stu laughed and looked at Holly.

"You'd better dump him as a partner. He can't even read a stupid seeding chart."

"You forget, Stu," Emily added, "he couldn't read one before the accident either."

Everyone laughed except Quinton.

"Ha ha. I'm ready to whip your butts," he challenged. "I still have some of that butane in my nostrils, Stu, and I'm gonna flame you."

"I don't think so," Stu said with his usual bravado.

Quinton shook his head and grinned.

"You can bet on it."

Gazing at center court, the audience eagerly awaited the

beginning of the next match. The crowd cheered as an official walked up to the podium. He began to speak through the P.A. system.

"Up next in this Miller Lite Co-Ed Challenge are the husband and wife team of Stu Gardner and Emily Roeg, playing against his partner Quinton Squid and women's number one player Holly O'Connor."

The official nodded to the referee standing on the platform.

"Gardner to serve," the ref said and tossed the volleyball to Stu.

Stu caught the ball and put out his hand to Quinton across the net.

"I'll take it easy on you, Q."

Quinton shook his hand and smiled.

"I wouldn't do that."

"Talk, talk, talk," Stu chuckled as he walked back to the serve line.

Stu served a floater deep court. Quinton easily got under the ball and bumped it. Holly received his bump and set him at the net. Quinton approached the ball with a loud banshee cry. He attacked and cocked his arm, appearing to go for the kill, but instead lightly dinked it past Stu's block. It hit the sand. Sideout. Quinton laughed at Stu's astonished face. Stu couldn't help but laugh as well.

"You loser. You total loser," he chided Quinton.

But the referee was quick to chime in.

"Sideout. Squid to serve."

Quinton turned to Stu.

"Angulated, man. You were angulated. Ha!" he said gleefully.

Stu tossed Quinton the ball. When Quinton caught it,

he searched his court for Holly's gaze. Their eyes locked. She smiled at him. He smiled back. She looked better every day.

An hour later found the quartet huffing and puffing in the middle of play. Holly hammered the ball down the pipe, between Stu and Emily. Stu lurched for the dig. He got it and passed the ball to Emily.

"I'm up!" he yelled to her as he stood up from the sand.

Emily set the ball right on top of the net. She saw Quinton go up for the block.

"On! Right on! He's up!" she yelled to her husband.

Stu lurched forward and attacked the ball. It hit Quinton's block but glanced off his arm and back into he and Holly's court.

"One!" Quinton yelled to Holly, letting her know it had touched him.

Holly dug the ball, barely popping it up.

"Two!" she yelled to Quinton.

They had one hit left. Quinton stood right under the ball. He opted to go for the rainbow shot.

"Three!" he yelled to Holly.

Quinton's ball arced beautifully over the net. It reached Emily, who passed it to Stu. Across the net, Stu saw Holly jockey for the block, so he set Emily for a cross-court slam.

"She's up! Cross-court kill!" he yelled.

Emily slammed the ball diagonally past Holly's block. It headed for the left back corner like a cannonball. Quinton was in the far right of his court, a good twenty feet from where the ball would hit sand. Without hesitation, he lurched left for the dig. He sailed through the air with his arms outstretched.

For a moment it seemed as though he would miraculously hit ground just in time to pop up the dig, but the ball was lifted by a sudden gust of wind, out of his arms' reach. In mid air he contorted his body to an upside-down position. Quinton hit the ball with a sweeping roundhouse kick from his right foot. The ball flew over the net, just grazing the left antenna, and landed in the opposite court, right in between a dumbfounded Stu and Emily. The crowd was hypnotized with disbelief. A shocked referee began to stutter.

"Th-th-that was an incredible dig, Mr. Squid...but it's still a fault. The ball is out, antenna. Point, game and match to Gardner and Roeg."

Stu stared over at his best friend and partner across the net.

"Quinton, what the fuck?"

Quinton lay back on the sand with his eyes closed, laughing uncontrollably.

Two hours later Stu still hadn't gotten the explanation he'd wanted. The foursome sat in Quinton's hot tub drinking Stu and Emily's Miller Lite winnings. Professional beach volleyball was not without its perks.

"Dude, I can't believe what I saw today. It was the most bizarre thing I've ever seen on the beach. And I've seen some bizarre shit," said Stu.

Quinton turned to him suddenly.

"Did I ever study any martial arts?" he asked.

With the straightest face he could muster, Stu answered. "Well, I think you studied the Kama Sutra..."

"Ha ha," said Quinton. Everyone chuckled.

"And practiced diligently on the Bikini Twins next door," Stu added.

Quinton splashed him with water. "Dick."

"Hey, I couldn't have seen the ride if you hadn't turned on the camera," Stu said, raising his eyebrows.

Quinton looked at him in disbelief.

"Bullshit. I would never do something like that."

Stu shook his head and grinned knowingly.

"I've still got the videotape. You certainly are a sight in the sack, old buddy. Muscles flexing. Amazing. Brad Pitt has nothing on you."

"He's screwing with your head," said Emily. "You were just such a prick before the accident he used to look decent next to you."

"Yeah, Quint. What did you do? Read a book by Marianne Williamson?" asked Stu.

Holly laughed.

"No. Just watched a lot of Oprah in the hospital," Quinton ribbed.

Emily turned to him.

"Holly showed me a little of what you did on the beach the other day. At least what she could imitate. What you did looks like Tai Chi to me," she said. "That would explain the breathing thing, too."

"Tai what?" asked Quinton.

"Tai Chi."

"Do some for us now," asked Stu.

"I can't. It just hits me in a wave. It's weird," Quinton explained.

"It's probably part of what's blocked in your memory," said Holly.

"But why would I have kept it a secret?" Quinton asked.

"Tai Chi is like a moving meditation," explained Emily. "It's generally viewed as something that's defensive, as opposed to offensive. Maybe you didn't want people to know you weren't always so *offensive*."

Everyone but Quinton found this amusing.

"How do you know all this?" Quinton asked Emily. "Did you study it, too?"

"No, not with a master per se, just book knowledge from teaching."

Quinton's eyes became fascinated with the jacuzzi's resurfacing bubbles.

"So," he said, staring at the bubbling water, "you're a teacher, Stu was a gardener, and Holly..."

He looked up from the water at her, smiling.

"...you're women's number one. You've probably been able to live off your endorsements for years now."

Emily laughed out loud. Beer flew out of her nose. Holly grinned at her. She couldn't help but laugh herself.

"Not exactly. Maybe now, but not a few years ago. Still, the men's and women's purses can't compare. I still keep up with the bar in case my rating slips. I'm a lawyer."

"No shit," Quinton said, intrigued.

Quinton looked at Emily, then back at Stu and Holly.

"Do I work?" he asked Emily.

"No. You get to live off your endorsements."

Stu was quick to chime in.

"Unless you start to fall below par in all your tourneys. The third seed is worth hundreds of thousands, but fifteen and twenty can't compare," he said.

"What about twenty-six?" asked Quinton.

Stu laughed. He shook his head.

"You'll be parking cars again. Or stealing lawn ornaments."

"Lawn ornaments?" Holly asked.

Emily laughed. Quinton glared at Stu.

"You told her?" Quinton asked.

"Told her what?" Holly asked.

Quinton took a deep breath.

"Well, you might as well know, too. My entire storage unit in Santa Monica was filled with stolen lawn ornaments and birdhouses. And don't even ask me why, because I have no clue whatsoever."

"Quinton," Holly said. "You certainly have gotten around in your life, haven't you."

"In more ways than one," added Emily. Quinton winced.

"I'm going to change the subject now...Everyone submerge. The first one up changes the kitty litter."

After some grumbling, they reluctantly took a deep breath and submerged underwater.

"Quinton, you really have to work on your breath control," Holly said, as she watched him change the litter box in the kitchen.

"How come Stu got his back so quickly?" Quinton asked.

"His injuries weren't as serious as yours."

Quinton shrugged. It seemed to make sense. The kitchen phone rang. Quinton was up to his elbows in kitty litter.

"I'll get it," said Holly.

She picked up the cordless phone.

"Hello...oh, hi...uh huh...just a second."

She held her hand over the mouthpiece.

"It's Ray from the DMV. I put this number on my machine in case my agent called. Hope that was okay."

"Of course," Quinton said. "Does he have something?"

"Yeah, he found a couple of Q. Davis' listed in southern California, but needs to know if there are any middle initials or anything else you might remember."

Quinton thought for a second. He kept his hands over the litter box.

"I don't know. I can't really think of anything."

"Where are those clippings? Maybe they have his height, or eye color. Something like that. Is there a picture?" she asked.

"Yeah. My hands are kind of a mess. The stuff is in the top drawer of my night table, to the left of the bed."

Holly put the phone back to her ear.

"Yeah, Ray. Hang on a second."

Holly went down the hall into the bedroom. She hit the lightswitch next to the door and the bedside table lamp came on. Quinton had nixed the lava lamp and all traces of Harry Connick Jr. Holly went to the table. Sitting on top was a micro-cassette recorder. She looked at it closely. It was voice activated.

She smiled and shook her head. She didn't know what he used it for. Maybe he would tell her someday – no, she didn't want to know. She opened the top drawer and took out the scrapbook. As she searched through the clippings, she came to the *Sports Illustrated* 'Remember When' article. She pulled it out and spoke into the phone.

"Hi, Ray...he's six-five, at least he was back in '64...I can't tell, it's a black and white picture...maybe dark brown hair and blue eyes. That's all I got...okay. Get back to me tomorrow if you can, or Tuesday. Appreciate it, doll. Bye."

She hung up the phone and flipped through more of the scrapbook clippings, but her eye kept wandering back to the cassette recorder. Curiosity got the best of her. She glanced back towards the kitchen, and rewound the tape for an instant. Careful to keep the volume low, she pressed play. Suddenly, she heard the recorded sounds of Quinton screaming in the middle of the night.

"No! No! Mom! Dad! NO!" he screamed through the tape recorder. She was momentarily wary of what she could be listening to. When the screaming was over she heard the sounds of labored breathing and mumbling as Quinton gasped upwards towards consciousness. As he woke, he began to address the tape recorder directly.

"Um, same thing. There's a new car, explosions, my mother and father are in the car. I don't know. It's the same thing. The same thing..." his raspy voice trailed off.

The recording ended with a loud click as the recorder's head stopped cold automatically. Holly put the recorder down. All was quiet. She looked toward the open doorway of the bedroom. Quinton was standing over her.

"What are you listening to?" he asked.

Holly didn't know what to say.

"I'm sorry, I was just –"

"Never mind. Just put it back in the drawer," he snapped.

"What was that?" she asked.

"Nothing. Just put it back in the drawer," he said sternly. She picked up the recorder.

"Do you have dreams like that a lot?"

"Look. I said forget it," he insisted, but she was persistent.

"You scream yourself awake sometimes, don't you?"

Quinton stared at her coldly. He didn't answer.

"You scare yourself so much you wake up. Don't you. What are you so afraid of?"

"I don't know."

"Quinton..."

"What?"

"There's something inside you that doesn't want to come out."

"What are you talking about?" he barked. He was starting to get irritated.

"Or there's something in there that doesn't want to let all of you come back out," she said.

He walked over to her and snatched the recorder from her hands.

"Enough of the psycho-babble, okay? You sound like –"

He didn't finish his sentence. She pried.

"Like who?" she asked.

"Like no one," he said, shoving the recorder into the drawer.

"Who, Quinton?" she insisted. She wanted so much to help him.

He so desperately wanted to confide in her.

He stared into her eyes. He wanted to trust her, but was still so afraid. She knew he must be in a hellish place, as she looked back into his tearful, frightened eyes.

"Dr. Collins," he said finally.

"The one in Boston?" she asked.

"Yeah. I started having the dreams a few weeks ago. He told me to keep a voice-activated tape recorder by my bed, so if I started saying something in my sleep I'd have a record of it. And to play it back for myself when I'm awake, to see if it triggers any memories."

She nodded. "That's a good idea."

"Yeah, well. It hasn't worked so far. All I have is this one piece of something that doesn't make any sense."

He sat down on the bed next to her.

"What do you mean?" she asked him. She stroked his back comfortingly. He didn't pull away.

His palms were beginning to sweat. He wiped them on the bedspread.

"It doesn't make sense at all. I'm much shorter than I am now, lower to the ground. What I see around me looks bigger, so I assume it must be when I was little. And there's this shiny new Cadillac convertible in a driveway. My mom and dad are sitting in it. I know they're my parents, but I can't remember their faces. There's something about it being a present from my Uncle Victor. When my dad turns the key, it explodes. A piece of metal comes flying towards me, and it hits the little boy in front of me. I don't know what it means."

"What does Dr. Collins say?"

"He thinks it's just, uh, what did he say? That my subconscious is trying to figure out what happened to me. To make sense of it all. My brain keeps giving out these displaced, fabricated memories because I can't remember who I am. Because my memory was taken away in the plane crash, my subconscious is trying to verify to my conscious mind that I never existed. That my parents were killed."

"Then how come you're standing there as a little boy watching them blow up?"

"I don't know. We haven't figured that part out yet."

"Do you have an Uncle Victor?"

"No. My father was an only child."

"Your mother?"

"Nope. Her too."

"Do you know anyone named Victor?" she asked.

Quinton shook his head.

"No."

"Victory Beachwear. They sponsor you," she said.

"No. That's Stu's."

Holly picked up the passport in the drawer. She opened it and looked inside.

"Who is Michael Delaney?" she asked.

"I honestly don't know."

"Then why do you have his passport?"

"I don't know. Somebody left it here."

"Who?" she asked.

"A burglar."

She looked up at Quinton, wide-eyed.

"A burglar?" she said.

"Well, it wasn't his passport. He didn't look like that."

Holly's forehead crinkled in confusion.

"Then whose passport is it?"

"I don't know. I guess it's this Delaney guy's. But the burglar said that I was him. That I was Michael."

Holly took a deep breath.

"This is getting weird, Quinton. I need some air."

She went to the sliding glass doors and out onto the deck.

"My life is the freaking Twilight Zone..." Quinton mumbled to himself.

He went into the bathroom and splashed water on his face.

Holly stood outside on the deck gazing at the moon. She thought about Quinton Squid. About what it must be like to know of no past. Especially if you were him. With his past. In all her travels, pro volleyball and legal practice alike, she could not recall coming into contact with someone in such a strange predicament. Common sense told her to run screaming from a man with such troubles.

But there was something about him. Something that seemed to click with something inside of her. He seemed so sweet underneath, so kind. Beautifully, legitimately so. And he was the sexiest man on the beach, to boot. Handsome and noble. He has no past, her heart told her, just potential.

Inside, Quinton toweled off and looked in the mirror. He couldn't help but stare again into his own eyes, still searching for hidden answers. He thought of Holly standing on the porch. He had fallen for her, hard. She's probably thinking up an excuse to get out of here, he thought. She must think I'm nuts. He pulled his eyes away from the mirror. No answers were going to be found tonight.

Sheba snuck through the open screen door and stood next

to Holly on the deck. Holly picked her up and stroked her dark silken fur. Quinton came out behind her. The sea breeze blew through their hair. He handed Holly a t-shirt to put over her bathing suit and goose-pimpled arms.

"Thanks," she said, and handed the cat to him.

Quinton took her gently. Holly watched as his eyes met Sheba's and lit up immediately.

"She's a beautiful cat," Holly said, warmer now.

Quinton smiled.

"And don't think she doesn't know it."

Holly reached over and scratched Sheba behind the ears. She purred rapturously. Holly looked at Quinton fondly.

"Most guys have dogs."

"I like dogs, but they don't really hit me. To me, cats are almost more than human. Sometimes you can look into a cat's eyes and see the 'moment that is everything.'"

"What's that?" Holly asked.

Quinton looked out at the ocean for a moment, then spoke.

"The idea that past, present, and future all happen at one instantaneous moment, but our minds divide it up into what we think of as time."

"Been watching a lot of *Nova* lately?" she asked. Who was this man, she wondered. He had really piqued her curiosity.

Quinton laughed. He put the cat inside and closed the screen door. He took in a long deep breath and stared out at the ocean.

"God, I love the nighttime air."

He pointed at the luminescent full moon high above. It reflected off the ocean.

"I think that's the Volley God too," he said.

"The sun and the moon?" Holly asked.

"Why not? It's nice to have two parents watching out for you."

Holly studied him for a moment. She smiled to herself.

"You know, you're not at all what I thought you'd be."

Quinton smiled.

"Why? What did you think I'd be like?"

"You don't want to know," Holly said.

"So what am I like," he asked.

"I haven't figured it all out yet."

"Tell me one thing you have figured out."

She looked up at him. Her five foot, nine inch frame was a good seven inches shorter than his. She could feel the warmth of his body next to hers.

"You're too tall," she finally said. She looked up at him invitingly.

Quinton bent down on his knees so that his head was below hers. He looked up at her, with a mischievous grin.

"Now you're too tall," he said to her.

She matched his smile and got down on her knees. Their shoulders were almost square. They looked into each other's eyes. Each could feel their resistance slipping away.

"Now we're relatively the same height," Holly said.

"I like this perspective," said Quinton. He felt the warmth of the energy between them.

"So do I," said Holly. As she stared into his serene eyes, a sense of peace began to overtake her.

They leaned toward each other slowly, as if drawn together. They kissed. They kissed again, then stopped.

"I've got to stand up," said Holly. She stood. She put a hand out to him. "We have to protect the knees," she said with a smile.

"You're right," he agreed, and allowed himself to be drawn upward by her.

They faced each other.

"But now I'm too tall again," Quinton said, basking in the warm glow of her eyes.

"You won't be if we're lying down," said Holly.

She led Quinton into his bedroom and closed the screen door behind them. They lay down slowly on the bed. They kissed, hands wandering over each other's bodies. They kissed some more. Their peaceful intimacy gave way to something more raw, more immediate. More hungry. Holly's t-shirt was tossed across the room. Bathing suits came off and fell to the floor. Suddenly, Quinton stopped.

He pulled back and sat up. He looked at her in confusion, mild panic playing over his face. Holly was perplexed.

"What's the matter?" she asked, stroking his calve.

He flopped down on his back, next to her. He looked up at the ceiling. They admired each other's moonlit forms in the mirror above.

"I don't know if I can do this," he said finally.

"Why? Did you have too much to drink?" she asked.

"No. I literally mean I don't know if I can do this."

It began to dawn on Holly. She tried to hide her smile.

"Oh, you mean…"

Quinton rolled his eyes.

"Yeah. I don't remember ever doing this before."

"Oh. This is interesting," Holly giggled.

"Don't laugh. This is not a laughing matter," he pleaded.

Holly slid on top of him.

"No. You're right. It's not a laughing matter. I apologize."

"Thank you."

"You mean," she reiterated playfully, "you don't remember ever doing this before."

Embarrassment played over Quinton's face. She held his hands. He could feel the warmth of her body over his.

"No," he confessed.

"Are you telling me the truth?" she asked.

"Is this something I would lie about?"

"No. I guess not. Okay. So. You're a virgin."

"There is no way I could be a virgin."

"No, no. I mean, at least up in your head. Do realize how many people would give their eye teeth for the chance to be a virgin again?" she said. She started to kiss his neck.

"Yeah. I guess you're right. I guess it would be okay."

"I'm not pressuring you am I?"

She kissed him full on the mouth then slid her way slowly to his ear.

"No. Not at all," said Quinton.

Holly switched off the lamp. They kissed a while longer. After a few seconds Quinton said, "I think I'm starting to get the hang of this."

"I think you are too."

"Just remember coach, you don't always get to be on top."

"Yes, sir."

26

In the middle of the night, the sleeping forms of Holly and Quinton seemed peaceful and at rest, but the stillness was deceiving. A volcano erupted deep below Quinton's surface. Desperate questions lay siege to his consciousness, like fireballs hurling at him from all sides. Through fragmented images, his mind struggled to come to grips with the reality of his situation.

Quinton's eyes twitched feverishly with REM sleep. Behind his eyes, he dreamt through those of a child. In the dream, the child saw Phillip Delaney looming over his head. He dangled a single, shield-shaped key in front of the boy. Mr. Delaney spoke.

"Look what Uncle Victor gave us," he said.

The boy's gaze shifted to the key hanging in front of his face. Inscribed just below the engraved coat of arms was the word 'Cadillac.'

The boy smiled. Pleased, he shifted his gaze back to the man holding the keys. But Phillip Delaney had vanished. This time the face looming above was that of the senior Quinton Davis. Panic seized the child as the stranger spoke to him.

"Look what Uncle Victor gave us," said Davis.

The boy threw his eyes shut only to find himself back in his driveway. Frantic, he looked to the top of the driveway for the Cadillac, trying to catch a glimpse of his real father. But it was too late. As his eyes reached his father's, the car exploded. Horrified, the child closed his eyes as the metal bumper hurtled toward him.

When the dreamer's eyes opened again, he found himself as Quinton the man, standing as the groom at the altar of a large Italian wedding.

The bride stood next to him, her face covered in a veil of white lace. All was quiet in the church. The dreamer hesitated. He looked at his best man. It was Michael Delaney. Looking into his eyes, Michael handed the groom the wedding ring and nodded. The couple silently placed rings on each other's fingers. The priest spoke.

"I now pronounce you husband and wife. You may kiss the bride."

The dreamer lifted the veil to kiss his bride. She was a stunning woman of Italian descent. But with the veil removed, Gina looked at him like the complete stranger he was. She gasped.

"You're not Michael!"

She turned to the best man standing beside him. "You are!" she screamed.

Michael Delaney looked at the dreamer, then turned and ran out of the church. Gina tried to run after him, but was unable to move. She watched him go, then turned back to her groom with a vengeance.

"Then I guess you'll have to do."

She readied her lips for a kiss. He leaned forward, but suddenly Gina's beautiful face turned into the ancient, creviced face of Nana Rosetta. He stepped away.

The dreamer was thrown back to Michael's childhood home. The young Frank and Michael stood at the end of his driveway.

"Ask your old man. He knows a lot about bugs," Frank said. Michael again heard the sound of an explosion. The bumper smashed into Frank's head.

The man struggling behind rapid eye movement was thrown into another, parallel reality. A severely burned Michael sat slumped in Nick's passenger seat clutching his dead cat. Nick rushed through traffic, playing connect-the-dots with passing hospital signs. He looked over at the barely conscious Michael.

"You're gonna be okay."

Michael fell unconscious.

The dreamer floated freely in empty space. As he opened his eyes, something appeared in the distant blackness. Something on fire. He began to hurtle toward it. It was a wall of orange flame, a portal of some kind. Something he hadn't seen in quite a while.

He flew through the flames. The blaze cleared to reveal another wall, this one made of brick. The dreamer flew toward it. As he neared the wall, he threw his arms up to shield himself from the impact. The textured pattern of the brick wall dissolved into a clear blackness.

Suddenly, the dreamer shattered through an invisible pane of glass. Broken shards reflected the orange flames receding in the distance behind him.

Without warning, he felt himself hit a large body of water with a splash. Under the water, moonlight shone down from above, illuminating the dark blue liquid. The coldness of the water seeped into him. In the distance he could see the ghostly form of a man floating supine in the water. It was Michael

Delaney. His eyes were closed, his face passive. Was he dead, or just asleep? The mirage faded.

The dreamer panicked. He tried to take a breath, but water filled his lungs. He began to scream, but water muffled the sound. His panic increased as he paddled frantically towards the source of moonlight.

After a few desperate moments, he broke the surface. He found himself in the midst of a pitch-black ocean, with no land in sight. A full moon provided the only illumination. He felt only fear. He continued to scream.

Quinton sat up in bed suddenly. His eyes darted about the room. He was in his bedroom. Good. He knew where he was. He hoped he knew who he was. He looked beside him. Holly stirred.

"What's the matter?" she asked, half asleep.

"Nothing," whispered Quinton. "Go back to sleep. Just got up to get a glass of water."

Holly rolled back over and fell asleep. Quinton stood up. He ran his fingers through sweat-soaked hair. He grabbed his bathrobe and put it on, went over to the glass doors, and out onto the deck.

It was still dark out. He knelt in front of the hot tub and dunked his head inside. After a moment he got up and shook his head dry like a dog. Quinton went down the deck stairs to the beach. He walked toward the water. He didn't notice the man following close behind him. By the time the stalker jammed a gun in his back it was too late.

"Don't turn around," Nick Avanti whispered loudly. "This ain't my dick you're feeling."

Quinton's vision became a purple haze. The ocean before him was replaced by the lobby of the Callabrisi office building. Nick threatened one of the Callabrisi's watchmen at gun point.

"Don't move. This ain't my dick you're feeling," Nick ordered.

Quinton's vision dissolved back to the Pacific Ocean. His eyes opened wide. He quickly turned around and looked at Nick. The look on Quinton's face was almost one of recognition.

"You must be the guy," Quinton said feverishly.

"I told you not to turn around."

"But you must be the guy."

"What are you talking about? Do you remember me, Michael?"

Quinton's voice began to raise in hysteria.

"Yeah. Yeah...You must be the guy that got hit with the bumper. You're the other guy!"

"Got hit with the what?" asked Nick.

"The bumper. After the explosion. When the car blew up," Quinton said, frenzied.

"Shh. Quiet. Shut up. Michael, will you shut the f–"

Quinton heard a thump. Nick's eyes widened and glazed over. He slumped to the ground unconscious. Holly stood behind him wielding the Louisville Slugger. Quinton jumped up and down excitedly.

"That was the guy! You hit the guy!" he screamed.

"Quinton. Calm down. What guy?" Holly asked.

"The robber guy."

"This is the robber?"

"Yeah. That's him. He left me the passport."

Quinton bent to the ground and picked up Nick's gun. He emptied the bullets onto the beach.

"Why would he come back?" asked Holly.

"My collar. He wants the cat collar."

"You're not making any sense. Why would he want the cat's collar?"

"Because it's made of diamonds. It's worth small fortune."

"What? You let the cat out all the time. Why wouldn't he just grab it?" reasoned Holly.

"I don't know. I just don't know," Quinton said, confused.

"This doesn't make any sense. Why would he give you a passport?"

"I don't know."

Quinton stared down at Nick's face.

"Why is he in my dreams..." he mumbled.

"He's in your dreams?" asked Holly.

The tumblers in Quinton's mind were desperately trying to fall into place. Progress had been made, but there was still such a long way to go.

He was struck by an idea.

"Don't call the police yet."

● ● ●

The morning sun broke out over the dunes. Nick lay on the beach near the edge of the water. Holly was nowhere to be seen. Quinton sat on the ground with his knees to his chest, pointing the gun at Nick. Nick lay belly down, unconscious, hands tied behind his back, stretched out on the sand. His feet pointed toward the dunes, his head faced the ocean. As the tide came in, waves crept ever closer to his face. Quinton looked on as the first wave reached Nick. Its icy foam slapped him hard across the face. He didn't wake.

The water fell back to the ocean. After a tidal beat it came up again and slapped Nick a second time. This woke him. He spit out salt water and turned over on his back. With a little wavering he managed to turn on his side, facing Quinton.

"Michael, what the hell are you doing?" he screamed.

Quinton was not in the mood to be fucked with. He flashed the gun at Nick.

"Shut up. Stay down. This ain't my dick in my hands," said Quinton.

"Oh, great. Now he thinks he's Cagney. Wake up, Michael. This ain't *White Heat*."

"Just shut up!" Quinton barked.

Another wave hit Nick.

"Holy shit, that hurts. You hit me twice with a baseball bat."

"I only hit you once. Holly hit you the other time."

"Mother of God, she's strong. I can see why she's number one."

"How do you know she's the number one player?" asked Quinton.

"I've been following your guinea wop ass everywhere. Don't you know when you're being shadowed?"

Another wave hit Nick.

"Ow! That salt hurts right where she whacked me. You know, last time you hit me I had to get six stitches," complained Nick.

"Can it!" Quinton screamed.

"Six fucking stitches!" Nick roared back.

"Why are you here?" demanded Quinton.

"I already told you, Gina and Frank –"

Another wave went over his head. The tide was rising, and this time Nick spent a few seconds under water. The wave finally rolled back into the sea.

"I think you should change your answer real fast," said Quinton. "Tide's changing, and you don't have gills,"

"Michael, I told you. I think Frank and Gina are coming to get you."

"I don't like that answer. I don't know Michael and I don't know them."

"Yes you –"

The next wave came up fast. It covered Nick entirely, then fell back to the ocean. Nick took a deep breath.

"This is your last chance," said Quinton.

"All I can give you is the truth. Cut me loose and I'll –"

"Not good enough! Who are you?" insisted Quinton.

Nick saw another wave coming towards him. He looked to Quinton, pleading.

"Michael, no! Stop!"

Nick's eyes were drawn suddenly to the top of the dunes. He craned his neck upwards to make out a figure towering over them. The figure cast a dark shadow over the two men perched at the edge of the sea. His form was silhouetted in the early morning sun. Nick tried to sit up, but another wave crashed over him. Quinton kept the gun trained on Nick. He turned around to see what had captured Nick's attention.

High above, the face of the silhouetted figure became visible. It was Frank Russo. Cradled in his arms was a large Uzi.

"Well, Michael, Nick. You certainly made it easy for me this time. Stupid fucks," he sneered.

He cocked the gun and began to spray Quinton and Nick with gunfire. They fell backwards as the bullets entered them. Their cries, along with the thunder of machine gun fire, echoed down the empty beach.

Quinton screamed himself awake, this time for real. He found himself frenzied and in a cold sweat. "Frank! Oh my god!"

Holly was startled awake by his cries.

"What?" asked Holly.

Quinton began to laugh nervously.

"It was so real. Did you hit some guy over the head with a bat last night?"

Holly was dumbfounded.

"What? No. Who's Frank?"

"Frank?" Quinton was in his own little world. He was starting to forget.

"It was a dream. It must have been a dream. Or a flashback. I don't know."

"Are you okay?" asked Holly.

"Goddamn. More weird shit. Really weird. Fragments, flashbacks…"

"So what's in these flashbacks?"

Quinton hesitated.

"Trust me," she said. "Tell me what you saw."

"There's a bunch. Bits and pieces. The Cadillac convertible in the driveway. My mom and dad sitting in it. I still can't remember their faces. Again, something about it being a present from my Uncle Victor. Like before, my dad turns the key and it explodes, and this piece of metal flies towards me, but hits the boy in front of me.

"And then I'm in a church getting married and when I lift the veil to kiss the bride, there is this beautiful young woman who screams at me: 'But you're not Michael.' Then she turns into an old woman before my eyes."

Holly laughed out loud. Quinton looked at her.

"I'm so glad this amuses you."

"I'm sorry. It's just all so strange," she said, trying to compose herself.

"And my best man is…the guy in the passport!"

Quinton got up and started to search the room frantically. "Where's that passport thing?" he asked Holly.

"In the top drawer where I found it."

He opened the drawer of the bedside table. He found the passport and pulled it into the light.

"What is it?" she asked.

Quinton rushed to the bathroom. He went to the mirror and opened the passport to the page containing the picture.

He held the picture up to his reflection in the mirror, and the two images stood side by side: the face of Quinton Squid and the picture of Michael Delaney. He stared at them. Holly came up from behind.

"Is there anything alike here? Anything the same?" Quinton asked her.

She studied the two images carefully.

"No. That guy doesn't look much like you."

"I know. But look closely," he said.

Holly looked closer.

"Something around the eyes maybe."

Quinton smiled.

"Exactly. Around the eyes. Will you get that picture of my dad?"

Holly went to the bedside table and pulled the picture of the senior Quinton Davis from the scrapbook. She brought it back to Quinton. Continuing to hold the passport against the mirror, he took the picture of his father and held it up to the other side of his face.

"How about now? Anything?" he asked her.

Holly looked at the picture. She stared at it pensively.

"You have your father's nose and cheekbones, jaw and basic facial lines."

"How about the other guy?"

"Maybe a little similar. All the eyes look alike, I think. Especially you and the guy in the passport."

"I think so too. You think this guy could be my brother?"

"But you're an only child."

"I know. But doesn't he look enough like me and a little like my father? He could be a brother."

"Well, yeah, I guess so. But there's got to be a better –"

"So maybe that robber guy is looking for my brother, right? He kept talking about people coming after me or something."

"I suppose, but..."

"But what?" asked Quinton.

"A lost brother, don't you think that's pretty unlikely?"

"What else, then?"

"I don't know, maybe this burglar guy is some weird fan screwing with your mind – I mean, your own best friend's wife tried to convince you you'd had an affair with her."

"So why would I dream about it, why would this Michael guy be in my dreams?"

"If you hear something long enough you begin to believe it. The power of suggestion can be a merciless thing. Especially for someone who doesn't have a memory."

"Maybe, but I just have a hunch. These things feel more like memories than dreams. I need that DMV address from Raymond. I have to talk to my father. I have to find him and see if I have a brother, Michael. See if there are people after him. But why wouldn't we have the same last names?"

"Maybe your father had him with someone he didn't marry, or he was put up for adoption. I don't know."

"Yeah, okay. That makes sense."

Quinton continued to hold up the two pictures, staring compulsively into the mirror. He was still clinging to the idea of finding some way to make sense of it all. Some way that would not destroy the fragile framework of the Quinton Squid reality, a reality he had gone to such lengths to reconstruct.

"Quinton," said Holly.

Quinton didn't answer.

"Quinton," Holly said again.

But he was someplace far away.

She gently pulled his arms down from the mirror.

"Quinton. I think you need to calm down. Now. Okay?"

"Okay. I know. It was just a dream, but it was so real."

"I know. I'll talk to Raymond in the morning. He'll get you that address."

Quinton finally turned away from the mirror to face Holly.

"Thanks. I'm sorry," he said.

"What are you sorry for?" she asked.

"I guess I'm not screwed on all that tight these days. You're probably not getting what you expected, are you?"

Holly smiled.

"You're right. I'm not getting what I expected. And with that, I'm very pleased. Come on, Quinton, let's take a shower."

She put the pictures down on the sink.

"I thought you wanted to calm me down," he said.

Holly smiled mischievously.

"Well, what I have in mind is relaxing," she said, edging him over to the shower.

"Yeah?" he asked.

"Oh, yeah," she said.

"You got a date."

27

Quinton plowed down the 405 South in his powder blue '67 Mustang convertible. Over the radio Clapton borrowed Robert Johnson's 'Crossroads.' The song was a bit too apropos for comfort. Quinton changed the station. He let it rest on 'Midnight at the Oasis,' then settled back into his bucket seat.

Through the lenses of his tinted sunglasses, the world seemed to glow with a green iridescence. He lowered them to read the sunbaked overpass sign. San Diego, it said. One hundred miles.

He looked down at the Olympic photo of Quinton Davis sitting on his lap. Clipped to the photo was a piece of paper with an address scrawled on it: 'Quinton Davis, 22 Ocean View Way, San Diego.' He picked up the picture and address. Quinton folded them together and put them in his shirt pocket. He wore a laguna blue polo shirt and khaki shorts; not his usual beach attire. He glanced over at Quinton Davis' Olympic Gold Medal, lying on the passenger seat beside him. Its reflection of the sun vibrated in rhythm with the engine.

An hour and a half later, Quinton pulled up to a small, weather-beaten two-story building by the seashore. A sign above the first floor read: 'Davis Bait and Tackle.' Quinton let his eyes wander over the building and up to the second floor. Cream colored curtains framed the windows inside. They blew gently in the warm ocean breeze. The second floor looked like a private residence. Quinton got out of the car and went up to the door of the bait shop. He held the folded picture and address in his hands. He opened the door and went inside.

Quinton took off his shades and dropped them in his pocket. He looked around the shop. It was your standard bait and tackle. A young boy of eleven stood behind the counter. The counter looked like a salad bar. There were a dozen open tins, and even a sneeze guard covering the entire ensemble. On each tin lay a faded piece of masking tape. Written on the tape in a child's scrawl were the usual at any all-you-can-eat buffet; earthworms, night crawlers, centipedes, dragon flies, caterpillars. Quinton didn't need to read on, he got the picture.

In the back of the shop an older man stood on a ladder stacking various canned goods. Quinton moved over to him. To the left of the man was an open storage closet. Quinton glanced inside. He was amazed by what he saw. His jaw dropped to the floor. It couldn't be! But, oh my god, it was. Birdhouses. Dozens of them.

Quinton stood behind the ladder and looked up at the middle-aged man. After a few seconds the man became aware of someone staring at him. He looked down to see who it was. Quinton saw the man's face. It was not unlike the image in the faded photograph, but showed the weathering of many years' time. The man stared blankly at Quinton Squid.

"Can I help you?" he asked.

"Are you Quinton Davis?" Quinton asked, then looked away.

"Yes, I am. And who are you?" asked Davis.

"Can I see you outside for a minute?"

Davis looked down from his ladder.

"Why?"

"It may be a little easier that way," said Quinton.

"What would?" Davis asked.

Quinton looked up at the elder Quinton Davis. He stared into his eyes for a moment, then slowly walked out of the store. Davis wiped his hands with a rag from his pocket. He carefully climbed down the ladder and went to the boy behind the counter.

"Sam, hold things down for a second, will you?"

"Okay, Dad," said Sam.

Quinton Davis followed Quinton Squid outside. They walked to a fence post by the parking lot. They leaned on it and looked out at the ocean. Davis turned to Squid.

"What's this all about?" asked Davis.

"That boy in there called you dad."

"That's because he's my son."

"Do you have any other children?" he asked.

"Look, maybe you better tell me what this is all about."

"Do you have any other children?"

Davis looked at him, perplexed.

"Yeah. I have two daughters. But what's this about? Is someone in trouble?"

Quinton turned and looked him in the eye.

"My name is Quinton Squid."

"The volleyball player?" asked Davis.

"Yeah. The volleyball player."

"I thought you looked a little familiar."

"You watch a lot of volleyball?" asked Quinton.

Davis shook his head.

"No. Not really. Now and again, I suppose. But Sammy's into the beach stuff. I used to play myself a long time ago. Not beach though."

"Yeah. I know," said Quinton.

"I figured you would. How did you find me?"

"Wasn't that difficult."

"You don't appear to be at all angry with me."

"I'm not," said Quinton. "From what I've read about you I know I should be, but I'm not."

Davis looked down at the sand beneath his flip-flops.

"You wouldn't even talk to me seventeen years ago when I tried to get custody from the courts. You wanted to stay with your foster family, you said. There were only three times after that I ever tried to get in touch with you, but you never answered my letters."

"Well, it doesn't matter anymore," said Quinton.

"Why?" asked Davis, as he stared at the sand beneath Quinton's leather sandals.

"Because I don't remember you. I don't remember anything from before that plane crash I was in. I don't even remember me. I just came here to ask you some questions and fill in some gaps. To find out what's going on in my head."

Davis looked up at Squid.

"You don't remember me? You don't remember anything from before the crash?" he asked.

"No. I wish I could, but I can't."

Davis shook his head.

"Man…"

"What?" asked Quinton.

"I think I'd rather have you remember me and be mad as hell than not remember me at all."

Quinton smiled.

"Well, look at it this way, if you help me remember something that clicks on some light bulbs from my past, I may end up hating you after all."

"Very funny," said Davis. "You have your mother's sense of humor."

"I don't even remember her," said Quinton.

"Nothing?"

"Only what I've read."

"That's a shame," said Davis, gazing out at the brilliant blue ocean.

A woman leaned her head out of the bait shop's second-story window.

"Quinton?" she yelled.

Both Quintons Davis and Squid turned to look at the person calling them. She was an attractive woman in her late thirties.

"Quinton, I need some help with Elizabeth," she yelled to her husband.

Davis turned to Quinton.

"Can you hang on just one moment?" he asked.

"Sure," said Quinton.

Davis walked around to the back of the building. He went up the outdoor staircase leading to the residence above the shop. Quinton noticed Davis' son, Sam, spying on him through the bait shop window. He called him over with an index finger. Sam came out of the shop and over to the fence where Quinton stood.

"You're Quinton Squid, aren't you?" asked Sam.

Quinton smiled.

"Yeah. You're right. What's your name?"

"Sam Davis," said the boy.

My half brother, thought Quinton.

"How old are you?" he asked Sam.

"Eleven."

"Eleven? You look like you're already about six feet tall."

"Well, only five-eight, but I'll probably still grow a lot more."

"You probably will."

"I see you all the time on TV playing volleyball," said Sam.

"Oh, you do?"

"Yep."

"You like volleyball?" asked Quinton.

"Yeah," said Sam.

"Not as much as my dad, though. You're my dad's favorite player."

"Really?"

"Yeah. You're the only player he ever really talks about. That's how come I started to like you."

"Well, thanks very much," said Quinton.

"You're welcome. My dad used to play volleyball too, you know."

"Yeah. I know," said Quinton.

"You do?"

"Yeah. I know he was on the Olympic Team in 1964, and he won the Gold Medal."

Sam was excited.

"Yeah, he did," he said.

Sam reached underneath his shirt.

"Hey, look at this."

The kid pulled something out from around his neck. Quinton could see it was a large blue ribbon.

"What's that?" Quinton asked.

"This is the ribbon my dad's Gold Medal used to be on."

"Oh, wow. He gave it to you." Quinton smiled. He liked this kid.

"Yeah. Just the ribbon though, not the Medal. He gave the Medal to someone a long time ago, before I was even born."

"Who?" asked Quinton.

"I don't know. It was someone though, because he said he gave it to him in exchange for a lot of bad stuff that he had done a long time ago. He said that my mom, the girls and I wouldn't have even recognized him back then because he was a really mean guy. But he's not anymore."

"No. He seems like a nice guy," said Quinton.

"Yeah, he's the best," smiled Sam.

"Who's Elizabeth?" Quinton asked.

"Oh, that's my sister. She's about a year and a half now."

Elizabeth Davis, thought Quinton. His mother's name. Strange, yet somehow fitting. Was the man searching for forgiveness? He didn't know. Quinton saw Davis coming back down the stairway. He called to his son.

"Sam, you think you could take care of Elizabeth for a while? I think your mom needs to rest a bit."

"Sure," said Sam. "Just hang on a second."

Sam went into the bait shop and ran back out again carrying a Mikasa volleyball and a magic marker. He ran up to Quinton.

"Could you sign this for me?" he asked.

"Sure," said Quinton.

He looked at the volleyball. Mikasa. Mi casa es su casa. Oh god. There it went again. His brain babbled at him furiously. He closed his eyes and signed his signature over the surface of the ball. He opened his eyes, then handed the ball and marker to Sam.

"You'll probably be as good a player as your dad someday," said Quinton.

"I hope you're right," said Sam. "Thanks. Bye."

Sam ran around the side of the house carrying the signed volleyball like a trophy. The two Quintons watched him walk up the stairs.

"Sweet kid," said the younger Quinton.

"Thanks," said Davis.

"So, how old is your other girl?"

"Oh, Jennifer? She's fourteen."

"So you got your second chance three times over."

"I guess you could say that. So, what can I do for you, Quinton? Can I call you Quinton?" asked Davis.

Squid smiled.

"Only if I can call you Quinton."

Davis smiled for the first time. "Okay," he said, and put his hand out to shake.

"Quinton Davis," he said, formally introducing himself.

Squid met the hand with his own.

"Quinton Squid," he said.

They shook hands.

"Nice to meet you," said Davis.

"Nice to meet you, too," said Quinton.

The two men smiled at each other.

"I'll grab us some sodas. We can head down the beach," said Quinton Davis.

He walked into the bait and tackle shop. Quinton could see him through the window. He reached into a corner fridge and took out two sodas. As he came out of the front door he turned the OPEN sign to CLOSED. He left the shop and locked the door behind him. He and Squid strolled down the beach.

The two men came to rest on a jetty a quarter mile from the shop.

The jetty was enormous; huge granite boulders stacked together to form a tidal barrier thirty feet wide and two hundred yards long. It was topped with smaller boulders and jagged stones to discourage beachcombers from walking on its dangerous sea wall. But that hadn't stopped Squid or Davis.

They sat at the far end of the jetty, atop an old signal tower at the very tip. The afternoon sun shone down on them. The ocean was loud, the waves thunderous as they slapped at the boulders with each tidal thrust.

The water was barren this far out, less the two surfers braving the sharp rocks and unyielding current to catch the best waves in the area. Davis sucked back the rest of his root beer. He turned to Quinton with a grin.

"You guys today…don't play volleyball like we used to. You get away with murder on the beach. You actually carry the ball on the set – deep dishing. That's bullshit," kidded Davis.

"You played indoor," said Quinton. "Indoor players are quick setters, it's true. But you still put a spin on the ball – that's excessive contact too, and not all deep dish is bullshit."

"How do you know so much about the game if you don't remember anything?" Davis asked.

"Well, the only stuff I remember is what I've learned since the accident."

"That's really strange," said Davis.

"I know. I'm getting really weird flashbacks, and I think I might've seen you in one of them."

"You've seen me in one of them?" asked Davis.

"Well, yeah. At least I think it was you. I can't remember the face, but I feel this person was definitely my father, and that's you.

"It was a white Cadillac convertible someone had just given us as a present. I think it was just you and my mother in the car. You turned the car over twice but it wouldn't catch. The third time it caught, but the car exploded. A big explosion.

"I don't remember much more about it, but I just needed to know if this makes any sense to you in any way, if you've ever been in a car explosion when I was younger, or anything like that. My doctor did his best to flesh it out in psycho-babble terms, but it feels too real to be something that my mind has fabricated. It feels more like a memory than a dream."

Davis looked at Quinton with concern.

"I never owned a Cadillac. Your mom and I in an explosion? God, no. Nothing I can think of comes to mind."

Quinton Squid nodded, then continued.

"And in this dream or memory or whatever it was, I'm standing there and I'm about eight years old. A little younger than Sammy is now. And I'm yelling and screaming at the burning wreckage trying to get to you, but the wall of flame is just too thick."

"Well, there's no way you could be eight years old with your mom and I in the same car. I left when you were three. She died when you were five."

"I know. That's why it doesn't make any sense to me."

Davis shook his head.

"I don't know."

Quinton reached into his pocket and took out the passport. He opened it and held up the picture page to Quinton Davis.

"What about this? Have you ever seen this guy before?"

Davis looked at the picture of Michael Delaney. He studied it closely. He looked back at Quinton.

"No. The face doesn't look familiar, or the name for that matter. Hold on a second."

Davis held the picture of Michael up to Quinton's face. He looked at the Delaney picture, then at Quinton, then back to the picture.

"But the eyes, they look like yours."

"And yours, too," said Squid.

"Mine?"

"Yeah. They do. That's what I thought, anyway. I don't know. Maybe not. I thought it might be my brother or something. We look so much alike in a very strange way, you know what I mean?"

Davis studied the two faces more carefully.

"Yeah. I know what you mean. I can sort of see it now," he said.

He looked at Squid with a seriousness in his eyes.

"If there's one thing I can tell you, son – can I call you that?"

"Sure."

"Thanks. If there's one thing I can tell you it's that no matter how much of a cold hearted, irresponsible son of a bitch I might have been, one thing I never was was promiscuous. I know it might sound silly from today's standards, but that's just the way it was. I've never been with anyone I didn't love. The problem wasn't the loving, it was the staying. The idea of permanency gave me the jitters. I know I can't justify my actions, so I'm not even going to try. I just have to do the best I can in the present right now."

Quinton could see Davis' lower lip tremble ever so slightly.

"It looks like that's just what you're doing," Quinton reassured him.

"Thanks," said Davis. "Quinton, I don't think this could be your brother, and I don't know who it could be."

Quinton tucked the passport back into his pocket.

"Long shot anyway, I guess."

"I'm sorry I couldn't have been more help," said Davis.

"No. You've been more than enough help. I don't remember what went on in the past, but right now there's a hurricane going on inside me, and you've done the best you can to help me sort it out."

"Thank you. That means a lot to me," said Davis.

"Me too," said Quinton.

They stood up from the tower. They hadn't noticed the sun go down. Traces of orange still lingered over the horizon.

"So, where are you going tonight? Back up to L.A.?" Davis asked.

"Yeah. Right back down the rabbit hole. I gotta go home and figure out what's going on inside my head."

"If I can ever do anything, you know where to find me," said Davis.

"Thanks. Tell Sam I said goodbye. And give him this."

Quinton took the Gold Medal from his pocket and handed it to his father. Davis held it in his hand.

"My Gold Medal. You kept it all these years. It's as shiny now as when I gave it to you."

Davis ran his fingers gently over the Medallion's surface. All those years, and not a scratch had touched it.

"Please," said Davis. "I want you to keep it."

"Thanks, but I can't. I think it belongs in Sammy's dreams now. Most of mine have already come true. At least I think so."

"Okay. Thanks, son. I'll give it to him."

"There is something you could do for me."

"Name it."

"I'd like to buy one of those birdhouses in your storage closet."

"You want one of my birdhouses?"

"Yeah."

"They're pretty old. I stopped making them about five years ago when my arthritis set in. They're not even for sale anymore. Used to have 'em out front. No one ever bought one. Not one. A young man tried to steal one once, a long time ago.

Pretty weird. I won't sell you one, but I'll give you the whole lot of them if you want."

Quinton smiled.

"If I came home with a carload of birdhouses in the back seat, the neighbors would start to talk. Thanks, but just one will do. And I insist on paying for it."

"All right," said Davis. "But I warn you, I'm going to charge you the full two bits, no family discounts."

Quinton laughed.

"I wouldn't have it any other way."

Davis stretched his arms above his head and inhaled the salty air. He looked out at the dark blue ocean.

"I'm always amazed at how truly beautiful it is. Whenever I close my eyes out here on the tower, man, I can feel the water churning below me, the current racing out to sea, and I want so much to be a part of it."

He looked over at his son and chuckled.

"I can't believe I just said that. You must think I'm a crazy old salt. Not the sharpest knife in the drawer."

Quinton smiled.

"No, not at all. The tide is pulled by the cycles of the moon. The body and soul are pulled by the ebb and flow of the tide. Water to water. Just like ashes to ashes, dust to dust."

Davis looked at him fondly. He seemed like a kindred spirit.

"You changed your name to Squid," he said. "It suits you."

"Why?" asked Quinton. "I don't even remember why I changed it. I don't know anything about them."

"They are the most mysterious of all the cephalopods," answered Davis. "Their shell is inside them. Their soft tissue outside radiates with a bioluminescence. Just like you – hard shell inside, all flash on the outside. They're quick like you too – the fastest of the invertebrates, faster than the octopus and the nautilus. The squid flies through the ocean, darting around on its self-propelled jet-stream of water. Just like you, digging on the hot beach sand. Quinton Squid, Deep Sea Diver. It suits you."

"I was told they were stupid. That they don't have to be caught, just hang themselves willingly on the fisherman's hook."

Davis laughed.

"I guess you could look at it that way. Candles that burn bright, burn fast. When they're hungry, they're hungry. They jump the gun. Like I said, quick. But sometimes too quick. They'll bite at any small moving object. A fisherman doesn't need bait to catch them. A squid will simply impale itself on a moving hook. That's you too – pulling the net down, punching the net ref, shooting your mouth off on TV. What makes a squid so incredible is also its fatal flaw. Don't let it be yours."

Quinton laughed.

"I don't think I'll have to worry about that. My performance hasn't been so incredible lately."

"It'll all come back soon enough, and when it does, just remember; act, don't react. There's a big difference."

Quinton could feel his mouth curl upward in a smile and his eyes fill with warmth. This is my father, he thought to himself.

"I'll remember that," Quinton said.

Their eyes lingered a bit longer on the open ocean, before they started on the treacherous trail back to the bait and tackle shop.

28

Quinton parked the car in his driveway. He walked up to the front door and went inside. Home. He flicked on the living room light and closed the door behind him. Sheba sat on the sofa. She looked up at him and meowed. Her green eyes reflected the scant light. He meowed back.

The answering machine's flashing red light caught his eye. He went to the desk and pressed play. The tape started to rewind. Quinton went to the kitchen and dropped his keys on the table. Sheba followed. He ran the faucet and patted his face with cool water. The machine beeped and the message began.

"Hi Quinton, this is Officer Riley, Pat. I have some information for you on that name you gave me, Michael Delaney. It was hard to track down, but I got it. Don't think it'll be too much help, though. You can call me at the station tonight, the 7421 number. I'll be here 'til eleven, extension 171."

Quinton scrambled for a piece of paper and a pen. He found them in the catch-all next to the silverware and scratched the number down. He grabbed the cordless off the wall and headed for the living room sofa. He lay back on the couch with a loud exhale. He dialed the number. One ring. Two rings. Someone picked up.

"LAPD, Santa Monica Precinct, how may I direct your call?" asked the operator.

"Extension 171, please," said Quinton.

One ring. Two rings.

"Riley," said a gruff voice on the other end.

"Pat, it's Quinton."

"Oh, hi," he said, his tone softening noticeably. "I have that information you wanted."

Quinton heard papers shuffling on the other end.

"I had to go through the Bureau to get this," said Riley.

The rustling of papers continued.

"I really appreciate it," said Quinton.

He could feel himself begin to sweat all over. The seconds ticked by. For god's sake, he wanted to yell, hurry it up. He had a conscious lock on his brain not to start counting. He tried to breathe instead. He could feel his clothes absorb the moisture suddenly covering his body.

The shuffling stopped.

"Okay, found it," Riley said finally. "Okay...Michael Delaney... died on December 22 of last year, at Beth Israel Hospital, Boston, Massachusetts. Actually, he was D.O.A... had two prior arrests for burglary, no convictions, blah-blah-blah...six foot four, tall sucker, twenty-eight years old...uh... okay, here we go, died in an explosion, a gas explosion in his apartment building. Coroners report says he died of complications from severe third-degree burns and head injury. What was left of the body was identified by a Victor Russo of Boston's North End, his former legal guardian, and a Gina DeMarco, of East Boston, his fiancée..."

"Gina and Victor..." Quinton mumbled under his breath. He took in a long, deep breath. He hadn't realized he'd been holding it for the past minute.

"What?" asked Riley.

"Nothing, just that the guy who broke in mentioned something about a Gina and a Frank."

"He may have been referring to Frank Russo, Victor Russo's son."

"Who is this Victor Russo?" asked Quinton. The name Uncle Victor rang through his head mercilessly.

"The head of a small-time racketeering family in Boston. Truck hijacking, stolen goods, that kind of thing. He was suspected but never implicated in the death of Michael Delaney, just as he was suspected many years earlier in the death of Michael's father, Phillip Delaney, in a –"

"– car explosion –," they said in unison.

Quinton began to breathe heavily.

"How did you know that?" Riley asked.

He heard Quinton hyperventilating on the other end of the line. "Are you okay?" he asked.

"Yeah," Quinton said. "Fine. The burglar said it, I think. Hey, my leg's cramping bad, can I call you back?"

"Sure, but I don't have too much else to tell, that's it."

"Great then, Pat. I appreciate your help."

"Sure, no problem. Anything else we can do, just let me know. Are we still on for that doubles match?"

"Yeah. Give me a call in a couple of days, we'll set it up."

"Sure. Talk to you then. Bye."

"Thanks. Bye."

Quinton hung up the phone. He dropped it on the coffee table. His breathing became less labored. He stared up at the ceiling. After a moment, he found himself counting the cracks. Fourteen. Fifteen. Sixteen…

"No!" he screamed aloud.

In the kitchen Sheba looked up from her waterbowl. She

came into the living room. Quinton was beside himself with confusion. He felt like he was drowning in his own sweat. He wanted to run, and run fast. But where?

Sheba jumped up on the sofa and spread herself out on his chest. Quinton closed his eyes and started to pet her. She purred in delight as he scratched behind her ears.

His brain was running a million miles a minute. That guy, the burglar guy, just has you confused with this guy who died. We were both there, in Boston, at the same time. It's all a mistake. Just a big mistake. But then how do you know about the car explosion – and what about the dreams? a voice inside of him demanded. No, it's just a big mistake. The power of suggestion. Just like Holly said. That's all.

The world behind his eyes was spinning. He continued to scratch Sheba behind the ears and under the collar. He felt his hands begin to tremble. Quinton opened his eyes. He felt something weighing down the cat's collar. He pulled Sheba closer and gingerly edged the collar around to the weighted object. Attached to the collar was a gold NBA Championship ring with an inscription reading: '86 Celtics.' Where the hell did this come from?

Quinton jerked upright. Sheba leapt off his chest. He made a bee-line to the living room door and flicked off the lights. He picked up the Louisville Slugger in the doorjamb and began moving across the floor.

His movements were fluid. He was quick but graceful. Quinton slid soundlessly through each darkened room, one by one, searching for the intruder, the burglar, but found no one. Satisfied he was alone, he turned up the lights. He sat at the kitchen table and leaned the bat against a chair. Sheba walked into the kitchen. He picked her up and set her down on the table. He gently removed her collar. He took the ring from the collar and placed the collar back on her neck. Sheba winked at him affectionately. Quinton stared at the gold ring.

"NBA rings," he mumbled to himself.

The ring dissolved before his eyes. He found himself in a purple-soaked Boston alleyway, outside the Callabrisi office building.

"What kind of plates?" asked Nick.

The purple haze faded and Quinton was left staring at the inscribed ring. But within a moment he was drawn back to the Boston alley.

Nick asked, "Why does he have a steel plate in his –"

A voice from deep within seemed to issue the response: "It's a long story."

Quinton's consciousness came back to his beach-front kitchen. Still staring at the ring he replied, "He was hit with the bumper."

Quinton felt himself starting to waver in and out of a trance-like state. He stood up quickly, tipping his chair backward. Sheba jumped off the table in alarm. Confused, Quinton grabbed the Louisville Slugger. Before he could move, the white Cadillac exploded before his eyes.

As the flames cleared he saw a large, shifty face looking down at him. It was the face of a much younger Victor Russo. Russo was surrounded by blackness, and spoke with a serious tone to his voice.

"Don't worry, son. I'll take care of you. Your father was like a brother to me," he said.

Quinton's subconscious thrust him back to Michael's childhood home. Frank and Michael stood in the driveway, arguing.

"Ask your old man. He knows a lot about bugs," cackled Frank.

Suddenly, all went black. Then, before Quinton's eyes, the blackness melted into a cemetery.

An eight-year-old Michael watched as two coffins were lowered side by side into two separate graves. Michael began to fidget. He tried to run towards the disappearing coffins, but Victor grabbed him, holding him back. Michael bit Victor's hand. He ran onto the thin strip of earth separating the two graves. He looked at his mother's coffin as it was being lowered into the ground.

"Mom!" he screamed.

He looked at his father's.

"Dad!" he yelled.

He looked from mother to father then back again. He wanted to jump down into one of the graves, but couldn't decide which one. Victor crouched to reach him at the edge of the graves. He spoke gently.

"Michael. Michael, come here. They're gone. Come to me, Michael."

"No!" screamed Michael.

He jumped onto his mother's coffin.

"Mama!" he yelled.

The pallbearers attempted to pull him from the grave, but he fought them, fists flailing.

"No!" screamed Michael. "No! They have to be buried together!"

He began crying, frantically grabbing at the thin wall of dirt between his mother and father's graves. Just as he managed to break through the gap separating the two, one of Victor's henchmen grabbed him from above and yanked him out of the hole. Michael flailed about, screaming at the top of his lungs.

"No! NO! I'm not finished yet!"

Quinton Squid was suddenly thrown back to his own reality.

"No! NO! I'm not finished yet!" Quinton screamed.

He opened his eyes. They grew wide, shocked at the decimation around him. The refrigerator, appliances, and counters in the kitchen were all dented and in pieces. Water spouted from a broken sink faucet. Quinton was out of breath. His whole body trembled uncontrollably. He looked down at his hands. They held a badly splintered baseball bat. Sweat trickled down his arms. He opened his hands and let the bat fall to the ground. He looked over at Sheba, huddling in the living room corner.

"Did I do this?" he asked her.

She didn't answer. He went to her with trembling hands. She hissed at him and ran into the bedroom. Quinton was left standing in the living room, alone. Just him, the television, and the liquor cabinet.

● ● ●

Quinton sat on the couch. He drained the last of a large bottle of tequila. Sheba was nowhere to be seen. He talked to her anyway.

"What should we do? Huhhh, Shebe? What should we do?" he slurred. "Oh, I know what we can do."

He searched the cushions of the couch and found a remote control. Quinton pointed the remote at the TV and hit the on button. Nothing happened to the TV, but the radio started to blare from the bedroom. A confused Quinton looked down and realized he held the stereo remote.

He stood up from the couch and headed to the bedroom, clutching the empty bottle of tequila. Sheba crawled out from under the couch and slinked after him.

Quinton stumbled into the bedroom. He stopped in front

of the stereo system and holstered the remote in the waistband of his pants. He put the bottle down and clicked off the radio.

He looked through a stack of CD's. Drunk, he flamboyantly picked one out and put it in the CD player. He programmed a song and hit repeat. He looked around for Sheba. She sat at his heels.

"There you are. Hey, I got the perfect song. We're going to listen to this until the end of time. Or at least until the electricity runs out."

It was 'Hotel California' by the Eagles. The CD player began to ooze its dreamy rhetoric.

Quinton started laughing to himself.

"Isn't this perfect? Isn't this fucking perfect?"

He swayed awkwardly to the music, doing his best to hum along.

Sheba jumped on the bed. Quinton lay down next to her. Staring up at the ceiling, he looked at his own reflection in the mirrors. Listening to the music he continued to stare at himself, drunkenly hypnotized by his own image.

The image began to go hazy for Quinton and his eyes began to close. Just before he passed out he could've sworn the face staring back at him was that of Michael Delaney.

As he lost consciousness in this world, he came to in a different one, Michael's. A fourteen-year-old Michael stood in Victor Russo's home gym, practicing on his Wing Chun wooden-man dummy. He practiced Tai Chi and Wing Chun blocking, trapping, and striking techniques. He was swift in action and deft in his accuracy.

A fifteen-year-old Frank entered the gym, just home from football practice. He wore his dirty uniform No.66 like a trophy. Michael could see where Frank had tagged on a third six with a permanent marker. Who did he think he was, the anti-Christ? Actually, thought Michael, he wasn't that far off.

"What are you doing with that wooden doll?" asked Frank snidely.

"It's a wooden-man, brainiac," said Michael, concentrating on his left palm brush-block.

"A woody man, huh? Whatsit give you, a boner?"

Michael looked at him with disgust.

"Dildo dick," he mumbled under his breath. Right parry, downward block.

Michael continued to hit the wooden-man. Frank stood there mulling over what he could say that would be even more nasty.

"...So, what? When you're done slapping it, do you suck it off too?" he finally said.

"Only if it buys me dinner first," retorted Michael. Upward parry, low backhand strike.

"You think you're pretty funny, huh?"

"Yeah. I'm funny." Sidestep, two-hand upward block. Focus.

"Come on. Show me some of that slope shit," beckoned Frank.

"It's Chinese," Michael said. "And no, I'm in the middle of practice." He continued.

Frank stood in front of the wooden-man. Michael stood back from his offensive practice stance.

"Come on, Frank. Move it."

"Make me," said Frank.

"I'm not gonna make you do anything. I'm asking you to move."

"Blow me," said Frank.

"Blow your mother," Michael said.

He started to walk away. Frank hurried after him.

"Man, you are such a wuss. You'll stand here and smack the shit out of this wooden thing, but take a swing at me? No way. Too much of a wuss."

Michael turned around. He had had enough.

"Frank, fuck you."

"Fuck me?" Frank asked.

"Yeah. Fuck you," Michael affirmed.

Michael turned to walk away, but Frank in all his football gear ran after him. He plowed into Michael from behind. Michael fell to the ground face-first. His nose began to bleed. Frank turned him over on his back and moved to punch his face.

"Don't ever say 'fuck you' to me again," threatened Frank.

Michael stared him in the eyes.

"Fuck you," he said in the most neutral monotone he could muster.

Frank belted him hard across the jaw.

"Apologize!" he screamed.

"Fuck you," said Michael softly.

Frank belted him again.

"Apologize, you ginzo wanna-be!"

Victor Russo slammed the door open. He saw Frank lying on top of a bleeding Michael. Victor started to yell at Frank.

"Frank! What the hell are you doing? Michael, are you all right?"

Frank released Michael and moved up and away. Victor stood Michael up and handed him a hankie. Victor walked over to Frank and began to slap him repeatedly in the face.

"Hey! Mister tough guy! What do you think you're doing, huh?" he said to Frank.

"He was just, he was…"

"I don't want to hear it!" interrupted Victor. "Go on, Frank, get outta here."

Frank slumped out the door. Victor went back over to Michael.

"Mike, Michael, you okay?"

"Yeah, I'm okay," said Michael. His mouth and nose dripped with blood. His left eye was beginning to swell shut.

"All right, that's my boy. Be a man. Be a man about it."

Victor patted him on the shoulder.

"Come on. We'll get some ice for that, okay?"

"Yeah…ice," said Michael, almost absentmindedly.

Michael looked back at the wooden-man fondly through his swollen, blackened eye, and followed Victor Russo out the door.

Quinton groggily opened his eyes and looked up at the ceiling mirror. He saw himself in its reflection. 'Hotel California' played on. The irony was not lost on Quinton. But he felt his frustration only compounded by the ambiguity of the lyrics and the confusion caused by his own brain's mental escapades. He sat up from the bed and looked around the room. He got up and grabbed the bottle of tequila next to the stereo.

Empty. Crap, that was the last of the liquor cabinet. He stumbled into the kitchen. There had to be something else to drink. Cooking sherry, he thought. Of course, cooking sherry.

He searched ravenously through kitchen cabinets, but found only cans of refried beans, rice, vinegar, and protein powder. He tore open the refrigerator door. At this point he would've settled for a six-pack of Utica Club Light. Or even Carling's Black Label. But the fridge was laden only with empties of Miller, Coors, and Bud Light. Why do all the tournaments promo light beer, he wondered, then closed the door in dismay.

"Alcohol," he said out loud.

Quinton stumbled down the hallway towards the bathroom.

"Ethyl or methyl," he mumbled.

Ethyl or methyl, which one could you drink? Which one was rubbing alcohol? Which one was Lucy Ricardo's best friend? Ethyl or methyl. Ethel Mertz or Methyl Mertz? his brain babbled, pointlessly. He walked through the bathroom door.

"Which one did that senator's son drink?" he wondered aloud.

He had been rushed to the hospital. Maybe this wasn't such a good idea. He looked at his face in the bathroom mirror. His eyes were already puffy and half shut. He was beginning to drool from the left side of this mouth.

He wiped the drool from his face with a towel and opened the medicine cabinet. A roll of Speedstick, a packet of aspirin and the last of a bottle of cough syrup. He picked up the cough syrup and turned it around and around. He held the bottle up to the light and squinted his double vision momentarily singular. 'Take one or two teaspoons every four hours as needed for cough. Do not drink alcoholic beverages when taking this medication.'

"Ugh," he said aloud, and let the bottle slip through his fingers, crashing into the sink. He put the packet of aspirin in his pocket, worked his way down to the kitchen sink, and poured himself a glass of water. The Eagles played on.

He chugged the glass of water and stumbled out onto the deck.

He was almost comatose as he looked up at the moon. He

stared at it yearningly, his eyes half-dead. The lone, brilliant moon shifted stubbornly into a double image of itself.

"Two moons," he said to himself.

An astonished Quinton walked to the edge of the deck. The water glass fell from his fingers, onto the tile edge and into the hot tub. Crash. Splash. Reaching for the sky, he stepped up on the bench lining the edge of the deck. Enraptured, Quinton addressed the double moon.

"Mom! Dad!" he screamed. "It's me!"

He lost his balance and fell over the railing onto the sandy beach below. He was out cold.

At eight in the morning, 'Hotel California' still blasted from Quinton's stereo.

Holly could hear it as she stood at Quinton's front door. She rang the doorbell, but there was no answer.

"Quinton?" she called out.

Holly peered into the side window, but the shades were pulled shut. She rang the doorbell again. She couldn't make out 'Bolero' over Don Henley's voice. Quinton probably couldn't either, she figured, and began knocking loudly on the door. The knocking turned to pounding.

Still no answer. She tried the doorknob. To her surprise it turned. She slowly opened the door and went into the living room. Holly saw the decimated kitchen.

"Oh my god."

Where was Quinton?

"Quinton!" she yelled and ran down the hallway into his bedroom.

The bed was still made and Quinton was nowhere to be seen. She walked into the bathroom. Nothing. An empty bottle of tequila and some bits of glass in the sink.

She walked back to the kitchen and scanned the

devastation. The refrigerator was dented, the kitchen table bashed in. The microwave was shattered and the countertop tiles were cracked in two dozen places. Water spouted from a pummeled sink faucet.

Holly went to the countertop, careful not to step on anything sharp. She knelt under the sink and shut off the water valve. She stood up and surveyed the floor. It was a bit slippery, but most of the water had gone down the sink drain.

Holly noticed the open sliding glass doors. She walked out onto the deck. Through the railing slats she could see a body lying on the sand below.

Holly rushed down the stairs. She ran quickly to the body and turned it over. It was Quinton. He looked dead, but she could hear him snoring.

"Quinton! Can you hear me?" she said, patting his face.

He didn't wake.

"Quinton," she said again, shaking him gently.

The music blared ceaselessly.

Holly fished the remote out of Quinton's waistband.

She studied it a moment and pointed it at the house. After pressing a few buttons the stereo ended its onslaught. She dropped the remote on the sand.

"Quinton," she said again, but there was still no answer.

She looked down at his sleeping form. He was completely covered in sweat-soaked sand. She couldn't help but laugh at this pathetic sight.

"Man, you are so corndogged."

She grabbed under his arms and pulled him up. Damn, he was heavy. She dragged him across the sand, up the stairs and onto the deck. On the deck, she hoisted him up and let him fall into the hot tub.

"Ah, Gina!" he screamed as he hit the water.

He opened his eyes and stood upright in the hot tub.

"Holly...where am I?" asked a disoriented Quinton.

"Who's Gina?" Holly asked.

Quinton started to climb out of the tub.

"Huh?"

"Who is Gina?"

"I don't know," said Quinton.

He began to remove his wet clothes and strip down to his briefs. Holly eyed him suspiciously.

"First it was Frank, now it's Gina," she said. "Who are they?"

"I don't know," he insisted. "Unless...the cops mentioned something about a Gina being the fiancée of the guy in the passport."

Before Holly could react, Quinton opened the screen door and went into the kitchen. He stopped dead in his tracks.

"Oh my god!"

"No shit," said Holly, coming in behind him.

"What the hell happened?"

Quinton looked over the mess in disbelief.

"I think a train hit my house."

Holly picked up the cracked Louisville Slugger and handed it to him.

"I think you were the train."

Quinton stuck his pinkie finger in his ear and shook it vigorously.

"What a mess."

"What happened last night?" asked Holly.

"I don't know. I really don't know."

Quinton picked up a bunch of empty liquor bottles from the kitchen table.

"Whatever it was, it must have started with a powerful thirst," he said.

Holly looked at him, incredulous.

"How could you drink all that without heaving?"

Before her eyes she saw Quinton turn green. He dumped his wet clothes on the kitchen table.

"You spoke too soon," he said and ran quickly for the bathroom.

Holly sat in a kitchen chair.

"How did you end up in the sand?" she yelled into the bathroom.

"I think I fell over the railing."

She heard the toilet flush. Quinton walked back into the kitchen. He wore a bathrobe over his boxer briefs.

"You have a game in two hours, you know," said Holly.

Quinton laughed out loud.

"Fuck that. Look at this place!"

He went to the table and searched his pants pocket for the aspirin. To his relief it was still there. At least his short-term memory was of some use. He grabbed a glass from the cupboard and went to the sink. He turned on the faucet, but no water came out.

"I turned off the valves," said Holly.

Quinton looked at her strangely.

"Why?"

Holly leaned back in her chair, reached under the sink, and turned the valve on. Water spouted from the faucet in every direction. Quinton began to laugh.

"Oh," he said.

An obliging Holly turned the valve off. Quinton sat down at the kitchen table next to her. He began to rub his aching head.

"Quinton, talk to me," she said.

He looked at her, frightened.

"I don't know what to say."

She put her hand on his back.

"Breathe," she said.

Quinton closed his eyes. His face scrunched up in turmoil.

"I don't know who I am, or where I've come from, or what I'm doing. I don't know what to say."

He opened his eyes and looked directly into hers. She could see a single tear roll down his face. His eyes were bloodshot.

"You don't have to say anything," said Holly.

She leaned over and gave him a hug. He accepted it.

"I love you, you know," she said.

He pulled back from her.

"How can you love me? Look around. I'm a maniac!"

"No you're not. You were obviously just very thirsty last night and things got a little out of hand."

He smiled. She smiled back.

"I got you to smile," she said.

Quinton's face turned serious.

"I might not be a top ten player for a while," he said.

"What you do doesn't matter to me."

"Then what does?" he asked.

"Who you are. Who you're becoming."

"But I don't know who I am. My memories are pulling me back to somewhere I don't want to be. It's like I've stepped into somebody else's life. Like there's two people inside me now, each grabbing one arm of my soul, but I don't know which one to give it to."

"Just give it time, Quint. It'll come," she assured him.

Holly looked at her watch.

"T-minus one hour and fifty-one minutes. Hermosa's calling. What do you want to do?" she asked.

"Get a broom," said Quinton.

"Wrong answer," said Holly.

"Get dressed?" asked Quinton.

"Ding! Give the man a prize."

"No. Give the man an aspirin," Quinton said as he moved towards the bathroom with his empty glass.

Holly picked up the phone and dialed. She smiled as somebody picked up on the other end.

"Hi, Em. It's Holly. Is Stu there?...hey, MC Juicemaster. What kind of concoction you got for a hangover...tequila, lots of tequila... yeah, I know."

● ● ●

Exactly one hour later Quinton sat in the player's tent at the Hermosa Beach Tournament of Kings Championships. He, Stu, and several other players sat around killing time before their games. Quinton drank a thick, broccoli-colored liquid from a glass.

"Jeez, Stu. What is this?" asked Quinton as he sipped the nasty concoction.

"Good stuff," said Stu.

"Be more specific," insisted Quinton.

"Finish it first."

Quinton quickly gulped it down, nearly gagging.

"Okay," said Stu. "Cayenne pepper, tomatoes, ginger, lemon, kelp –"

"Kelp?"

"Seaweed," explained Stu.

"Oh, god."

Stu continued.

"...wheatgrass, watermelon rind, blue-green algae, shark cartilage, and a pomegranate."

Quinton was speechless. His mouth gaped open.

"Oh, and a few Alka-Seltzer," added Stu.

"I'm gonna hurl, man."

"No bud, you're gonna dish some serious 'in-your-face action' on the court today, got it?"

"Got it," Quinton said listlessly. Somehow, he didn't feel that convinced.

Stu and Quinton sat netside waiting for their first game to begin.

"We just have to burn through the three other teams in our pool to advance to the quarters. You think you can make it?" Stu asked.

"Three, huh?"

"Yeah. Then single elimination."

"For the quarters and semis tomorrow?" asked Quinton.

"And finals."

"Well, I'm sure I'll be watching that on TV. We'll be lucky if we get through two teams today," scoffed Quinton.

"Always the optimist," said Stu.

"No. The realist."

"You like parking cars?"

"All right, screw it. Let's earn some money today," said Quinton.

"That's what I like to hear," said Stu.

And earn money they did. A couple of hours later they sat netside at center court, waiting for their final matchup of the day.

A Hermosa official walked onto the court. The game was about to begin. He stood in front of the sideline mic. He turned to the four players sitting behind him.

"Okay guys, this one's being covered by the cameras, so let's keep it clean," he said to them off-mic.

He turned and addressed the crowd sitting in the bleachers.

"The AVP is pleased to announce that this fourth pool final matchup of the Hermosa Beach Championship is being broadcast live on CSN. And tomorrow's quarterfinals and semis will continue their all-weekend coverage of the Tournament of Kings, concluding with the Hermosa Finals at four p.m. The team that wins this match will win themselves a place in tomorrow's quarterfinals. Net referee Steve Vaughn will now introduce the two teams."

Steve Vaughn stood on the raised ref's platform wearing a headset mic.

"Center court, we have the matchup of the No. 12 seeded team of Rocks Lee and Raymond Wiles, their toughest kill of the day being their match over Gull Becker and Derrick Billings, as they try to outdig crowd favorites and No. 3 seeds Quinton Squid and Stu Gardner, who barely made it here from their win over B.J. Aaron and Steve Aimes. Wiles to serve."

Vaughn tossed a new AVP game ball to Ray. Quinton turned to Raymond.

"Thanks for that address, man."

Ray smiled.

"Anytime, dude. Good luck today."

"You too, man."

Ray Wiles backed up to his serve line. The game began. Ray served it hard and deep. Stu caught the serve and passed it to Quinton. Quinton approached the ball with his hands in a set position, but instead faked the set and tapped it cross-court. It hit the sand like a feather. Sideout.

"Sideout. Gardner to serve," said referee Vaughn.

Stu poked Quinton in the ribs with his elbow.

"Wise guy. Hit like a man," he joked.

Quinton smiled.

"Bite me."

"Slice and dice, all day long," Stu egged him on.

"You wanted the serve? You got the serve. Serve the ball."

The match had been one hell of a battle. Quinton's cut shot points had been numerous. The teams were tied, one game all. The next game would determine who would move on to the coveted quarter final bracket. The four men had pounded their hearts and souls into that ball. They had hit it with everything but the kitchen sink. The contest was close. The deuces had been many. By the thirty-seventh combined point both teams were ready to suck back a few cold ones.

In the middle of play for the thirty-eighth point, Quinton and Ray jumped up to the net at the same time – Ray to crush the ball, Quinton to block it out of his court. Ray was a brawny guy whose sense of timing was not particularly stellar. Quinton was fairly stout, but Ray was a bulldozer. Quinton threw his arms up for the block. He was too busy concentrating on his jump to realize his arms were a bit too far apart. Ray blasted the volleyball with all the force he could muster. The ball crashed between Quinton's arms and into his face – six-packed. Quinton went down hard into the sand. The ball went with him.

"Quint! Quint! You okay? Time out," called Ray.

"Time out's been called. Point to Lee and Wiles. Fourth deuce at nineteen-all," said the referee.

Quinton lay on his back. He lifted his head out of the sand and shook it fiercely.

"No...I'm okay," said Quinton, getting his wind back.

Ray put an arm out to help him up.

"Are you sure?"

"Yeah. Dude, you're strong," said Quinton as he stood up.

Ray tried to brush some of the sand off of Quinton's back.

"Sorry man."

"It's okay. It's in the job description," Quinton said, and dusted himself off.

Stu came over to Quinton.

"You okay, Q?"

Quinton wiped the sand out of his eyes. "Yeah. I'm fine. Let's rock and roll," he said.

"Okay," said Ray.

The buzzer sounded.

"Time is called. Wiles to serve," said ref Vaughn.

Ray Wiles jump-served the ball hard with his sledgehammer of a fist. Stu got a piece of the cannonball and passed it to Quinton to set. Quinton stood primed at the net. He looked toward the sun over the bleachers. He squinted painfully, waiting for the passed ball to fly through the glare of the sun. He would track its emerging silhouette to calculate where to intercept the ball. Suddenly, someone in the top bleacher moved in front of the sun, throwing Quinton off.

It was Frank Russo. Quinton couldn't help but stare at him. Their eyes locked. Quinton froze.

Before his eyes, the sun-drenched beach became swallowed up by thick purple fog. The crowded bleachers were replaced by the cold North End alleyway behind the Callabrisi office building. In the foggy distance Quinton could see a large form enter the alley carrying two metal cases. As the figure grew closer he could see it was the man Michael would have known as Frank Russo.

Quinton shut his eyes quickly. He knew he wasn't standing in a North End alleyway. He was on Hermosa Beach in the middle of the championships. He opened his eyes. He was back at the beach, but not Hermosa. He was at his beach house in Santa Monica. He saw himself pulling Nick Avanti's head out of the hot tub.

"Michael...I've been...keeping an eye on you. I hear that Frank and Gina are getting itchy...," Nick said, gasping for breath.

Quinton closed his eyes urgently only to open them again in the alleyway. The purple fog continued to roll through the alley, but it was now devoid of Frank's hulking form. Quinton blinked feverishly.

When his eyes finally reopened he found himself standing in reality at Hermosa Beach. The ball hit the sand right in front of him. Quinton stood there frozen, looking towards the sun. Frank was gone.

"Point to Lee and Wiles. Twenty-nineteen. Match point. Lee to serve," said the referee.

"Time out," called Stu.

"Time out has been called," said referee Vaughn.

Stu ran over to Quinton.

"Quint! Q, are you all right?" he asked.

"What?"

"What's the matter, man? Come on, we're doing good," said Stu, somewhat irritated.

"I know. Something shook me. I don't know what it was."

Quinton's eyes searched the bleachers for Frank, but he was nowhere to be seen. Quinton glimpsed the sun, then quickly closed his eyes.

"Don't do that, man. You shouldn't look into the sun like that. It's too fucking bright," said Stu.

"Yeah. Okay," mumbled Quinton.

Quinton shook off his momentary flashes of confusion. The buzzer sounded.

"Time," called the referee.

Rocks Lee picked up the volleyball and headed to the back-court line for the serve.

Thirty yards down the beach, the live broadcast of the game was being displayed on a tiny black and white Sony Watchman. Onscreen Lee continued his walk to the serve line. The TV announcer's voice issued from the Watchman.

"...Gardner called a time out for his partner, Quinton Squid, who appears to still be reeling from that pounding six-pack by Ray Wiles."

The owner of the Watchman began to snicker. It was Frank Russo. He lounged on the beach under an umbrella, wearing a particularly tacky Hawaiian shirt and tres-gauche gold necklace.

The game continued center court.

"Lee to serve. Match point," said Steve Vaughn.

Rocks Lee jump-served the ball hard. It flew over the net and then down the line, deep. Stu dove for the rocket, but couldn't get to it in time. Ace.

"Ace. Match to Lee and Wiles. Twenty-one to nineteen," said referee Vaughn.

The crowd began to howl in approval. That AVP game ball had gotten one hell of a workout from the four players. The two teams approached the net to shake hands.

"Good game, Quint," said Lee.

Quinton shook his head and smiled.

"You were passing nails, man. Just too damn good."

"I saw you got your revenge on the 'Double A's' earlier," said Ray.

Stu laughed.

"They crashed and burned, man. Redemption in the eyes of the Volley God."

"No lie. Aaron and Aimes are a couple of tapeworms," said Ray.

"Fuckin' A," agreed Stu.

"Good luck tomorrow, guys. We'll be watching," said Quinton.

"We'll make you proud," Rocks said.

The four men headed for their seats.

30

The post-game ritual was alive and kicking in Quinton's jacuzzi. Quinton sat in the hot tub, his back to the beach, arms stretched out across the railing behind him. Emily and Holly sat on either side of him. The three had already thrown back a few beers.

Stu sauntered out of the kitchen carrying a large bag of ice chips. Quinton dropped his arms from the railing and brought them around Holly and Emily's shoulders. He flashed his eyebrows at Stu. Stu was not impressed. He dumped most of the ice into the beer cooler next to the tub. He kept a small portion in the bag, and tied it into an ice pack. He tossed it to Quinton.

"Here."

Quinton lifted his arm from around Emily and caught the ice pack.

"I said I didn't need one, Stu."

"Yes, you do," Stu insisted.

"No I don't."

Quinton passed the ice pack back to Stu. Stu slid into the hot tub.

"Tough guy, huh? Your nose is already beginning to swell.

You're gonna have one hell of a six-pack headache tomorrow. See if I'm sympathetic then."

He handed the ice pack to Emily.

"Here honey. Go house."

Emily unwrapped the pack and began eating the ice chips.

"Bad habit," she garbled through a mouthful of ice.

"Craving ice means you have an iron deficiency," commented Stu.

Quinton looked at him, incredulous.

"Where do you get all this stuff ?"

"Common knowledge," said Stu.

Stu took a cold beer from the ice chest and held it to his forehead.

"Man, that feels good."

Quinton turned to him.

"Okay, I'll take it."

"Too late. Em's eating it."

Emily tied the ice pack back together.

"Here Q."

She handed it to him.

"I can always find something else to eat," she said, making eyes at Stu.

Stu looked downward and began to blush.

"Oh my god, he blushed," said Holly.

"He vacuums too," said Emily.

They all laughed. Quinton lay the ice pack over his eyes and forehead.

"Too bad he can't dig," he said as he leaned back against the railing.

"Yeah. That last ace was a heartbreaker," said Emily.

"King of the Corndogs, my man," Quinton said to Stu.

Stu made an old lady face.

"Ha ha. Have your fun. We're gonna smoke 'em next year," said Stu.

"I don't know, Stu," said Quinton.

"Shit!" Stu exclaimed suddenly.

"What?" asked Quinton.

The hot tub began to bubble up a pale red.

"I think I stepped in some glass," said Stu.

"Glass?" asked Emily.

"Stu, hang on a second," said Holly.

She stood up carefully in the tub.

"Holly, sit," said Quinton. "I don't want you to –"

"Q, I'm the closest to the steps."

She carefully made her way to the tiny steps leading out of the jacuzzi.

"Q, float him over here," she said.

"I can do it myself," Stu barked.

He put some weight on his foot and moved toward the steps.

"Oh, man!" he yelled out.

"Stu, give me your hand," said Holly.

Stu reached his hand out and Holly pulled him to the steps. She helped him out of the tub and sat him down on the deck.

"Is he all right?" asked Emily.

"Hang on a second," said Holly. "Don't you guys move yet. There might be some more glass down there."

"I think I dropped a glass in here the other night," said Quinton. "When I was trashed."

"Real bright," said Stu.

Holly inspected the foot. There was a large superficial cut on the ball of it. She dragged the ice chest over.

"Here. Stick your foot in this."

She lifted Stu's foot and gingerly put it into the ice.

"That hurts!" Stu exclaimed.

Quinton turned to Emily.

"He's such a whiner."

Emily laughed.

"Et tu, Emily?" said Stu.

"I'll get a bandage," Holly said.

"Is there glass in my foot?" asked Stu.

"I didn't see any," said Holly.

She turned to Quinton and Emily.

"I'll get a trash bag. Q, see if you can pick up the rest of whatever he stepped on."

Holly went through the glass doors into the kitchen. Quinton and Emily bent down into the hot tub. Quinton shut off the bubbles and scanned the bottom.

"Yeah, it's a glass," said Quinton.

"Q, don't let her pick up any more shards," said Stu. "She has a tournament next weekend. You don't have one 'til next season."

"He's right, Em. What would he do if you lost? He'd have to get a real job."

"Here," Emily said with a smirk as she handed him the bits of glass she'd collected.

Quinton took a deep breath and submerged under the water. He searched the bottom for all the glass he could find. Eighty-four seconds later he surfaced. A stunned Holly stood over him.

"My, you certainly have worked on your breath control," she said.

She held a trash bag in front of him. Quinton dropped the shards he'd gathered inside.

"Thanks," he said, and winked at her.

She winked back.

"Is it all out of there?" asked Stu.

"As much as I could see," said Quinton.

Stu took his foot out of the ice.

"Good enough for me. I'm freezing."

"Wait. Let me get a bandage on you," said Holly.

She put one on his foot and he slipped back into the hot tub.

"Are you sure that's smart, Stu? There might still be glass in there," Holly said.

Quinton could see her shivering. The wind was picking up. Goose bumps covered her skin.

"Get back in here, Holly. You'll freeze to death."

"Oh hell," she said, and joined the other three.

Quinton turned the jets back on. He leaned against the deck railing and put the ice pack back on his face.

Stu turned to Quinton.

"So, as I was saying dude, we could be seeded number three or four again in no time."

"You think so?" asked Quinton.

From just below the deck a fifth voice answered the question.

"Yeah. You're getting pretty good, Michael."

Quinton felt the cold metal barrel of an automatic pistol press into the back of his head. He heard the pistol's slide pull back slowly and then release, placing a bullet in the chamber. The hammer clicked firmly into place.

Quinton removed the ice pack from his face. He saw two hulking, no-necked monsters standing at the top of the deck stairs. Each pulled out a matching snubnosed revolver. Quinton didn't quite recognize Carlo and Muncie, but they pointed their guns at him nonetheless. He felt the cold steel leave his head. A moment later, he heard a large man coming up the stairs. The man reached the top. Quinton recognized him as the one who had blocked the Hermosa sun. Frank Russo moved slowly over to Quinton. He crouched on the deck in front of the hot tub.

"Saw that six-pack on TV. Must've hurt like hell. But probably not as much as this."

Frank took the butt of his gun and whacked Quinton hard across the forehead. Quinton was sent reeling back into the railing. He was knocked out cold.

Quinton awoke to a bizarre and menacing sight. Stu, Holly, and Emily sat in the hot tub, their mouths gagged with tape, their hands bound behind their backs. Carlo and Muncie stood over them. Muncie held a live toaster over the hot tub. It was plugged into an extension cord coming from the kitchen. Quinton could see the red glow of the toaster's heating element. Holly, Stu, and Emily were being kept at bay by threat of electrocution.

Quinton slowly got his bearings. He realized he must've been hauled out of the hot tub and dumped in a deck chair. Frank sat on the deck table next to the tub and looked at Quinton. He smiled mischievously as he rubbed the buzz cut on top of his head. Quinton tried to stand up.

"Sit down Quinton," said Frank.

"Who the fuck are you? What the hell do you–"

Frank pistol-whipped him across the face with his gun. Quinton's cheek and jaw began to bleed.

"I said sit down!" yelled Frank. Quinton complied. Frank paced in front of Quinton.

"Still don't remember me, huh?"

"No," said Quinton. He knew Frank was familiar, a vague image in his dreams, but could remember nothing of the context of their relationship.

"Maybe we need to jog your memory," said Frank.

Frank hit Quinton square on the forehead again, with the butt of his gun. The blow tipped Quinton over in his chair. Quinton started to bleed from a large gaping cut above his left eye. Frank bent down and pulled him up by the back of his neck. He threw him back into the chair. Frank studied the wound over Quinton's eye.

"That's about where I got it. How 'bout that? Did that help your recollection any, 'Quinton'?" asked Frank.

In Quinton's mind's eye he saw the Delaney childhood home framed in purple fog. The Cadillac was ablaze in the driveway. He saw the blonde boy in front of him get hit with the car's metal bumper. All traces of the purple hue disappeared. But the memory lingered a moment longer. Something clicked. Quinton zoned back to the beach house.

"So it wasn't the other guy. It was you," Quinton said.

"What was me?" asked Frank.

"You. You're the one who got hit with the bumper."

Frank smiled.

"Very good. We're making progress now, huh? Thanks so much for ducking."

Frank hit the right side of Quinton's face with his knee. Quinton's face contorted in pain. Frank screamed at him.

"You were a coward then! You were a coward at the Callabrisi's! And you're a coward now!"

Quinton sat up in his chair.

"I'm not a coward."

Frank raised an eyebrow.

"Oh, yeah? So you're just sitting here letting me beat the shit out of you. Is that right?"

Quinton looked over at his friends being detained in the hot tub. Frank slapped him across the face. Quinton was silent.

"Michael, are you a martyr?" Frank asked sardonically.

Quinton's jaw began to tighten.

"Fuck you."

Frank pushed the deck table in front of Quinton. He grabbed Quinton's right hand and placed it on the table, palm up.

"You're a right-handed player, aren't you?

Quinton's vision blurred. He felt light-headed.

"Yeah. I serve with my right hand," he said in a near whisper.

"Well then, this will be quite a sacrifice."

Frank held his gun to the center of Quinton's palm. He stared into Quinton's eyes. Frank looked back at Quinton's friends in the hot tub. They were horrified. He laughed.

"Always nice to have friends, isn't it Michael? But we were never friends, were we? And because of your little stunt, the Callabrisi's had us all by the financial balls. Just the plates, he said. But you couldn't listen. You had to take the stones, too. And you knew Pop would blame me for it, you mongrel dago-mick."

Frank started to squeeze the trigger ever so slightly. Through the blood on Quinton's face he could see a drop of sweat fall from his nose. Frank backed off the trigger.

"Ooh. You're sweating now, huh? Any of this making sense yet, Quinton? Jarring your memory? This isn't going to be any fun unless you remember. No fun at all. So raise your hand if you do. Your other hand, that is."

They stared into each other's eyes. Quinton began to look faint as blood ran slowly from his head.

"I just came in from Tahiti. Turns out the Callabrisi's had their plates all along. And most of the diamonds. It was Nicky, that piece of work. He knew they wanted my father's cajones in a vice, and where else was he gonna sell the shit anyway?"

Quinton stared blankly. But something else clicked in his head.

"Nick…"

Frank nodded.

"Yeah, Nick Avanti. Oh good, it's starting to come back. Let's help it along."

Frank drove a knuckle into Quinton's left temple. Quinton winced.

"Nicky left quite a trail to their summer home. Old man Callabrisi wasn't too pleased when I told him how easy it was to find. But then again, he wasn't too pleased when I shot him either. He's a 'cup is half empty' sort of a guy."

Quinton swooned, about to faint.

"Wake up!" screamed Frank.

He drilled the gun barrel into Quinton's palm. It began to bleed. Quinton screamed.

"That's better," said Frank. "You know, Nick sort of vanished after Tahiti. I don't think I would've found you, if it wasn't for Gina and the Cable Sports Network. You've got to learn to control that tic better, Michael."

Quinton's head nodded as he began to pass out. Frank slapped him, but Quinton continued his weave towards unconsciousness. Frank walked to the ice chest full of beer, picked it up, and dumped the entire contents over Quinton's head. Quinton woke up, shocked.

"Hey, bro. It would be nice if you could stay conscious for most of this," said Frank.

Quinton's eyes darted about the deck. It was all starting to come back to him now. The violence was just too familiar.

"Frank, let them go," he said.

Frank bent down to him with a curious expression on his face.

"You remember me?"

Quinton carefully palmed the can of Miller Lite which had fallen into his lap.

"Yeah. I remember you," he said fiercely, through suddenly gritted teeth. "Let them go, Frank."

Frank turned to Carlo and Muncie and pumped his fists with glee.

"He remembers!" he yelled, raised his Beretta into the air and squeezed off several shots through the silencer.

Quinton slipped the can of beer under his thigh.

Several houses down the beach, Nick Avanti's head popped up from behind a barbecue grill. He had heard the stifled chirp of the shots. It was a sound he knew well. He took note of Frank standing on Quinton's deck, then quickly ducked back behind cover.

Frank turned to Quinton.

"Okay, I'll let them go. One for every one of your aerial roundhouse kicks that hits my plate. You're gonna do it Michael. You're gonna kick me. You're finally going to fucking fight me."

Quinton didn't move. Frank slapped him across the face. Quinton didn't flinch. An angry Frank slapped him again, harder. Quinton's eyes burned, but he still didn't move. Thoroughly frustrated, Frank belted Quinton hard across the jaw. His neck buckled backwards then forward, sending his skull into the table.

In his mind's eye he saw the Cadillac convertible explode before his eyes. When he blinked, a nine-year-old Frank stood in front of him at the end of the Delaney driveway.

"I find bugs, then I burn them," Frank said.

Quinton was thrust back to the beach house deck. He raised his head to stare at Frank absently.

"I find bugs, then I burn them. What does that mean?" asked Quinton.

Frank smiled lasciviously. He was enjoying this. He yanked Quinton's head above the table by his hair.

"Information's expensive. It's going to cost you."

"What's it going to cost me?" Quinton asked in a faint mumble.

Frank let go of Quinton's head and let it fall back on the table. Once again he pointed the gun at Quinton's right palm.

"How about I pull the trigger and we find out."

Quinton wearily lifted his head from the table. The two stared into each other's eyes. Frank pulled the trigger and shot a hole clear through Quinton's hand. Quinton's jaw clenched, but his eyes barely flinched.

"You gotta scream! You gotta scream or it doesn't count!!" bellowed Frank.

Quinton pulled his hand back. Blood poured down his wrist. Stu, Emily and Holly looked on in horror. Holly began to feel around the bottom of the hot tub with her foot for a stray shard of glass. Stu and Emily took the hint and searched as well.

Quinton picked up an old pair of sweatpants from the deck and wrapped them around his bleeding hand.

He started to scream.

"Answer my question! I paid the price, now answer my question! What did you mean about 'I find bugs, then I burn them?!' " Quinton yelled.

"You had Nick hit me with a crow bar!" Frank howled.

"It was a flashlight!" Quinton shot back, amazed at how clear his memory of this fact suddenly was. "Now answer me!"

Nick serpentined his way down the beach and snuck

himself under Quinton's deck. He crouched in a corner, careful not to let his shadow spread out onto the beach behind him.

In the tub above, Stu's body shuddered. His eyes widened and he gritted his teeth. A momentary blur of red bubbled to the surface in front of him. He had found a piece of glass. Holly and Emily stared into his widened eyes. Holly looked at the two thugs standing guard above them. The toaster still hovered overhead, but little mind was being paid to the hot tub. The antics a few feet away were far more interesting.

"I can't believe you just did that!" screamed Quinton.

Even Carlo and Muncie winced.

"No shit, huh? Jesus Christ, Frank," said Muncie, almost clucking in disapproval.

"You two tried to blow him up!" insisted Frank.

"But that was orders," said Muncie.

"I didn't think even you were that much of a fucking maniac!" Quinton screamed at Frank.

"Yeah, well school's open!" Frank yelled back. "I was playing in the warehouse one time, around my dad's office. You know, checking out the cockroaches, trying to figure out where they lived."

"You always loved bugs."

"Yeah, but this time I came across some other kinds of bugs. You know, the electrical type. I told my dad. He called the exterminator."

"What does that have to do with my father?" asked Quinton.

"Uhn-uh, that's another question. Give me your left hand."

"No."

"Oh, for crissake," yelled Carlo.

"You fucking shut up," growled Frank.

Frank turned to Quinton.

"You'd rather it be a foot then?" he asked.

Quinton reluctantly put his left hand on the table. Frank stared at him. Quinton closed his eyes. Frank slapped him across the face.

"Oh, no. I want to see your eyes when I pull the trigger," screamed Frank.

They stared into each other's eyes. Frank pulled the trigger. This time Quinton screamed out in pain. Frank bellowed with delight.

"That's more like it."

Underwater, Holly tapped Stu's foot with her own. She turned slightly and flashed her tape-bound wrists at him. Stu nodded. Holly made eye contact with Emily. She motioned her eyes upward at Carlo and Muncie, clearing her throat. Emily nodded. It was all agreed. Stu bit down hard on his teeth as he grasped the shard of glass with his toes. A bit more red burst to the jacuzzi's surface.

Under the deck, Nick whipped out his pocket knife. It was a small Swiss Army knife with a nail file, scissors, cork screw, and tiny one-sided blade. Great for little emergencies, but not an inherently good weapon. He searched the sand next to Quinton's barbecue for a poker, or anything else he might use as a weapon.

Emily's eyes were intent on Carlo and Muncie. Holly turned her back ever so slightly in Stu's direction. He strained to get his foot to her hands. Lucky he was limber. Stu's toes gently fed Holly's fingers the piece of glass. She grabbed the shard and turned back around.

Nick found something in the sand and picked it up. It was Quinton's stereo remote. A diversion would be good, he thought, and began to press buttons at random.

Holly cut at her wrist bindings. The glass was sharp. Good

for slicing tape, bad for wrists and fingers. She sawed at the tape quickly but carefully, quietly hoping with each stroke she wouldn't hit an artery.

Nick continued pushing combinations of buttons, but with no luck. He stared up at Quinton and Frank anxiously through the slats in the deck.

Quinton wrapped both hands in the sweatpants. Frank brought his head down to Quinton's level. He spoke in a soft whisper.

"Your father was a lily white wuss. Yeah, him and the old man started the trucking company together, when it was legit. Didn't make much money in the beginning, did they?"

Stu and Emily looked on in earnest. They turned to Holly, a red film floating to the middle of the tub from behind her back. What was she doing back there? Stu moved his foot to and fro to dilute the blood's concentration. Emily kept an eye on their captors. Holly turned her head to Quinton. Blood spattered the deck below him and covered his bare chest and legs. She turned away and stared straight ahead through the deck railing at the cool blue ocean, listening, yet not listening to the conversation a few feet away.

"...then all of a sudden, things started to pick up. There was more money around, more money to spend. And your dad thought it was all legit. What an idiot. When he found out my dad had gone in with the Callabrisis, and their trucking was a front for highjacking, he didn't like that very much. Didn't sit too well with his conscience, I guess. So he started playing footsie with Federal investigators. Your father was a snitch, Michael. A motherfucking snitch."

Quinton stared up into Frank's spiteful gaze.

"What?" he said.

"What? You didn't like my answer, then ask me another

question. When Pop found out, he blew your father's ass to hell."

In what Quinton now knew to be Michael's mind's eye, he saw the Cadillac explode.

"I was supposed to be in that car too, wasn't I?" Quinton asked.

Frank shook his head evasively.

"That's another question, Michael. What are you gonna give me this time?"

"For God's sake," Quinton screamed. "I'm running out of blood! Just answer my fucking question and shoot me! You're going to anyway. Was I supposed to be in that car or not?"

"No. No, you weren't, Michael."

"Why not?" Quinton asked.

"That's another question –"

"Answer it, Frank!" Quinton screamed.

"You're beginning to remember," said Frank.

"Yeah. I remember."

Frank smiled.

In the space between the edge of the deck and the railing, just behind Muncie, Holly saw what looked like a human head begin to emerge. Blonde hair. With suspiciously dark roots. A forehead. Thick eyebrows. A man.

The head rose slowly. It stopped when the eyes were level with the deck floor. The man's eyes darted back and forth across the deck, assessing the situation. Holly stared at them intently. She made eye contact.

Holly's eyes bulged wide. The man stared directly into them. He raised his head a few more inches and put a finger to his lips. Shh. Holly relaxed a little. He must be a friend. She hoped.

"How many," Nick mouthed silently.

Holly slowly blinked three times. He nodded. Nick scanned the deck. Three of them. Three armed and hulking North End Tonys vs. a bleeding amnesiac, three bound Californians in a hot tub, and an East Boston grifter with a Swiss Army knife. Nick looked back at Holly. He couldn't help but notice the maroon film glistening through the jacuzzi's bubbles. Were Carlo and Muncie blind?

"Keep cutting," he mouthed to her. His head popped back under the deck floor.

Holly continued on as sweat trickled down her face. The burn of the chlorine digging into her raw, lacerated hands was becoming unbearable. Oh god, it couldn't be much longer.

"Answer me, Frank!"

"That's why I was there. My father gave me ten silver dollars to go down and play with you that day, to make sure you didn't get in that car."

"Why would he do that?"

"I don't know. But ten bucks was ten bucks. And by the way, you little turd, I really appreciate you telling me to duck, too!"

Frank kneed Quinton's bunched-up hands. Quinton yelled out in pain.

"I spent six months in the hospital thanks to you!" screamed Frank.

Quinton screamed back.

"Don't piss on me, Frank! It's thanks to you my parents are d–"

"Shut up!" Frank screeched.

Holly burst her bindings.

Frank grabbed a piece of tape from Carlo and put it over Quinton's mouth.

Nick's head popped back up above the deck. Holly immediately made eye contact.

"Hands free?" mouthed Nick.

Yes, nodded Holly.

Nick lifted his Swiss Army knife into her field of vision.

"This is all I have," he mouthed.

Her eyes widened. Was he fucking kidding?

"Wait for my move, then improvise," he whispered.

Nick studied the toaster's extension cord. There was no way for him to get to it, no way to cut it. At least not fast enough. He'd have to snatch the toaster out of Muncie's hands. But something would be needed to slow the big guy down.

Nick slowly extended the corkscrew from his Swiss Army knife. He quietly drilled it into the deck railing, through a fold in Muncie's polyester pants. Holly did her best not to stare.

"Get ready," Nick mouthed, then disappeared below the deck. Holly kept her free hands behind her back. She watched as Frank continued his diatribe.

"But all that stuff doesn't really matter now. Your final betrayal is what matters, Michael."

Quinton tried to talk through the tape. He tried to bite his way through it. Frank laughed.

"Those Celtics rings were to be my father's pride and joy. The only thing he cared about more was you, and you knew it and you used it."

Quinton managed to bite off a piece of the tape covering his mouth. Not believing his ears, he yelled at Frank.

"That's what this is all about? Because you think your father liked me better than you?"

"No, it's not that at all Michael," snapped Frank. "It's just the simple fact that I hate your fucking guts. I always have. You and your whole fucking family. You're a pussy, Michael. You've always been a pussy. You'd stand around and slap that wooden thing. Play Bruce Lee while you shadow boxed. But you're just a passive-resistant little fuck."

"And you're a confrontational, fuck-head maniac."

"You're getting mad now, aren't you Quinton? Or is it Michael? Which is it, anyway? Huh? Who are you? Who the fuck are you, you piece of shit!"

Quinton could feel the cool beer can waiting next to his left thigh. He wanted to smash it with all his might into Frank's skull. But not yet. Patience. Breathe.

Frank looked over at the three in the hot tub.

"All you gotta do is kick me three times. Three times and they're outta there. Or I'll plug you and you'll never know what happens to them."

Out of nowhere, 'Hotel California' began to blare from inside the house. Frank froze, his gun to Quinton's head.

"What the hell is that?" Frank whispered to Quinton.

Below the deck Nick dropped the remote in the sand. He inched his way up to the railing, right behind Muncie.

Quinton tried to speak.

"Shh. Don't say a word," Frank whispered. "Don't even breathe, or they'll drop the toaster in the hot tub." He backed through the kitchen's sliding glass doors and into the house.

Holly looked at the railing before her. Nick crouched behind Carlo and Muncie, barely balanced on the edge of the deck behind the railing. Quinton looked over in disbelief. He readied the beer can in his right hand. He let out a yelp as the cool metal touched his raw wound. Carlo and Muncie looked over at Quinton. Nick deftly reached out his arms towards the toaster. Holly readied her hands for action. Quinton let out another yelp as a distraction.

"Shut up!" Carlo yelled.

Nick snatched the toaster from Muncie's hands. A startled

Muncie tried to turn around, his pants caught on the corkscrew. Suddenly unbalanced, he wobbled. Holly crouched and leapt out of the tub.

She grabbed Muncie by the lapels and pulled him back into the tub with her, tearing his pants from the corkscrew. He hit his head on the tub's tile edge.

Carlo turned to the railing, reaching out to grab Nick. From out of nowhere, a beer can flew like a bullet at Carlo's head. The impact sent his large mass careening over the railing, past Nick, and onto the sand below.

"Holy shit!" Nick cried out, climbing over the railing onto the deck, toaster in hand.

Quinton, half-conscious, moved towards the hot tub. Through his pain, he smiled at Nick. Nick felt a slight tug on the toaster. He looked to the glass doors. Frank stood there motionless, a CD in one hand, the extension cord in another. Frank yanked the cord, hard. The toaster popped out of Nick's hands and flew towards the hot tub.

"No!" Quinton screamed.

Strength dwindling, he ran headlong toward the tub and dove for the toaster. Sailing over the tub, he caught it in mid air, crashed through the railing, and fell with it onto the beach below. The extension cord, pulled from its wall socket, flew past Frank.

"Michael!" screamed Nick.

Frank pulled his gun and came back out on the deck.

"Shut up, Avanti, you little fuck."

Frank made his way to the edge of the deck. He surveyed the wreckage on the ground below. Quinton lay there unconscious, deck railing and toaster scattered around him. Carlo lay next to him, out cold.

Frank held up the Eagles CD.

"Never did listen to new music, did you? Why is that Michael?" he asked, then turned back to Nick.

"Well, if it isn't the Sundance Kid. I was hoping you'd show up. All tanned from the Islands, I see. And a shitty dye job, to boot."

Frank inched his way towards the jacuzzi. Two of his three captives were still bound and gagged. Holly, still gagged, used her free hands to hold an unconscious Muncie above the water. Frank shrugged. He continued.

"By the way, Nicky, old man Callabrisi asked me to say hi. But I figure you'll be able to say hi to him yourself soon enough."

Frank reached the edge of the tub. He looked down at Muncie again. Out cold. He spoke to Holly.

"Hey, you, sand bitch. Let him go."

Holly hesitated. Frank pointed the gun at her.

"Now," he insisted.

Holly let go of Muncie, and he slipped under the water. After a moment he woke, became frantic, and pushed himself to the surface. He blinked and looked around, dazed.

"Muncie," said Frank.

Muncie looked up at Frank.

"Yeah, dipshit, it's me. Get your wet ass outta there and go drag Michael and Carlo back up here."

Frank turned to Nick.

"Boy, these CD's can be sharp things, huh? I wonder how sharp they are?"

Frank bore the edge of the CD hard across his own forearm. To his amazement it began to bleed.

"Ha! Look! I'm bleeding. Pretty sharp."

Muncie dragged himself out of the tub and dripped down the stairs. Frank moved closer to Nick, near the edge of the deck.

"I wonder if it could cut a jugular, huh? Let's find out."

Frank put the CD to Nick's throat and held the gun barrel to his temple.

"Drop the fucking gun," a woman's voice called out from behind. Frank smiled.

"She has balls, Michael, I'll give you that. Just like Gina," he yelled over the side of the deck.

Behind him, he heard a revolver's cylinder and hammer click into place. Frank stopped smiling. Still holding the gun and CD to Nick's head and neck, he turned half-way around. From the corner of his eye he saw Holly in the hot tub holding Muncie's snubnose. It was trained at his head. He saw water drip from the barrel. The smile returned to his face.

"Don't know much about firearms, do you?" he said.

"Maybe I do, maybe I don't," she said. "Don't know about you, but I just heard the hammer and barrel click. Guess the chlorine didn't have enough time to bind the grease. Wonder if there was enough time for water to seep into the shell casings. Maybe the powder's wet. But then again, maybe it isn't."

Frank turned to face her. He kept the CD at Nick's throat, lowering his gun.

"Hurts like hell to rip that tape off your mouth, don't it? Ever kill anyone?" he asked, moving his gun slowly in her direction.

"Ever get capped?" Holly asked.

Frank forced a wry smile. Was she serious?

"You don't see me limping, do you?" he said, still inching his gun towards her.

"Yeah, well. Limp away asshole."

Holly aimed the gun at his kneecap and quickly pulled the trigger. Frank closed his eyes and winced. But no bullet came.

"Shit!" Holly screamed and cycled the trigger five times at his chest. Nothing. From beneath the banister, a crimson-soaked hand reached up for the Swiss Army corkscrew stuck in the railing. Holly saw it. She knew that hand.

"Guess the powder was wet," said Frank.

Holly dropped the snubnose on the deck.

"Guess it was."

The hand carefully unscrewed the knife from the railing.

"Blondie, before that attempted capping, you were just an innocent bystander. And what about trying to empty that load into my chest? Pretty fucking hostile. You're in the game now, sweetheart. Muncie, grab Michael and we'll toast them all in the tub. Muncie?"

Frank started to turn around, CD still to Nick's throat. Quinton freed the corkscrew. He looked up at Frank's gun. It dangled limp.

Quinton silently lifted the corkscrew and let it come crashing down on Frank's foot. Frank screamed and dropped his gun. He pivoted towards Quinton, slicing the CD hard across Nick's throat. Nick fell to the deck floor, bleeding. Quinton jumped up, grabbed Frank by the collar, and pulled him over the railing. Frank fell to the ground below. Quinton fell on top of him, knocking him out with the blunt handle of the Swiss Army knife before passing out himself.

Holly rushed out of the jacuzzi, over to Nick. She quickly brought a hand towel up to his neck.

"Hold this here, with pressure," she said.

Nick looked faint. He tried to speak, pulling the hand towel from his neck. Holly pressed it back on.

"No, keep pressure on it. I'll get some ice before your throat swells shut."

She ran into the kitchen. Nick spotted Frank's automatic

a few feet away. He crawled towards it. Holly burst out of the kitchen. She knelt at the tub.

"Stu," she said, knife in hand. "Raise your arms in back."

He did. She sliced through the tape and handed him the knife, nodding toward Emily.

"Cut Em loose and get out of here."

She turned to Nick. He was slumped against the railing, automatic in one hand, towel to neck in the other. Holly removed the towel and examined the wound.

"It's not deep. You're lucky the CD wasn't any sharper than he is. It's swelling. Keep the ice on it and you won't choke." She attached an ice pack wrap around his neck lightly.

Stu and Emily scrambled out of the hot tub. Stu headed down the stairs after Quinton. Emily lurched for the cordless phone. Holly yelled to her.

"Em, it's dead, I already tried the other one. Go for help. Now. Please."

"What are you going to do?" Emily asked.

"I don't have a clue," said Holly.

"Okay. Don't worry, help's coming," said Emily, as she took off, running.

Nick turned to Holly.

"Holly, n-no cops...b-bad for me..." he pleaded.

"Look, I don't know who you are, but we don't have any choice. We got three armed freaks of nature running around down there."

Nick looked over at Muncie's water-logged revolver, and at Frank's Beretta in his hand.

"O-O-Only one," he said, and tried to stand.

Quinton, Frank, Carlo and Muncie lay unconscious on the sand below. A prune-footed Stu disarmed Carlo and cocked the hammer of his snubnose. He gently slapped Quinton awake.

"Is everyone all right?" Quinton asked.

"A bit water-logged, but we're okay," answered Stu, his gun pointed at the three thugs. Quinton crawled off Frank's body and onto the sand next to him. His hands bled into the ground.

"God almighty," said Stu. "Look at your hands. You're still losing blood."

"I can't feel them anymore," said Quinton. He patted Frank down for weapons, staining his clothes with blood.

Frank's eyelids began to twitch. Unaware, Stu put the revolver down and tied Muncie's hands with his own belt. He picked up the gun and stood over the quartet.

"What the fuck's going on, Quinton? Who are these psychos?"

"Your worst nightmare, Gardner," Frank said, as he thrust his foot into Stu's kneecap with a loud crack.

Stu screamed and fell to the ground. Quinton and Frank scrambled for the gun. Frank pounced on it, sending Quinton reeling back against the deck stairs. Quinton looked over at Stu. He was unconscious. The femur of his left leg stuck out from beneath the skin.

From the deck above, Holly looked down in terror. She ran for the stairs. Nick stood and drew Frank's automatic. He let it come down on Holly's head. She fell to the deck floor, out cold.

"Sorry Holly," whispered Nick, "Just can't let you get hurt."

He took the ice pack off his neck and slid slowly down the stairs, behind Frank. He pressed the gun into the small of Frank's back.

"Drop it, Frank."

"Why, you got the one with wet powder?"

"No, you piece of shit. I got your Beretta."

"Prove it," said Frank.

Nick fired one stifled shot into the air.

"Well, you're right," said Frank. "That's my Beretta 21 all right. Too bad it only holds seven rounds, and you just pumped off the last. Shouldn't have wasted those first few shots, but I didn't know you were coming."

Nick pulled the trigger at Frank's back. The chamber clicked, empty. He pulled back on the slide and clicked the trigger again. Nothing.

"You're a real coprolite, Frank. A real pre-historic piece of shit," Nick said, raising the gun above Frank's head. Frank shifted, making a quick, pivoting turn on his left leg, throwing his right into the air for an aerial roadhouse kick. He hit Nick's head dead-on, driving him into the sand. Frank slapped a fresh clip into his pistol, stripping a round off the magazine into the chamber. He faced Quinton again, gun loaded, aimed right at him.

"See Michael, I learned some of that gook shit too. You're not so special after all."

"Who said I was special," Quinton asked calmly.

He looked down at Frank's feet, noting most of his considerable weight rested on the left leg.

"Everyone. Nana Rosetta. The old man."

"What is this Frank, a Smothers Brothers routine – 'Mom always liked you best?' "

"No," Frank said, agitated. "It's just that –"

In one fluid motion, Quinton dropped to the ground, his legs parting in a sudden split. He turned on his side, and swept Frank's left leg with his own. Frank fell to the ground, gun still in hand.

Quinton kicked Frank's wrist and the gun hit the sand. Both men stood, regaining their ground. They circled each other, fists poised for battle. Frank looked at the sand below, eyeing the Beretta.

"You touch it and I'll kick you into tomorrow," Quinton warned. Blood trickled down his arms.

"You getting mad now, Michael? Mad enough to fight me? Mad enough to hit me? Even with those fists?"

"I'm not mad."

"You're full of shit."

"Anger is the enemy, Frank."

"No, you're the enemy."

Frank lurched for the gun. Quinton met him with a hook kick to the knee. He followed through with a side kick to the shin, and a frontal roundhouse to the head. Frank fell backward beneath the deck. He felt around aimlessly in the sand for a weapon. Quinton spotted the gun. Before he could react, Frank lurched for him, delivering a powerful blow to Quinton's solar plexus with the stereo remote. Quinton buckled over. Frank kneed him in the chin.

Quinton hit the ground and was thrown into the past. A twelve-year-old Frank and eleven-year-old Michael faced off in Victor Russo's living room.

"You want a cat instead of a dog? You kick me right now," ordered Frank.

Quinton was thrust back to the beach.

Crouched on the ground, he jabbed his knuckle into Frank's knee cap, sprang himself into the air, and caught Frank's neck with a spinning back kick. Frank teetered. Quinton's hands bled feverishly.

Wavering between worlds, he was pulled to the memory of his parents' gravesite.

"Michael. Michael, come here," beckoned Victor. "They're gone. Come to me, Michael."

"No!" Michael screamed.

"No!" Quinton screamed out loud as he came back to the moment.

He stabbed Frank in the face with a straight lead punch, a back fist, then an upward palm stroke. His hands screaming from the punishment, he followed through with an aerial reverse kick to Frank's head. Frank plunged to the ground. He fell on his back, his face bloodied. Quinton leapt on top of him as if possessed by demons. He positioned his hands for the kill – one fist on Frank's throat, the other pulled back taut. Like a bow and arrow, ready for the thrust, he could crush Frank's trachea with one concentrated blow. He hesitated. Frank spoke through choking gasps.

"Kill me, Michael. Kill me by your hand and let me finally be in my father's favor. You can't, can you? You never had the balls, Michael. You never had the guts. You can't even kill me, and I killed your fucking parents."

The agony in Quinton's face was overwhelming. It took every vestige of his dwindling self-control not to let the arrow fly. Quinton wavered, covered in blood. He was barely conscious himself as he looked down at Frank. Someone spoke from behind.

"It has nothing to do with guts, Frank. And nothing to do with balls." Nick stood over the two of them, pointing the Beretta down at Frank. He continued.

"How does it go, Michael?…'Renounce your pride. Forgo victory and defeat. Defend yourself as the moment calls for, with skill and resolve. But do not be attached to the outcome, for then you may have already lost.' In his mind, to fight you the way you fought him would make him no better than you. For Michael, fighting has always been the last resort. For defense only. Strength through discretion, not aggression.

"You never understood why he couldn't be part of our shit-dyed little world, Frank, and you never will. I'm dirty. And so are you, fucking pazzo. But he is his father's son. Not Victor's. He's better than any of us. Michael wasn't raised by a waste of life like Victor, and so isn't one himself. Even Victor knew it. Still knows it. And that's why he favored him. It's so simple, Frank, but you never got it, did you? And the reason you didn't get it is the same reason you are who you are. You created your own circle."

"Screw you, Avanti," was Frank's response.

Sirens began to sound in the distance. Nick looked back towards the street. He could see flashes of red and blue glimmering in the hazy distance. He turned back to Frank.

"This time I'm going to get it right. Left or right, Michael?"

"Right," said Quinton.

"Right," said Nick as he let the butt of the gun come down on the right side of Frank's head. Frank went limp, out cold. Nick helped Quinton off of Frank's body. The sirens grew close.

Nick walked Quinton to the deck stairs. He helped wrap his hands with the sweatpants.

"I gotta go," he said. "Still have a few warrants out."

"I remember," said Quinton.

Nick shook his head.

"Too bad, maybe it all would've been best left forgotten, Mikey."

"How else do we learn, except from the mistakes of our past?"

"Hey, you sound like Michael again," Nick said with a quick chuckle.

"He's in here somewhere."

"Tell him I said goodbye," Nick said as he edged his way down the beach.

"Naw, he knows you'll be back around soon enough," yelled Quinton.

"He's probably right," yelled Nick.

"Paesan, Nicky!"

"Paesan, Mikey!"

Nick was gone in a flash.

"Mr. Squid, Mr. Squid, it's Officer Riley," a voice bellowed a moment later from inside the house.

Quinton passed out on the beach.

31

Quinton lay in his bed asleep. Holly lay next to him. As he turned from side to side, his eyes caught a glint of the early morning light as it spilled through the bedroom curtains. He covered his eyes with his bandaged hands and allowed them to open slowly. Morning.

God, what a night. He looked over at Holly. Had it all been a nightmare? No. The bandages on her forehead and fingers were a sobering reminder that it had not. He looked down at his own hands. The left was in a cast. Two metacarpal bones had been splintered by the bullet. In eight weeks he would know if the surgeon's work had repaired the damage fully. The doctors were optimistic. Quinton was just glad his serving hand hadn't borne the brunt of the damage. Almost impossibly, that bullet had shot clear through his right hand without hitting bone. The right hand was lightly bandaged, and for some reason throbbed more than his left.

He didn't want to see his face. He hadn't looked in a mirror yet. He just couldn't bear to see what Frank had done to the face that had taken him what seemed a lifetime to heal. The damage wasn't extensive, mostly cuts and bruises. Still, he didn't want to look in the mirror until Holly told him his wounds had healed.

Holly. He looked over at her again. God, she was beautiful. He kissed her gently on the forehead and slipped out of bed. He put on a pair of boxers and went out on the deck.

Quinton looked out at the ocean. As he took in a long, deep breath, he felt himself slip softly into an old memory. It was effortless. His mind was beginning to remember the past. And was accepting it.

On a crisp autumn day an eight-year-old Michael sat on the back steps of his home with his father. Phillip Delaney took a long puff on his pipe. He spoke to his son.

"Your Uncle Victor breaks the rules sometimes, and I can't. So we might have to leave here sometime soon."

"Breaks the rules?" Michael asked.

"Like in Chi Chuan class yesterday."

"When Jimmy Myers kicked Joe in the balls...uh, nuts?" Michael asked.

"Yeah," Mr. Delaney smiled. "You've got to pick your rules and stick by them."

"But I thought you wanted me to learn how to fight."

"No, I want you to learn how not to fight."

Michael pondered this for a moment. He turned back to his father.

"Is Uncle Victor my real uncle?"

Phillip Delaney took a drag on his pipe.

"No, just a business partner."

As the memory faded, the crisp autumn wind slowly dissolved into the sound of seagulls crying in the saltwater distance. Quinton took a deep breath of ocean air and let his moist eyes dry in the breeze.

He turned back inside. He closed the door, sat down in the chair across from his bed, and watched Holly as she slept.

Holly. Quinton stared at her intently. His jaw grew tight, and his heartbeat quickened. He thought he might drown from the questions that flooded his mind. And the numbers, the counting that interwove through all the questions.

Who. What. Where.

When.

Why.

How.

How could she still love him? What did she see in him. One, two, three...When exactly was he going to lose his mind? Would he. Why wasn't she afraid of that? Four...What would he do if she left?

Who exactly was he, and where did he belong? He was more than a man without a country, he was a man without an identity. Seven, eight, nine...He was neither Michael now, nor Quinton. He was a hybrid.

Ten. Would it all fit together? Whose memories were whose? Whose qualities were whose? What was learned, what was he born with, and what had he actually experienced. Just close your eyes, he told himself. Breathe.

"Breathe, Quinton," he whispered aloud. He concentrated on his breath. He could feel the throbbing in his right hand begin to subside. He opened his eyes and exhaled, body and mind in unison. He felt his breathing pattern gently reverse. He let it go. A calming energy overtook him. Who, what, where, and why didn't seem to matter anymore. Deep inside, something told him it would all work out.

Just exist. Here and now.

An hour later Holly woke. Her arm reached across the bed

for Quinton, but he wasn't there. She turned over and looked up. She saw him sitting in the chair, smiling at her.

"Good morning," she said.

"Good morning."

"How are you doing today?" Holly asked.

"I'm okay."

She studied him a moment. He felt a pang in his stomach. He knew she was going through her own litany of hows and whys. Just let her do it, he told himself. Let her feel it. Then if she stays, it will be for you, not some idea of who you're supposed to be. Let her be. Trust it. Trust her. She stared at him, more intently.

"What are you thinking about, Michael? Your name is Michael, isn't it?"

Quinton smiled.

"I guess so. I don't know. Michael, Quinton. Somewhere in between."

Holly smiled back. Who was this man she just knew she loved? Who was anyone, really? This man had touched her heart. That's more than a simple name could ever do.

"Well, whatever your name is, get right back here in bed with me."

He lay down beside her. She pulled him close and kissed him.

"I love you Holly," he said.

"I love you too, whatever your name is."

She kissed him again and pulled the sheet over their heads.

In the late afternoon Quinton and Holly sat on a piece of driftwood in back of Quinton's house. They held each other on the sun-drenched beach, gazing out at the restless ocean. An open cooler sat next to them. There was nothing left to say that hadn't been said already.

Suddenly, a shadow loomed over them. They turned around. Quinton stiffened.

In front of them stood Gina DeMarco, her gold-tone pant-suit reflecting the late afternoon sun. As she stood, her three-inch heels sank into the sand. Sunglasses covered her eyes.

"Hey...you're that volleyball player, aren't you?" she asked.

"Yeah."

"Nice place you have," she said matter-of-factly. There was almost a warmth to her voice.

"Yeah. I paid a lot for it," said Quinton.

"So I hear," she said. "You like it here?" she asked, suddenly serious, as if a lot hinged on his answer.

"Yeah. I do," Quinton said.

Gina was quiet for a moment.

"I guess...I could see how you could like it here. But I myself prefer the East Coast. The hustle and bustle of Boston's North End. The smell of pastries and green peppers that fills the air. The fog that rolls in from Boston Harbor after it rains...The leaves are changing colors now. The snow will be falling soon enough. I wouldn't know what to do with a sunset like this. To me, it's Siberia with palm trees...You have no family out here."

"I know," said Quinton.

"So who will take care of you?"

"I'll take care of me. Whatever I can't, the sun will provide."

Gina smiled.

"That sounds like something someone I used to know would say."

"Who was that?" asked Quinton.

"A boy who was like a friend to me. And later, a beautiful lover."

"Was?" Quinton asked.

"He's gone now," said Gina.

"Where did he go?"

"He died. In a fire. I guess he's moved on to another life."

"Reincarnated, you mean."

"Yeah. Something like that."

Silence. Gina looked down at Holly, then quickly looked away. Quinton stood up.

"Don't hurt her, Gina."

"I have no reason to hurt her, Michael."

Quinton stood his ground. In the distance behind Gina, a large black Lincoln pulled into view. Quinton saw someone sitting in the driver's seat, their identity concealed by the tinted glass. He looked away from the Lincoln and back at Gina.

"It's Quinton," he said.

Gina nodded.

"Frank says you remembered."

"Most of it," said Quinton.

Gina took something out from behind her back. A red rose. She handed it to him. He hesitated, then accepted. He lifted the rose and inhaled its fragrance.

"Watch out for the thorns," Gina warned.

"I always do," said Quinton.

Holly stood.

"Let me go put that in some water," she said awkwardly.

Quinton handed Holly the rose. Holly looked into Gina's sunglass-covered eyes. Gina took them off. The two regarded each other for a moment.

"Thank you," Gina said to Holly.

Holly walked away with the rose. She went inside the house. Quinton and Gina were left staring at each other, unsure of what to say.

"You look different," Gina finally said.

"I am different," said Quinton.

"So you are."

Gina bent down to the cooler and took out a beer.

"Can I have one of these?" she asked.

Quinton smiled.

"Yeah, crack one for me too."

Gina sat down on the log. Quinton sat on the sand, facing her. They drank their beers. Quinton looked up at her.

"You look understated as always."

"At least all my parts are real. A rarity in this part of the country, I hear."

Quinton looked over at the Bikini Twins' house. Lori and Tango were coming out of their abode wearing bright new matching bikinis. They waved at Quinton.

"This is true," said Quinton, and waved back at them.

Quinton looked back from the momentary distraction. He put his beer on the sand and looked at Gina.

"How'd you find me?" he asked.

"That damn tic of yours. It was all over Cable Sports. Every time you got nervous."

"But I could've been just an ordinary jock," Quinton said, "cleaning sand out of my ears."

"No, Michael. I know that tic, you've been doing it since you were eight, since your parents –"

"Yeah, I know," he interjected. She continued.

"It was also your eyes. You have such beautiful eyes."

Quinton scratched the inside of his ear with his pinkie. Gina caught it.

"Oh, Jesus, Michael, don't worry. I'm not here to jump you."

"Then why are you here? Kill me if you want, Gina. Just don't keep me waiting for it. The waiting is the real killer."

"I don't want to kill you. I never wanted to kill you. I just want to go home."

"I can't come with you," he said.

"I know that," she said, and looked at the ground. "You're rooted in this sand now, not in that compost pile anymore."

"I wasn't ever rooted in that, Gina. It was never really a part of me. I belong to my father, not to Victor."

"No. You belong to yourself, Michael. Quinton. Can I call you Michael?" she asked.

Quinton stared at her blankly.

"The Michael you knew is dead."

"He's still alive in my memories," she said.

Quinton paused. He picked up his beer and slugged down a large gulp.

"Mine too," he confessed.

"What do you see when you look in the mirror," she asked him.

"Well, I don't see Michelangelo's 'David.' "

Gina smiled.

"No. No more Sistine Chapel face."

"It'll take some getting used to," he said.

"She seems to like it," Gina said, nodding toward his house.

"She's a good person. She reminds me of the way we were, before."

"Before what?" she asked.

"Before the compost pile."

"I don't know you Quinton, but I've never felt Michael so close as I feel him right now. I am so angry at you, yet...I don't want to hurt you. It's strange. I never understood before how you could feel those two things at the same time. But you, you weren't afraid to cause injury, you just chose not to. And Frank, well, Frank..."

"...is in jail."

"I know. We have to go bail him out. Frank pushed you,

Victor pushed you, I pushed you. But you never budged. You just breathed. Your crazy dan tien."

"Who is Dan Ten?" asked Quinton.

"It's not a who, it's a what. Your Taoist breathing, your meditation."

"Ah," he said, it finally dawning on him. "Dan tien."

"Yeah, you always said it was what gave you the strength not to push back at the lot of us. I was just on the receiving end of one of Frank's pushes. When he gets in the car, I'm gonna shave him bald again. 'Cause I'm not where Michael was. I still need to push back."

"We all do what we need to get by," said Quinton.

"I still love you, Michael," she confessed.

"I don't know if I ever loved you, Gina."

"I know."

"I'm sorry," said Quinton.

"Don't be. We all do what we need to get by."

In a gesture which seemed foreign to her, Gina cautiously put out her hand to shake. Quinton took her hand and they shook. Gina stood up. She turned to leave, then turned back.

"I found my diaphragm."

Quinton laughed.

"Where?" he asked.

Gina smiled.

"Nana Rosetta was using it as a sink stopper to wash her woolens."

Quinton smiled.

"Her house still smell like mothballs?" he asked.

"Yeah. If she has her way, she'll be buried in them. By the way, Nicky says hi."

"Where is that little wop? He just took off."

Gina grinned slyly.

"Don't know where he is right now, but around two a.m. he'll be above my bed on a bungie cord."

Quinton laughed.

"And for Christ's sake Michael, put on some sun block. When you tan you age," Gina kidded.

They smiled at each other. Gina turned to leave. Before going, she pulled something out of her purse.

"Victor wanted me to give this to you," she said. "But I don't want to."

"Why?"

"Bad memories."

She handed him the object. It was an old, smoke-stained, shield-shaped car key. Inscribed below the char-burnt coat of arms was the word 'Cadillac.'

"He said he's sorry," she explained. "For everything you lost in the fire."

Quinton turned the key over and over in his hands. Something struck him.

"Only when you see the truth can you let go of the feelings that empower the pain."

"I don't understand," said Gina.

"I tried to run away from the pain. Away from the past. Part of my mind even tried to protect me from it. But it followed me here, into this other life. Now I need to face it. Only then can I ever let it go. Only then will it have no more power over me. Then I can truly live my life."

Gina looked at him. Her eyes were uncharacteristically moist. A lone tear trickled down Quinton's cheek.

"Will your hands heal soon?" she asked, as gently as she could.

"So they say."

"Then I'll look forward to seeing you play on CSN next year."

"Stranger things have happened."

"Not in this family...Goodbye, Michael...Quinton."

"Goodbye Gina."

As she turned and walked quietly back to the waiting car, Quinton sat down on the log. He continued to turn the key over and over in his hands. He looked back at the black Lincoln in the distance. The driver's tinted window slowly rolled down. A man leaned up to the window. Through the simmering heat of the beach, Quinton recognized the man's face. It was Victor Russo. He looked at Quinton, then down at the key he was holding. Their eyes met. Knowledge seemed to pass silently between them.

Victor nodded, then looked quickly away. Quinton slowly nodded back. The tinted window rolled up again. Gina got into the Lincoln and it disappeared down the road. Quinton, dwarfed by the hazy sunset, stared after them. He put the key in his pocket.

Holly came out of the house and down on the beach. She sat on the driftwood next to him.

"What was that all about?" she asked.

"Old debts being paid off, I guess. Or old confessions."

"I don't understand."

"I'll tell you about it tomorrow. But right now I just want to see the sunset, and be here in this moment, with you."

They looked at each other and smiled. Quinton leaned over and kissed her. They fell backwards off the log into the sand and looked up at the sky.

"So, what am I supposed to call you," Holly asked.

"Call me Quinton Squid...for now anyway."

She kissed him. The sun disappeared over the horizon.

ABOUT THE AUTHOR

BURNING SAND is the first novel from R.J. Ruggiero, a screenwriter and playwright living near Boston. R.J. has written and developed screenplays for the Academy Award-winning producers of *Rocky, Raging Bull, The Right Stuff,* and *Ender's Game,* and was a comedy writer for *The Tonight Show with Jay Leno.*